REBEL OBSESSION

SAINT VIEW REBELS #2

ELLE THORPE

WWW.ELLETHORPE.COM

Copyright © 2023 by Elle Thorpe

All rights reserved.

No part of this book may be reproduced in any form or by any electronic or mechanical means, including information storage and retrieval systems, without written permission from the author, except for the use of brief quotations in a book review.

Editing by Studio ENP.

Proofreading by Barren Acres Editing.

Original cover by Elle Thorpe. Photo by Wander Aguiar.

Discreet cover by Emily Wittig Designs.

For Dana, who is always ready to beta read the next book. Thank you for your enthusiasm, your advice, and your friendship.
Elle x

1

VAUGHN

I didn't stop for red lights.

I didn't take my foot off the accelerator for corners or intersections. I blew through every single one, my need to get to Rebel more powerful than any concern for my own safety.

Caleb's taunts rang in my ears.

Cry for them, baby. I bet they like it, too. You know she screams when you take her hard and fast? Oh, of course you do, she lives with you. You probably fuck her tight little cunt like that all the time, don't you?

"Faster," Kian muttered from behind me. He leaned forward, his head coming between the two front seats. "Fuck, Vaughn. You're driving like my grandma."

"My foot is already on the floor, asshole." My teeth ached from gritting them. My dentist would have heart failure if he could hear the way they gnashed against each other.

Fang, sitting in the passenger seat, didn't say a word. But his body language told me everything his mouth wasn't. He was stiff as a board, his gaze trained on the dark road ahead of us, every muscle primed and ready to fight.

I focused on how far we had left to drive. Five streets maybe? Fuck. Why did it feel like they were all a million miles long? Why did a hard-down accelerator still feel so slow?

Caleb's Halloween party played over and over in my head. A security guard forcing us to sign a waiver as we'd arrived. Taped-off areas Caleb clearly hadn't wanted people in. Women outnumbered ten to one. I'd put that down to Caleb being a boy's boy and girls never really liking him once they saw past his all-American good looks.

I'd assumed he'd just had no female friends.

That had been a mistake.

I'd underestimated how truly reprehensible he was. All too soon, his friends had shown their true colors.

They'd called it a 'primal' party. A throwback to caveman days where taking what you wanted, whether she wanted to give it or not, was the norm.

It was nothing more than an excuse for gang rape. Or watching others do it.

Bile churned in my stomach at the memory of them holding women down. Ripping at their clothes, forcing them to give up parts of themselves that hadn't been offered. We'd been outnumbered, but I would have stepped in anyway, no thought to the consequences.

If Caleb hadn't taken Rebel. If he hadn't dragged her into his car and driven her back to our house.

I had no idea why he'd go there, of all places. But I knew what he was going to do to her if we didn't get there in time to stop it. He'd already hurt her once. Him and his friends.

Kian, Fang, and I had promised revenge for the things they'd done to her. The deal was we'd have her back, but taking them out, making them pay, was all hers.

My fingers tightened on the steering wheel. "I know we said she could be the one to kill him..."

"He's mine," Fang practically growled, so low and deep even I shuddered at the pure malice in his voice.

"Make it hurt." Kian cracked his knuckles.

I couldn't have said it better myself.

I didn't care about Caleb.

All I cared about was her. The woman I'd been calling Roach for the past few weeks, ever since I'd found out she was my new stepsister. The woman I'd comforted when our parents had been murdered.

The woman I'd watched ride Fang's face until she came, and who I'd developed a serious case of feelings for. Ones that were decidedly unbrotherly, step or otherwise.

I didn't exactly know how she'd crept up on me so fast. One minute we were strangers—an attraction between us, no doubt—but I was married. Separated, and very much out of love with my wife, but still married. And Rebel...she had been so very broken.

But somehow, I'd found her living in the house I shared with Kian. Found myself aware of her every time we were in the same room. Day by day, the attraction grew harder to deny, until she was all I was thinking about, even if she was with Fang.

That didn't matter anymore. Not when she was in danger. All that mattered was getting to her.

The tires screeched as I took a corner too fast. I barely managed to keep control of the car, coming out of the turn in a wild fishtail. My heart rammed against my chest, but nobody told me to slow down.

In the distance, sirens wailed. Caleb had said he'd paid off the police, and I knew he probably wasn't lying. He had the connections to force them to look the other way. So thinking they were coming here was probably too much to hope for.

If they weren't, I prayed they were back at Caleb's party, helping the victims we'd left behind.

Guilt stabbed through me. "Those women..."

"Don't think about it," Kian said quietly. "We were outnumbered, and we've called the cops. We can't help them and help Rebel too. We have to hope the police will actually do their damn jobs for once. Think about the one person you can save."

I hated he was right. I glanced back at him. It had been a decade since we'd last lived together. He'd been a daily fixture in my life from the time I was a kid, right up until I'd moved across the country, cutting him out of my life completely.

But I still knew that look. It was the way he looked when he cared about someone. It was the way he'd once looked at me.

The driveway to our house was at the end of the street. "Is her phone still registering as being there?"

Kian checked the app he'd used to track down Rebel's location. "Yeah. We're right on top of her signal."

Fang's fingers moved to the door handle.

Kian braced himself on the two front seats.

I spun the wheel, taking the sharp corner.

And came face-to-face with Caleb Black, sitting behind the wheel of his car, engine on.

Our gazes collided. Even through the darkness and windshields and space between us, the evil in his eyes glinted.

It was in every inch of his smile. The lazy grin, so full of arrogance. The laid-back casualness that belied the immoral things he did.

Fang and Kian were out of the car before I'd even put it in park.

I was only a second behind them, not bothering to turn off the car. I let the engine idle, a background grumble to Fang's bellow of outrage.

"Where is she?" His fist pounded against the driver's-side window of Caleb's car so hard I was surprised it didn't shatter.

Kian went for the passenger-side door, yanking on the handle to no avail. He peered into the back seat, cupping his hands around his eyes and pressing them to the glass. "She's not there!"

I stood in front of the car, staring evil right in the eye. "Check the trunk! She's small enough to fit."

Kian ran around the back and slammed his fist down on the metal. "Rebel!"

Caleb's voice was muffled from inside his car but still loud enough to make out. "Get out of the way, Vaughn. I don't want to have to run you over. I just had this car detailed."

Which meant he could hear me too. "If you've laid one finger on her, I'll kill you," I promised.

His only answer was to gun the engine again.

I knew without a doubt he'd run me down. There had

to be a reason he hadn't already.

A blood-curdling scream from the backyard had all of us snapping our heads in that direction.

Kian's eyes darted to me. "Was that—"

I was running before he could even finish his question. The thumps of their boots on the ground behind me told me they'd followed my lead.

I prayed I hadn't made a fatal error. If Rebel was actually in the trunk and this was some sort of decoy to let Caleb slip away with her, I'd never forgive myself.

But gut instinct told me he hadn't brought her here for a quick pit stop before he went on his merry way.

He'd brought her here for a reason.

I had a sinking suspicion it was so we'd see whatever he'd done to her.

I steeled myself as I pumped my legs, pushing them to get around the side of the house to where the scream had come from. She needed me.

The thought almost stopped me in my tracks. She needed *us*. I wasn't her man. That was Fang's role.

So I switched my brain off. There wasn't space for that sort of thinking. Not here, not now, not tonight.

But nothing could have prepared me for what I saw around that final corner.

If I lived to be a hundred, I was sure nothing would fill me with as much terror as Rebel tied to a chair, at the bottom of the swimming pool.

2

REBEL

I wasn't sure how I'd lost my breath.

It might have been the cold punch of water. Or the sharp pressure of it smacking against my spine after Caleb shoved me backward into the pool.

Maybe it was the panic that set in, even through the copious amounts of drugs he'd injected me with.

It could even be thanks to a probable concussion, courtesy of the blow to the back of the head when he'd found me hiding in his basement, along with another woman he'd been keeping prisoner.

She was still down there.

If I drowned in this pool, there'd be no one to rescue her. That gnawed away at me like a rat. I'd promised her Kian, Vaughn, and Fang were coming and that they'd get us out.

Both of us.

Caleb had beat them to it, and now it was too late.

Water rushed around me, filling my ears and nose

and mouth. It was a pretty aqua color thanks to the pool lights, but deadly nonetheless.

I fought against the restraints, yanking my arms, scraping my wrists and ankles, but it did little good. I was too weak to loosen the ropes. Attached to the heavy outdoor chair, I hit the bottom of the pool quickly, the metal back scraping along the tiles. The surface was probably ten feet above my head.

Super great. Just fine and freaking dandy.

They'd come.

Fang and Kian and Vaughn.

But it would be too late.

I hated that for them, that they'd get here and see me like this. Halloween costume cut up so Caleb could get off on my exposed body. Tied up and drowned.

What a great way to go out. At least my mom wasn't alive to see it.

Vaughn had already seen more murder than any regular person should. He'd lost his dad at the same time I'd lost my mom, the two of them poisoned on their wedding day. I knew he'd blame himself for my untimely end too. I wished I could tell him not to. I was the stubborn asshole who'd insisted on him taking me to Caleb's party. He hadn't wanted to, but I'd been hell-bent on finding the men who'd attacked me.

I couldn't even bring myself to regret it. Splitting up from Fang and the others at the party? Yeah, that wasn't my finest hour. I regretted that. But even now, with my lungs screaming for air, I didn't regret the desire to make Caleb and his friends pay for what they'd done to me.

Someone had to.

My need for revenge apparently outweighed even my need for air.

I'd thought drowning would feel worse than it did though. It was oddly peaceful beneath the water. Darkness flickered at the corners of my vision, unconsciousness beckoning.

Wouldn't be long now. Any minute, and the darkness would engulf me.

"Rebel!"

It was a muffled shout. One I would have put down to a hallucination if it hadn't been accompanied by an arm spearing through the water toward me. Curiosity sent the darkness receding just enough that I could watch the arm blindly groping for me, but a good few feet off target.

I had the strange desire to laugh. Funny, bodyless arm.

Floppy, weird-looking thing.

The water rippled around me wildly, and hands grabbed at my arms.

For a millisecond, I thought it was one of the guys.

But her hands were too small. The face that loomed over me wasn't Fang's permanently grumpy scowl or Kian's playful grin or Vaughn's too-sexy smirk.

Sasha's panicked face swam in front of my eyes.

I'd only met the woman once, when I'd gone next door to borrow an egg for a cake I'd been baking. But I would have kissed her if I'd been able to move.

With her hands around my arms, she got her feet beneath her and pushed hard on the bottom of the pool.

The two of us, along with the chair, shot up above the surface.

"Rebel!" Sasha spluttered. "Are you okay?"

My body took over, trying to suck in air while painfully vomiting water at the same time.

All too soon we sank beneath the surface again. This time we only fell halfway before she pushed off the bottom and sweet, blessed air kissed my face.

"Shit, this was not my best idea. I can't swim very well." She gasped, face barely above the water with the effort of keeping me above it.

I couldn't help her. No matter how hard I tried to get my arms and legs free, I was completely at her mercy. I sucked in another breath but then the weight of me and the chair dragged her down again.

She pushed off the bottom once more, but she was getting tired.

I was going to drown us both.

The second my mouth was out of the water, I pushed away the desire to take huge, gulping breaths and forced out choked words instead. "Let me go."

"No!"

"Let me go or we both drown."

There was fear and confusion in her eyes. Then suddenly, determination. Instead of letting me go, she opened her mouth and screamed.

We both sank beneath the water again.

Her next push off the bottom wasn't strong enough to get us all the way up.

Every sliver of hope inside me died.

Inch by inch, second by second, the darkness came for me again.

All I could do was pray Sasha was strong enough to get herself out. She was too young and innocent to be caught up with my crap.

I wouldn't even get to tell Fang I loved him. He'd poured his heart out, and I'd been too chicken to say it back. Even though I felt it. Fuck, I felt it so hard.

Vaughn's face swam in front of mine.

I smiled.

Hallucinations of hot men were nice. Much better than the burn of ropes or the agony in my lungs. The pain seeped away, but so did the Vaughn image, darkness trying to consume me whole.

So quiet.

So dark.

So dead.

We broke the surface, and noise exploded around me.

"I've got her! I don't know if she's breathing!"

Hands reached for me. Fang's terrified face flashed by. Then Kian's.

"Get those ropes off her, Kian! Hurry!"

That was Vaughn's voice.

I couldn't work out what was going on. Only that suddenly, everything somehow hurt more than it had a minute ago.

I crashed down onto the ground none too gently and with no idea if I'd fallen or been tossed there. Pain scraped along my arm, tearing at what was left of the stupid Catwoman costume. My head flopped down on the hard poolside tiles. My body convulsed painfully, water pouring from my mouth. I moaned miserably, my stomach clenching in on itself to release the liquid I'd consumed.

"She's breathing!" Kian crowed in victory. He pummeled my back, forcing more and more water from inside me. "Someone check on Sasha."

The vomiting and coughing felt never-ending.

But the pain told me maybe I wasn't dead after all.

"Sasha is fine," she said from somewhere behind me. "But where the hell is the ambulance? One of you called one, right?"

I didn't hear a reply. Fang knelt and covered me in a towel and his jacket. He looked absolutely destroyed.

I was pretty sure my tears mingled with the pool water on my cheeks. I wanted to reach out to him, tell him I was okay, except I wasn't sure if that was true.

All I could do was cough and moan and plead with my eyes for him to not leave me.

I didn't know when exactly Fang had become my safe place.

But he was.

"Love..."

The words were barely more than a gurgle around a cough.

"Don't try to talk," he soothed.

"Love you," I choked out, pain in my throat. "Don't want to die without you knowing that."

He put one warm hand to the side of my face, his fear melting into something warmer as he held on to me. "You tell me that now, Pix? When this lot are all here listening and you're puking pool water?"

I was pretty sure I was just dribbling water now but still managed to mumble, "Your timing wasn't much better." He'd confessed he loved me in Caleb's house, while we'd been standing on the spot where I'd been attacked.

Hardly romantic.

He shook his head slowly and then leaned down and

placed a kiss on my forehead. His voice went croaky. "I love you so fucking much. You scared the shit out of me, Pix. I thought you were dead when we got out here and you were at the bottom of that pool. I thought we were too late."

A siren sounded from somewhere out front, and he glanced over his shoulder then gazed back down at me. "I'm gonna go get the paramedics. You keep breathing. You are not dying, you hear me? I won't fucking let you. So help me, if I come back here and find you didn't listen, I'm gonna spank your ass."

Everything in me wanted to sass him with a witty reply about how much I liked a good spanking, but telling him I loved him seemed to have taken up all my energy.

Fang got up and jogged to the edge of the house, disappearing around the side that would lead him up to the road.

It left space for me to notice the state Vaughn was in. He paced up and down the poolside, dripping wet, hands to the back of his neck. He kept shooting panicked glances my way, at least three of them before he realized I was watching.

He dropped to his knees in front of me, and then down onto his stomach so our faces were level. "Hey, Roachy. You okay?"

I think we both knew I wasn't. But I tried to nod anyway. "Sure. Was just inspecting the bottom of the pool. There's a few broken tiles that could use replacing."

Behind me, Kian sniggered, his palm still running up and down my back.

But Vaughn's mouth pressed into a line. "Don't joke. You were about two seconds away from drowning."

Ugh. He had his bossy older brother voice on, which he knew annoyed me. He wasn't that much older than me, and he wasn't my brother. I mustered up enough energy to tell him where to go. "If I want to make jokes about my failed imitation of a mermaid, then I will. Thanks, *brother*."

His eyebrows furrowed. "Seriously? You're giving me attitude five minutes after I save your ass from drowning?"

Sasha cleared her throat. "Hey, I helped! Quit hogging all the credit."

Kian glared at her. "You nearly drowned yourself in the process. See now why I wanted to teach you how to swim last summer? What the hell were you thinking, jumping in that pool, Sash?"

If gazes could set a man on fire, Kian would have gone up in flames.

Sasha's gaze was scalding. "Oh, I don't know. Maybe I was thinking I didn't want to see you cry because the woman you have the hots for sank like Jack from *Titanic*."

Kian gasped. "Sasha! You did not just go there! You know how I feel about that movie. Rose totally had room on that bit of wood, and you know it!"

I would have laughed if Fang hadn't come running with the paramedics at his heels. Vaughn scrambled out of the way.

The female paramedic cast a watchful eye over the entire scene before she focused on me. "I'm Claire. Where are we at?"

Kian's face sobered. "She puked water for a good few

minutes, but she's breathing and talking," he informed them. "Not sure how long she was under...Sash?"

She lifted a shoulder. "Maybe a minute?"

Claire looked at her. "Were you here when she fell in? Are you sure it was only a minute?"

Sasha's cheeks pinked. "Actually, I was next door... But it was definitely only a minute. I ran right over as soon as I saw her go in." She glanced over at me. "Sorry. I didn't mean to be a Nosey Nelly. But that guy..."

I tried to smile at her while the paramedic put a mask blowing oxygen on my face. "I'd be pretty dead right now if you hadn't. Thank you."

"How exactly did you fall in?" Claire asked, picking up on Sasha's comment about a man. The paramedic glanced at the rips and tears on what was left of my costume. With shrewd eyes, she studied the three men standing around me and then lowered her voice. "If you need help..."

"It wasn't them," I said quickly.

She checked my expression, and her worries must have been settled by whatever she found there. "Okay. I believe you. We can talk about calling the police when we get you to the hospital."

I clutched at my towel tighter, a new spike of fear tearing through me at the mention of the hospital. Leonn, one of Caleb's buddies who'd attacked me, worked at the hospital as a doctor. Fang had kneecapped him pretty bad earlier in the night, so there was a very high probability he'd be there, in the ER, getting medical attention of his own.

I shook my head. "No hospital."

Paramedic Claire frowned. The woman should have

been a schoolteacher. She had that 'I'm disappointed in you' scowl down pat. "Your oxygen levels aren't too bad, but you need to come in and get a full work-up. You're at risk of secondary drowning."

I'd heard of it. Where water in your lungs drowned you while you were on dry land. "How do you diagnose that?"

"Observation, mostly."

I jerked my head at the three guys hovering around me like mother hens. "Pretty sure they're willing to observe me."

Claire looked up at them with a sigh. "Don't suppose any of you want to help me out and talk her into going to the hospital?"

Fang and Kian would go along with whatever I wanted. But Vaughn wasn't always so easily swayed. He stared at me. I gave a tiny shake of my head and mouthed, "Please."

I couldn't go there. Not as weak as I was. They wouldn't let the guys stay with me since it was past visiting hours, and I didn't want to be helpless and alone anywhere near Caleb's friends. I wasn't giving up on my revenge plan. But confronting them right now wasn't the way either.

I'd been given a second chance at getting it right.

I wouldn't fail again.

3

REBEL

Vaughn convinced the paramedics to give me some fluids without taking me to the hospital. I had no idea what they put in those squishy bags, but they helped with the disjointed, drunk feeling the drugs had caused. Finally, the paramedics checked Sasha over and grudgingly left, the woman side-eying me like she wanted to sling me over her shoulder and carry me inside the ambulance against my will.

As soon as they were out of earshot, Sasha spun on the four of us. "Does somebody want to tell me what the hell happened here tonight?"

The guys all turned to me.

I sighed, appreciating they realized it was my story to tell. But I was exhausted and cold, despite the insulated medical blanket the paramedics had wrapped around me. "It was no big deal."

Sasha gave an overstated blink. "Rebel. That guy tried to murder you. Who was he?"

I shook my head. "You have that 'I love true crime'

glint in your eyes."

"The only thing in my eyes is chlorine."

Sasha was early twenties at most, and in the very brief conversation we'd had, she'd already admitted to being a podcast junkie. I loved a good murder mystery as much as anyone, but the one I'd found myself in the middle of was distinctly less fun.

And a whole lot more dangerous than listening to psychopath stories while you cleaned your house.

I didn't want to drag another person into all of this. "He's dangerous, Sasha. Please don't be offended when I tell you I'm not telling you."

She huffed and pushed to her feet. "Fine. You save a girl's life and you don't even get the inside scoop to sell to the tabloids. Rude. I'm off to have a shower then." She paused at the edge of the pool. "I really am glad you're all right."

I smiled at her. "I'm really glad you were snooping. That's as far as you take it though, okay?"

She rolled her eyes and flounced away. "You're about as much fun as my parents were. I thought you were cooler."

Despite the guys' best efforts to get me inside for a shower, I refused to move until I'd made sure she was safely to her house. Fang checked the entire perimeter and assured me Caleb's car was nowhere to be seen, but I didn't quite believe he wasn't still hanging around, hiding in the bushes. He wouldn't have wanted to be caught, but I knew him.

Watching me drown would have been something to write about in his diary. I could just imagine him going home to his gigantic, too-modern house and pulling out a notebook from beneath his mattress. *Dear Diary. Today I outdid myself on the vile factor. Think I might have set a new record for evil. Didn't even get caught. Just destroying lives one after the other, like a complete and utter pro. More despicable acts to come! Stay tuned! XOXO, Caleb.*

Ugh.

I really fucking hated that guy.

"She's inside." Fang scooped me up from the lawn chair I was huddled on. Not the one that had taken a dip in the pool with me. It was shoved to the side in disgrace, but it didn't help much, since all the chairs were identical.

I wasn't sure I'd ever swim in that pool again. Or any pool. The memory of no air in my lungs came back all too sharp and real, bringing a racking bout of coughing with it. Any peace I'd found in the bottom of that pool had been all in my head. Because my body felt like it had been hit by a Mack truck.

Fang carried me to the house, keeping my blanket wrapped around me tightly, muttering about calling the paramedics back and forcing me into the ambulance, even though we both knew he wouldn't. Kian and Vaughn followed a few steps behind us. I peeped over Fang's shoulder as the coughing subsided, watching them walk side by side.

"Hey." Kian reached a pinky finger out to Vaughn, brushing it over the back of his hand. "You okay?"

Vaughn pulled his hand away sharply, then shook his head.

"She's alive," Kian whispered. "She's here. We got her back. Stop beating yourself up. It wasn't your fault."

Vaughn just kept staring at me.

Guilt punched me right in the stomach.

I turned away.

A few feet from my bedroom door, Kian jogged ahead, opening it so Fang could carry me through. Kian and Vaughn followed, the three big men inviting themselves into my room.

I raised an eye at Vaughn and Kian. "I need a shower."

It was only then they seemed to realize where they were. Kian nodded respectfully and moved toward the door.

But Vaughn stood his ground. "We need to talk about what happened tonight and where we're going from here. I don't know about the rest of you, but this isn't some revenge game anymore. Caleb is dangerous. I fucked up tonight, taking you there."

"So did I." Fang clutched me tighter. "I should have never let you go back in that house, Pix. I'm so fucking sorry."

They were both ridiculous. Neither of them had done anything wrong. I looked at Kian, paused in the doorway. "You got anything you want to unnecessarily apologize for?"

Fang and Vaughn frowned, but Kian's lips curled up in a half-grin. "I'm really sorry I was a little off-key on that Taylor Swift track the other day. Those high notes get me every time."

I fought back a snigger, but Vaughn and Fang remained unimpressed.

I sighed. "Neither of you are at fault. Stop taking the blame for my actions. I'm a big girl. I can admit when I fucked up. It's not your job to stop bad things happening to me. Especially when it's me who put myself in that situation."

Vaughn seemed like he wanted to argue, but I gave him the fiercest 'I am woman, hear me roar' expression that I could muster up, and he left the room with a shake of his head.

Kian watched him go, then turned back to me. "Take your time in the bathroom. Get warm. I'll use the one downstairs."

I thanked him. Then I was alone with Fang, for the first time since I'd blurted out I loved him.

I wrapped my arms around him and pressed my lips to his neck. "Hey, you," I said softly.

He carried me through the bathroom door and sat me on the vanity. But when he pulled back, he didn't look particularly happy. "Don't 'hey you' me."

I peered up at him, surprised by his tone. "You mad at me?"

"Yes." Then his shoulders slumped, and he brushed a strand of my hair behind my ear. "No. I don't know. Don't tell me it's not my job to protect you, Pix. It is my fucking job. If I'm your guy...one of your guys..." He frowned trying to label himself.

"You're my guy," I assured him quickly. "My only guy. Kian and I are just friends. Vaughn is...I don't know. My brother, I guess."

Even I heard the uncertainty in my tone.

He strode across the bathroom to the shower and turned on the hot water. "You rode my face while club girls sucked his cock. Hell, Pix. You came that night because he told you to. That is not what people do with their brothers." He waved a hand beneath the water and flinched at the temperature before he stepped back and offered it to me. "There you go. Scalding hot, just how you like it."

I dropped the blanket, and Fang's gaze dipped to the rips and tatters of my costume and my scratched-up skin beneath it.

"It's okay," I assured him. "I'm fine. Don't look."

But that was like telling the sun not to be bright.

Fang's eyes traced every injury on my body. He slowly peeled off the last tatters of fabric, leaving me completely naked.

But I didn't feel exposed the way I did when it was Caleb ripping my clothes off.

Fang's lips touched the scratch on my neck and then ghosted over the graze on my shoulder. He kissed every scrape and bump, ending with the tiny cut at the corner of my mouth. "You know I'd do anything for you, right?"

I put my fingertips to the sides of his bearded face and stroked. "I know."

"Even share you."

Oh, boy. "I can't ask that of you."

"You aren't. I'm offering. I keep fucking up with you, Pix. Letting you get hurt. When all I've ever wanted to do is make you happy."

My heart swelled. Damn. This man would be my undoing. "I don't understand how some woman hasn't already claimed your heart. Big scary biker on the outside. Sweeter than any man I've ever known on the inside." I pressed my lips against his again, but he wouldn't let me deepen the kiss.

"There's something between you and Vaughn." From anyone else it would have been an accusation. From him, it was just stating a fact.

I shook my head. "It doesn't matter. It's just attraction. It's you I want to be with. You're my safe place, Fang. That's all I could think about when I was trapped on the bottom of that pool. I love *you*."

It should have been weird to say those words to a man. I'd never said them to anyone but my mother.

But I meant them. When he stared at me like that, with his whole heart wide open and on display, telling him I loved him back was the easiest thing in the world.

His lips on mine were featherlight. "I love you too. And that's why I'm not tying you down."

Panic lit up inside me, and I inched back. "What does that mean? Are you breaking up with me?"

I couldn't bear to hear the answer. This was why I'd been terrified to ever commit to a man. To ever tell one I loved him. Love was too big a feeling. Too all-encompassing. It had destroyed my mother over and over, and I had never wanted it to do the same to me. I had no one to pick me up the way I had for her. I didn't get the luxury of loving someone so wholeheartedly it could devastate you if it went away.

His eyes went big. "Fuck no. We talked about this before. I'm just saying it better now. I'll be here. Always. You've owned my heart from the minute I met you and you'll have it 'til the minute I die. There's no one else for me. But even I can see something between you and Vaughn, and I think you're kidding yourself if you think there's only friendship between you and Kian." He ducked his head and stared deep in my eyes. "I'm saying that for as long as I'm breathing, I'm always going to be here. But there's room for them too. If that's what you want. The life I lead... Fuck. We both know what it is. You might need them one day."

I didn't want to think about that. I wrapped my arms around him and pulled him close. Something deep inside me knew he knew me better than I knew myself. He was giving me the permission I needed to build a support system. To build relationships that would hold me up if I gave in and admitted that what I needed was him and the way he loved me. When he said he was going to love me forever, I knew he meant it, but we both knew what he did for a living. He lived a dangerous life. One fraught with bad people who wouldn't think twice about putting a bullet through his brain if the desire took them. The Slayers had lost their prez just months ago, and though his wife was a strong, badass woman, there was something a bit smaller about her ever since. She might not have been on the bathroom floor like my mother had a tendency to be, but she was broken in her own way.

It was the daily reality of loving a man who lived outside the law. It came with taxes that weren't paid to the government.

"Shower, Pix. You're freezing." He rubbed my arms briskly.

I hadn't even noticed the goosebumps that had popped up all over my skin. I slid off the vanity and stepped into the hot, misty water.

I wasn't sure anything had ever felt as good. But as soon as I was warm, I turned it down and beckoned to him through the glass. "Come here."

He stood slowly, stripping off his jacket and undid the Velcro fastenings on the Batman costume he'd worn to Caleb's Halloween party. He slid it down over his shoulders and abs. I wasn't sure if the sudden shaking in my legs was because of leftover drugs still wandering their way through my system or because Fang was the hottest man I'd ever seen naked.

I couldn't help the urge to tease him. "Ooh. Take it off, Batman."

He raised an eyebrow. "This doing it for you?"

"Just a few inches lower and it will be."

He dropped the costume low enough to free his erection.

My mouth went dry, and I darted my tongue out to catch some water before groaning, "Get in here."

The shower screen creaked when he opened it, but then his big body was inside the little cubicle and towering over me.

I reached for his cock, the need to please him rapidly rising inside me. He'd just said I could explore things with other men. At the very least, that deserved a blow job.

But he caught my hands. "Not a chance. You just nearly died. We aren't doing anything tonight. I just want to take care of you."

I let my hands fall limp at my sides. "I don't get you."

He reached for the bottle of shampoo, squirted some into his palm, and then rubbed it through my hair. "I'm not that complicated."

But he was.

I'd barely scratched the surface and I was already in love with him.

The thought was terrifying. If I loved him this much now, how much harder would I fall when I knew every little detail?

4

VAUGHN

I showered in record time, not wanting to use up all of the hot water when Rebel had been in that pool so much longer than I had. I dried off and crawled into bed, listening to the old pipes squeak and complain while the others used the bathrooms.

But the longer I lay there, the stronger the urge was to get up and scrub my hands again. Not because they were dirty, but because the back of my hand burned from where Kian had touched it. I couldn't stop thinking about the way his skin felt against mine. Familiar and yet so foreign.

Scrubbing it raw felt like the only way to get the feeling to stop.

I'd been so careful not to touch him since I'd moved back here, knowing the reaction it created.

It was a reaction I'd fought most of our teenage years.

One that was an automatic reaction to resist even now.

I tossed and turned, the sheets too smooth, too soft.

Nothing like Kian's calloused fingertips, rough from the physical labor he did every day.

I flipped onto my stomach and groaned into my pillow. Only that was worse. Because now my dick was rubbing against the sheets and the mattress. I was hard and desperately wishing there was a person beneath me.

All because he'd touched the back of my damn hand.

I was a joke if one tiny touch could have this much effect. I didn't want it. I *couldn't* want it.

Yet, I knew exactly what I was going to do. I shoved my knees up, resting my weight on one forearm and making enough room to get my other hand beneath me.

I fisted my cock viciously, giving in to the desire that had flooded in the moment Kian had shown even the tiniest bit of affection.

It was like being transported back to my teen years, including the rushing need to come way too quickly.

But I kept going, not wanting to draw it out. Not wanting to take pleasure in wanting him the way I did.

Nothing good came from the two of us. It never had. Caleb and his friends were proof nothing changed in this town. The same people were still doing the same fucked-up shit, while the cops looked the other way.

Starting something up with Kian would only end the same way it had last time.

I couldn't do that again. To either of us.

But it didn't stop my body from wanting him.

I jerked my shaft, stifling noises of pleasure I didn't want to feel.

A knock at the door froze me in place. Shit. Had I even locked it?

"Busy," I ground out.

But the door handle turned anyway, and I frantically flipped onto my back, yanking the covers up over me. "What the fuck? I said I'm busy."

Kian pushed open the door, the smattering of freckles across his nose and cheeks evident, even in the dim light. His bare chest still glittered with water droplets that had flicked off his hair.

Without any permission from me, my gaze rolled down his body. Over well-defined pecs, abs, and those lines that ran either side of his hips, dipping below the white towel wrapped around his waist.

He smirked when my gaze finally lifted to his face. "Heard you making all sorts of noises. Just came in to make sure you were okay."

I hoped it was dark enough that he couldn't see me blushing. I was sure I was, my cheeks blazed with heat. "Stubbed my toe." It was a ridiculous excuse, but it was the best I had on short notice.

Much like mine had, his gaze tracked down, heating a path of fire over my naked chest.

He stopped when he got to my dick, only harder now for having him in the room. He raised an eyebrow. "Stubbing your toe gives you a hard-on?"

I squeezed my eyes shut. He always did this. He lived to call me out and wind me up.

There was no point in answering that. All I could do was try to change the subject. "Why did you touch me back there?"

He chuckled. "I haven't touched you 'back there' in a really long time, Vaughn."

My dick kicked at the memory.

For fuck's sake. This was mortifying. "I meant in the hallway," I choked out. "You touched my hand."

"Is that illegal?"

I clasped my fingers around the edge of my sheet and pulled it a little higher on my chest, trying to cover up how very naked I felt. "Don't do it again."

He folded his arms across his thickly muscled chest. "Don't offer you a tiny bit of concern after a really shitty night? I barely brushed your fingers. Is that seriously what you're asking?"

I swallowed thickly, knowing that actually wasn't what I meant, but it was the only thing I could voice. "Yes."

Something changed in his eyes. His jaw hardened, and he moved forward, sleek, like a panther, until he was right at the edge of my bed. Before I could stop him, he reached out and caught my wrist. "Or what?"

My breath sucked from my lungs. His fingers were too warm. Too rough. Too fucking tight around my wrist, preventing me from pulling away.

At least that's what I told myself. That I couldn't get away, even if I wanted to.

His thumb rubbed over the same place he'd touched me earlier.

Just like before, it burned.

Just like before, that tiny touch did things to my dick that it had no business doing.

His left hand wrapped around my other wrist. He pried my fingers away from the sheets and pinned them down on the mattress, sliding them up until they were either side of my head.

"Or what, Vaughn?" he asked again. "If I touch you like this, what are you going to do?"

Absolutely fucking nothing.

"Stop," I begged.

He put one knee on the edge of the bed and leaned over me so our faces were mere inches apart. "If I thought you meant that for even half a second, I would." He threw his other leg over my hips, straddling me, his towel loosening in the process. But if he noticed, he didn't show it. Inch by inch, so slowly it was maddening, he lowered himself on top of me.

We both hissed at the contact, my erection grinding on his.

He was as hard as I was.

"I don't want this," I managed to get out around pants of breath that easily gave away the lie.

Kian rubbed his dick against mine. The sheet and his towel were an unwanted barrier, but my dick didn't seem to care. Precum wept from my tip, wetting the sheet with my need for him to keep going.

He dipped his head and licked a path up my neck until he got to my ear.

I waited for it. For him to whisper something dirty. For him to kiss me there while he groped, pulling the barriers away so we were skin to skin.

It was the same old dance we'd done a bunch of times before, only now we weren't eighteen, sneaking around, hiding from our parents.

I wanted him. There was no doubt about it. I moved against his dick shamelessly, wanting more.

His teeth clamped down on my earlobe, and warning

tones went off in my head. I was going to come, and he'd barely even fucking touched me.

"Say you want it."

"I want it," I admitted, desperate for him to touch me properly. "Fuck, Kian. I want it."

Kian ran his tongue around the shell of my ear. "Too. Fucking. Bad."

I blinked.

In the next second, he was off me. The sheet had slipped low enough to reveal my cock, wet with my own arousal, hard and aching for him. "What the fuck?"

Kian just walked out, like we'd been playing Monopoly and the game was over. He glanced over his shoulder before he closed the door. "It's not so fun to be the person left behind, is it?"

The door closed.

All I could do was stare after it.

5
―――
REBEL

I woke in the middle of the night and instantly knew something was wrong.

Fang's body radiated heat behind me, his breathing slow and regular in sleep. The house around us was silent, the only noises a muffled croaking of a frog somewhere outside.

But the longer I lay there, the more I sensed something was out of place.

I pried Fang's arm from around my middle and gently pushed it back toward him. He stirred and rolled over but didn't wake. I should have just woken him, but he'd looked exhausted by the time he'd tucked us both into my bed. I just didn't have the heart.

Whatever didn't feel right was probably all in my head.

But a gut feeling said I was being watched, and there was only one person creepy enough to do that.

Caleb.

It was a ridiculous thought. Caleb would have to have

balls the size of Texas to try coming into this house with Fang, Vaughn, and Kian all here. Especially after the shit he'd pulled tonight. He had to know we'd be coming for him. It would be suicide for him to return to the scene of the crime.

I was letting residual fear from earlier take over my common sense. The fact my mouth was dry with fear right now while Fang slept in my bed was so stupid, I was embarrassed. I needed to get up and go grab a glass of water from the kitchen. That would prove to my overactive imagination there was nothing to worry about here.

And that I hadn't completely lost my nerve.

I lifted my head from the pillow and squinted into the darkness.

A man sat in the corner, staring at me.

I opened my mouth to scream, but only a squeak came out.

"Just me, Roach. You're okay."

I slumped back in relief at Vaughn's familiar voice. But then I picked up a throw cushion and hurled it across the room at him. "What are you doing, sitting over there like a complete and utter voyeuristic creeper? Did you change your name to Caleb? You scared the shit out of me, Vaughn!"

I was whisper-shouting so I wouldn't wake Fang, but I really wanted to yell. Loudly.

Vaughn caught the pillow easily and placed it on his lap. "Just wanted to make sure you were okay. Someone needs to watch you for secondary drowning."

"Fang's right there." I flicked my head toward the sleeping man-giant next to me.

"I could hear his snoring from down the hall. He's

hardly watching to make sure your lungs aren't defective."

"My lungs are perfect. I'm not even coughing, and he doesn't snore. So you can go now."

The man didn't so much as move a muscle.

"Seriously. I'm fine."

"If I go back to my room, I'm just going to toss and turn all night worrying about you."

I folded my arms over my chest. "Since when do you care about anyone but yourself?"

He rubbed his bare arms briskly. "I care about people. You, in particular."

"Because I'm your sister?"

"You're not my sister." He shivered in the darkness.

I took in what he was wearing. A pair of flannel pajama bottoms and a white wifebeater singlet. "You need a robe and slippers."

"I'm not eighty."

"You are cold though."

"I'm fine. Go back to sleep."

I sighed, knowing there was zero chance of rest while he was sitting there in the corner. "Are you really not going back to your bed?"

"Not until Fang wakes up and is actually keeping an eye on you."

I rolled my eyes and raised the edge of the blankets. "Get in then."

He raised an eyebrow. "Are you serious?"

"I can't handle watching you sitting there shivering. It was probably your chattering teeth that woke me up in the first place."

"It was probably Fang's fart that woke you up, actually. Echoed right around the room."

I fought back the urge to laugh. "Just get in."

To my surprise, he pushed slowly to his feet and padded across the thick carpet. He stared down at me and the space I was offering him in the king-size bed. Fang and I took up most of the room, but there was enough for Vaughn if he decided to take it.

Some part of me really wanted him to take it.

Probably the part that got horny just looking at his biceps.

"If you try to Dutch oven me so I have to breathe in Fang's fart stench, I'm not going to be impressed, Roach. I will drag you under with me so fast. Just watch."

Despite his protests, he slid into the bed, and I dropped the blankets over his shoulder.

Like they had a mind of their own, my fingers sought out his arms. Maybe to rub away the cold.

Maybe because it was a good excuse to touch him.

But I recoiled the minute my fingertips met his skin. He was icy.

"How long have you been sitting there watching me sleep?"

"Hours."

My heart squeezed. As much as he'd surprised me, there was something about the way he wanted to care for me that was anything but creepy.

We lay on our sides, facing each other, barely a few inches between us. But the darkness made it less weird. Even this close up, I couldn't see every detail of his face.

It was some other sense that told me he wasn't okay. "Did something happen?"

"Other than Caleb trying to murder you?"

I trailed my fingers over his skin. "Yeah. Something feels off with you."

"I'm fine."

"People who say they're fine never actually are. Tell me. I'm a good listener." It was true. I talked a lot, loudly, at a million miles an hour, but I knew how to shut up when I needed to.

He twisted, trying to get comfortable. "I fucked up with Kian."

I groaned softly. That was not what I wanted to hear. There was something between Kian and Vaughn neither had admitted to, and I'd been quietly rooting for the two of them for weeks. "Seriously? How do you fuck things up in the tiny amount of time between me nearly drowning and you sneaking in here hoping I was sleeping naked?"

He glared at me. "Do you want me to tell you the story or do you want to keep making jokes at my expense? Where are those listening skills you seem so proud of?"

He had a point. "Continue then."

He let out a heavy sigh. "I always fuck up with him. Now. Back when we were teenagers... I just keep making the same mistakes."

I tucked my hands into a prayer position and then slid them under my face, giving him my full attention. I knew I was supposed to just be listening, but I couldn't help asking another question. "What the hell happened with you two?"

His gaze flickered up, somewhere above my head. "So much and not enough all at once."

"You guys hooked up?"

"What's your definition of hooking up?" His tone was curious.

"Kissing?"

"Yeah."

"Hand job?"

Vaughn nodded slowly. It was hard to be sure, but I had a feeling his cheeks might have been pink if I'd been able to see them properly in the low light.

Not caring that I sounded like a fifteen-year-old drilling her bestie for the details of the night she'd lost her virginity, I kept going. "Oral?"

"Do you really want a blow-by-blow description of every sexual thing we did?"

"I very much do."

He chuckled. "We didn't have sex."

I pouted at him. "No peen in ass? No cock sliding into the henhouse? No dick taking the old dirt track..."

He made a face at me. "No. But..."

"You would have?"

He lifted a shoulder in a shrug. "I think so. Everything we'd been doing up until that point led in that direction."

"How old were you?"

He gave a half shrug of his one exposed shoulder. "Started when we were seventeen or eighteen. Though we'd been skirting around each other long before that."

"Why'd you stop?"

Vaughn's face clouded over. "I took him to an Edgely party."

The name was familiar. "That fancy rich boys' school in Providence?"

"Yeah. That's where I went. Kian was over at Saint View High. We didn't run in the same crowds, but we lived together so there was no avoiding each other. We'd been getting closer all through senior year, despite the fact I had a girlfriend, and by the end of the summer, I just wanted to be with him. Some of the guys threw a party at the beach. One last hurrah before we all went off to different colleges. I tried to ditch the party so I could wait for Kian to get home from his summer job. My friends wouldn't take no for an answer though, so I texted Kian and told him to meet us there when he was done."

I could tell where this was going. "Your friends didn't like him?"

Vaughn shook his head. "Actually, they loved him." He shoved a bit more of the pillow beneath his head. "Kian hasn't changed. He's always been outgoing, and he had them all eating out of the palm of his hand, telling them stories about the shit that went down at Saint View High. Drug raids. Public sex. Teachers hooking up with students. Football team drama."

"I sense a but coming..."

Vaughn's soft, warm breath brushed over my cheeks. "I loved that he was getting along with my friends. I was drunk and horny and fucking stupid. I dragged him out of the party, down along the beach..."

A sick feeling swirled in my stomach.

"We were laughing about something. I can't even remember what anymore. Kissing. Sloppy as fuck, but all over each other. He tripped over his own feet and fell. I tried to pull him back up, but he batted away my hands and undid my fly instead..."

I pushed away the thought of Kian down on his knees in front of Vaughn. It was hot, but now wasn't the time.

But Vaughn kept going. "He said if he wasn't going

to see me every day, then he was sending me off in style. Then gave me the best blow job of my life. Right there on the beach. It was dark, and there was no one around, but at the time, it was the hottest thing I'd ever done."

He squeezed his eyes tight for a moment before he continued, still keeping his voice low. "It wasn't enough. I wanted to go all the way before I went to college. I was staying local but moving out of my dad's house. Kian was going off to play ball. I didn't know how much we'd see of each other after that night. I didn't want to regret not going there with him."

I swallowed thickly. "What happened?"

Vaughn's mouth pressed into a hard line. "I left him there on the beach while I went to find my friends to say goodbye. I was only gone for a few minutes, Roach. I swear. But by the time I got back, two guys had Kian down on the ground, kicking and punching him."

I gasped quietly. "What? Why would they do that?"

"They were calling him a faggot."

I clapped a hand over my mouth. "They saw the two of you?"

He nodded. "I shouted that I was going to get my friends if they didn't stop, and that was enough for them to run off. But the damage had already been done. He was messed up, Roach. Really bad. I moved into my dorm room while he was still in a coma."

My eyes must have been as wide as dinner plates. "What happened after he woke up? Did you two date?"

Vaughn's dark-eyed gaze flickered away from me. "No."

"Why not?"

"Because I never went back to see him after he came to."

I squinted at him in the darkness. "Why?"

He shifted onto his back and stared at the ceiling. "The simple answer? Because I was an asshole."

"I already know that, so how about you give me the complicated answer too?"

His voice was tight with emotion when he finally spoke again. "He was so damaged. Bandages, bruises, surgeries for internal bleeding... I barely recognized him, lying so still in that hospital bed he may as well have been dead. At first, they warned his dad that he might never wake up. So I visited every day, watched him fight until his vitals improved, and eventually they started saying he was going to be okay. But once I knew that, I couldn't go back. He would say it wasn't my fault."

"It wasn't."

His head jerked to the side, and even though it was dark, there was a wealth of pain behind those eyes. "If I'd gone back there to see him, he would have forgiven me in a heartbeat, and we would have picked up right where we left off. Then I would have spent every day of my life terrified of that happening to him again. Every time we held hands. Every time we went to a restaurant. I couldn't risk it. Providence was too stuck in the Dark Ages to accept the two of us."

He touched his fingertips to mine in the darkness, and I grabbed them tight, hoping they provided comfort, if that's what he was searching for.

Vaughn took a deep breath before he continued. "Kian has such a golden view of everything and everyone. He never would have believed it. But I knew. I grew up here. I'd heard my father's business partner making homophobic comments. I'd heard the way the guys at school talked about 'faggots.' I should have known better than to do anything with him in public. I knew better, and one of us had to think with a level head. Someone had to end it." He pulled his hands away and pressed the heels of his hands to his eyes. "Seeing him in that hospital bed, with machines keeping him alive... I've never experienced anything that bad. Except maybe you at the bottom of that pool, your wrists and ankles tied."

Despite keeping his voice low so we didn't wake Fang, there was a change in his tone. One that sounded like he was barely keeping it together and punishing himself further by not letting me comfort him.

I couldn't help it. I pulled his hands back to me and squeezed them. "You were seventeen."

His eyes were miserable. "I was old enough to know better. I did that to him, Roach. I might as well have been the one planting my boot into his face."

"That's not true."

He closed his eyes, like the memories caused him pain. "And now he hates my guts."

I frowned at that. "Kian doesn't hate anyone. Especially not you. I think you'll find he doesn't blame you for the attack."

He sighed softly. "Maybe not. But he blames me for leaving. For staying away."

"That's probably warranted."

Half his mouth lifted in a smile. "Probably." He looked past me and over at the Fang-shaped lump on my other side. "Is Fang going to punch me when he wakes up and finds me here?"

"I don't think so."

"I'm in his bed having 2:00 a.m. conversations with his girl. I'd punch me."

I stifled a laugh. "It's my bed. I'm free to invite anyone I want into it, thank you very much."

"Does Kian sneak in here at night?"

"No."

"Just me, huh?"

"Just you."

Something flickered in his eyes. "I like being in your bed, Roach. This one. The one at your apartment. Your sheets smell like you."

"I thought they smelled like Fang's farts." I could barely keep in my laughter.

Vaughn's grin turned boyish. "Just said that to make you smile."

I slapped his arm. "Is that how much you think of me? That fart jokes amuse me like they do three-year-old boys?"

"Was I wrong?"

He had a point.

A silence fell over us, but it wasn't uncomfortable. I was warm with Fang's heat at my back and Vaughn's at my front. There was something nice about being sandwiched between them. Caleb couldn't get to me here.

Unless I let him into my head.

I locked up.

"What just happened?" Vaughn squeezed my fingers. "Where'd you just go?"

I tried to push it away. Tuck it into some secret spot in my brain where it wouldn't hurt me. "Nowhere. I'm squished between two huge bed-hogging men."

He wouldn't let me dodge the question. "You thinking about Caleb?"

A tremble shuddered through me. "Please don't say his name."

"We need to though, Roach. We need to talk about what we're doing in the morning."

I swallowed hard, forcing out the words I'd already decided on. "We need to go to the cops."

"They won't do anything. They're so firmly in Caleb's pocket."

I squeezed his fingers back. "We need to go back there."

His eyes sharpened. "Not a chance in hell."

I knew he'd say that. But I knew what I had to say next would change his mind. Because even though he'd left Kian alone on that beach, he'd gone back for him when he was in trouble. He might have walked away once he knew Kian was going to be okay, but that was only because he'd convinced himself Kian was in danger with him around.

Vaughn protected those he cared about, just as much as Fang and Kian did.

I just hoped that protection could extend to someone he didn't know. "Caleb has another woman locked in his basement."

"What!" Vaughn shouted.

Fang was awake in an instant, flicking on the lamp beside him. A second later, Kian came crashing through the bathroom we shared.

Vaughn didn't even seem to notice. He just gaped at me, wide-eyed.

Kian took in me, Fang, and Vaughn in the same bed,

blinked twice, then rubbed his eyes. "You guys had a sleepover without me? I could have brought s'mores and my blow-up mattress."

Fang stared at Vaughn, a growl in his voice. "Why are you in my bed?"

"My bed," I corrected. "And quit it with the growling. You just said there was room for them."

Kian let out a confused laugh in Fang's direction. "Did you just offer us a foursome, bro?"

Fang rubbed his hand through his hair. "I need coffee to have this conversation."

Kian let out a low wolf whistle that was completely obnoxious at this time of the morning. "That wasn't a no."

The two of them went back and forth while I just looked at Vaughn, whose dark-brown eyes had me in their grips.

Vaughn pulled his gaze away and got out of the bed, putting distance between us. "Rebel just told me Caleb has another woman held captive in his basement."

Fang and Kian fell silent, both their heads whipping toward me.

"Is that true, Pix?" Fang cracked his neck audibly. "Please tell me that's not true."

"Why didn't you tell us this before?" Kian groaned.

I stared at him and answered with a flat, deadpan tone, "Sorry. Was a little busy trying not to get murdered. Forgive me if my own survival was at the forefront of my mind. Incredibly selfish of me, I realize."

He backed off. "Sorry, sorry. I know. What the hell are we going to do now?"

It seemed obvious to me. "We go get her. We all know

the police are going to shut right down the minute I mention Caleb's name."

Vaughn's eyes were stony. "*We* go get her, Roach. Not you. You aren't going anywhere near him."

I'd thought we'd been making some sort of progress, huddled in bed together, whispering secrets. But now we were right back to him acting like my bossy, overbearing brother.

"We go before dawn." Fang gritted his teeth and grabbed his phone from the bedside table. "I'm calling War. This is bigger than just us."

I wanted to wail for him not to. If he told War, War would tell Bliss, and I'd been trying so hard to keep her out of this mess. She would blame herself for everything Caleb had done to me. She was pregnant. I didn't want her putting that sort of stress on herself. I would never forgive myself if something happened to my future niece or nephew.

But I also knew there was no getting around it. I didn't want them going to Caleb's place without backup. "Tell War to tell Scythe. Or Vincent. Whichever of his psychopathic personalities is in residence at the moment. They think Caleb is a scared, harmless little boy who ran off with his tail between his legs after everything he did to Bliss. He'll want in."

Fang left the room to make his calls. Kian mumbled something about putting some clothes on and disappeared through the bathroom.

Leaving Vaughn and me alone.

He stared at me from where he leaned on the wall. "Promise me you aren't going to try to follow us."

I scowled back. Only partially because I had been planning to do exactly that. "I hate the big brother act."

"That's not why I'm protective of you."

Something flickered low in my stomach at the change in his voice.

He crossed the space between us and put his finger beneath my chin. "I wouldn't crawl into bed with my sister, Roach."

"We weren't doing anything."

"I wanted to."

My mouth dropped open. "What did you want to do?"

He smirked. "I've got to go deal with Caleb. So you're going to have to wait until next time I crawl into your bed to find out."

6

BLISS

It was two in the morning before I closed the door after the last guest left my sex club. I leaned back on the solid wood, my feet aching after being on them all night.

War got up from a couch and wandered over, immediately slipping his fingers to the back of my neck and rubbing out the tension that had formed there over the past five hours I'd been working. "You sure you don't want to start your maternity leave yet, baby girl? None of us expect you to keep working. You know that, right?"

I smiled up at his familiar, handsome face so full of concern for me. "I know. But I'm only a few months pregnant. It's too soon. I'll go crazy just sitting at home all day while the three of you galivant around."

"I could go on maternity leave too," Scythe called from behind the bar. "I know many a way to keep you entertained all day. Most involve my tongue."

War raised an eyebrow at me. "He makes a tempting offer, don't you think?"

It was. Scythe was good with his tongue. All my guys were. But I already had that on tap. Between them, I could have a guy between my thighs twenty-four seven if I so desired.

Heat flared between my thighs at the thought.

War grinned like he could read my mind. "You need something from us, baby girl? I know that look on your face."

I tried to school it into something a little less obvious. "It's two in the morning. We need to get home."

Nash glanced up from counting the money we'd taken that night. He had a thick wad of cash in his fist, which was a turn-on in itself. He grinned when he saw I'd noticed. "Good night. Very good, actually." He tucked a rubber band around the bills and put it back into the register before he came around the other side of the counter, a playful grin on his bearded face. "Could make it an even better night if we want to hang out here for another hour or so."

Scythe rolled his eyes. "Excuse me, but I'll need more than an hour with her. Don't taint me with your premature ejaculation problems, old man."

I bit my lip to keep from laughing. Scythe loved nothing more than to rib on Nash, who had recently turned forty. We all knew Nash had no such problems.

But something gleamed in his eye anyway. "I do love when you lay down a challenge."

Scythe winked at him before grabbing my wrist and drawing me into him.

I laughed. "Don't use me as a pawn in your games. I'm going home and going to bed."

Scythe stepped in closer so his breath tickled over my

ear. "Give me five minutes to change your mind." He kissed the side of my neck, soft and sexy.

Like they had a mind of their own, or one that only listened to Scythe's commands, my nipples hardened.

I almost groaned in annoyance. I'd been ready for pajamas and bed.

But one whispered sentence, and all those plans went out the window.

His touch slid up my arms and across my chest so he could take big handfuls of my boobs. He pinched my nipples through my lacy lingerie and smoothed his thumb over them. "Do you know how hard I've been all night, getting little glimpses of these when the lights hit you just right?" His lips trailed up my neck while he worked to free my tits from my top. He got the knotted halter neck undone, and my boobs fell free and heavy into his hands.

I'd never been small there. I wasn't small anywhere, with plenty of curves and thick thighs and a jiggly ass.

I hadn't always loved myself, but I'd found three men who did.

Four if you counted Scythe's alter ego, Vincent.

Scythe rubbed his thumbs over my nipples some more, eliciting a little gasp of pleasure because pregnancy had made them super sensitive. He caught my pleasure with his lips, kissing me until I gave in to this happening, just like he'd known I would.

I could never resist them. Any of them. At any time. Even on my most exhausting nights, one soft kiss, one dirty look, and I was throwing aside any plans for a *Golden Girls* binge.

Scythe got shitty if I watched that without him anyway.

His tongue prodded my lips, and I opened for him, the kiss deepening until I gripped the sides of his face and held him tight to me.

He groaned, and I pulled away only to have War claim my mouth. He stood behind Scythe, sandwiching him between us. Scythe dropped his head back on War's shoulder while War and I kissed, tongues moving together in a practiced rhythm we'd done so many times before.

By the time we broke apart, he had Scythe's black work pants undone and his underwear halfway down his ass so he could jerk Scythe's cock from behind.

Another round of heat surged through me. I loved when the two of them touched each other. Could literally sit there and watch them with popcorn if they didn't always end up dragging me into it too. They were both so strong and sexy, and everything about the two of them together turned me on.

Nash knew it too. He mirrored War's position, coming in behind me and dragging my panties down my thighs.

"You're wet," he murmured in my ear. "Your panties are soaked."

"She's always horny when I'm around." Scythe's hips jerked lightly with every pump War gave of his cock.

"She's always suffocated by your ego when you're around," I sassed him back before War shut me up by claiming my lips again.

Nash found my clit and started up a slow, torturous pace that set the ball of nerve endings on fire. I kissed

War back while reaching behind me for Nash's fly. With his help, I freed his cock.

He was the biggest of the three, though none were a slouch in the dick department. The size of him no longer bothered me though. I'd had all of them in every part of me. Not one of them had ever caused me any pain. They knew me. They knew my body and the things I liked. None of them ever took without giving me a hundred times more first.

Nash's dick moved between my legs, not pushing inside my opening but coating himself in the arousal building there. Every rub of my clit had me wetter and wetter, and he ground his dick back and forth, torturing us both until I was mewling, begging one of them to give me more.

"I need someone inside me," I groaned. "Quit torturing the horny pregnant woman."

I reached down between me and Scythe and covered War's hand with my own. Together we guided him to my entrance, teasing his head in my wet warmth until he surged his hips forward. War and I got our hands out of the way so Scythe could sink inside me.

The relief was nearly instant. Him filling me in the place I so desperately needed him. Scythe fucked me slow, pulling one of my knees up, so he could get deeper inside me while standing. He was thick and hard, stretching me so perfectly little moans of ecstasy escaped my lips.

I held on to him, digging my nails into the solid muscle of his back because I knew he got off on a bit of pain.

"Your pussy is so sweet, Bliss," he whispered in my ear. "So fucking tight and warm."

War kissed his neck. "Much like your ass."

Both Scythe and I groaned at War's dirty words.

Scythe reached behind him, his arm moving rapidly, telling me he was jerking War off. "Fuck me," he groaned to War. "I need you in me while I'm in her."

But War slowed him down, stepping backward. "Let me get some lube."

In a sex club, we had copious amounts of the stuff. There were tubes of it on every other surface. War grabbed the closest one and coated his cock in thick, slippery gel.

Then with a wink at me, tossed the tube to Nash.

Nash's tongue licked up my neck, and he nuzzled in there, his free hand coming around the front to rest lightly on my throat. "You want that, Bliss? Can you take both of us still?"

I moaned my permission. "Fuck. Please."

He groaned. "You're such a good girl."

It didn't matter how many times they'd called me that. I still got off on every one.

The lid on the lube bottle cracked open, and then Nash's fingers were between my cheeks, spreading me, lubing me up. Scythe's thrusts were slow and deep, jolting me back against Nash's fingers, each thrust taking them deeper. He rimmed my back hole, working the tight opening in just the way I liked, while an orgasm built somewhere behind my clit.

"I need to come," I moaned, unable to move as the orgasm barreled down.

The only leg I had weight on trembled, but Scythe

and Nash had me, their strong arms keeping me steady while they drove me higher and higher with their hands and cocks and tongues.

I cried out at the loss of Nash's fingers, but a second later he replaced them with the thick head of his cock.

"Watch me, Bliss," War demanded.

I opened my eyes, and my gaze met his. They blazed with need, and he grabbed my chin, kissing me roughly, sloppily, but I loved every second.

Then he bit down on Scythe's shoulder and thrust in hard.

Scythe's moan of ecstasy hit some place deep inside me. Nash pushed in at that same time, and I clamped down on both of them, my pussy and ass spasming with the force of the orgasm. I held Scythe for dear life, taking every thrust, every pump, from the front, from behind. I took War's kisses and his dirty words while he fucked the man he loved. I took his whispers of love for me and stored them deep in my heart. I took Nash's 'good girls' and Scythe's cum when he couldn't hold on another second.

All four of us joined in a pleasure that not one of them alone could deliver.

Spent, Scythe slipped from my body, leaving a sticky mess between my thighs. Nash used the opportunity to lean me over the back of the nearest couch, pushing me down with a hand between my shoulder blades and drawing my hips back and up.

Beside us, War did the same to Scythe, both of them fucking us from behind.

Scythe turned his head toward me and watched Nash take me in the ass. Despite War pounding into him, he gave me a wicked grin and reached across, and then between my legs to stroke my clit.

I shouted and instantly fell into a second orgasm, while Scythe chuckled victoriously.

Nash dug his fingers into my hair and pulled, forcing my back to arch and my head to tilt back.

If I hadn't already been in the middle of an orgasm, I would have come again. Buried deep inside me, Nash came hard, his shouts of ecstasy mixing with War's. The two of them drove home in unison, all raw masculinity and sex appeal that made me question why I'd ever even considered going home to bed when this was on offer.

Nash's movements eventually slowed, and he pressed a kiss to my spine as he withdrew from my body.

War and Scythe had already finished, and War walked over to me, wrapped me in his arms, and kissed me deep. "Proud of you."

A sudden wave of sleepiness came over me. "What for?"

"The way you don't hold back with us anymore. Look at you, standing there with their cum between your thighs and one of our babies in your belly." He dropped to his knees and placed kisses across my bump. "You're the best thing that ever happened to me, baby girl. I can't wait to do this with you for the rest of my life."

Scythe raised a lazy eyebrow from where he lay sprawled on the couch, still completely naked. "This a marriage proposal? Your cock ring doesn't count as an engagement ring, you know."

War flipped him the bird. "You're just jealous because I'm not down on my knees for you."

Scythe grinned. "I fucking love you on your knees for anyone, War."

War glanced at Nash. "I think he just gave me permission to give you a blow job."

Nash laughed from where he stood running his fingers up and down my back. Nash enjoyed our foursomes as much as any of us did, but he'd never wanted one of the guys the way War and Scythe wanted each other. He loved them. But not like that. "Not sure your jaw could take me."

War cocked his head, and for half a second I thought he was considering having a go.

But then Scythe growled. "Don't even fucking think about it."

The corner of my mouth lifted at his little display of jealousy.

War walked over and kissed him. "Yours is the only cock I want." But they were interrupted by War's cell phone ringing.

Scythe groaned. "Ugh. Leave it. I'm getting hard again."

But War pulled away and glanced over at his phone on the bar top. "I don't like calls at this time of the night. Makes me think someone is dead."

I stood a little straighter, a sudden chill falling over me.

War strode across the room, yanking his jeans up but not bothering to do up his belt. It jangled as he picked up the phone. "All good. It's just Fang. Probably club stuff."

My shoulders slumped in relief.

Nash kissed my cheek. "I'm grabbing a shower before we go home."

I smiled up at him. "I'll come with you."

I linked my fingers between his but stopped when War let out a whistle, stopping us both in the doorway. When I looked back, he was holding up one finger. A clear sign for us to wait.

"Is she sure?" War asked, that frown line between his eyes deepening. "Absolutely no doubt?"

He paused, waiting for Fang to fill him in on whatever it was.

That rising sense of dread came back with a vengeance. This was clearly not club business if he wanted us to stay. War wasn't exactly secretive about what was going on with his club. If he could safely tell us what they were up to, then he did. But there was a lot he was too afraid to tell us. We'd learned not to push.

"Okay. We'll be there in thirty. Don't fucking do anything without us, all right? Yeah, I'll bring Bliss." He ended the call without saying goodbye.

With my heart thumping, I bit my lip. "You'll bring Bliss where?"

He turned to Nash. "Can you grab her a blanket? We need to talk about Caleb."

I blinked in surprise, but it was all too quickly replaced by a dark, heavy feeling I hadn't felt in a while. I didn't like thinking about my abusive ex anymore, now that he was out of my life for good. "What about him?"

War's mouth tightened into a line. "He tried to kill Rebel tonight."

"What!" I yelped.

But War continued without reacting. "She's okay. But she thinks he has another woman locked up in his house. Fang wants backup to go in and try to get her out."

Scythe sprang to his feet like he'd been waiting all his life to be called up. "Put me in, Coach. I'm your guy." He rolled his head to one side, his neck cracking audibly. "It's been too long since I had some fun with our little friend."

War looked to Nash. "You want in too?"

Nash wasn't as bloodthirsty as Scythe, nor did he lead the same sort of violent lifestyle War did, where killing was just part of his job as an MC prez. But Nash's eyes narrowed. He loved Rebel like a sister and he hated Caleb as much as the rest of us did. "Fuck. Yes." He shook his head. "This is our fault. We should have ended him permanently after what he did to Bliss."

Scythe frowned. "Pretty sure I was the one who suggested murder and mayhem, and you went all dad mode on me and said I wasn't allowed."

Actually, that had been me. Caleb was an influential businessman. He had connections to powerful people and parents who would notice if he suddenly went missing. Killing him wasn't as easy as taking out some trailer park trash who everyone expected to die of an overdose anyway. It had been me who'd talked them out of going after him. I'd been scared. I had everything I'd ever wanted in these three men. Love. Security. A home, and a baby on the way. Caleb had been out of our lives. Too scared, I'd thought, to try anything again. I hadn't wanted my men hurt or back in prison. Not when we had so much to look forward to.

I'd just wanted them out of danger. Safe with me and here to watch our baby grow up.

A tear rolled down my face at the thought of Rebel being hurt by my lack of action. She was my family as much as these three were, and yet I'd left her vulnerable and unprotected.

With hate in my heart for what Caleb had turned me into, I steeled myself for words I never thought I'd say about a man I'd once loved. "Kill him. End this once and for all."

7

REBEL

It was still dark when Vaughn opened the front door to our house.

Bliss shoved him out of the way, barreling forward into the entry way, not even bothering to say hello to him in her haste to get inside. "Where is she?"

"Up here," I called to her from halfway up the staircase.

She lifted her gaze, and instantly her face crumpled, her shoulders shaking.

"Oh, Bliss." I hurried down the stairs and swept the taller woman into the tightest hug I could muster, ignoring the sting of pain from my injuries. "It's okay."

She dropped her face into the shoulder of my sleep shirt, crying hard enough that the wetness seeped through the fabric. "I'm supposed to be the one comforting you," she wailed.

I rubbed a soothing hand up and down her back. "I'm not the one crying like it's an Olympic sport and you've been training for gold."

She sniffled. "Don't make jokes."

"She's good at that," Vaughn mumbled.

I gave him a pointed look. "Don't you have a bad guy to go catch, Robin?"

Bliss glanced between the two of us, confused. "Isn't his name Vaughn?"

I sniggered. "Long story. Has to do with a Halloween party. But come up to my room and I'll tell you all about it." I peered around her shoulder and gave a small wave to Nash, War, and Scythe, all standing in the foyer, looking stupid in their all black getups, balaclavas included.

My three weren't any better.

"Wannabe stealth ninjas, much?" I gave my best martial arts yell. "Kiiiiiya!"

No one laughed at my teasing. They were all too busy with working out the logistics of how their little raid was going to go down. Scythe ran a blade through his fingers absentmindedly while Fang filled everyone in on the plan they'd come up with.

"Tough crowd," I muttered. "Well, enjoy your Caleb hunting."

There was a sincere hint of bitterness in my tone. I knew what was going to happen next. They'd go to Caleb's, put a bullet in his head, or I guess a knife, if Scythe got to him first. Then they'd pat themselves on the back for a job well done.

If that got the woman out of Caleb's basement, then it would be a good thing. She had to be the priority.

But there was a wounded part of me who knew it should have been my kill. Who knew I needed it if I was ever going to feel whole again. He'd stolen my power. The only way of getting it back was making him hurt as much as I had.

A bullet was too kind. Too simple and easy.

Too painless.

I wanted him to die in agony.

I should probably ask Scythe for a blade to play with, considering I was clearly as batshit crazy as he was.

Kian stepped in front of me and squeezed my biceps. "Your face is scaring me. Are you going to murder your friend if I leave the two of you here alone?"

"Of course not," I scoffed. "That's fucking insulting." I side-eyed Bliss. "Unless she drinks the last of the milk before I get to put any in my coffee."

Kian nodded. "Okay, good. Just checking." He leaned in and brushed his lips over my forehead.

Vaughn paused on his way to the door too. "Don't follow us, Roach. I know you want to."

I gave him my most innocent expression. "I don't know what makes you think I'd do that."

He reached for my hand, wrapping his fingers around my clenched fist. Slowly, one by one, he pried my fingers away, revealing the contents I'd been trying to hide from him. He plucked the car key from my palm and let it dangle from his fingertips. "I'm taking your car keys with us."

I glared at him. "I have the Uber app, you know."

He shrugged. "Hey, if you want to explain this whole situation to your driver, good luck. I hope he doesn't mind you making him an accessory to murder. Poor innocent driver. Just trying to make ends meet for his hungry wife and children left at home. I mean, they'll probably all die from starvation while he's in prison, but sure. Call an Uber."

My mouth dropped open. That was a bit over the top.

He leaned in and placed a kiss on my cheek. Was it my imagination or did he linger there longer than he needed to?

"Stay here, Roach. I mean it. For her, if not for yourself. We can't focus on her if we're worrying about you."

It pissed me off, but he was right. "Fine."

Fang was last. He just tilted my head up and pressed his mouth down on mine.

Instantly, all of the cold parts inside me melted.

"I love you," he whispered over my lips before he pulled away.

"I love you too," I whispered back.

I caught the look that passed between Bliss and War and if I hadn't been sending my guys off to murder a man, then I might have cared we'd just pretty publicly announced we were a thing.

Bliss said goodbye to her guys, and they all filed out into the darkness of the early morning, with the first rays of the sun barely nudging the horizon.

I closed the door behind them, and half a second later, Fang growled from outside. "Lock it, Pix."

I rolled my eyes at Bliss and made a show of flicking the locks.

All while knowing that wouldn't keep Caleb out if he really wanted to get in here.

But Fang had already thought of that. "War called up Aloha, Ice, and few of the other guys from the MC. They're all stationed up on the road and in the woods around us."

I huffed out an irritated sigh. That explained why they were all happily heading out and leaving me behind. "I hate feeling this helpless," I complained to my best friend. "We're just princesses locked in a tower while the men go out and do all the knightly bullshit. Feminism died a thousand deaths in this house tonight."

Bliss put her arm around my shoulder. "Or it's alive and well, and you're just letting someone else take care of you for once."

"That makes me uncomfortable," I grumbled.

She towed me into the living room. I hadn't spent much time in here, because it was on the formal side. I wasn't used to couches that were hard and uncomfortable because they were meant more for decoration or perhaps a polite tea and scones, rather than kicking your shoes off and flopping onto one with a beer and a football game. All the little breakable trinkets stressed me out. Intrusive thoughts really made me want to pick one up and hurl it onto the floor.

I had no idea what that was about.

She perched on the edge of an overstuffed, floral couch and pulled me down next to her. She twisted to face me. "I hate you didn't tell me it was Caleb who hurt you."

"I didn't want you putting any blame on yourself when nothing he did is your fault."

"It is, though! I should have let Scythe take care of it ages ago."

I picked up her hand and squeezed her fingers. "I know you would have if you'd known what he was going to do to me."

"He hurt me too," she said softly. "Raped me, I mean."

I put my arms around her again, and this time, my tears joined hers. "I didn't say anything either. It's my fault he has another woman."

Bliss shook her head forcefully. "It's not either of us. It's him."

I nodded in agreement. "Can we talk about something else?"

She wriggled back against the couch, trying to get comfortable. "You can tell me why Fang..." She cocked her head to one side. "Does Fang even have a last name, or is he like Cher? And Beyoncé?"

I giggled. "I don't even know."

She raised an eyebrow. "You just told the man you love him and you don't even know his last name?"

I grinned. It didn't even bother me. I might not have known that, but I knew other things. Like how he made me feel safe. Like how I knew, without a shadow of a doubt, he'd always have my back.

I didn't need to know the name he used on his driver's license in order to love him. "His first name is Milo though."

She frowned. "I wouldn't have picked him as a Milo in a million years. That's such a..."

"Unintimidating name?"

"Yes! Exactly. And he is anything but."

I shrugged. "One of the guys gave it to him, apparently. Colmillo means Fang in Spanish. It came from that, if you believe the legend."

She smiled widely at me. "But you love him?"

I nodded without hesitation.

She squealed and clapped in excitement. "We can have a double wedding!"

I widened my eyes at her. "A what? Whoa. Hold your horses." I scanned her fingers. "Are you planning on marrying one of those three men who follow you around like lovesick puppies?"

Bliss got a dreamy look in her eye. "Well, no. But War was down on his knees today—"

I sniggered. "Scythe is around. Of course he was."

She slapped my arm. "Stop. You're as bad as he is. War was kissing my belly, actually. It was so sweet. Kinda made me think about one of them actually proposing."

"How would that even work?"

She shrugged. "Just a commitment ceremony, I guess. It's not like the four of us can have something legal. If any of them actually ever ask me, I'll let you know. Since it seems you might have the same problem someday."

I shook my head quickly.

But Bliss was all over me. "They all kissed you."

"They're my friends."

She scoffed. "They're out trying to murder a man for you, Rebel. That is not friend-only behavior."

"I'd kill a man for you."

She smiled softly at me. "Yeah, but we're soulmates. Kian kissed your forehead. That's like, the universal symbol for 'she's mine.' It's distinctly un-friend-like."

My forehead still burned from the brush of his lips. "That's not true," I protested weakly.

Bliss kept pushing. "Nash has been your friend for years. Has he ever kissed you on the forehead?"

She had a point. Forehead kisses did seem just a tad more intimate than the half-arm hugs Nash usually threw my way. If Nash kissed my forehead the way he kissed Bliss's I would be entirely weirded out.

Bliss knew she had me. She side-eyed me. "What's going on with Vaughn?"

I flopped back against the couch. "I don't know. He's so hot and cold. One minute he's crawling into bed with me—"

She raised an eyebrow.

"Fang was on the other side."

Bliss's mouth dropped open. "Get me some popcorn and tell me more."

"There's not much more to tell, honestly. Nothing happened. We just talked."

"But you wanted more? Even with Fang there?"

I picked at a stray thread from the couch. "Fang has been hanging out with War too much. He offered the same sort of deal you and War have."

Bliss's eyes couldn't have been any bigger. "He offered to share you?"

I lifted a shoulder. "Sounds a bit gross when you put it like that."

But Bliss was like an overexcited dog with a bone. "Word it however you want. But essentially, if you'd climbed on top of Vaughn when he'd been in your bed earlier and ridden his cock, Fang would have been cool with that?"

Heat blasted through me at the thought of slipping a leg over Vaughn's muscled thighs and sinking down on him. "Yes."

Bliss eyed me with the shrewd gaze only a best friend could have. "Oh my God! You wanted to!"

I frowned but found I couldn't deny it. So instead, I brushed it off. Again. "Kian and I are just friends. And it's just attraction with Vaughn. You're in love with all three. I only love one. Totally different situation."

"I loved War before I loved Nash or Vincent or Scythe. Feelings grow. They change. If you let them have the room to do so."

The thought was vaguely terrifying. It was scary enough to love one man. But to feel like that about multiple felt like a recipe for disaster. "I just need to screw Vaughn and get it out of my system, I think."

"So do it."

The thought was tempting.

"Do Kian while you're at it." She wriggled her eyebrows suggestively. "Or do them at the same time."

I laughed at her very out-of-character behavior. Normally it was me egging her on. "Who are you, and what have you done with my prudish best friend?"

Bliss shrugged. "You wore off on me."

"In a good way?"

She leaned over and kissed my cheek. "In the best way." She glanced around the room, her gaze coming to rest on a framed photo of my mom and Bart. Bliss stood and went to inspect it, her T-shirt clinging to her little baby bump.

She picked up the silver photo frame and smiled wistfully at it. "Your mom was really happy."

Emotion clogged my throat, the same way it did every time I thought about her lately. The grief was too raw. Too new for me to be able to just skim past it. "I think she'd finally found a good one, you know? I hate that it was all cut too short."

Bliss put the photo frame down, adjusting it so it was

exactly where she'd found it. "Do they have any leads on her murder?"

"Besides me, you mean?"

Her face morphed into a grimace. "You haven't been arrested yet, so that has to be good, right?"

"Can't be a bad thing, I guess. But I don't know that the cops are investigating any other options with too much vigor."

She made a face. "That was my experience when Axel died too. They're completely incompetent."

"The woman next door thinks it was Kian."

Bliss's mouth dropped open. "That big teddy-bear-looking man? What on earth would make her suspect him?"

I shrugged. "I thought the same thing, but there is an unusual number of photos of Kian with Mom and Bart."

"He lived here. They hung out. That's not so unusual."

I nodded, hoping that was all it was too. I'd barely had a minute to think about Sasha's accusations before everything had happened with Caleb. "She said there was screaming in the nights before the wedding too. Not the good kind."

"We should search his room," Bliss said suddenly.

I stared up at her. "That sounds like something I would suggest and you would talk me out of. What are in those pregnancy hormones?"

"Beyond an overactive sex drive? I don't know. But what I do know is I don't want my best friend going to jail and getting preyed on by a butch lesbian named Biff."

I frowned at her. "I think I'd much prefer a lipstick lesbian named Leslie if I was going down that rabbit hole, but can we not get so ahead of ourselves? I'm not going to jail."

Bliss's smile wavered. "Of course not. But I still think we should search his room anyway. You don't have to do anything. I'll do it all." She headed toward the stairs.

I grabbed her arm. "You know something."

Bliss shook her head. "No, I don't."

I knew when she was lying. "Swear on your unborn baby."

Her mouth dropped open. "Rebel! You can't make me do that."

"It won't be a problem if you aren't keeping anything from me! But you totally are or you would have already done it!" I searched her face. "Did you talk to Liam?"

Liam Banks, my lawyer, was a friend of Scythe's. Bliss had called him when I'd been taken into the police station for questioning.

Bliss sighed. "Fine. I spoke to Liam. He couldn't really say anything, and I don't want to stress you out. But he did kind of insinuate if we could produce some sort of evidence that would force the police to look beyond you, it would be helpful."

We'd heard as much before, but I'd put it to the back of my mind, distracting myself with hunting Caleb and his friends down.

That might have been a mistake. I knew I was an easy target for lazy cops and a jury could easily find me guilty. Hell, I had means, motive, and opportunity.

Bliss cocked her head. "Are you hesitating because you don't want to invade his privacy? Or because you think you might actually find something?"

The answer instantly popped into my head. I didn't like it.

"The latter," I admitted.

Bliss rubbed her hand up and down my arm sympathetically. "You like him. You don't want him to have been involved. I totally get it. But as your best friend, Rebel, come on. You need to know who you're living with. If he did this...you're living with a murderer."

That was a tad worrying. I'd moved myself in here, with next to no knowledge about either man sleeping beneath this roof.

Bliss knew she was getting close to convincing me and put the nail in the coffin. "If you're even considering Fang's offer to let Vaughn and Kian in, you have to know who you're getting in bed with."

"Shit," I muttered. "I really hate when you're right."

Kian and I might not have acted on whatever was quietly building between us the way Vaughn and I had, but it didn't mean it wasn't there. I was trying so hard to convince myself we were just friends, but really, we weren't even that. We couldn't be.

I didn't trust him. I wanted to. I wanted to focus on the sweet way he'd secured a lock to my bedroom door so I'd feel safe. Or the way he'd supported my desire to learn how to fight.

But ever since Sasha had put her seed of doubt in my head, I'd been putting up walls with him. Holding him at arm's length.

I pushed up off the couch and held a hand out to Bliss. "Okay. We're doing this."

"Yes! Wait. Should we get gloves? Fingerprints and all. Do we have enough time? What if they come back. Oh

God, that would be so bad if he busted us in there." She wrung her hands. "Is going through someone's room a crime? What if doing this with a baby in utero sets him or her up for a future life of crime?"

I glanced back over my shoulder at her. "Seriously? You're worried about that when she might have gotten half her genetic makeup from Scythe and Vincent?"

"You have a point."

Bliss was always more cautious than I was. She was the good girl to my morally gray. We sat nicely in those roles, and it was actually comforting to be back in them.

I grabbed her arm and dragged her toward the stairs. "Come on. You put this idea in my head so you're coming with me."

She complained the whole way that she must have had temporary pregnancy-induced delusions but followed me into Kian's room and stood in the middle while I started snooping.

"What exactly are we searching for, do you think?" Bliss squinted around at Kian's perfectly tidy bedroom. She trailed a finger along his bookshelf, then held it up to her face, inspecting it. "Damn, it's neat in here. He even dusted."

I rifled through a stack of PlayStation games, sitting on his bedside table. "I don't know. A murder confession would be great though."

Bliss sniggered and pulled open Kian's top drawer. "Money maybe? Or something else inappropriate that might prove he was more than just friends with your mom and Bart?"

I lifted the corner of his mattress to peer beneath it. "Inappropriate like these, you think?"

On the slatted bedframe was a couple of porn magazines.

Bliss turned around and wrinkled her nose. "Oh, ew. Who still uses magazines to get off? That's so seventies. Get a Pornhub subscription, Kian."

I didn't disagree, but part of me was curious. I picked up the little stack and let the mattress drop back.

Bliss smacked the magazines out of my hand. "Oh my God, what are you doing? You know what he was doing while he was looking at these, don't you?"

My mouth went dry thinking about it. Kian sprawled out on his bed. Magazine open to a centerfold of a naked, big-breasted woman staring poutily at the camera.

His hand around his shaft, slowly moving up and down while I was in the room next door.

Bliss snapped her fingers in front of my face. "Where did you just go in your head?"

I blinked. "Someplace very, very dirty." I knelt to pick up the magazines, knowing I couldn't just leave them there on the floor, even if they did have traces of Kian's spunk on the pages. I closed the first one, ignoring the lewd position of the couple, and reached for the second that had slid partially under the bedframe.

There was a bright-yellow Post-it note stuck to the cover. Handwriting scrawled across the front.

In an instant, my heart sank.

"This is my mom's writing," I said quietly.

Bliss paused, mid rifle through Kian's underwear drawer. "How do you know? Why would Kian have a porno with a note from your mom on it?"

I shook my head. "She puts love hearts above her i's like I do sometimes. I picked that up from her. More disturbing though, is what the note actually says." I peeled it off and handed it to her.

Bliss read it aloud. "Thought this might help. Come to my room when you're ready."

Her eyes went huge, but she tried to cover up her initial reaction with a more diplomatic one. "That note might have originally been stuck on the vacuum cleaner. Maybe he was cleaning his room with a...broom? And she brought him the vacuum and she just meant to do her room next..."

I looked at her.

"Yeah, okay. That's weak."

"Anyone our age wouldn't have a porn mag, Bliss. You said that yourself. But Mom's generation..."

"She wasn't that much older than you."

"Old enough. I remember finding pornos all over our house when I was a kid. Still no idea if they were hers or her boyfriends', I didn't want to know, but that generation was raised on magazines." I screwed up my face and tossed the offending items onto Kian's bed. "Oh God. She gave him those, didn't she? As a come-on? Go get horny then come to my room!" Bile rose in my throat, and I made a choking noise as I gazed at the ceiling. "That's sex predator behavior, Mom! He's young enough to be your son. So gross!"

Bliss fingered the note, then sat on Kian's bed. "Kian isn't a kid. He's well over twenty-one. Let's not taint her with the sex creep brush. For all we know, Kian was the one who started it."

I squeezed my eyes shut tight. "So you think they were sleeping together?"

"I'm not sure when else you'd give someone porn and an invitation to your bedroom."

I sank down on the bed beside her, the mattress dipping beneath my weight. "Do you think Bart knew?"

She shrugged. "Seems like it would be pretty hard to miss something going on right under your own roof. Maybe he liked to watch..."

I gagged. "Oh, gross. I do not want to think about my mother and Bart and a guy I might want to have in my bed in a threesome."

"So you do have the hots for him!"

I waved her away and flopped backward on the bed. "This is so bad. I wish we'd never come in here."

"Do you think Vaughn knows?"

I shook my head. "No. There's a weird tension between him and Kian. But it's the kind that comes from seeing the other naked, and instead of thinking, *geez, bro, put it away,* you think, *damn, bro, put it in.*"

Bliss flopped back with me, both of us lying on our backs and staring at the ceiling.

"Okay, but as much as we were maybe hoping to find nothing, this cements the idea they were having an affair. An affair is a strong motive for murder. What if Kian wanted more than just some spicy nights with your mom? What if he offed Bart in a jealous rage?"

I peered over at her. "How many daytime soaps did you watch while you were off with morning sickness?"

"God, so many. But I'm serious! We should at least tell the cops."

I held up the little yellow square of paper. "That we have a Post-it note for proof?"

"Doesn't sound great when you say it like that."

"How else are we going to prove it? We've searched his room. There's nothing else here that points at the two of them having an affair. Vaughn and I went through our parents' room too. All we got from that was photos."

"You need to go through his phone. That's where all the juicy stuff will be. Nudes. Love letters. Creepy stalker pics he might have taken of her while she was in the shower."

I huffed out a sigh. "I just can't imagine Kian doing any of that."

"Explain the Post-it then."

I couldn't. "How am I supposed to go through his phone? Just come right out and ask him for the passcode?"

Bliss twisted onto her side and propped up her head on her hand. "You need to get closer to him."

"I already live with the man."

"Closer." She grinned at me. "Good excuse to sleep with him if you ask me."

I shoved her shoulder, and she toppled back onto the bed with a laugh.

"Two problems with that. One, he could have murdered two people. And two, we just found evidence he could have been sleeping with my mom!"

"Let me throw a little one-two back at you. One, that could be all coincidence. Two, you think he's insanely hot and you're looking for an excuse to moan his name." She lifted her head. "Seriously, though, I want you to be safe. Maybe you should come live with us. At least for a little while."

I shook my head. "I can't. You're right."

She raised an eyebrow. "About sleeping with him?"

"About getting closer. If he has something to hide, I'll find it."

"Naked."

"Not naked!"

Bliss made a knowing sound at the back of her throat. "Mmm-hmm. We'll see about that."

She could see about that all she wanted. I had my hands full with Fang and Vaughn. Until I knew for sure Kian was innocent, I wasn't getting in any deeper with him.

No matter how much certain parts of me protested.

8

FANG

Scythe danced around on his toes like a fighter, his eyes slightly crazed. "Are we standing around singing camp songs or are we going to go storm the castle? Let's go."

War held up a hand in a stop motion. "Hold on to your bloodlust for just a minute, would you? We need a plan."

"There's six of us, one of him. At worst, his friends are still there, so that's three. We've got the numbers." Vaughn recited the stats to the other guys, sparking a debate over where we parked the cars and who took what entrances.

I tuned out. All I wanted was a cigarette. Or really just anything to do with my hands. I eyed the way Scythe was fingering his blade and understood why he did it.

I couldn't stop thinking about the woman tied up in Caleb's basement.

It could have been Pix.

At one point, it had been. Maybe not tied up exactly,

but they'd kept her in that house, hurting her instead of letting her leave. I hadn't been there to save her. The very fucking least I could do was save another. Maybe it would help ease my guilty conscience.

"Fang. Ride with us."

I glanced up at my name to see War flick his head toward Nash's Jeep, parked in the dark across the road from Rebel's place.

Vaughn and Kian hesitated on their way to Kian's truck, waiting for me to decide who I was riding with. After the night we'd had, and knowing what we were about to do, it didn't feel right to just leave Kian and Vaughn to themselves.

We might not have been true friends before last night, but something had changed in those few hours.

But when your prez gave you an order, you followed.

"Go on ahead," I called to Kian. "We'll meet you there. Park down the road a way, okay?"

They walked off into the slowly lightening darkness, and a moment later the truck doors slammed.

I fell in line with War. Nash and Scythe drew ahead of us, discussing something I couldn't quite hear because War slowed our pace until it was really just the two of us walking together.

He glanced over at me with a half-smile. "She loves you back, huh? 'Bout fucking time you told her."

I wasn't generally one for smiling, but this time I couldn't help it. Hearing her say she loved me in front of our friends was better than any other feeling in the world. I'd almost expected her to want to hide the fact we were together. I would have gone along with it.

I wanted Rebel in any capacity I could have her.

I always had.

But War's smile faded. "You haven't been around the clubhouse much lately though. There was a meeting last night you didn't show for."

I blinked and pulled out my phone, scrolling down through the messages, and sure enough, there was one from War.

"Fuck, boss. I'm sorry. I didn't even see it."

He clapped me on the shoulder. "I get it. I get it. Women got a way of stealing your focus sometimes. Guilty of that myself with Bliss. But I needed you last night."

"Won't happen again. What did I miss?"

"We're going after the Sinners. It's time, brother. We can't hold out anymore."

I'd been waiting for this. If War hadn't been so caught up with Bliss and her pregnancy, it probably would have come a lot earlier.

Not all that long ago, War's parents had been in a terrible car accident when one of the club women had tampered with their brakes. She'd had reasons of her own for wanting them dead, that none of us had seen at the time.

Fancy, War's mom, had been knocked out cold but survived.

War's dad—Army, our previous prez—had been found at the bottom of the cliffs by a hitman who'd put a bullet through his brain.

That hitman had been Scythe. The man War was already in love with.

Hadn't that been a fucking shit show.

I ground my teeth together. "Agreed. It's time we took

care of it. They ordered that hit on your old man. One of their own admitted to it. Even if it was Scythe who'd carried out the actual kill, they gotta know we don't take that shit lightly. We going for their leader?"

War puffed on his cigarette, blowing a stream of smoke into the darkness around us. "Scythe never got the guy's name when he took the job, but we know it was one of them. I'm holding their leader responsible. You know him?"

I shook my head. "Not really."

War touched the screen of his phone. It glowed yellow, lighting his face, and he turned it around to show me.

It was a mug shot of a man who looked vaguely familiar.

"Hayden 'Chaos' Whitling." War's voice was barely calmer than a snarl. "Low-level gangbanger until he balled up and offed their leader so he could take his spot."

"Vicious."

War punched my shoulder. "If one of you did that to me, watch me come back and haunt your asses."

I couldn't imagine anyone doing that to War though. He was well liked, both inside our chapter and with the other Slayers' clubs. It was sometimes hard to believe he was Army's son.

The two of them were nothing alike.

War might have idolized his old man, and I'd been as loyal to him as I was to War, but Army had a coldness to him I'd never seen in his son. A ruthlessness to get to the top and to make sure nobody ever saw him as weak.

Under his command, I'd done things I didn't want to think about.

War gave me a shove toward Nash's Jeep. "Come on. Head in the game. Tonight, we end this thing with Caleb. Tomorrow, we worry about the Sinners and Hayden 'Chaos' Whitling."

9

KARA

She wasn't coming back.

I'd waited for hours, while Caleb's Halloween party continued outside the four walls of the house I was kept prisoner in. Feminine screams shattered through raucous male laughter and heavy, thumping music. I folded in on myself with every one, until I was curled up in a ball in the corner of Caleb's basement dungeon.

It was sick that I seemed to be safer in here than the women outside. I couldn't even bear to think about what Caleb and his friends were doing to them.

If it was anything like what they'd done to me, God save their souls.

Was one of the women screaming Rebel? She'd promised help. That she had men on the outside who would come and free me. But Caleb had taken her somewhere, and now I was more alone than ever.

Time ticked by slowly. I was exhausted, but I couldn't sleep. The little baby inside me kicked and rolled and punched, completely unaware of the danger I'd so stupidly put us in.

Gradually, the party noise outside died away, leaving me in a silent house.

Exhaustion crept over me, and sleep beckoned.

His footsteps on the stairs shattered any hope of rest. Instinctively, I wrapped my arms around my belly and turned away from the door.

I didn't even need to look up when he undid the locks. Rebel had been gone too long. He'd either killed her, or she'd been smart enough to get away and never ever come back here.

I hadn't been as clever. Just like my father always told me. All I was good for was my pretty face.

"Get up, slut."

I shook my head. I'd been praying to get out of the windowless room for days, and now that I had the opportunity, I didn't want it. Not when it meant going with Caleb. If there was even the slightest chance Rebel was still trying to free me, I needed to be here. If he took me somewhere else, I was right back to square one.

"For fuck's sake. Did I offer an alternative? Get up."

I tucked in on myself even farther, praying he'd lose interest and just go away.

I was never that lucky.

Sharp fingers wrapped around my upper arm, and I yelped in pain when he roughly yanked me to my feet.

"Please don't," I begged.

He shoved me toward the open door, the basement stairs looming beyond. "If you don't want me to kick the shit out of that bastard baby growing in your belly, you'll do as I say."

I stared at him. I couldn't help it. The pure malice in his tone, the evil threat, it was beyond comprehension. I was sure he couldn't mean it. No human could.

But there was something distinctly cold in his eyes. Something unhinged. "Keep your eyes on the floor, slut. You don't deserve to see anybody after the way you've acted."

I dropped my gaze, realizing in that moment he would carry out his threat if I didn't obey. He wasn't bluffing.

I shuffled to the stairs and took them one at a time, his chest brushing my back the entire time as he hurried me up them, no care given to the fact I was so heavily pregnant and climbing stairs wasn't exactly easy for me anymore.

"Fat bitch. Move your ass." He shoved me forward.

I barely caught the railing to stop myself from hitting the floor.

The house was dark and quiet, but beyond the glass doors was the evidence of a huge party. Empty beer bottles and red Solo cups littered the yard. Halloween decorations were tipped over, and uneaten food sat spoiling on platters, barely picked at.

My stomach grumbled, reminding me I hadn't eaten since I'd been taken. "Can I have some water, please?"

It seemed a simple enough request, but it earned a sharp yank on my ponytail. Pain spliced through my scalp, and I let out a whimper.

"Why would I give you anything after the way you turned up here, acting like you had some sort of claim on me? I'm owned by no woman. I owe you nothing. Not even water. Sluts like you don't deserve it."

I licked my dry lips, refusing to beg or cry. He'd just get off on it. I wouldn't give him that.

He dragged me to the front of the house and peered out the window. "Fuck!" He took his phone out of his pocket and tapped the screen before holding it to his ear. While he waited for whoever he'd called to pick up, he twisted my hair tighter and tighter until tears rolled down my cheeks.

He leaned in and licked one. "Exactly what I wanted. I love when you cry for me."

I wanted to vomit.

"Hugh. Where the fuck are you?"

The sun was barely starting to flicker over the horizon, so it had to be early morning. I stood there at the window, hoping I'd at least get to see the sunrise. I'd always loved them. Back home, I was expected to be up and helping out on the farm before dawn, and I'd grown to love the vibrant displays.

I wasn't guaranteed to see another sunset. But if I could just stand here long enough to see it rise...

Of course, he wouldn't even let me have that. He dragged me away to a panel by the front door and stabbed at the buttons, changing the image, until he swore again.

But the image filled me with hope.

Three men dressed all in black, exiting a vehicle. I squinted at the screen, trying to work out where they were. It didn't seem to be the front of the house. Maybe from a camera pointed down the street.

I went to scream, but Caleb clapped a hand over my mouth and tsked in my ear. "Now, now, remember our deal."

His hand dropped to my swollen belly, and I froze.

He rubbed his hand all over it, finishing with a vicious pinch of the already stretched skin.

I stifled a sob but didn't fight when he pulled me away from the window and to the back of the house. Another check of a security camera panel attached near the back door, and he was pushing me out into the early morning air and into the thick bushes that lined his property.

We were barely concealed before another man crept down the side of the house and into the backyard.

With his hand still on my belly, Caleb simply gave a silent shake of his head.

I didn't make a noise. The instinct to protect my child was too strong.

In silence, we watched the men storm the empty house.

Caleb laughed softly in my ear. "So fucking stupid. Come on."

With the men preoccupied inside, he hauled me away through neighboring properties. I stumbled over tree roots and uneven ground, trying to keep up with the punishing pace he set, until we stumbled out onto a road.

Caleb looked around, clearly trying to get his bearings before getting out his phone again.

I didn't bother listening to his conversation.

I focused on the sunrise and each new ray of light that streaked across the sky.

When a car stopped in front of us and he shoved me into the back seat, I went, just grateful he hadn't put me into the trunk where I couldn't see out of a window.

I barely noticed the houses outside changing from million-dollar mansions to average suburban homes, and then to run-down shacks that made our old farmhouses back home seem luxurious.

When our driver stopped at our destination, I focused on the sky and how beautiful it was, not the ramshackle building I'd been taken to.

Knowing the alternative, Caleb needed no other threats to get me out of the car and up to the front door. He banged his fist against it, paint flaking beneath the force of his blows. When nobody came, he switched to bellowing, "Hayden! Get out here!"

Eventually, the door opened, and a deep, sleep-laced voice grumbled out from the depths of the house. "What the fuck? What time is it?"

Something about his voice pulled me out of the safe space my brain had created. I finally dragged my gaze away from the sunrise.

Hayden was the most attractive man I'd ever seen. Tall. Broad-shouldered. A maze of tattoos all over his tawny skin. His dirty-blond hair was just long enough to put into a ponytail at the nape of his neck, but it was messy from sleep. Tight black boxer briefs clung to his muscled thighs, but that was the extent of his clothing.

His gaze collided with mine.

He looked me up and down, his gaze coming to rest on my belly before sliding back to Caleb sharply. "What the hell is this?"

Caleb shoved me forward, and I stumbled over the threshold, not realizing there was a step.

Hayden caught me, strong arms wrapping around me. "Whoa. You good?"

Caleb pushed in behind us and took one last glance at the street, searching both ways before he closed the door. His friend's car had already disappeared. "Get your guys up and watching."

Hayden still hadn't let go of me, but all his attention was on Caleb. His eyes narrowed. "Why? What have you done?"

Caleb didn't answer, only screwed his nose up at the vaguely musty scent that seemed to cling to the old house. "It reeks in here."

Hayden glared at him. "We could go crash at your place instead, if you prefer."

Caleb scoffed. "Be my guest. I can't go back there anytime soon. Not until I get a few little problems straightened out." He looked at Hayden properly for the first time since we'd arrived. "Which is where you come in. I need you to do something for me. A job."

"What is it?"

"I need protection."

Hayden's jaw clenched. "For her too?"

Caleb sniggered. "What? No. I couldn't care less about her. You can have her."

Hayden glanced at me, then back at Caleb. "To do what with exactly?"

He shrugged. "Whatever the hell you want. I'm sure a man like you has needs."

"She's fucking pregnant, Caleb!"

Caleb seemed as bored as if Hayden had just suggested he watch paint dry. "If you don't like her, just keep her with the others."

For the first time since we'd left the house, I couldn't keep my words inside. "The others?"

But Caleb had already lost interest, wandering away

through the quiet house and leaving me alone with the other man.

Hayden watched him go and then turned to me with a sigh. "Are you okay?"

I shook my head. "Please let me go."

"I really fucking wish I could. Come on."

He pointed toward the hallway, but he let me walk of my own accord. At the end, he opened the door.

Four other women slept on mattresses on the floor.

One lifter her head sleepily and blinked an eye. "Chaos? What's going on?"

Through gritted teeth, Hayden, or Chaos as this woman seemed to be calling him, leaned on the doorway. "Caleb just dropped her off. Take care of her, okay? She's pregnant."

He closed the door behind me.

Leaving me alone with 'the others.'

10

KIAN

Rebel and Bliss stood in the foyer when we returned, anxious expressions firmly in place. Rebel's big eyes flicked from Fang to Vaughn to me.

"Well?" she asked, a hint of breathlessness in her voice. "Did you find her?"

The others didn't answer. The mood had been so low in the car that I hadn't even suggested karaoke for fear someone might stab me since they hadn't gotten to take their frustrations out on Caleb.

Nobody else seemed willing to answer, so I filled them in. "The place was empty."

Rebel's face fell. "You searched the basement? There are multiple rooms..."

"We searched them," I assured her. "There was no sign of a woman being held there."

"No sign of Caleb either," Scythe complained with a toddler-like pout. "Worst killing expedition ever!"

We all glanced over at him.

"What? So I'm dramatic." He flopped down on the couch, only further proving his point.

The rest of us ignored him.

"So what now?" Rebel asked. "That girl is still out there somewhere. He has her."

Fang cleared his throat. "We'll keep searching. He can't hide forever."

"But no more tonight," I added on. "None of us have slept, and we have no idea where he is."

Rebel buried her face in her hands. "This is all my fault. I should have told you all straightaway. I shouldn't have let him take me in the first place."

"You didn't *let* him take you anywhere," Vaughn corrected. "You were taken against your will. Nobody is blaming you here, Roach."

But it was clear Rebel was very much blaming herself. I didn't like the way that made me feel. I'd very quickly come to hate when she wasn't smiling.

"I've sent a few of the guys from the club over to watch his house," War assured the women. "He'll come back eventually. Or someone will. When they do, we'll be ready."

It was all that could be done for now, when everyone's tanks were running on empty.

War, Nash, Bliss, and Scythe said goodbye, Bliss wrapping Rebel in a long hug and whispering something in her ear I couldn't make out.

Fang was next in line, sweeping her into his arms and kissing her mouth. "War needs me at the clubhouse. Stay here. Sleep. Heal. I'll be back as soon as I can." He held her tightly, and she melted right into him.

A pang of jealousy coursed through me. Just like it did every time another man touched her.

Lucky assholes.

If she'd been single, I would have been actively pursuing her. She was a stunner, with her tight little body and big eyes and sassy attitude. She made my palm itch for wanting to spank her ass before I plowed into it.

I swallowed thickly and breathed through my nose, trying to clear my head of thoughts that weren't going to serve me well. This was around the time of day I woke up with morning wood. I hadn't been to sleep, but I still had the hard-on.

"I'm going to bed for a while," I announced, not tired but knowing if I stood around watching her any longer when I was this fucking edgy, I was going to do something I regretted. I'd been expecting a fight tonight. I'd geared myself up on the way over to Caleb's house. Let my body fill with adrenaline, only to have it all go nowhere.

This had happened when I'd been professionally fighting too. The opponent would concede or just not turn up, and I'd go from super amped to fight to super amped to fuck.

It didn't help that there were two people under this roof who were viable candidates for the latter.

Shame one was taken and the other was firmly back in the closet.

I left the others in the foyer and took the stairs two at a time. When I got to the second floor, I snuck a glance back down at my roommates.

Rebel watched me.

She turned away but not quick enough that I hadn't seen it.

Fuck.

I slipped into my room and closed the door behind me. I leaned back on it, ignoring how hard my dick was. Having her living here was a recipe for disaster. She was with Fang. Fuck, I even liked the guy. We got along well. I didn't want to be making moves on his girl.

I'd been stupid enough to let my dick rule my head once, and it had ended really freaking badly. I didn't want to do it again.

My dick ached for how bad I wanted her though. It wasn't just the leftover adrenaline. It was how strong she was. How determined to set wrongs right. Yet there was a softness to her that set off every protective part of me. Something broken that needed shielding so she could rebuild and regroup.

I knew what it felt like to have your entire world turn upside down in the blink of an eye. I'd had no one to have my back when it had happened to me.

I didn't want that for her.

I pushed off the door, headed for my bed, but stopped a few steps in. Everything was wrong. There was a crinkle in my bedspread. The top drawer was open just slightly. I could have sworn the air smelled different. Not in a bad way. In a nice way actually.

I stuck my head out into the hallway again, but everyone had disappeared. Knowing Fang had left and I wasn't about to walk in on the two of them having sex, I strode through the open bathroom door, and finding hers open, I leaned on the doorway. "You and Bliss have fun while we were gone?"

Rebel lay on her bed, scrolling through her phone. She shrugged. "Sure, I guess so. We haven't had much girl time lately."

I folded my arms over my chest. "Mmm-hmm. Have fun going through my bedroom?"

She glanced over at me. "What makes you think we went through your room?"

"There's a wrinkle in my bedspread."

She snorted on a laugh. "So?"

"Have you not noticed how tidy I am? I'm insulted you think I would make a bed and leave wrinkles. My top drawer was open too."

She twisted to roll over onto her side and propped her head up with one hand. "You don't think you might have done those things yourself when we were hurrying to get ready for Caleb's party last night? Or after the whole pool debacle?"

She had a point. I had been a little preoccupied. It had been the middle of the night when we'd finished up with the paramedics and I'd come back to my room after having a shower. I supposed it was possible that I might not have taken as much care as I normally did. "Why does it smell like perfume in there?"

"I sprayed some deodorant earlier. Your bathroom door was open."

Well, shit. That made sense. I rubbed the back of my neck. "Sorry."

She shrugged and went back to her phone. "No sweat."

"You need anything before I get some sleep?" She seemed pretty healthy for a woman who we'd found at the bottom of a swimming pool not all that long ago. "Still no coughing?"

"No secondary drowning here. My lungs are good. I'm good. Just tired."

"I'll leave you to it then. Get some rest." I pushed off the doorframe and went back through the bathroom. This time I shut the door.

I stripped off the all-black getup and pulled on a pair of flannel pajamas with Taylor Swift's face all over them. They'd been a gag birthday gift from Miranda and Bart, but they were super comfy, so I wore them regularly. I got beneath the blankets and tried to sleep, but it didn't seem to matter how long I lay there, the need to fight or fuck wouldn't go away.

I tossed and turned, getting hotter by the second. It was like someone had lit up the fireplace in the corner of my bedroom, except the flames were inside me, heating from the inside out.

I knew there was no way of getting any sleep when I was like this. I could get up and run, but my body was exhausted. Getting off was the easier option. Caving in to the need I'd been trying to ignore, I stripped off my pj's. Taylor didn't need to see what was about to happen here.

I got back beneath the blankets and palmed my already hard cock. I closed my eyes while I stroked myself, but the instant I did, Rebel popped into my head.

I didn't want to disrespect Fang by thinking about his girl while I did this. So I closed my eyes again, willing myself to think of anyone but the sweet little brunette in the bed just feet away.

The next image in my spank bank was Vaughn.

I twisted onto my side with a groan. That was so much worse.

I grabbed my phone, ready for some inspiration that were not images of either of my roommates, who were both frustratingly unavailable.

The screen was black. "Nooo," I groaned softly. "Turn on."

The stupid thing was completely dead. It hadn't been charged in over twenty-four hours, so it was hardly surprising, but the timing sucked. I tossed it across the room, knowing the carpet was thick enough to soften the fall. I'd charge it when I woke up. I rolled over and lifted the corner of my mattress, fumbling beneath it for the stash of dirty magazines I kept there for such situations.

I came up empty-handed. Frowning, I groped around some more and then checked the other side, thinking maybe I was losing my mind. I always slept on the left. Which meant my stash was always on the right. They weren't on either.

I found them at the bottom end of the bed and got back beneath the covers. But my mind was whirring a million miles a minute, no longer thinking about my dick but why the hell my room felt so wrong.

"Rebel!" I bellowed.

"What?" she yelled back.

"My porn collection? Seriously?"

I waited for her to deny it. But a minute later, the bathroom door slid open and her head poked in. Her gaze darted to the porn collection in my hand and then back up at my face.

Her guilt was written all over her features. "Okay, so

fine. Maybe Bliss and I had a very quick poke around your room."

"I knew it! You little gaslighter! You seriously had me thinking I was turning into a slob."

She frowned at me. "Jesus, Kian. If one wrinkle in your bedsheets and a slightly ajar drawer constitutes being a slob, I think we need to get your OCD checked."

"My OCD is just fine. What on earth made you want to go through my room?" I wasn't exactly mad. I had nothing to hide. If she'd just asked, I would have let her look at whatever she wanted. But I was curious to know what she'd been searching for.

I kinda hoped it was porn. Damn, that was hot.

She raised a shoulder. "I just realized I barely know you. Or Vaughn. But Vaughn wears his heart on his sleeve, so I feel like I at least know what makes him tick. You hide yours."

The idea was baffling. "I'm an open book. What do you want to know?"

She raised an eyebrow. "I can ask you anything?"

"I need to sleep, so limit it to your top three."

She wandered over and perched on the edge of the bed. I tried not to notice her smooth, bare legs as she crossed them up underneath her. An oversized sleep shirt swamped her slight frame, and she tucked her arms inside it while she mulled over her questions. "You'll tell me the complete and honest truth? Even if I don't like it?"

"Sure."

"Have you ever had an affair?"

I blinked at the shot she'd fired. "Okay, not going to lie, I didn't' realize we were going deep right off the bat. I thought we were going to talk favorite colors or foods, but sure. Let's rattle some skeletons in the closet."

"You're hedging."

She was right. I was in avoid mode while my brain worked overtime. "I'm just trying to work out how best to answer the question so you don't hate me."

She bit her lip. "Just tell me straight."

I sighed, really wishing she hadn't gone there until she knew other things about me. The less douchey things in particular. "Yes. I've had an affair. But in my defense, it wasn't me in the relationship. They were, I wasn't. Doesn't excuse it. I knew they were with someone else."

She didn't say anything. Her face became totally unreadable.

"Do you hate me now?"

I almost didn't want to hear her answer. She'd barely been in my life a couple of weeks, but in that tiny space of time, she'd become someone I didn't want to disappoint.

She shook her head. "No, of course not. But this is what I mean by I don't know you. I wouldn't have picked you as the type."

Guilt swirled in my gut. "I'm not. I made a mistake. With one person. I never did it again. And I don't plan to."

She nodded, but I could see she wasn't quite convinced.

"Ask me your second question then."

I needed the chance to prove to her I was more than just that one mistake.

"I asked you this once before and you turned it into a joke. But now I'm asking seriously. Was there something going on with you and my mom?"

The question rang in my ears. "Miranda?" I choked out. "Are you seriously asking if I was sleeping with your mom?"

Rebel nodded.

I laughed. I could hear the relief in it. "Your mom loved Bart more than life itself."

"People have affairs behind the backs of people they love all the time."

Yeah, they did. Just ask Vaughn. I'd been sucking his cock while his high school girlfriend got drunk with her friends in the next room. But that hadn't been Miranda and me. She'd adored her fiancé. "Your mom was one of the good ones. She never would have cheated on Bart."

Rebel hugged herself a little tighter. "So you didn't kill her then?"

I let out a low wolf whistle. "Wow. How long have you been wondering that?"

She gave a small shrug, her petite shoulders rising then falling. "I don't know. But I really want you to tell me I'm crazy for even considering it."

That was easy. I grabbed her chin and held her firmly. "I didn't kill your mom, Little Demon. And I have no desire to hurt you. You're safe in this house with me. Those locks I put on your doors were just to make you feel better. You don't actually need them."

The relief on her face was obvious. It flooded her eyes as she nodded.

Fuck, she was beautiful, staring up at me like she was. I wanted to pull her onto my lap and wrap my arms around her tight. Trail my hands up and down her spine and run my fingers into her hair.

I dropped my gaze to her lips and was rewarded with her pink tongue poking out to wet them.

Fuck. I'd just sworn to her that I wasn't ever going to make the same mistake twice. Yet all I wanted to do in the moment was tilt her face up and claim her mouth.

Distract her from the fact I hadn't actually answered her when she'd asked if there was anything going on with her mom.

There hadn't been an affair. Being the other man wasn't something I wished to repeat. Being Vaughn's dirty little secret had been enough to last me a lifetime.

But things had gone on. Things that would send the cops in my direction if they realized I had a perfect motive for murder... I liked Rebel a lot. I didn't believe for a second she had anything to do with her mother's death. I would help her find another suspect.

But I didn't want that person to be me. We needed to find the real murderer.

"Last question," I managed to get out, even though she'd already had her three.

She nodded.

She looked over at my porn collection. Then at my bare chest, then lower, at the blankets barely covering me. In the wake of her questions, I'd forgotten I was naked.

Slowly, her mouth lifted in a half smile. "Were you spanking the monkey just now?"

I was grateful for the easier line of questioning. We'd slipped straight back into our usual friendly vibe.

I grinned at her. "Actually, I was just searching for an article to read. There's informative stuff in these, I'll have you know."

She raised an eyebrow in challenge and reached across the bed for the nearest magazine. She flipped it open to a random page and read the heading. "Sixty-nine ways to make her come."

"See?" I chuckled. "Informative."

"Number One. Put your finger in her ass." She tossed the magazine straight back at me with an eye roll. "Oh, come on. This was written by a man who still lives in his mother's basement and only touches blow-up women. Good Lord. How is that number one?"

This felt like much safer ground, and she was cute as hell when she was all scowly and pissed off. But more than that, her reaction made me curious. "You don't like anal? Damn, girl. You don't know what you're missing. And I say that as a man who has been in that position."

She glanced up at me. "Never said that."

My dick gave a kick of excitement.

Enough for her to notice. She rolled her eyes. "Clearly, you like anal."

"Probably wouldn't fuck men if I didn't."

She cocked her head to one side. "You prefer that? Men over women, I mean?"

"Didn't say that," I echoed back her earlier statement with a wink.

She glanced down at her hands with a smile. I couldn't help reaching over and tracing it with my thumb. It was nice to see after the worry she'd had there when she thought I was banging her mom. "What's the smile for?"

"Nothing."

"Bullshit. You like that I'm bi."

My thumb trailed to her lips, and she sucked in a breath. "I want you to like whoever you want, Kian."

She was so close. Her vanilla-and-peaches scent all up in my nose and making my head spin. If she'd started this little conversation as a distraction from the bigger secrets between us, it was now becoming a problem of its own. My dick strained in her direction. I was still covered by a blanket, but it left little to the imagination.

I did nothing to cover it up. But for the sake of not making the same mistake twice, I needed to end this now. I liked Rebel. I didn't want to ruin the friendship we'd started building.

I wanted to one day be able to tell her the full, complete truth.

"You should go back to your room, Little Demon. Fang wouldn't like that you're in here with me."

Her gaze was trained on my dick. "Fang and I have an understanding when it comes to you and Vaughn."

I nearly fell off the fucking bed. "Does that mean what I think it means?"

"Probably."

I brushed a finger over her bare knee, unable to stop myself now that she'd half waved a green flag in my face. What the hell was Fang thinking? Surely, he didn't mean what I was imagining. "Okay, so let me just say the most out-there thing I possibly could, and you can tell me if your agreement covers it."

"Go on then."

I stared her dead in the eye. "If I flipped you onto the bed, spread your legs, licked your sweet slit until you gushed on my face, he'd be cool with it?"

She eyed me without saying anything, and damn if it didn't feel like a challenge.

One I was totally up for. "What if I then rolled you over and slid my dick into your pussy and fucked you hard and fast while I kissed you slow, he'd be cool with that?"

Still no denial.

"Fuck," I groaned. "So just to clarify, you're saying if I laid you over my lap, spanked your ass, then took it with my cock, until you screamed my name loud enough for the neighbors to hear, he'd just be like, hey, cool, Kian. Nice work, bro?"

Her lips parted softly on a pant. "If I was cool with it, he'd be cool with it."

"Are you cool with it?"

"Keep talking like that and I could probably be persuaded."

I groaned. "Leave the room, Rebel."

She frowned. "Seriously? You say all that and then you tell me to go away?"

She had a point. But so did I. "You also said you don't feel like you know me."

"Since when do you need to know someone to do...that?"

But I needed it. "Despite rumors you may or may not have heard, I actually don't really like one-night stands. I'm kind of a relationship guy."

She smiled at that. "So no sex unless I'm your girlfriend, huh? If I took this shirt off right now, you wouldn't touch me?"

I shook my head.

She pulled her shirt over her head, leaving her sitting on my bed in nothing but a pair of panties.

I groaned at the sight of tight little tits, a perfect perky handful I could devour with my tongue. I instantly reached for her without a thought to whatever the hell bullshit I'd just been preaching. It hadn't been a lie. But Rebel on display for me was too much to resist.

She pushed to her feet and strolled toward the bathroom, dodging my greedy fingers. "Shame. But I respect your boundaries, Kian."

"Fuck my boundaries," I groaned. "Get back here."

She shook her head as she walked into the bathroom. A moment later, a buzzing sound floated back. "My vibrator and I will be respecting your boundaries from all the way over here in the bathroom." She closed the door.

I was not a murderer.

But I was an idiot.

11

VAUGHN

Laden down with a dozen reusable shopping bags, I struggled through the doorway and unceremoniously dumped all twelve on the kitchen floor.

"What's all that?"

I spun around and found Kian lying on a yoga mat in the open-plan living room. He had his head swiveled in my direction, but his legs were in some sort of pretzel position that had to be insanely painful.

"Groceries." I pointed at the food cupboard. "We were getting pretty low."

Kian unraveled himself only to twist into a different, even more awkward position. "Yeah, I noticed, but we've run out of the money that was in the household account. Your dad's business partner seems to have put a stop to the regular payments that used to go in there."

I swore beneath my breath. "I'll get it fixed. Just tell me if you need money."

Kian bristled, like I'd somehow managed to insult

him in the three sentences I'd uttered since walking in here. "If you just paid me for the work I'm doing, I wouldn't have to, Mr. Moneybags. My wages haven't been going into my account either."

I sighed. I was probably more broke than Kian was. I'd been living off the tiny amount of money I'd managed to salvage from my trust fund after I'd realized Brooke had happily spent ninety-five percent of it without my knowledge.

Kian pointed to a package sitting on the dining room table. "That came for you while you were out by the way."

I squinted at it. "What is it?"

"I'm already your currently unpaid housekeeper. Do you really want me to be your receptionist too?"

I glared at him. "What's up your ass this morning? I didn't mean it like that."

Kian pushed to his feet, a sheen of sweat glistening on his lightly freckled skin. "I'm going to see if Rebel wants to go for a run."

I watched him walk up the stairs to her room. I might have been amused by her loud complaints at being woken up for cardio if I wasn't so busy hating on the fact Kian was clearly pissed at me.

I was the one who should have been pissed. It was him who'd walked out after grinding on top of me, then leaving me with a case of blue balls.

But I knew that was nothing compared to the way I'd walked out on him ten years ago. He'd denied sex. I'd denied our entire fucking relationship—years of friendship and months of slowly becoming more.

I sighed and picked up the package from the table. There was no return address, but the postmark was from

California. In an instant, I was on edge, knowing it had to be from my wife. "What now, Brooke?" I muttered to the empty kitchen.

The package was legal-sized but oddly light when I picked it up. I shook it, but it didn't make a sound, so I dug through the top drawer and found a pair of scissors. The sharp blades made quick work of the plastic mailer, and I tipped the entire thing upside down to empty it onto the table.

It took me a minute to realize the long golden strands falling from the package were hair.

I didn't know how long I stared at the pile before I dared to reach out for the card nestled amongst it.

But my heart pounded when I turned it over to read the scrawl of letters written across it.

You can pay what your woman owes. Or we can continue sending parts of her. This is a warning. The next one won't be.

My stomach swirled with nausea. I'd thought Brooke had been overexaggerating when she'd claimed these men she owed money to would kill her if I didn't pay.

I tried to convince myself it wasn't her hair. It could be any blond woman.

But what if it was?

Kian's sneakers squeaked on the grand staircase behind me, and I quickly swept the hair and the card into my palm before I turned around.

Kian was alone.

"You couldn't get her emo ass out of bed?" I asked, trying to hide the tremble in my fingers.

He scowled in a very un-Kian-like fashion. He was normally all sunshine and rainbows and positivity. But apparently not with me. Not anymore since I'd reopened

Pandora's box by practically begging him to fuck me the other night.

Awkward.

He put his hand on the doorknob and turned, letting in a gust of cold, morning air. "At least get her to eat something, would you?"

He disappeared outside, the door banging shut behind him.

Rebel peeked over the top of the banister as I was brushing Brooke's golden hair into the bin. "Is he gone? Have I managed to escape the torture?"

I glanced up at her, trying to calm my breathing. The combo of Brooke's hair and Kian's slightly sweaty body were too much. "It's safe to come down. Come get some breakfast. I bought a bunch of different things."

Kian wasn't the only one who'd noticed Rebel never ate.

I had three different cereals, eggs, bacon, hash browns, and toast all lined up on the counter for her perusal by the time she made it down the stairs, an oversized hoodie swamping her petite frame. "Take your pick."

"Cocoa Puffs for the win."

She pulled the box toward her with a grin. "Kian would be horrified about the lack of protein and the abundance of sugar, I'm sure."

"I just want you to eat something. I don't care what." I took a white bowl from the cupboard and spoon from a drawer and pushed both of them across the counter to her.

She bristled as she poured a ridiculous amount of

Cocoa Puffs into her bowl and added a heavy-handed pouring of milk. "I eat."

I wasn't going to argue with her. "What are you doing today?"

Her spoon paused midway to her mouth. "Kian is right. I do need to do some exercise. I've been lying around the house for too long. I need to work on my fitness and strength. But ugh. Running is the worst. You know if you don't let him shout encouragement at you, he just sings instead? I honestly don't know what's worse."

"The singing. Definitely the singing."

A gold strand of hair glistened on my sleeve in the morning sunlight. My hand started up a new round of the shakes. Did they have her somewhere? Or had they just jumped her on the street and lopped off her ponytail? Brooke was obsessed with her hair, treating it with all sorts of lotions and oils and spending hundreds every time she went to the hairdresser. She'd probably have preferred to lose a toe than to have all her hair hacked off like this.

I didn't want to be married to her. I'd come here, swearing her problems were no longer mine.

But she'd been a part of my life for a decade. I didn't want to see her hurt. I couldn't just walk away, even if I wanted to.

Rebel watched me while she ate. "Are you okay? You look pale and off in your own head."

I wasn't okay at all. But I didn't want to pile my shit on top of her shoulders. She already had enough of her own things going on. "I need to swim."

I hadn't thought about it before the words had fallen

out of my lips, but even the idea of diving into a pool sent a dose of calm through my system.

Swimming was what I knew. It was where my head cleared because all that mattered was kicking and stroking and keeping myself from drowning. The harder I pushed, the more I thought about sucking in air every time I turned my head.

I'd spent a lot of time doing laps after I'd moved to California. I'd spent hours a day there, away from Brooke's nagging and her constant whining that I was no fun.

I was no fun because all I'd thought about was Kian. Even though by that point, I hadn't seen him in years.

I poured myself a bowl of Cocoa Puffs. "Do you want to come with me? Swimming is cardio."

Her eyes went big, and she dropped her spoon, sending chocolate-flavored milk sloshing over the side of the bowl. "God, you're an asshole. I nearly drowned a few nights ago, Vaughn."

I shoved a spoonful of sugary cereal into my mouth, chewed, and swallowed. "So, what? You're never going to swim again?"

"Exactly."

I shook my head. "We live minutes from a beach."

"Good thing I'm so *emo* then, huh? We don't like the sun much."

Clearly, she'd heard me talking with Kian. But I shrugged. "If the shoe fits. Go get your probably all-black swimming suit on and let's go."

She shuddered. "I can't."

I didn't like the way she trembled. I reached a hand

out to steady her. "Hey. Are you really going to let him take this from you?"

Her jaw hardened. "Why, Vaughn? Why say that? I really hate you knew that was probably the one thing you could say that would get me to go."

My smile widened, and I tugged her hand toward the stairs. "I just wanted to see you in a bikini, Roach. Don't read too much into it."

She shoved me but ran up the stairs. When she hit the landing, her little smile gave me one of my own. She had a light in her that had a way of making everything better. Even the mess I'd made with Kian. I didn't want to see that light go out.

The indoor swimming pool was surrounded by a vague haze of chlorine. Rebel wrinkled her nose. "Why does the oversized bathtub of death smell so bad?"

It had been a very long time since I'd been to the aquatic center here, but nothing had changed. I strode toward the changing rooms. "So you don't get sick from all those little kids peeing and pooping in it."

Her mouth dropped open, and she stared over at the handful of kids playing in the knee-deep water of the kids' section. "You're joking, right?"

"Not really."

She trailed after me. "And yet you still get in there willingly?"

"It's worth it. I need to swim, and the ocean is too cold this time of year."

I dumped my sports bag down on a bench seat outside the changing rooms then pulled off my hoodie. My sneakers and sweatpants came next.

Rebel sniggered. "Nice Speedo." But her gaze dipped down my body, rolling slowly over my abs, and then lower, along the trail of hair beneath my belly button. She coughed. "They don't leave much to the imagination, do they?"

"Are you complaining?"

She dragged her gaze back up to my face, but it was with clear reluctance. "No, sir, I am not."

Fuck. If she kept looking at me like that, I was going to want to do a lot more than swim with her. I cleared my throat and distracted myself by digging through my duffel bag. "Get your gear off. I brought you my extra pair of goggles. I've got a swim cap in here somewhere too, if you don't want to get your hair wet. Is that what you're swimming in?"

She'd stripped her warm outer layers and stood in a black pair of running shorts I was sure had never been used for their intended purpose. On her top half was an oversized black T-shirt that might have actually been one of mine she'd swiped from the laundry.

"Yes."

I shook my head. "That shirt will drown you."

She shoved her hands on her hips. "I'll be fine."

I pointed at a sign. "You can't wear T-shirts in the pool anyway. The colors leech out and ruin the pool's pH or something like that."

She scowled at the sign that did indeed state regular T-shirts could not be worn into the pool. Specific Lycra swim shirts were fine, but what Rebel was wearing was not.

She shoved her hands on her hips. "That just seems like a ploy by some pervy old guy in management who wants to see some skin. Sexist creep."

"At the risk of sounding like that guy, what have you got under that?" I asked.

She grinned, looked around, and noticing no one was behind me, lifted her shirt to flash me.

It was a well-designed flash. All I caught was a glimpse of her bare underboob. No nipple. But it was enough to send blood rushing to my dick.

Not wanting to terrify the children across the other side of the pool and their bored mothers watching, I turned and dove into the pool. I flinched at the temperature. It was heated but still a bit of a shock to the system. The water rushed around me, filling my ears, and I blew out to keep the water from going up my nose. I hadn't even put my goggles on, so I had to squeeze my eyes tight. I swam blindly to the other end of the pool, did a neat somersault, and was halfway back before I had myself under control. I slowed my strokes, treading water while I swiped at my eyes.

Rebel wasn't standing at the other end.

I used my hands and feet to propel me in a circle, searching for her, but couldn't see her mop of dark, short hair anywhere. "Rebel?"

In the deep end of the pool, tiny bubbles rose to the surface.

Ice froze over my gut.

"Oh Jesus, fuck. No."

My legs felt disjointed. Like no matter how hard I

kicked, the water kept pushing me backward. I turned my head and gulped for air, forcing my arms to spear through the water to get me there quicker. Water streamed into my eyes, stinging them, but I couldn't close them. Not until I got there. Not until I knew if I'd been making up those bubbles I'd seen.

Rebel sank slowly toward the bottom of the pool, her black T-shirt billowing out around her. Small bubbles leaked from her nose and mouth, but her eyes were closed.

She made no move to swim. No effort to propel herself back up to the top so she could breathe.

How long had she been down there? Ten seconds? Thirty? A minute? Maybe more?

I swam harder, panic fueling my kick. A few feet away, I took a breath then dove beneath the surface, kicking down until my fingers touched her skin.

She didn't react.

I wrapped my arm around her bare waist and dragged her up. We broke the surface, and I sucked in a lungful of air, simultaneously shaking her.

"Rebel!"

Her eyes flew open, and she shook her head, water droplets flicking me in the face. "Yeah?"

The adrenaline departed my body in an instant. I shoved her away from me, my chest so tight I couldn't breathe let alone hold us both up.

Treading water easily, she watched me with big brown eyes.

I swam away.

I swam as far as I could with trembling arms. At the opposite end of the pool, I grasped the edge and tried to breathe normally but I couldn't. It fucking hurt too much.

A minute later, a soft voice came from behind me. "Vaughn."

I spun around, suddenly way more angry than scared. "What the fuck was that? You just play dead now?" If she hadn't been treading water in the middle of the lane, blocking my escape, I would have swum straight past her again.

She shook her head. "I was just...I don't know. It's peaceful down there."

"Peaceful!" I exploded, words fueled by fear. "Sure, real fucking peaceful down there where there's no goddamn air! You know, that thing you need to breathe?"

She reached out and touched my chest. "Hey. I had air. I wasn't tied down. I was coming back up."

I tried to breathe normally, but it was like it was me who'd been the one drowning, my lungs filling with water. I grabbed the edge of the pool, shaking my head. "What were you thinking? You think you were the only one who suffered a trauma that night? You weren't, Rebel. Do you know how useless I felt, realizing no matter how fast I drove, I probably wasn't going to get there in time? How guilty I felt when I saw what he'd done to you? If you wanted to punish me, you picked the best fucking way to do it."

Her arms came around my neck from behind, her chest pressing to my back, her lips at my ear. "I'm sorry. I didn't think."

Her lips touched the side of my neck.

I froze.

She did it again.

Her lips were soft and warm but insistent. She kissed a trail up the side of my neck, mumbling the word 'sorry' in between each kiss.

I reached behind me and grabbed her thigh. In a second, I had her swiveled around in front of me, her back hard up against the side of the pool. She gasped when I dragged her thigh around me, but an instant later, her other leg mirrored the action, and she linked her ankles at my lower back.

My barely covered dick pressed to her running shorts.

"I'm sorry," she said again, mouth an inch from mine while she searched my face. "I wasn't thinking. I didn't plan it. I just jumped in. I'd planned to swim…but then I just…didn't."

I couldn't hear it. Couldn't bear to think about the way she hadn't even tried to swim. I tightened my grip on the backs of her thighs, pressing her tighter to the wall so she couldn't slip below the surface.

My dick hardened against her core, grinding on her soft, sweet parts.

Her breath hitched. Her gaze dropped to my lips. She leaned in, but I dodged, not ready to forgive her.

The rejection should have stopped her. Most other women would have swum away, hurt.

Not her. She gripped the sides of my face, keeping me in place. "Kiss me," she whispered softly but fiercely. "You don't get to rub all up on me like this, turning me on, and then not kiss me."

Oh, that was rich. Her making demands when she was the one sinking to the damn bottom of the pool. "Then stop trying to fucking die on me! You don't get to do that anymore! You hear me? I don't even know what I'd do if..."

Her fingers stroked through the wet hair at the back of my neck, her gaze searching mine. "What you'd do..."

I didn't even know what I'd been trying to say. But whatever it was felt big. Too much. Too soon.

I slammed my mouth down on hers instead.

She scrambled in my arms, wrapping hers around my neck and pulling me impossibly tighter. She kissed fiercely, just like I'd thought she would. She moaned into my mouth, and the noise went straight to my dick. It surged with need for her, and fuck if I wasn't tempted to reach between us and push aside her shorts.

It was a bruising kiss, both of us fighting for control. Our tongues dueled, our lips battled. Her hips rocked against mine until I trailed my lips off the side of her mouth and bit her neck. "Stop moving or I'm going to come."

Her breath left on a hiss. "Keep going. The chlorine will take care of that too, right?"

We both stopped and stared at each other.

Then burst out laughing.

"That is so disgusting, Roach," I complained. "What is wrong with you? You're a total vibe killer."

"What!" She shoved my chest, pushing me away, but you couldn't wipe the smile off her face. "You're the one who said it got rid of pee and poop germs. Cum doesn't count?"

A mother from the other end of the pool gave an overexaggerated cough with a glare in our direction.

It only made me want to swim right back to Rebel and do a whole lot more than kiss.

Rebel seemed like she was thinking the same thing. "Can we pick this up in our backyard pool?"

"The one Caleb tried to kill you in?"

She shrugged. "I could use some new memories to replace those ones. If you're up for it."

"That pool isn't heated. And it's winter."

She licked a droplet of water from her lip. "I'm so horny right now, Vaughn, I don't think I care."

I dove beneath the water and swam to the opposite end of the pool before I could find out if chlorine was really as effective as I hoped it was.

12

REBEL

Vaughn drove home from the pool with a smile on his profile that I was sure matched the one on mine. I sat on a soggy towel, with his hand clamped on my thigh, thumb rubbing absently over my bare leg. Every mile we drove closer to the house, his thumb crept higher and higher up my leg, a silent promise of what was to come as soon as we got in the door.

I couldn't stand the anticipation.

My nipples were hard beneath my oversized hoodie, and I reached up inside it, grasping one between my fingers and tweaking.

Vaughn watched me from the corner of his eye, his gaze flicking between me and keeping us on the road.

"Watch where you're going," I admonished him. "Nothing to see here."

"Lay the seat back. Take off your hoodie."

I widened my eyes at him. "It's broad daylight, Vaughn."

"Don't care. I want to see you play with your tits."

Heat soared through me.

I lowered the seat right down so I was lying. I could no longer see the other cars and houses flashing by outside while Vaughn drove. I could only hope they couldn't see me either.

"Take it off, Roach," he mumbled. "I can't wait until we're in the house. Need to see you now."

The hoodie came off over my head, leaving me topless but shivering in the cool air of the car. I pulled the hoodie over me like a blanket.

Vaughn leaned over and cranked up the heat. Then he snatched the hoodie away. "Don't freaking hide from me. Let me see you."

"I wasn't hiding. I was cold."

"Then do something to warm yourself up." His thumb moved quicker on my leg.

I took my breasts in my hands slowly and pinched my nipple between my thumb and forefinger.

Vaughn groaned, sneaking little glimpses at me out of the corner of his eye. "I'm tempted to pull this car over. If it wasn't the middle of the day, I would."

I tweaked my nipples, rolling them and molding them as hard as I dared and getting a jolt of pleasure every time. "Drive faster. This isn't helping my horniness any."

He chuckled. "Join the freaking club. I'm so hard right now I'm surprised there's not a hole in my Speedo."

"You want me to check?"

"I very much do, but I don't want you moving your hand off your tits either." He took a corner. "As soon as we're home though..."

I dragged a hand down my stomach toward the waistband of my shorts, but his hand covered mine. "We're nearly there."

I reached for my hoodie, but he squeezed my thigh. "Who said you could put that back on?"

I let out a whimpering noise. I might hate when he was in bossy big brother mode, but fuck it was hot right now.

But he drove into the driveway and swore softly. "Shit. Kian is working on his car. Put the hoodie on." He tossed it in my direction.

I slunk lower in the seat, not wanting Kian to see me all bare tits and flushed face.

Vaughn parked the car and got out.

I followed a minute later after putting the seat up.

Kian wiped his hands on an oily rag and looked between the two of us. "What was going on there?"

Vaughn shrugged. "We went swimming. She was tired. Took a little nap in the passenger seat."

Kian glanced at me. "Really?"

I was a terrible freaking liar. I always had been. "Yeah. Sure."

Kian glanced between us, then focused on me, obviously detecting the lie. "What were you really doing?"

"Foreplay."

Vaughn groaned.

Kian pursed his lips together and nodded at him before turning back to his car. "Righto."

I squinted at Kian, who was trying very hard to busy himself. Then over at Vaughn who was standing as far away from me as humanly possible without running across the yard screaming. I pinned him with a glare. "What the hell, Vaughn? You were all over me like a rash and now suddenly you're embarrassed for Kian to know what we were doing?"

He shoved his hands in his pockets and stared at the ground. "That's not it."

But it was. Obviously. Irritation flickered inside me. "And you!" I pointed at Kian. "You reek of jealousy. Please don't forget that you were the one who rejected me last night."

Kian opened his mouth, probably to argue that in the end, it had been me who'd walked out to go play with my vibrator, but that was only because he'd put the brakes on in the first place. I wasn't about to lie there, begging him. I held a hand up, cutting him off. My cheeks flamed hot, and suddenly I'd had quite enough of both of them. "Stop. I don't want to hear it. I'm going upstairs."

Vaughn took a step to follow me, but I whirled and glared at him. "Don't even think of following me after that. Either you want me, Vaughn, or you don't. I'm not going to be anyone's dirty little secret."

I got upstairs and slammed my bedroom door. I went straight for the bathroom, locked both the door to my room and the door to Kian's, and then stood in the shower for an obnoxiously long time, washing off every trace of chlorine and Vaughn's fingers.

I was irrationally annoyed. Mostly because I was horny.

By the time I dragged myself out of the shower, the bathroom was full of steam. I traced an immature message onto the mirror for Kian to find and went back into my room.

Fang was sitting on my bed.

I stopped in my tracks. "Hi!"

He gave me a soft smile. "How you doing, Pix?"

God, the man made me happy. As soon as I laid eyes on him, all my frustrations with Vaughn and Kian melted away. I tucked my towel beneath my arms and sat next to him. "Better now you're here. But I thought you were helping War with club business?"

"Vaughn texted. He said you needed me."

I raised an eyebrow. "Did he say what for?"

Fang smirked and ran his index finger along the edge of my towel. "His text was pretty specific, actually."

I was sure my eyes went wide. "It was not? Show me!"

Fang unlocked his phone then handed it over.

I practically dove on it but stopped before I hit the message icon. "You don't want to like, delete a whole bunch of stuff? Tell me not to snoop in certain places?"

"I'm an open book, Pix. You want to know something, just ask me. You don't have to go through my phone."

"I wouldn't do that," I assured him, not wanting to seem like a jealous psycho girlfriend.

He inhaled the freshly washed scent of my hair. "Wouldn't care if you did. But look at the message Vaughn sent me."

I leaned against him and rested my head on his shoulder while I opened his messages. True to my word, I ignored the ones from War, Queenie, and a host of other names I recognized as guys from the club. There were a few I didn't know as well, but I figured if he hadn't told me who they were, they either weren't close friends or weren't my business.

Vaughn's message thread was at the very top, the most recent message Fang had received. I tapped it and read the message, my face pinking with every word. "I'm going to kill him."

Fang chuckled and took the phone back. "Why? Did he lie? You aren't horny as fuck and need some dick?" He could barely contain his laughter.

I groaned. "If that was all he'd said I could have handled it. It's the rest of the message that's bothering me."

Fang leaned in and kissed my neck. "You don't like that he sent me a blow-by-blow instruction list of everything he wanted to do to you?"

"Yeah, that."

Fang drew his tongue up my neck. "I think it's kind of considerate of him to think of your needs and want them fulfilled, even though you won't let him do it himself. Why exactly are you not letting him do it, though?" His tongue swirled around my ear.

All rational thought up and left the building. "No idea. Let's stop talking about him. Put the phone down and do that thing with your tongue some more."

Fang did it again but whispered, "What if I put the phone down with it recording? Just in case you want to show Vaughn later? Seems mean that he started all this but doesn't get the reward."

I groaned when he sucked on my neck. "Vaughn doesn't deserve to watch."

Except just the thought of it had me squeezing my thighs together, trying to find a little relief.

Fang stood and set his phone down on the chest of drawers. "Last chance for me to hit record. 'Cause once I get over there and start acting out this list he gave me, I'm not stopping."

I eyed him to see if he was serious.

It appeared he was.

Without waiting for me to say yes, because he probably already knew from the way I was panting like a slobbery dog, he hit the record button.

My breath quickened. He came to sit on the bed next to me again, but something was different this time. His gaze was hotter. Needier.

Or maybe that was just me.

Partially for Vaughn, for not actually leaving me as high and dry as I thought he had.

But a lot for Fang who had dropped whatever the hell he was doing, and ditched whoever he was with, in order to be with me for something as ridiculous as scratching a sexual urge.

I reached over and popped the button on his dirty black jeans and then drew the zipper down.

Fang watched me. "This wasn't in Vaughn's list of instructions."

I leaned over and wrapped my hand around his cock, pulling it out. "No, but it's in mine." I stroked his length, watching it get harder and bigger and thicker with every touch.

Fang shifted on the bed, lifting his ass so I could drag his jeans down farther, and then leaning back on his hands. "I'm so sad for Vaughn, missing out."

His snigger of amusement told me he wasn't sad at all.

And his dick told me he was pretty damn excited.

I checked the phone, making sure it was still standing up and recording. Because fuck Vaughn. Let him see what he was missing.

Fang reached over and untucked my towel from beneath my arm.

I sucked in a breath while he slowly unraveled the damp fabric from around my body, letting it fall onto the bed beneath me.

I was on full display for the camera. There was no one standing behind it. No one ever had to see it if I didn't want them to.

But I could feel Vaughn's presence like he was standing right there, watching me with heated eyes.

"Spread your legs for him, Pix. Let him see what he's missing." Fang clearly felt Vaughn's presence in the room as much as I did.

I spread my legs.

Fang's hand found my clit instantly, starting up a slow rub that matched the pace I stroked him.

I leaned over, seeking his mouth, and he delivered, placing his lips down on mine while he played with my pussy.

"He got you all wet and needy. I could take you right now, Pix."

He could have. I'd been aching for it since Vaughn had me playing with my nipples in the car.

It was one of his text messages. Suck her nipples.

Fang stood, brushing my hand away from his erection. He put one hand to the back of his shirt and dragged it over his head. I helped him out with his jeans, shoving them the rest of the way down his legs until he toed them off, along with his socks. He must have already left his boots downstairs.

Fang went into director mode. "Get up on your knees. I want him to be able to see your face."

I knelt on the bed, facing the camera. He knelt on the floor, his back to it.

Fang's lips wrapped around one nipple. He squeezed the other with his fingers, rolling and massaging it. "I brought you something." He kissed the swell of my boob before sucking the nipple back into his mouth.

I dug my fingers into his wide, muscled shoulders, and held on, arching my back, just to get him exactly where I wanted him. "What is it?"

He reached for his jeans pocket and produced a set of nipple clamps, attached by a silver chain.

"That wasn't in Vaughn's text either."

Fang chuckled, attached one to my nipple, and tightened it while watching my face. When I gasped, he stopped and set to work on the other. "He'll like it if you like it."

The clamp bit down, sending a spark of pleasure with it. "Tighter," I urged him.

Fang kissed me deeply, his tongue exploring my mouth, while he gripped the back of my head, holding me in place. My nipples tingled from the clamps, little pulses of pleasure cascading down from them and congregating in my clit.

I needed more. I was already so turned on from Vaughn, and now from the clamps. I pushed down on Fang's shoulders, and he chuckled.

"Needy."

"Very," I gasped. I was desperate for more.

He produced a third clamp and held it up. "For your clit."

"Yes," I moaned. I moved his hand down, making no secret of what I wanted.

He lowered his head to my pussy, kissing my bare mound, spreading my lips.

The pinch of the clamp around my clit had my eyes rolling back.

"You like that," Fang announced as more of a statement than a question.

But my moan of, "Yes," made it clear he wasn't wrong.

"Good."

He flicked his tongue against the clamped bud, and I gasped at the contact. The beginnings of an orgasm built low in my belly, but Fang wasn't close to done. He put his face between my legs, tonguing at my opening, tasting my arousal.

"You're wet enough to take us both." He pressed a couple of his thick fingers up inside me. "We could both be in your sweet slit with how wet we have you." He trailed his fingers back to my ass and rimmed the tight hole with my arousal. "Or do you want one of us here? Fucking this ass until we fill it with cum?"

My legs trembled, not at the dirty words, but more at how much I wanted it. Both. Despite a pretty active sex life that included group sex, I'd never taken two men at once. I'd never trusted anyone to have that much access to my body. That much control.

But if Vaughn had been in the room right then, I would have given it up in a heartbeat. "Both," I whispered on a broken breath, desperate and aching to come. "I want to do both. With both of you."

Fang groaned. "Watching your pussy stretch for both of us, fuck, Pix. I can't stop thinking about it. Ever since I got you off while he was watching, I've wanted to do it again."

I grasped both sides of his face and tilted it up so I could steal his kiss. Then whispered, "Then make me come now. Make me come, knowing he's going to watch you get me off."

He removed the clamp from my clit, and I moaned at the sensation of blood rushing back in. But then his lips were around the tiny bud, sucking and licking, his fingers deep inside me, fucking me until I couldn't fight back the orgasm a minute longer.

I came around his fingers with a shout of ecstasy. I ground against his face, letting him draw out every ounce of pleasure he could before he laid me back on the bed, covering my naked body with his. He ground his erection between my thighs, thrusting lightly against my entrance.

"Want to fuck you bare, Pix. I want to see my cum inside you." He buried his face in my neck. "Need to know you're mine, even if I'm sharing you."

It was a bad idea. But I couldn't deny I wanted it too.

I let him push inside me, enjoying how warm and thick and hard he was.

"Want to see those clamps on your tits while you ride me." He rolled us so I was on top, straddling him, his dick fully seated inside me.

I glanced over at the camera.

Fang followed my line of sight and swiveled us so I faced the camera. His fingers dug into my hips and forced me to rock over him.

I started up a slow rise and fall on his dick, moving my hips so every time I sank down on top of him so he hit my G-spot. His fingers moved to my clit, rolling and rubbing it, building me up only to stop when my moans got too frantic, then started again once I had calmed down.

I used his strong chest to steady myself, and he surged his hips from beneath me, both of us working in tandem to get off. My breasts ached with need, my nipples throbbing pleasurably from the clamps. I chased down my second orgasm, moving faster and harder, Fang grinding and grabbing, fucking me perfectly because, damn, if I didn't need it to get over the line again.

He released the nipple clamps and sat up, wrapping his arms around me tighter, kissing my neck while I dug my heels into the mattress to use them as leverage to bounce on him.

"Come again for me, Pix. Just for me while I come."

My gaze met his, and suddenly it was just the two of us. Me needing him as much as he needed me.

"I love you," I whispered, kissing his lips, his beard rasping over my soft skin.

"Love you too. Always."

For once, the word didn't scare me.

We kissed as we came. I clamped down around him and moaned into his mouth at the added sensation of a second orgasm. He came without a noise, just a desperate embrace and obsession with having me closer.

Once upon a time, this sort of intimacy would have terrified me.

But with everything else in my life so out of control, he was the one thing I could count on. My safe place.

Sated, we slowed our movements, the two of us whispering words in between soft smiles and kisses, Vaughn completely forgotten.

Until Fang pulled from my body and stared down at the place we'd been joined.

I didn't move. Just let him drink in the sight.

Slowly, he backed away toward the phone and picked it up. He brought it to the bed. He watched me through the camera lens, focusing first on my face, then lower on my pinked, slightly swollen nipples, then finally, on my pussy, dripping with his cum.

He ended the video.

"Send it to him," I whispered before I lost my nerve. "I want him to see what he has to live up to."

Fang's smile was tinged with pride when he hit the send button.

13

REBEL

I let Fang snuggle me for as long as he wanted. I was warm, well satisfied, and content to lie in his arms for the rest of the day while I silently plotted the things I wanted to do to my attackers. Caleb was the worst of the three, and I mentally planned out all the most gruesome ways to murder someone. Hugh wasn't any better and deserved the same treatment after hearing about his 'primal parties,' which should have been relabeled as rape parties.

Nobody would miss either of them when they were gone. They were a shit stain on society.

But I couldn't stop thinking about Leonn's kids. His wife. The patients he helped. The way he'd pathetically cried when Fang and I had caught him outside Caleb's party. I still wanted him to suffer for what he'd done. I wanted him to look at the photos of my injuries and really see what he and his friends had done to me. If I couldn't bring myself to kill him, at the very least, I wanted him to rot in jail for the rest of his life where he couldn't hurt anyone else.

After twenty minutes or so, Fang kissed the back of my shoulder. "I need to get back to the clubhouse."

I rolled over so we were facing each other and pouted at him. "Stay a bit longer? I haven't had enough of you.'

He brushed a thumb over my bottom lip and smiled wistfully at me. "You have no idea how long I've wished for you to say that to me. Normally, I'd stay here and hold you until you kicked me out of bed." He replaced his thumb with his lips. "And we all know that will be in about twenty minutes anyway because you cannot snuggle long."

"I'm getting better," I complained. "I like *your* snuggles anyway."

"Good. But War needs me."

"Secret MC business?"

"We're planning how to go after the Sinners. Their prez, or leader. I don't know what they call him. But he's the one who set up the hit on War's dad. It's time we settled the score."

I stroked fingers over his bare chest, trailing my touch over his black and gray tattoos, and the thick, raised scars that ran all over his skin.

As damaged as he was, he was still perfect for me. "I don't want you to get hurt."

"I can't promise you that."

"I know, and I know I can't ask you not to do this. But you're starting a war."

Fang shook his head. "We're ending one. The Sinners started it months ago when they ordered our prez be killed."

I wasn't really sure there was a difference, but I knew this was the life I was choosing by being with him. The thought of losing this...him holding me. Loving me. Now that I'd had a taste, it was almost unbearable to think about never having it again.

Like he could read my mind, he kissed my forehead. "Let Kian and Vaughn look after you while I'm gone. I don't like the idea of you being alone in this room, worrying about me."

"What if I want to just stay here and worry about you?"

He shook his head softly. "Please don't. I can't afford to be distracted. If I'm thinking about you being sad, my mind isn't out there on the streets, protecting myself and my brothers."

That was the last thing I wanted. I didn't want to lose him. But I didn't want him losing anyone either. The only family Fang had was his brothers at the club.

And now me.

"I'll hang out with Kian and Vaughn. I won't be alone. Don't give me another thought until you're back in my bed, okay?"

He rubbed his nose against mine. "Impossible. But I'll be back soon."

He slipped out of the room, closing the door behind him. Soft conversation floated back from the landing outside. I burrowed my head beneath the blankets, cheeks flaming, knowing he was probably talking to Vaughn.

We'd sent him a sex tape.

I was desperate to know if he'd watched it.

I didn't know whether I wanted him to or not.

The thought of staying in bed and hiding was all too tempting. But after an hour of trying to psych myself up about facing Vaughn, I dragged myself out from beneath the covers. I'd promised Fang I wouldn't hide in here, and I wasn't about to start breaking my promises to him.

I found Vaughn and Kian watching football on the big-screen TV in the den. Despite being in the same room, there was a distinct frost in the air between them. The two men sat on couches at opposite ends of the room, as far away from each other as possible. Both had their gazes trained on the screen, neither talked or laughed or smiled. They had laser vision, pointedly not looking in the other's direction, even though they clearly both wanted to watch the same game.

"What happened between you two?" I asked. "You were okay, and now suddenly you're not."

Vaughn glanced over at me. If he'd watched the tape, he showed no sign of it. "Nothing. We're fine."

Kian snorted without taking his gaze off the screen. "Vaughn begged me to fuck him. I wouldn't, because I don't trust him not to just up and leave again like the last time he wanted that. We're not fine."

I gaped at Vaughn; my little sex tape suddenly not even close to the most interesting unspoken thing in the room. "You what?"

Vaughn glared over at Kian. "Fuck, you're an asshole. You ever thought maybe that was a private thing between me and you?"

"There's nothing between you and me, Vaughn. Private or otherwise. You made that very clear."

I sat on the couch in the middle of the room and

tucked my feet up beneath me. "We need popcorn for this."

Kian went back to watching the screen. "No popcorn. There's nothing to see here."

I slumped my shoulders. "Boo. That was just getting interesting. But speaking of popcorn. I have a shift at Psychos that finishes at eleven. There's a movie marathon showing at the Saint View Theater. Starts at eleven-thirty."

Kian was suddenly interested. "They're showing *The Crow*, right? And *Interview with the Vampire*? I wanted to go, but my truck is off the road."

"If you drop me at work in my car and pick me up, we can go straight after." I could have gone alone, but I'd just promised Fang I'd let them take care of me. Walking around after dark in Saint View wasn't always the smartest idea. Saint View was home, but calling it a rough neighborhood was an understatement.

"It's a deal. You starting soon? I'll get my shoes and drop you off."

"Perfect. Thanks." I glanced over at Vaughn, mentally reliving the attraction that had spilled over between us at the pool. Then the way he'd made sure I was satisfied, even when I wouldn't let him touch me. I could cut the guy some slack. "Vaughn, do you want to come, too—"

Vaughn opened his mouth to answer.

Kian cut him off before he could get out a sound. "No. He doesn't. He's busy."

Vaughn abruptly shut his mouth and nodded. "You two go. Have fun. I've got some stuff to take care of."

He stood stiffly and walked away.

I watched him leave through the den doors and

waited until he was out of earshot before I shot Kian a look. "That was mean."

He shrugged. "Yeah, well, so was him abandoning me when I was in a coma, hurt and confused, and in desperate need of a friend. So was him leaving for ten years while he ran off and married some woman he didn't even like. So was him jerking away like I'd burned him when all I did was touch his damn hand and ask if he was okay. The nice guy finished last, Little Demon. I'm sick of being the nice guy."

I couldn't argue with any of that. He was one-hundred-percent entitled to those feelings. Vaughn had fucked up. And Kian had paid the price. "Do you need a hug?"

He stared up at me. "You don't strike me as a hugger."

"I'm totally not. But Fang is, and I think he's rubbing off on me. I even hugged Vaughn."

"What was that like?"

"Awkward at first. Kinda nice after."

He nodded wistfully, and I wondered if he'd had a similar experience. But before I could ask, he pushed to his feet and strode to the doorway.

"Where's your keys? I'll drive you to work."

I guess that was a no to the hug.

Kian walked into Psychos ten minutes before closing time and immediately picked up a cleaning cloth and spray and got to work wiping down tables. I was the only one left in the bar, though Nash was in back in his office, despite my assurances I was fine closing up alone.

"This place is probably going to really hurt your OCD," I warned him. "No matter how much you clean, it's still a dive bar. The other side where we throw the parties is much nicer."

He raised an eyebrow. "You offering to show me where you hold sex parties?"

I winked at him. "If you play your cards right on this getting-to-know-you thing, maybe."

He rubbed at a sticky spot where someone had spilled a beer earlier. "Is that what we're doing tonight? Getting to know each other so you can get in my pants?"

I tossed my dishcloth at him. "You wish. Leave that. It's clean enough."

He frowned. "Your cleaning standards disturb me."

"That's kinda how I feel when you're vacuuming at five in the morning."

He scowled. "Well, if you and Vaughn would just take your shoes off at the door..." He looked over at the sound of my laughter and dropped his cleaning spray onto the table. "Oh, you're making fun of me, huh? You want that ride to the movies or not?"

"You drove my car here!"

"And I'll drive it right back home if you don't watch your mouth, Little Demon. You did skip out on our run. One on the way home now is just as good."

"I swam with Vaughn instead."

The playfulness in Kian's expression clouded over. "No talking about him tonight. Let's just go watch the movie."

That was probably safer. The theater at Saint View

wasn't far from Psychos, so we walked the couple of blocks. Something I never would have done without him beside me.

"I'm jealous you don't even have to worry about getting jumped out here alone at night."

He glanced down at me. "You do?"

"Always." I pulled my knuckle-dusters out. "These do help me feel a bit more secure. I didn't have them that night when I really needed them though."

"You needed a gun that night. Nothing else would have stopped them."

I knew he was right. "Soon," I murmured. I already had the gun, on permanent lend from my old neighbor. It held bullets mentally engraved with Caleb's, Leonn's, and Hugh's names.

Kian's gaze burned through me, but I didn't look up at him.

"We're here. After you." Kian held open the door to the theater.

The inside was nothing fancy. Deep-red carpet with an elegant gold swirling pattern covered the floor. It had probably once been stunning but now it was dirty from the feet of thousands who'd watched movies here over the years. There were marks that even Kian wouldn't have been able to remove with his selection of special chemicals and powders. One young woman worked behind the counter that served as both a ticket booth and a candy bar, and she busily served the short line of people waiting.

Kian and I joined the end of the line, behind an older man standing alone. He turned around and smiled when we stopped behind him, and I flashed one back.

The man did a double take and opened his mouth like he was about to say something but then just smiled again and faced the front once more.

I stared at his back. There was something familiar about him, and the way he'd reacted had been odd. But Kian hadn't said anything, so maybe I was imagining things.

We inched forward, and the man spoke with the girl behind the counter, ordering a ticket for the movie marathon playing in the other theater opposite the one we were going to, as well as a popcorn and a drink.

She took his money and handed him his purchases. He walked away, but I didn't miss the little look he shot me over his shoulder.

"Do you know that guy?" Kian asked, pushing some money toward the woman after ordering our tickets and snacks. He watched over my shoulder in the direction the man had moved. "He keeps staring at you."

I shook my head. "I don't think so."

Kian's frown deepened. "Should I go tell him to back off then? I don't like how much he's looking at you."

I gripped his arm before he could, a gut instinct fueling the action. I could feel the man's gaze, but it didn't feel creepy, like he was checking me out. More like he was trying to work me out.

Even weirder was the urge to do the same to him.

We eyed each other across the lobby, both of us waiting for the theater doors to open and our showing to begin.

At eleven twenty-five, an employee opened the theater doors from the inside, locking them into the open position so we could walk through. I was just about to enter when a hand grabbed my arm.

"Rebel?"

I spun to find the man from the line.

Kian knocked his hand away. "Hey. Don't touch her."

But the instant the man had said my name, I knew who he was. It jogged loose a myriad of old memories, ones I wouldn't have been able to recall if you'd asked me, but they all came flooding back from the sound of my name on his lips. "Dad?"

Kian froze, but I couldn't worry about him. The older man beamed at me and nodded quickly.

"Yes. Torrence. Wow. I can't believe you remember me. But I thought that was you. You're so grown up."

I swallowed thickly, a cloud settling over me because this wasn't going to be the happy reunion I'd once hoped for. Too much time had passed for that to be a possibility. "That's what happens when you don't see someone in twenty-five years."

The smile fell from his face. "I know. It's been a long time."

"Understatement of the century." I was being sassy and rude, I knew, but this man wasn't my father. He might have been the person who'd donated his sperm to create me, but he wasn't my parent.

To be fair, my mom hadn't been much of a parent either, and I'd still loved her.

But at least she'd been around.

Torrence had disappeared when I was five or six and never came back.

"What are you doing here? Do you live in Saint View?" That didn't seem possible. I'd lived here my entire life and I was sure I hadn't seen the man since he'd walked out all those years ago. If he lived here, I would have run into him before now.

He shook his head. His hair was completely gray and on the long side, so it bounced around. His eyes weren't mine though. His were a catlike green. It was how the child in me remembered them. Mine were more like my mom's.

His eyes crinkled at the corners. "No, I haven't lived in Saint View for a very long time. Not since your mom kicked me out."

I prickled at the lie. "Mom never kicked you out. You left. Don't blame it on her now. That's a shitty thing to do."

Kian put his arm around my shoulders and squeezed, supporting me quietly. "We can go if you want, Little Demon. Just say the word and we can go sit in the dark, or I can take you home. Whatever you prefer."

But I shrugged him off. I hadn't seen my father in so long. I wasn't letting the opportunity pass to tell him exactly what I thought of him. My voice rose. "You broke my mother's heart when you left. And mine! You didn't even say goodbye. Don't you dare tell me my mother kicked you out when I had to watch her lie on that dingy, gross, government housing floor and cry until she passed out."

I expected an argument.

I didn't expect the way his face crumpled. He reached out his hand to touch my arm, but I flinched away.

The man nodded in understanding. "I'm sorry. I didn't know about any of that. But, Rebel, you have to know, I didn't leave willingly. She didn't want me in her life, or yours. If she cried after I left, I don't think it was because she missed me. She could have had me all along. I never would have left you if I'd had the choice."

His words hurt. They confused. This wasn't the story I knew. This was all wrong.

But my mother had kept things from me before. Bart being one of them. Maybe this was another.

"Where did you go when you left?" I asked. "Why are you back?"

He cleared his throat. "I saw news of Miranda's murder. It was all over the national papers back home."

I narrowed my eyes at him. "So, what? You thought you'd come back and see if there's some sort of inheritance for you?" Opening credit music was starting up inside the theater, but it was like my feet were glued to the spot. I couldn't move until I'd worked this guy out.

The man stuck his hands into his pockets and looked down at the stained carpet. "No. I know Miranda had nothing to her name. I don't know why I came here, honestly, Bel. Some part of me thought that maybe, now that your mother is gone, that you might need me. Not the other way around. I just got in the car and drove, and the next thing I knew, I was here, back in the places we used to go." He gave a tiny smile. "I used to bring you here. Do you remember? To watch kids' cartoon movies."

I opened my mouth to tell him off for calling me Bel, and to tell him he was full of shit. I couldn't remember coming here once as a kid.

Except then I did remember.

Sitting in the darkness. A Disney movie on the screen.

A man next to me, offering me candy and popcorn, his green eyes bright in the dark room.

I did remember.

Shit.

"Bel, I don't want anything from you. I just thought I should be here. In case you wanted something from me."

Suddenly, all the times my mother had told me my father never gave a shit about me seemed questionable. Did a man who never cared take his kid to a movie? Did he come back when her mother died just in case she needed him?

I didn't want to consider that Mom could have lied about something this big. Or that she could have kept away a father who just wanted to be in his daughter's life.

I jerked my head toward the movie theater. "We should go inside. Our movie has already started."

Torrence nodded. "I'm in that one over there. But, Bel? Could we meet? I'm sticking around until your mother's funeral. I want to pay my respects. But I'd really like to talk to you before then. I can come to you. Or we can meet at a café…"

I shook my head on instinct. "I don't…"

He jumped in before I could say no. "You have a family you haven't even met, Bel. Sisters. I married again after your mother…"

I blinked at him. "You had more kids? I have siblings?"

He smiled proudly and pulled out his wallet. "Here's my business card. My cell phone number is just there. If you have a spare afternoon, or even just an hour, I'd love the opportunity to tell you about them."

My fingers trembled when I took the card and tucked it into my palm. I'd never had siblings. I didn't know what that relationship was like. But I'd seen the way Bliss had loved her brother, Axel. How strong that bond was. How it tethered them together, through thick and thin.

I had Fang and Kian and Vaughn. My friends at Psychos.

But what Torrence was offering was different.

It was blood ties. A different kind of family. The type I'd craved as a kid, when my mother was on a bender and her friends were partying in our house, and I was hiding in my closet, scared to come out in case one of her friends gave me the sort of look that made me nervous.

The card in my hand represented the childhood I'd never had the chance to have.

It represented a family I wanted the chance to know.

Kian and I watched both movies in silence. Or at least he did. I was there, my eyes wide open, but I wasn't sure I was registering anything on the screen.

I toyed with the edge of Torrence's business card, tucked into the pocket of my hoodie, my head filled with questions about who he'd become after he'd left.

I couldn't stop thinking about the fact I had siblings. Sisters. Plural. That's what he'd said, hadn't he? That meant at least two. Maybe more. Torrence clearly had the breeding thing down pat.

"Did you like the movie?" Kian asked as the lights came on. He stretched his arms above his head and yawned.

I blinked in the sudden light after sitting in the darkness for hours. "Yeah, sure. It was great."

Kian offered his hand, and I took it so he could pull me up to my feet. He tossed some leftover popcorn into his mouth.

"I really liked the bit where the dinosaur ate that woman. How good was that!"

I nodded distractedly, edging my way out of the seats and into the aisle. "Yeah, sure. Awesome."

Kian sniggered behind me. "There was no dinosaur."

I glanced back at him. "There wasn't?"

"You have no idea what we just spent the last couple hours watching, do you?"

The crowd thinned out as we made our way into the lobby again. Sunlight streamed through the dirty glass windows. Around us, people dragged themselves sleepily to their cars.

Despite being awake all night, I was the complete opposite of sleepy. I was wired. "I have zero idea. I spaced out."

Kian strolled along beside me while we walked back to Psychos where we'd left my car. There was an early morning chill in the air, but I liked it. It was invigorating.

"Thinking about your dad?"

I shrugged. "More like thinking about the fact I could have had this whole other life, you know? I have siblings. A stepmom. His business card has gold foiling on it. That probably means he has enough money to buy a nice home somewhere, right? Not a mansion like Vaughn's maybe. But a nice suburban home with a big kitchen for family dinners, and a backyard with a dog..."

"I think you're reading a lot into a single business card."

I waved him off, not ready for the fantasy bubble to break. "If he'd taken me with him…"

We got to my car, but Kian paused, not getting the key out of his pocket. "If he'd taken you with him, you wouldn't be you."

I swallowed thickly. "Would that be so bad?"

If I wasn't me, I wouldn't have had to go through being gang raped by Caleb and Leonn and Hugh. If I wasn't me, I wouldn't have to know they held another woman captive, in a location no one had been able to find, even though War had his guys searching.

Kian reached over and tilted my chin. "Hey. Look at me. Yes, it would be bad. Because you, Rebel Kemp…you are pretty damn awesome." His thumb stroked the side of my face. "If you hadn't grown up here in Saint View, taking care of your mom and bossing everyone around at Psychos, you wouldn't be half the badass you are right now. Show me that card."

I produced it from my pocket and handed it over.

Kian squinted at the tiny writing. "He's a small-town farmer from the middle of nowhere. Can you really see yourself out there on a farm, getting up at the ass crack of dawn to plow the fields?"

I wrinkled my nose. "The only time I like being awake at that time of morning is if I'm the one being plowed. And even then, you better be making it worth my while."

Kian eyed me. "Are you saying I just have to give you a double orgasm to get you out of bed to run with me?"

I glanced at him. "You could try it and see what happens?"

He groaned. "I'm gonna pretend you didn't say that. Back to my petition for why you wouldn't want to live in

Hicksville. Their idea of a fun Friday night is probably cow tipping. Do you like stepping in cow poop in the middle of the night? And getting chased by farmers with shotguns?"

That sounded awful. "No," I admitted.

"No offense, but he seems like the sort of person who says grace before meals."

"The great Almighty would probably strike me down if I tried that."

Kian chuckled and ruffled my hair affectionately. "See? You're just fine the way you are, Rebel. You're a strong, badass woman, and I respect the hell out of you."

I swallowed thickly. "You do?" I wasn't sure anyone had ever said that to me before.

"It pains me you would think I wouldn't."

"Most people don't. They just see the mouthy trailer trash girl who works at a dive bar sex club. No education. No money. Just scraping by..."

Kian stepped in closer. He trailed a finger down the side of my face. "Then they're fools for not seeing what's right in front of their noses." His gaze dipped to my lips. "I see you, Rebel. The real you. I have ever since you busted into my house for a peek at my dick."

I bit my lip, trying to hold back a smile. "Not exactly how it happened, if I recall correctly. But thank you."

He suddenly seemed nervous. He took a deep breath before words spilled from his mouth. "Okay. You know what? I need to say something. This is not how I practiced it. I was going to do this whole thing at the movies, but then your dad showed up, and I know this is all sorts of messed up, because of Fang and Vaughn. I don't want to be the guy who takes advantage of you when you're in a vulnerable position. I also don't know if you've put me in the friend zone. Maybe it's too late, and I missed my shot, but—"

I put my finger to his lips and smiled. He was so damn cute when he was nervous. "Kian. Can you quit babbling and just kiss me?"

His eyes widened. "Oh, awkward. I was actually going to ask for a blow job..."

I glared at him.

He chuckled and put his arms around me, drawing me closer against his chest. "Just joking. I want to kiss you, Little Demon. I've just been waiting for you to say I can."

He lowered his head and put his lips on mine.

His lips were soft and sweet, just like his personality. He kissed me slowly, not caring we were in the middle of a deserted parking lot, with a scary clown mural on the wall just to our right and trash blowing around in the crisp morning breeze. He took his time, kissing my lips and holding me close until he slanted his head and opened his mouth. His tongue sought mine, but it was gentle and slow, a flickering of him against my lips until I let him in.

He pulled back before I'd had enough.

His soft smile was boyish and almost shy.

I grinned up at him. "You're really freaking cute, Kian O'Malley. Just a kiss? No trying to feel me up? No trying to fuck me in the back seat?"

His hand slipped from the side of my face and down my arm until his fingers tangled between mine. "As tempting as that sounds, I just want to hold your hand right now."

I couldn't remember the last time someone had just held my hand. No strings attached.

It was oddly nice.

He squeezed my fingers. "I meant what I said before. I think you're a badass, just the way you are."

"Do you truly mean that?"

He nodded. "Of course."

I hoped he was serious. "There's something I want to do before we go home. I know you're probably exhausted."

He shook his head. "I'm fine. Whatever you want, you got it. Breakfast, maybe? Oooh, or we could go for a run?"

I shook my head. "Your cardio obsession disturbs me, as usual. But I have something else in mind." I pulled out my phone and checked the time on it. "Leonn has a shift at the hospital in about forty minutes."

Kian's smile fell. "Leonn who attacked you? That Leonn?"

"The one and only."

"How do you know his work schedule?"

I stared at him. "I told you I needed to know everything about these guys so I knew how best to destroy them. A man's work schedule isn't that difficult to find out."

Kian's expression morphed into one of worry. "I thought you were leaving this whole revenge plan alone. After what happened at the Halloween party..."

"I never agreed to that. You all tried to make that decision for me."

Kian opened his mouth to argue but then abruptly shut it. "We did kind of do that, didn't we?"

"Yes."

He sighed heavily; his breath just barely visible in the cold morning air. "I'm sorry. It wasn't our place to do that, was it?"

"Nope. But you also don't have to be involved in the next step if you don't want to be. I know I'm asking a lot..."

Kian took the car keys out of his pocket and tossed them at me. "You drive."

I caught them with a grin but really hoped he wouldn't regret that. "It involves some illegal activity." I unlocked the car with the beeper dangling from the key ring.

Kian opened his door and gave me a rueful smile. "Then I really hope you've planned it out enough that we don't get caught. But you can't scare me off. If revenge is still what you want, then who am I to tell you you can't have it."

God, he made me feel like I was invincible. And that even if I weren't, he'd be right there behind me, ready to glue me back together. "If there wasn't my junk bucket of a car separating us right now, I'd kiss you again."

"Save it for after whatever it is we're doing."

We both got in the car, and I started the engine. It didn't take us long to get to where we needed to be. Saint View and Providence shared a border, and the closer we got to Leonn's fancy house in the center of Providence, the bigger and grander the houses became. Derelict properties gave way to middle-class suburban homes then mansions, until Leonn's place loomed in front of me. I jerked my head toward the two-story mansion that sat in the middle of a large block of land. A short driveway turned into a circle that swept around the front of the property, Leonn's black Jag sitting in the middle of it.

"Newer than our place," Kian commented. "Sweet lawns. I wonder who their gardener is. I should get their number. We're going to need someone."

I frowned at him. "What? We are? What about you?"

He shook his head. "It's not just the money in the household account that's dried up. I haven't been paid since Bart died either. I've tried getting it straightened out, but all my calls to Bart's business partner go unanswered."

I frowned. "I'll talk to Vaughn. He can talk to Harold and get the money sorted out…"

Kian shook his head. "Please don't. I don't want to keep arguing with him, and it doesn't matter anyway. I can't keep working there with Vaughn back in town. I can't handle him being my roommate and my boss."

I wanted to argue, but I could see how that would be a problem. "As long as you aren't moving out…"

I really didn't want him to go. Despite the kiss, Kian was my friend first. I liked seeing him every day, and having him in the house made me feel safe. As long as I didn't think about the fact he was possibly a suspect in my mother's murder.

That little ole thing.

"I'm not going anywhere," he promised.

A tiny, panicked part of me settled at his reassurance. It wrapped up my concerns about his relationship with my mom and Bart and smothered them.

Now wasn't the time. I reached across the center console and took out the photos I'd stashed there after thinking about it earlier. We needed to get on with this. If

Leonn decided to leave for work early, this entire thing would be a waste of time.

"Cover me." I clutched the photos between my fingers and squeezed the door handle with my other.

"Wait!" Kian yelped. "Cover you? With what, a blanket? I'm not armed. What are you doing?"

I flashed the photos at him. He'd seen them before. They were copies of the Polaroids I'd taken of myself after the attack. My face bruised and battered, my skin ripped and torn. My eyes looked dead. Completely soulless because three men had taken every scrap of dignity I'd managed to scrape up over the years. Plus, I'd added a message from myself in blood-red Sharpie. "I'm reminding our friend I haven't forgotten what he did."

Before Kian could argue, I was out of the car and striding down the gravel driveway.

Kian hissed for me to come back, but I wouldn't. I wouldn't rush or hurry. I walked down that driveway like I was a six-foot model on a Victoria's Secret runway, owning every step, my damn head held high.

If Leonn had cameras I'd be on them. But what was he going to do? Go to the cops? I doubted it. That would mean he'd have to tell his wife and kids about it. I suspected Leonn wasn't quite that brave.

Every step I took stoked the fire inside me. Caleb might have tried to drown it, but I was still here, ready to show them nothing had changed. I wasn't going away. I was still determined to make them pay so they never hurt another woman the way they had me.

It was the driving force that pushed me on.

Nobody else could suffer like I had.

Like the woman Caleb held captive right now.

It hadn't been part of my plan, but a few steps from his car, I stooped to scoop up a handful of little rocks. The anger was too much to contain. I jostled them around in my loosely closed fist, almost like they were dice and I was about to throw a lucky hand.

Then ran them up the side of Leonn's shiny car, taking scrapes of paint off as I went.

I waited for someone in the house to hear the obnoxious noise, but there was no movement from behind the windows of the massive house. I dug the rocks in harder, scrubbing off as much paint as I could in the time it took me to get to the front of the car.

I dropped the stones by the front tire, and they blended back in seamlessly with the rest of the driveway. For a second, I thought about breaking into the car and leaving the photos all through the interior. But I didn't want Leonn getting in the car, where the dark tints would shield him from view.

I wanted to see his face when he saw the photos.

I wanted him to know I hadn't forgotten what he'd done. That even though the cops wouldn't touch a well-respected doctor from Providence, I wouldn't stop.

Not until I'd destroyed him the way he'd destroyed me.

I lifted the windshield wiper and tucked the images beneath it.

Kian's eyes were wide when I got back inside the car, but he held up his hand for a high five. "See what I mean, Little Demon? You're a total badass. Now what?"

I reached behind me and pulled over the leftover tub of popcorn. "Now we sit here, eat popcorn for breakfast, and wait."

Kian shoved his hand into the oversized bucket and tossed a handful in his mouth. He munched it around a grin. "Seriously? We're just going to hang out here, right in front of his house? You don't even want to move the car a bit so we aren't so obvious?"

I chomped a piece of salty, buttery goodness in half. "Nope... Oh look! The door is opening. Is it wrong to hope his wife might be the one to see them first? I'd love to watch him try to explain that to her."

Kian pointed to Leonn walking out his front door, dressed in business pants and a hospital polo shirt that tugged tight over his rounded gut. He had one armful of paperwork and juggled his keys and a coffee with his other hand. He was so distracted; he didn't even notice us sitting up on the road in my car with our snacks.

Leonn put the coffee down on the roof of the car so he could beep the locks. He was busy tossing papers into the passenger seat when he paused and pulled the photos off his windshield.

I leaned forward, barely breathing, desperate to see his reaction.

Leonn stared down at the images and dropped them quickly, as if they'd been on fire.

Kian shook his head. "What did you write on them?"

I shrugged. "Just a small reminder that he could turn himself into the cops with a full admission of the things he and his friends had done, or this was just the beginning."

Leonn clearly realized he couldn't leave the incriminating photos in the middle of his driveway for his entire family to find. He bent to retrieve them and shoved them into his car with a vicious thrust.

Then he looked around, left to right, his gaze finally coming to settle on my car. He froze.

I didn't. I'd been waiting for my moment.

I rolled the window down. Made sure Leonn had a good, clear look at my face. Then waved.

I was sure I could see the blood draining from his rosy cheeks, even from this distance.

Fuck if it wasn't the most satisfying thing I'd done in weeks.

I turned the car on and drove away.

Kian sat back and let out a low whistle. "He just shit his pants. That was great."

I glanced over at him. "You up for round two? Because I know Hugh's address too."

He leaned over and kissed me softly. "I'm up. Just watching you take back your power is hot."

I kissed him back, feeling it too. Power was everything.

In that moment, I could almost understand why Caleb got off on it.

14

REBEL

Fueled by the tiny reign of terror I'd started the day before; I got up by eight and snuck downstairs into the den Bart had used as an office. His laptop sat in the middle of a big, solid wood desk. I sat my ass down in a chair that was much too big for me and powered up the computer.

While it was going through its start-up process, I helped myself to the bottle of scotch I found in the second desk drawer. What I wanted to do down here felt like it needed a bit of Dutch courage. Even if it was for breakfast.

I was pleasantly surprised to find Bart's computer didn't require a password. But emotion hit me in the gut when the background image loaded and it was a picture of him and my mom on a beach, their hair windswept, but their smiles happy.

"You really loved him, huh, Mom?" I whispered, tracing a finger over her face. I was glad she'd finally found a man who'd loved her for who she was. I was just sorry she hadn't found it earlier.

I wondered if she'd approve of what I was about to do. A huge yes instantly sounded in my head, which was comforting, even if it was just my own subconscious telling me things I wanted to hear.

I poked around Bart's computer but found nothing of interest. Just a lot of boring files and spreadsheets with his company logo on them. I wasn't surprised. I doubted anyone who didn't password protect their laptop had anything to hide.

Everything about Bart screamed of him being an honest, genuinely decent guy.

"Sorry to defile your computer with my darkness, Bart," I muttered, opening a word processing program and cranking the font size up to one hundred. "Real freaking sorry. But this needs to be done."

I opened a web browser and went searching for what I needed.

Caleb was easy. His portrait was on the front page of his website. "Ugh, could you be any more all-American? You just need a football under your arm, you fake."

I swore to never trust a man with such perfect teeth ever again.

Finding a photo of my second attacker wasn't much harder. Leonn's photo was on the hospital's staff page, a list of his qualifications in small writing beneath it.

Hugh was the hard one. I knew he worked for Caleb, but Caleb didn't have a pretty page of employee achievements the way the hospital website did. Probably because there wasn't room to share the limelight with his big head. So that was a no-go.

I searched Instagram and found an account that might have been his, but I couldn't be sure because the profile was locked, and the profile picture was of a dog.

I didn't want to think Hugh could have an animal. He didn't deserve one.

I checked Facebook, but it was more of the same. The same profile name on Twitter had a lot of anti-feminism bullshit though, which I gave the middle finger to, and after scrolling for a while, I found a photo of him holding a fish.

It was as tiny as his pecker-sized dick.

I dragged all three onto the document and hummed beneath my breath while I arranged blocky text around it. It was no masterpiece, but I hit print, and a printer in the corner whirred to life.

It was slow, but minute by minute, the printer spat out hundreds of copies of a flyer that spelled out exactly what Caleb and his friends had done. I'd spared no punches. 'Rich, White, Rapists' was the heading, and beneath it detailed exactly what they'd done to me. I'd even included an accusation of them keeping a woman against her will.

I'd laid it all bare, for everyone to see.

The cops might have been in Caleb's pocket, but I wasn't. I was done being quiet. Being small.

"What are you up to in here, Roach?"

I snatched up the papers from the printer and held them to my chest. "Nothing. Go back to bed. You're tired."

Vaughn padded across the room in nothing but pj pants and reached over me to pluck the piece of paper that was rolling out of the printer.

I tried to snatch it back, but he held it above my head, and there was only so much spring in my short legs.

He tilted his head back to read it.

A second later, he dropped his arm and glared at me. "Are you serious?"

I'd known he wouldn't like it. "I gotta do something. Women here aren't safe. They need to know."

"I agree, but what are you going to do with these?"

"Go down to the hospital and stick them on every car in the parking lot."

He groaned. "Roach, there's cameras there. They'll be able to ID you. Do you have a plan for when they sue you for defamation? That can be proved a lot easier than your accusations. It sucks, but it's true and you know it."

I went quiet. He didn't know what I'd already done at their houses with Kian. "It'll be worth it."

Vaughn's shoulders slumped, and he handed me back the page. "I'll go get my shoes on then."

"What for?"

"You've printed about a billionty of them. You're going to need help handing them out."

I beamed at him.

He groaned again. "Fuck, Roach. Don't smile at me like that."

"Okay." I kept smiling.

He shook his head, his own smile lifting the corners of his mouth. "You're the worst."

"I'll wear that title with pride. But, Vaughn?"

"Mmm?"

I stepped in close and pressed up on my toes to brush my lips over his cheek. "Thank you. After this, I swear I'll be good."

I went to step back, but his arm circled around my waist, holding me close.

"Don't make promises you can't keep."

I should have pushed him away. Tried to step out of his embrace, but I couldn't even pretend I didn't like how close we were. "I can be good," I said softly.

"What if I like it when you're bad?"

My breath hitched.

"You've been drinking," he murmured, running his nose up the side of my cheek. "I can smell it."

"A couple of swallows." My voice was barely more than a whisper.

His lips brushed my neck. "Fuck, don't talk to me about you swallowing."

Heat bloomed inside me. I trailed my fingers down his naked back, the long, toned muscles reacting to my featherlight touch.

It wasn't the only thing that reacted. His dick stirred beneath his pajama pants.

He didn't look away from me, though.

"I need to tell you something," I whispered.

He didn't say anything, just waited.

"That night at the clubhouse. With Fang, and the club girls…"

He froze. "Yeah. I remember."

"When they sucked you…"

"It got you wet."

I swallowed thickly. I was so sick of beating around the bush with him. We'd been dancing around each other for weeks. "Just like I am now."

His hand slipped from my waist to the side of my leg and moved up beneath the long-sleeved, oversized sleep shirt I'd worn to bed. It inched higher and higher up my hip, until his fingers tangled in the cotton of my panties. "I want to feel it."

"I want to suck you."

He dipped his hand inside the triangle of cotton covering me, over my mound, and parted my pussy lips. We groaned in unison at his first touch of my clit, but his fingers kept going, searching lower for the wet silkiness pooling at my core.

His lips pressed properly against my neck, and I let my head fall back in ecstasy. He used my own arousal to rub the bundle of nerves, and little moans started up at the back of my throat.

"I want to hear those noises around my dick, Roach. I've wanted to hear it ever since the other morning at the swimming pool."

I shoved his pajama pants down, freeing his erection, then knelt at his feet, my knees sinking into the plush carpet. It wasn't the first time I'd seen his cock, but it was the first time I'd seen it up close. Precum leaked from his tip, and before I could do anything about it, he stroked himself with the fingers he'd had in my panties, coating his head with my juices, mixing them with his.

"Open, Roach."

I gripped his base and opened my mouth for him.

He slid inside, hissing out a breath as he glided along my tongue. At the same time, he put his fingers into his mouth, licking them clean before shoving them into my hair. "You taste so fucking sweet. I can't wait to put my tongue between your legs."

I moaned around his dick, closing my lips to form a

seal. He pulled back, and then pushed in slowly, giving me a chance to adjust to his size. The next time he pulled out, I licked and sucked the tip of him until he couldn't stand it anymore and thrust all the way back in.

"Fuck, you're good at that," he groaned.

The praise went straight to my core, tingling and teasing it. I was hollow, but with every dirty word and every thrust of his dick, he had me aching to be filled. He fucked my mouth slowly, letting me taste every inch of him. His precum mixed with my own arousal he'd coated himself with.

I liked giving him head. Bringing him pleasure.

"Need more of you on my tongue, Roach. Reach between your legs. Finger your sweet pussy."

I moaned but shoved my fingers inside my panties.

I was so wet. The fabric was coated. I gave a quick rub to my clit, while I sucked him deep into my mouth, but I needed something to ride.

Two fingers weren't enough, but it took the edge off the torture. I rocked my hips, twisting my hand in just the way I liked so I could hit the spots that made me cry out with need.

I was going to come. He was too much. Who knew the little rich boy from Providence had a dirty mouth when he was getting laid?

Who knew I would like it this much?

I rode my fingers until my legs trembled. I moaned around his cock, the noises more like gasps.

Until he circled his fingers around my arm and stopped what I was doing.

I looked up at him in question.

"Let me taste you."

He lifted my arm and sucked my fingers inside his mouth. His tongue swirled around, licking them clean. "Not enough, Roach."

He bent and put his hands under my arms. In a second, he had me up, sitting on the edge of his father's desk, my legs wide so he could kneel between them. He pressed his mouth to my inner thigh, and then higher, kissing me through my panties.

He moved them aside, and his next kiss was firmly on my clit. Open-mouthed. Wet and full of tongue.

Just how I liked it.

"Is this what Fang did to you?" he asked between long licks and strong sucks. "I told him to go down on you slowly. Savoring every taste of you until you begged to come."

I ran my fingers through the short lengths of his dark hair, fighting the urge to come right now. "Didn't you watch the video?"

Vaughn practically growled into my sensitive flesh. "I started…"

I tilted his head up. "You started, but…"

He pinched my clit.

If it was supposed to be a punishment, it wasn't a very good one. It felt amazing.

"I watched him clamp your tits and got so fucking horny I had to go take a cold shower."

I slapped the side of his face gently. "Good. 'Cause that's exactly how I felt, standing in that shower after you kissed me at the pool but were then too embarrassed to take it any further."

A little stab of pain splintered through my good mood.

That had really fucking sucked.

Vaughn stopped. "I wasn't embarrassed by you." He rocked back on his heels. "Fuck, is that seriously why you were mad at me?"

I shoved him back and squeezed my legs closed. "It was pretty obvious you were."

He pushed my legs open again. "That had nothing to do with you and everything to do with me fucking things up with Kian. Again. I saw the jealousy on his face when you and I came in and I just...I don't know. I couldn't hurt him again. But I didn't mean to hurt you either."

A little of the fire went out of me. Kian and Vaughn had been so young when things had gone so badly for them. I hated how much their past was hurting them. Kian's attack reminded me too much of my own. It wasn't Vaughn's fault, no matter how much he blamed himself. Kian knew that.

Vaughn shifted uncomfortably. "Do you think he'll ever forgive me?"

"He already has."

Vaughn shook his head. "For leaving, I mean."

I honestly didn't know. "I hope so."

Because there was an energy between the two of them that couldn't be denied. One that was strong, and tangible. Maybe it was frayed, but I didn't think it was broken.

"We don't have to do this," I said to Vaughn. "I don't want to be your consolation prize." I went to get down off the desk, but he caught my leg.

"You would never be anyone's second choice, Roach. I want you."

Tingles started up deep in my core. "What about Kian?"

Vaughn trailed his fingertips around my clit before rubbing over it. "We don't work."

I tried to hold back the shiver his touched caused me. "You could if you tried again."

He shook his head. "I want his forgiveness. I do. But I don't think we can get back what we had. Not in the same way we had it in the beginning, anyway. Too much time has passed. There are too many hurt feelings." He paused, gaze intent on me. "And then there's you. There can't be anything between Kian and me if having him means giving up you."

I had no idea where I stood with him. "You and Kian had a good thing once, right? You and I? We kissed once. We aren't anything."

His brown-eyed gaze bored into mine. "Aren't we? Say that looking into my eyes. Tell me there isn't something here worth pursuing."

I couldn't say that. I'd called it attraction over and over again, but it was more. It was a pull to be near him. An urge to battle so we could make up. A desire to get beneath the front he put up and see the kindness he'd only shown glimpses of.

There was a good man in him. One he hid with arrogance and attitude.

But I didn't think the apple fell too far from the tree. My mom had found a good one.

I suspected I had too, in the form of Bart's son.

"There's something between us," I admitted.

Vaughn gave me an arrogant wink. "Told ya."

I shook my head with a sigh. "You're the most irritating person, Vaughn. Lick me some more so I don't have to hear the rubbish that comes out of your mouth."

"Thought you'd never ask." His tongue flickered over my clit.

I lay back on the desk and took what he offered.

15

VAUGHN

I managed to convince Rebel to at least wait for the cover of darkness before she went handing out her flyers. But I was aware I probably only won that argument thanks to the fact she was a little tipsy and more agreeable after the oral-induced orgasm I'd given her.

Satisfied she wasn't going to rush out and do anything crazier than her norm, I went to the pool and swam myself into oblivion, reliving her down on her knees in front of me while I plowed up and down the pool.

Best swim of my life.

I drove home from the aquatic center in a hoodie and a towel, flip-flops on, even though it was cold out. For as long as I'd been training, I'd always hated sticking my barely dried feet back into socks or Ugg boots like everyone else on the various swim teams I'd been a part of over the years.

It just begged for a case of tinea if you asked me.

Fungal foot infections aside, I loved everything else

about swimming. From the fact it kept me fit and let me eat whatever I wanted. To the way my head cleared when I dove into the water. I'd always found clarity while staring at the black line on the bottom of the swimming pool.

I'd left feeling Zen.

Only to pull into my driveway and find it strewn with oily car parts and tools that set me instantly on edge.

A familiar set of legs stuck out from beneath Kian's truck, his feet clad in work boots. I couldn't see his chest or face, but even from behind the wheel of my car, I caught a glimpse of his abs when his shirt rode up.

"Fuck," I muttered, déjà vu washing over me at the familiar scene.

It was like Kian and I had time-warped straight back to our high school days, with me coming home from training and him out here working on whichever junk bucket car he'd managed to scrounge up enough money to restore.

I'd spent hours out here with him, slowly learning the names of tools as he'd called them out then laughed at me because I hadn't known one end of a wrench from an oil filter.

It was like he'd been born knowing and loving all things mechanical. He'd tried teaching me, but I'd never really picked it up.

I'd liked watching though.

Watching him.

My phone rang through the speakers of my dad's car, and I forced myself to quit staring at that little peek of abs and the light dusting of hair beneath his belly button.

I knew exactly where that led.

I swallowed thickly and answered the call, trying not to pant into the speaker. "Yeah?"

"Vaughn. It's Harold Coker."

I dragged my gaze to the display and forced myself not to groan. That was what I got for getting hard over Kian working on his car instead of paying attention to who was calling. If I'd realized it was my father's business partner, I would have let it go straight to voicemail.

Then conveniently not listened to it for several days.

"What can I do for you, Harold?"

"I've been waiting for your call, but apparently, you're just as irresponsible as you always were. There are things that need discussing, Vaughn."

"I'm aware." Like whether he had an alibi for the hours before my father's murder for one. It was on the tip of my tongue to ask him right now, but I wanted to see his face when I put that question to him.

It would be harder for him to lie while looking me in the eye.

Harold cleared his throat. "You'll come in this morning then."

"Happily. As soon as I've had a shower."

"I'll be waiting. Wear a suit, Vaughn. Don't disrespect me by turning up here in your jeans and motorcycle jacket."

He hung up before I could respond.

Pompous old asshole. I'd never liked the man, and he'd never liked me. I'd never understood why my father had gotten into business with him. He might have had money and connections, but he was an insufferable fool, and my father had known it too.

He'd just worded it more diplomatically than I did.

Dad had never minded if I turned up at his office in jeans and a leather jacket. He'd always just been happy to see me.

The same could not be said for his scowling business partner.

I got out of the car and took my time walking past Kian's makeshift workshop.

When I neared, he rolled out from beneath the vehicle raised on ramps.

He didn't bother adjusting his hoodie to cover up that damn sliver of skin though. "You went swimming."

"Soggy towel gave me away, huh?"

Kian grinned and sat up on his creeper, rocking it in minuscule movements with his hips.

I was sure he was aware that if he'd made the movement bigger, it would have been a thrust.

He rested his forearms on his widespread knees and pointed at my face. "Nah. You always get goggle marks around your eyes."

Once upon a time he'd liked to trace them, while informing me if I continued to wear them so tight, they were going to leave permanent indents.

But then again, once upon a time he would have seen me coming in after swimming training and quietly followed me up the stairs into the shower.

Heat ignited at the back of my neck.

We'd been stupid kids, just fooling around.

Until it had become the most important relationship in my life.

"Do you ever think about us?" I blurted out.

Kian's smile fell.

I held up a hand, the heat moving to my cheeks. "Fuck. Don't answer that. That's embarrassing. I need a shower."

I was almost at the front door before he called back, "All the time."

I stopped and turned around.

His gaze burned me. It wasn't hot with passion or anger.

He just saw me.

He always had.

"I have to go take a shower. I've got a meeting with my dad's business partner this morning."

Kian wiped a wrench with a rag. "Can I ask a favor?"

"Sure."

"Could I get a lift? I've got a job interview at eleven. It's not far from your dad's building. They only just called, and I already had the truck in pieces. I'm not going to have time to get it back together before I'm due to be there."

An uncomfortable feeling settled over me. "You're quitting?"

He pushed to his feet and shoved the oily rag in the back pocket of his jeans. "I need to get paid, Vaughn."

I squinted at him. "You still haven't been?"

He shook his head. "Not since your dad died. I'm surprised Rebel didn't tell you."

"Why didn't *you* tell me? I would have gone to see Harold sooner." I was horrified I'd been so selfish and privileged that I hadn't even thought about where his paycheck was coming from. "I thought that had just been a delay while they adjusted to my dad being gone, but you should have been paid by now, delay or not. I'll fix it, okay? Today. I'll make sure you get everything you're owed."

Kian nodded slowly. "I'd appreciate that."

A 'but' lingered in the air between us.

I sighed heavily, knowing exactly what that 'but' was. "You're still going to interview for the other job, aren't you?"

He nodded. "I can't keep working here."

"Because of me?"

"Yes."

He'd always been honest to a fault. Even if it hurt. Which this one did.

He ran his hand through his hair and cocked his head slightly, studying me. "That bother you?"

"That you don't want to work here because I came back?" The hurt part of me was as honest as he was. "Yeah, Kian. That bothers me."

He took a step closer, gaze flickering over my face. His voice dropped an octave. "You like bossing me around?"

Heat flared inside me at the unspoken sexual undercurrent. "From what I remember, it was the other way around."

His gaze dipped to my lips, and he ran his tongue over his. "I remember you liking it."

I had to stifle a groan as the memories flooded back. Him with his fingers fisted in the back of my hair. Guiding my mouth up and down over his lap. Teaching me.

I swallowed hard, like I had back when my mouth was full of his cum.

Shit.

I needed to walk away before he noticed how hard I was getting. "Meet you back out here in twenty minutes."

"Need a hand in the shower?"

I couldn't answer for fear I might say yes. I was sure he didn't mean it anyway. He'd probably just get me hot and then walk away again. But if he did mean it...

I couldn't go back there with him, no matter how much I wanted to. Last time had ended so badly it had almost killed him.

Nothing had changed in this town. Caleb and his friends were all still the same scumbag human beings. The cops were still incompetent and prejudiced.

All that was different was I was no longer the naïve kid who had hoped for more.

I walked away without answering.

The drive to my father's office in Providence wasn't long in terms of the miles passing beneath the car's tires, but with Kian sitting in the passenger seat next to me, freshly showered and smelling vaguely of cologne, it seemed like it was on the other side of the country.

I flicked on the radio to fill the painfully awkward silence, and Kian grimaced at the rave techno mix that came through the speakers.

"You still like this shit?"

I glanced over at him. "Sorry it's not Whitney."

He shook his head sadly. "Me too. Me too."

We didn't say anything for the rest of the drive, but I did lean over and push a couple of buttons on the dashboard until I found a pop station playing an old Mandy Moore song.

A smile flickered at the edge of Kian's lips, but neither of us said anything.

I pulled up outside my dad's building and sighed, staring up at the five stories that made up Weston and Coker Investments.

"You always hated this place." Kian leaned over the center console to stare at the offices with me. "Nothing's changed, I see."

"Only my dad isn't inside anymore."

"He was the only thing that made the place bearable."

I nodded.

Kian punched me lightly on the arm. "Hey. You're not a kid anymore. You don't have to go in there if you don't want to."

Except I did. I owned half the business. Even if I didn't want it. "I need to get you paid."

Kian unclicked his seat belt and let it roll back before shrugging. "Don't worry about me. I'll be fine. Don't go in there just because Harold Coker is a stingy bastard."

"I need to talk about what we're doing with the business moving forward anyway. I can't keep putting it off. If he's not paying you, who else isn't he paying? My dad would have never stood for that. He loved his staff like family."

"Fine. So you do need to go in there." He shoved me toward the door again. "Go on. You got this. Rip the Band-Aid off. Tell him who's boss. Seize the day!"

I frowned at him. "That was a lot of live, laugh, love type exclamations in one breath."

Kian paused, considering that. "Okay fine, how about

a realer one? It's not going to be like the last time you were there."

There it was. The real reason I didn't want to go inside that building.

Kian opened the passenger-side door and jogged around the front. To my surprise, he opened my door for me. "Out. Let's go."

I peered up at him. "Don't you have an interview to go to?"

"Not for another forty minutes. I can come with you first."

I got out slowly, embarrassment creeping up the back of my neck. "I'm being ridiculous."

Kian shook his head softly. "You're not. I remember how bad it was last time. How much it affected you. Not wanting to go back there now is totally warranted. The guy is a flaming homophobe and a piece-of-shit human being on top."

I nodded.

We walked through the lobby doors, me in jeans and a leather jacket just because Harold had told me not to. Kian in his dirty work boots and a flannel shirt.

We were at complete odds with the hustle and bustle of well-dressed businesspeople inside the building.

Kian grinned over at me, and it suddenly felt like it had years ago. Me and him against the world and fighting tooth and nail to stay out of my father's business, even though everyone expected it of me. Especially Harold Coker. He'd never had any children of his own, and his interest in me had been laser focused. He'd been grooming me to take a role within the company since I was ten years old.

I was sure it was just because he thought I was easily controlled.

The elevator binged open, and I strode across the space to the receptionist. "Hi. I'm Vaughn Weston. Harold is expecting me."

The woman looked up, and her eyes widened. Then filled with tears. "Oh, I'm sorry! You're so much like your dad! I wasn't expecting it." Her tears spilled over, and she let out a loud sob.

I glanced over at Kian with a panicked expression, and he shrugged.

I patted the woman on the arm awkwardly.

Harold's office door opened, and his gaze dropped to the woman staring at me with tears running down her face.

She instantly stopped, wiped her eyes quickly, and lowered her head to stare at the floor. "My apologies, Mr. Coker. Vaughn Weston is here to see you."

Harold's gaze slid to me, but his disgusted expression didn't lift. He jerked his head in my direction, indicating I should go into his office, but his comment to the receptionist was scathing. "Get yourself together, woman. Or find a new job."

"Yes, sir. Won't happen again, sir."

I frowned at her as I passed by and took a seat in Harold's office.

I remembered the woman's face, even though I couldn't recall her name. She'd been with my father for years. I'd only ever seen her smiling.

But then my father didn't speak to her the way Harold did.

He closed the door and took the chair across from me.

His seat was twice the size of the one I sat in, with a tall, imposing back that somewhat resembled a throne.

I'd sat here once before, while Harold handed me some 'truths' he thought I needed to know. Ones my father apparently agreed with but wouldn't voice because he was too soft when it came to his only son. Harold's words, not mine.

At the time, I'd found Harold intimidating. Overbearing. He'd seemed powerful, with his ability to run a company and manage floors filled with staff.

Now he just seemed like a little man, trying to make himself seem big.

"Don't talk to her like that again."

He paused in putting on his glasses. "Excuse me?"

"The receptionist." I racked my brain for her name. "Glennis, right? Don't talk to her like that again."

His gaze narrowed. "I'm going to pretend you didn't just say that. Because, frankly, I have better things to do."

I sat back and folded my arms across my chest. "Do tell me why you've summoned me in here then."

"Your wife is causing problems."

I blinked. That had been the last thing I'd expected him to say. "For who, exactly?"

Harold picked up his pen and pointed it at me. "You. Me. Want to explain why I had to take a call from her last night, crying hysterically down the line and making all sorts of outrageous claims about my business and what it owed her."

I raised an eyebrow. "Your business? Last I checked, I owned fifty-one percent. Making me the majority shareholder."

Harold tsked and shook his head. "You own half of fifty-one percent. Your new stepsister owns the other half. That makes me the majority shareholder."

"That's a matter of paperwork."

"Maybe so. But we'll see. Right now, the bigger problem is your wife. She claims you've cut her off financially."

"Not that it's any of your business, but yes. I did."

He scowled, his gaze shifting past me to the glass walls beyond where Kian sat waiting. "I suppose that out there has something to do with it?"

"That out there? He has a name, and you know it."

"That out there has been a massive problem for you in the past, and I see nothing has changed." Harold huffed out an angry breath. "You aren't a child anymore. You want to take over this business, Vaughn? Sort your shit out with Brooke. You need her and her family's connections if you want to walk in your father's shoes. You need to prove you're a family man who can be trusted. Jesus Christ, I thought we were done with this. Clearly, ten years and your own bankrupt business did nothing to make you grow up. You're still the selfish, spoiled little brat you always were."

The anger bubbled up inside me. "Then buy me and Rebel out. We'll take the money, and you'll never see me again. While you're at it, you need to pay Kian the money he's owed. As well as anyone else you've been stiffing since my father died."

Harold stared at me like I was an exhibit in a museum. "You've started up with Kian again, haven't you?"

I ground my teeth. "Even if I have, that's not your concern."

Harold just shook his head and laughed bitterly. "I won't have my company associated with men like that."

"Men like that?" I spat back at him. "What the hell does that mean?"

"It means pull your head out of your ass. I can't just buy you out. Don't you think I would if I could? You think I have millions, just sitting in my bank account, ready for me to put in your pocket? It doesn't work like that, you ignorant child."

It was the first inkling I'd heard of the business maybe not being as profitable as it seemed. But a lot of businesses had cash flow problems when all their wealth was tied up in assets. I refused to let him take advantage of me, or of Rebel and Kian. "Then sell something."

He scoffed. "Like what? The building we work out of? We're mortgaged to the hilt. You're in this as much as I am, Vaughn. You can thank your father and his lack of business sense for that. The only way either of us is coming out of this with any money is if we make it now that he's out of the picture."

Shock punched me in the gut, but it was just as quickly replaced with suspicion. If what he'd said was true, he'd just admitted he had a motive for murder.

If he noticed his slip, he didn't mention it. "Sign your portion of the business over to me. Or wake up and act like an adult. You don't get the luxury of doing whatever you want anymore. Our entire business runs on word of mouth and the relationships we build with clients and other CEOs. It's all about who lets you sit at their table. You think any of them will want to work with you if they're constantly thinking you want to stick your dick in their asses?"

I sat forward in my chair and gripped the edge of the desk. "Wow. You really went there, huh? You sure you aren't just worried someone might think you caught the gay from me?"

There was barely concealed anger behind his eyes. "We talked about this when you were younger. You knew what was expected of you, and you agreed. You married Brooke." He leaned toward me, resting his elbows on the desktop and jabbed a finger in my direction. "Keep her happy. We lose her family connections, then you might as well kiss seventy percent of our business goodbye. You're worried about me making the receptionist cry? Or not paying your little friend? Imagine devastating seventy percent of the staff when we have to lay them off."

I cracked my knuckles, knowing he was right but hating every minute of it. "Don't put all of that on my shoulders. It's not my fault if you can't hang on to clients without me marrying their daughters. My father wasn't married for most of his career. He still managed to build this business into what it is."

Harold slammed his fist down on the table. "I built this company into what it is by keeping your father out of those meetings! I've clawed it back from the brink of his disasters time and time again. He got to la-di-da around with his trailer trash girlfriends, while I did all the fucking work, fixing everything he broke! While he was telling you to marry for love, it was me arranging your marriage, making the connections you needed to take over for him. Now that it's time for you to step up, you throw it back in my face?" He pushed to his feet, leaning heavily on the desk. "Every cent you've ever spent was thanks to me. That house you live in. That car you drive. I tolerated your miserable fucking father every day to get this company to where it is. But I won't do that again with you. You'll sign over your share, or you'll fall in line and do as I say, Vaughn."

I stood, mirroring his aggressive posture. I didn't believe for a second there was no money. He was a con man through and through. Anger pulsed inside me, hot and violent. "I'll fall in line? Or what, old man? What the hell are you going to do?"

His smile was one of a snake. He'd clearly already thought this through. "Does your friend out there have an alibi for your dad's murder? The police chief and I play golf together regularly. Would be real easy for me to plant the idea Bart's live-in surrogate son was fucking his pretty new fiancée. Seems like a good motive for murder if you ask me."

Ice filled my veins. There was already evidence that pointed to Kian. He couldn't afford any more.

Harold eyed me with a look that was stone-cold determination. "There's more than one way for me to make sure you keep Brooke happy, Vaughn. And away from Miranda's little ho of a daughter."

The tentative hold on my anger snapped the moment he mentioned Rebel. In a heartbeat, chairs went skittering across the room, and I fisted my fingers in his shirt, hauling him up and against the wall. "You don't know a thing about Rebel, so keep her name out of your fucking mouth."

The door flew open behind me, but I barely noticed. I was too caught up in defending what was mine.

"Kian is the best man I know. He's good and honest and so fucking kind he'd probably forgive you for the shit spewing from your mouth. If you knew anything about him, you'd see in a heartbeat he's a better person than Brooke could ever hope to be, and yet you dismiss him, just because he's a man? You hypocritical, homophobic piece of shit." I drew one arm back, my fist shaking, just begging to be let loose.

"Do it," Harold sneered. "Go on, Vaughn. You know you've always wanted to. Ever since you were a boy. I'm more than happy to have a potential assault charge to use as leverage to get you to do exactly what I want."

Kian's arms came around me from behind. One across my chest while the other untangled my fingers from Harold's shirt.

"Let him go," he said softly in my ear. "He's right. This entire office is filled with witnesses, and they're all staring. Let him go."

I couldn't. The rage had a grip on me I couldn't release.

Kian only held me tighter. "Your dad wouldn't have wanted this. Whatever is going on, we'll work it out."

I let go.

Harold chuckled, like he'd gotten exactly what he wanted. "See you soon, Vaughn. Get Brooke out here. We should set up a meeting with her parents. I'm sure they'd love to see their son-in-law now that he's proudly taken the reins of the family business. We've all been waiting for this for a very long time.

"Get me out of here," I murmured to Kian. "Before I do something I probably won't regret."

He herded me back through the office, scattering a

small crowd of people who had gathered to watch the showdown with open mouths.

The elevator was already waiting, the doors binging open the moment Kian punched the button. He pushed me inside and waited for the doors to close.

And then his lips hit mine.

16

KARA

The 'others' had names.

Winnie. Vivienne. Georgia. Nova.

After days of being locked in a small room with them, I'd learned all sorts of things. Winnie liked country music and line dancing at her local bar. Georgia loved horses but couldn't ride, because her family had never had the money for lessons. Vivienne was stunningly beautiful and came across like a stuck-up ice queen, but she was actually sweet and kind if you gave her a minute. And Nova had a self-deprecating humor that was funny, even in the situation we'd found ourselves.

They knew nothing about me though.

Because what was there to say? I was a stupid girl who'd thought she could take on a man like Caleb Black? I was ashamed of myself in so many ways. Landing myself in here was just another to add to the already long list of failures.

I shifted uncomfortably on the bed that had been brought in for me.

"You okay?" Winnie asked.

"I'm fine." The words came out sharper than I intended, and I was instantly regretful. "I'm sorry. I didn't mean to snap. My back is just killing me from this mattress."

She got to her feet and crossed the little room to sit beside me. The mattress in question squeaked beneath her weight. "Just hang in there. It won't be like this forever. Hayden promised he'd get us proper beds as soon as Caleb is gone."

I flinched at the mention of the two men keeping us hostage. "I wouldn't count on it."

Winnie twisted so she was half sitting behind me. "Where does it hurt? Here?"

I nodded when she prodded my lower back with strong fingers. But the kneading felt great.

Until it didn't.

I groaned loudly. The pain lasted a minute or so then subsided.

She paused, watching me. "Are those pains coming and going?"

I nodded miserably. "Sorry. You don't have to keep massaging my back. I'm not a complainer normally, I swear. I don't know what I've pulled, but it's bad."

Winnie exchanged a look with Georgia before picking up my fingers. "Babe. Is there any chance you could be in labor?"

I shook my head. "I'm not due for another three weeks, and this pain is pretty firmly in my back. Not my stomach. I've just twisted something."

Georgia bit her lip. "I've watched enough medical

procedure shows to know that back pain is a sign of labor too."

Winnie nodded in agreement.

I glanced between the two women. "Seriously?"

Georgia knelt in front of me, rubbing her fingers over mine. "Didn't they teach you that at those parent-to-be classes?"

Just further proof I was a naïve, stupid little girl who was way out of her depth. I didn't know anything about that. "There's classes? My family always just gives birth at home. So does everyone else I know. The women all attend..."

I groaned as another pain splintered through my lower back. "Oh, my. That really hurts. Is there any Tylenol here?"

Vivienne got up and crossed the room to the door. "I'll ask Hayden."

I shook my head viciously. "No!"

All four women stared at me.

I lowered my voice. "Please, no. If you're right and this baby is coming now, they can't know."

For the past few days, Nova had given off an air of "I don't care." She'd refused to join in with conversations she didn't deem interesting enough and spent hours with her nose stuck in one of the few books we'd been given. But now, her book was tossed to the side, completely forgotten. Apparently, me giving birth was more interesting than whatever she'd been reading.

She scrunched her face into an expression that clearly made out she thought I was crazy. "Honey, if you have a baby in here, there ain't gonna be any hiding it. You have seen a baby, right? Small, squawking things? I might not have seen any human babies being born, but I've seen enough animals. Blood. Shit. God knows what other fluids. Plus, you're already squealing like a stuck pig. Once that baby is coming out your hoo ha, you really think you're going to be able to keep quiet?"

I had to be.

Caleb had already threatened my child once. I rubbed my hands over my bump protectively. Once he or she was born, Caleb would take them from me. If we were separated, I would never know if they were properly taken care of. If they were even alive or dead.

He wasn't taking my child.

I didn't care if this baby was half his.

He or she was all mine. "Just give me something to bite down on. I can be quiet."

Winnie looked around. "I don't see anything."

Georgia did the same. "A sock might do? Hayden brought in some clean ones yesterday."

"Yes!" Winnie stood and opened a chest of drawers. "They're clean, Kara. I promise."

How clean the sock was didn't matter if it did the trick.

Vivienne's eyes went wide with panic. Her gaze darted around the cramped, dirty room. "Wait. We aren't seriously doing this here? In a dingy old bedroom? The water in the bathroom doesn't even get that hot. This isn't sterile!"

"Sterile?" Georgia asked. "We got bigger problems than that. Are we forgetting the fact none of us are doctors? Or even mothers. We don't know what we're doing. I'm getting Hayden. He's been good to us."

I gaped at her. "Good to you? He's keeping you prisoner, not putting you up in a hotel. Besides that, if he's friends with Caleb Black, he's a monster. All men are."

Another contraction hit me, this one stronger than the last. Despite myself, a scream tore from somewhere deep inside me.

The door crashed open, and the man who'd let Caleb put me here stood in the doorway, muscled chest heaving. "What the hell? Is someone hurt?"

His dirty-blond hair was tousled like he'd only just woken up. But his blue eyes focused in on me, and then down at my belly when I let out a guttural groan. "Oh, fuck. Please tell me this isn't what I think it is."

"She's having the baby," Nova announced in a bored tone.

I shot her a dirty look.

"What?" She folded her arms beneath her breasts with a pout. "He would have worked it out. You're the one who screamed."

"If you'd just given me the sock quicker—"

Hayden's gaze flickered between us. "Sock?" He shook his head. "Never mind." He came over to me and indicated for Georgia to move out of the way. He took her place on the bed beside me.

I flinched away. "Don't touch me."

His lips pursed. "Can't do that, sweetheart. If you're having a baby, we gotta get you to the hospital."

I blinked in surprise. "You'll...take me?"

His eyebrows furrowed together. "Of course. I don't know what I'm doing here—"

I screamed again; the pain so intense I was scared I was literally going to rip in two. "Something is wrong," I cried.

Winnie got one of my arms around her shoulders, while Hayden did the same on the other side. The two of them heaved me up, Winnie's eyes huge with panic. "This seems to be happening too fast. Aren't you supposed to get a warm-up? Some small contractions before the screaming starts?"

"My back has been sore all night—ooowwwww." I couldn't hold my weight. It hurt too much. I let Winnie and Hayden carry me back to the bed. There was so much pressure in my back. Instinctively, I crawled onto my hands and knees and rocked back and forth.

"What the hell is going on here?"

Caleb's voice had me flinching away, even mid contraction. A chill rolled down my spine that had nothing to do with the drafty room and the ice on the late fall air outside.

"Call an ambulance," Hayden barked at Caleb. "We can't move her. She's too close to having the baby."

Caleb snorted with derision. "She'll deal with it. I need you. We have another...shipment coming in today, and you have to handle it."

Hayden stared at Caleb. "She'll deal with it? Caleb, she's having a baby. And by the look of her, she's barely older than a baby herself."

I was twenty-two but I didn't have the energy to argue with him. It didn't matter anyway. The pain swamped me again. I was barely getting any time now between contractions, and each one felt like I was splitting in two. I howled at the pressure, the pain that had been localized to my back now spreading to my belly, my arms, my legs. Every muscle in my body was locked tight. It wouldn't have mattered if Caleb had allowed an ambulance to come and get me. I wasn't moving. This was where my baby was going to be born.

Surrounded by four women I barely knew. A man I was scared of. And pure evil himself.

I suddenly wanted my mom.

But of course, she'd abandoned me as wholeheartedly as the rest of my family. Disowned me rather than stood up for me.

I had no one.

No one but this baby.

I couldn't have her here. I hung my head and was shocked to see my thighs coated with blood. "I can't," I moaned. "Please. I can't do this."

Hayden muttered angry words to Caleb, but I barely heard them. The other women patted me on the arm or the back, but every time I looked their way, all I could see was the terror in their eyes.

It only fueled my own. "I don't want to die," I begged them. "I don't want my baby to die."

Nova's expression made it obvious I wasn't the only one worried about the blood. I begged her with my eyes. Begged for her to reassure me and tell me everything was going to be okay.

She turned away.

I bit down on my lip. I needed to push, but fear overcame me. I couldn't do anything. I just knelt there. A prayer fell from my lips, a mumbled rush of words I'd been drilled on over and over as a kid. Words I'd known by heart since before I could remember my own name.

I didn't know that I believed in a god anymore. I didn't know that I ever had. It was why I'd left my family. But now I fell back on the familiar words, taking comfort in them when everything else was out of control.

"I can see the baby's head," Winnie breathed. "Kara, can you push? It's right there."

I shook my head.

"The head keeps slipping back. I don't think that's a good thing. Come on, Kara. Try to get him or her out, okay?"

I couldn't. As soon as it was out, Caleb would take it from me.

Or God would.

It was my fault.

My punishment for leaving. All of it because of my actions. "I'm sorry," I whispered. "I'm so, so sorry." I stared down at the mattress beneath me, gaze tracing over the swirling pattern on the sheet.

Two fingers came beneath my chin and lifted it.

Hayden's sea-blue eyes stared into mine, his expression fierce. "Hey. Kara, right?"

I nodded.

"Listen to me. You aren't dying here in this shitty room and taking that baby with you. You understand? You're going to push, and you're going to get it out."

I glanced toward the doorway.

Caleb watched silently. His eyes sharp, like he fed on my pain and fear.

Hayden turned my face back to him. "Hey. Don't look at him. Look at me. I'm not going to let anything happen to you, okay? You or your baby."

He seemed so honest. So open. I could see why the other girls liked him. On the outside, with his skin covered in tattoos and piercings in his ears and eyebrow, he screamed bad boy. He screamed fear and danger.

He and Caleb were polar opposites. Caleb could run for president with his preppy clothes and clean-cut style.

But their eyes gave them away. Hayden's were kind and calm.

Caleb's were blank of anything good. They were soulless pits that would surely lead straight to Hell.

I focused on Hayden. "Do you promise?"

He didn't hesitate. Not even for a second. "I promise. You're going to be okay, and so is your baby. I give you my word."

We stared at each other.

Maybe it was stupid, but there in that moment, in the sudden quiet of the room, I nodded.

A silent acknowledgement that I believed him.

He nodded back. "Okay. We're doing this then. Push, Kara. Let's meet your kid, okay?"

17

VAUGHN

One minute I was contemplating throwing punches at my father's business partner.

The next I was being shoved up against the wall of an elevator, Kian's lips hard on mine.

In an instant, every old memory flooded back. Kissing him now was like kissing him for the first time, only we were better at it. There were no braces bashing, no mangling of lips or too much tongue.

His kiss was different, but it still had the same effect it always had.

I fucking wanted him.

I grabbed his face and kissed him back, taking as much as giving, opening my mouth and letting in his tongue before pushing back so I could taste his lips.

He ground on me, his dick pressed to mine, both of us instantly hard and desperate for more.

"Fuck, I've missed you," he whispered urgently.

I couldn't even voice words. I just wanted more of his

lips on mine. I took what I wanted, cutting him off, silencing him with a touch that made my head spin.

The elevator doors binged open.

I drew up every ounce of willpower and pushed him away.

He blinked in surprise, but I tore my gaze away from him.

"We need to go. Come on."

I strode through the lobby and back out onto the street, practically running for the car.

"Vaughn."

I didn't stop. If anything, I picked up the pace. Suddenly, the safety of the car felt very far away, and I was completely exposed. I glanced up at the building we'd come out of, knowing Harold Coker was up there, probably watching down from his office like a hawk, ready to swoop and snatch up an unsuspecting mouse at any moment.

Kian was the mouse.

Despite his size and how violent he could be in a fight, Kian was vulnerable. Harold had warned me away from him once, and I'd ignored him.

That had ended with Kian in a coma. I'd never been able to prove it, but I was sure with every beat of my heart that Harold had been the one to instigate the attack. It had been a show of power. Proof I was Harold's puppet and he had ways of making me do whatever he wanted. I was sure he'd paid those guys to follow us and attack Kian, as a warning to me to do as I was told.

I had no business starting anything up with Kian again. Not when it put him in danger. Not when it was doomed to fail.

This time, I'd protect him. Rebel too.

Behind me, Kian's boots quickened on the pavement. "Vaughn!" His fingers bit into my arm. "Fucking hell, would you stop?"

I jerked out of his grasp and kept going, but he followed with a dogged determination. When I reached for the car door handle, he walked straight into the back of me, pinning me to the metal body.

His dick was still hard, and it ground against my ass.

I fought back the urge to moan. "Get off me," I demanded. But it was a weak request, and we both knew it. My knees were wobbly at the thought of him hard behind me.

"What the hell just happened in there?"

I didn't try to turn around. I didn't want to see his face when I broke his damn heart again. "I shouldn't have let you kiss me."

His breath tickled over the side of my neck. "Why?"

I breathed out slowly, trying to get myself under control. When what I really wanted to do was spin around and kiss him some more. Put my hand between us and feel how hard I made him. Drop to my knees and pay him back for the blow job he'd given me on the beach that night, so many years ago it felt like another lifetime.

That night before Harold had proved exactly how much control he had over me.

"We can't do this again." The words came out harsh and forced. I was practically begging. "Let me go."

"Not until you tell me why."

If I told him the truth, he'd say he didn't care. That Harold could go to hell and he wasn't scared of him.

I was. Not for myself or anything he could do to me.

But I'd seen what Harold was capable of, and I believed him when he said he'd make me fall in line by using Kian.

I couldn't have him hurt again. Or watch him go to jail for a murder he didn't commit. Kian might have been happy to bet on Harold being all talk, but I would never forget Kian's broken and bruised body hooked up to machines. The days I snuck into his hospital room and begged for him to wake up.

"I don't want this," I protested.

"Bullshit. You kissed me back."

"I shouldn't have." I forced out words I'd never wanted to say. Not back then. Not now. Back then I'd run away instead of saying them, but I couldn't do that again. I couldn't live with myself. I'd grown up in the ten years I'd stayed away and now I had to man up and say the things I should have had the guts to say back then. "I'm with Brooke. I'm staying with her."

Kian backed off, and I turned around slowly.

"You're going back to Cali?" He said the words like an accusation.

I hadn't planned on it. There was nothing for me there. But what choice did I have? Until they found the real murderers, Kian was in danger if I didn't keep Harold happy. I didn't want all those people my father had loved losing their jobs. Fuck, I'd already been so selfish, I couldn't let him down again.

"As soon as I can. I'll stay for the funeral."

Kian's eyes blazed with hurt. "What about Rebel?"

There was a silent add-on. *What about me?*

I ached at the thought of walking away from Rebel

before I could even really start anything. Kissing her had awoken something in me that had felt dead for a very long time. I wanted more of her kisses. More of her lips around my cock. More of my head buried between her thighs. She made me laugh in a way Brooke never could. Fuck. Even when she was annoying me or trying to get herself killed, I wanted her.

But Rebel was here, with Kian. Harold might not have known much about her yet, but he'd find out. When he did, I had no doubts he'd make similar threats against her.

Harold wanted me with Brooke. There was nothing I could do to stop it. There never had been.

"I need to go." I unlocked the car and opened the door.

Kian just stared at me. "You're doing it again. Running. I don't know why I expected anything less."

I nodded. He was right. There was no point denying it.

"You're a coward."

I swallowed thickly. I could barely stand to look at his expression. "Kian... I'm sorry."

He held a hand up. "Save it. I really don't want to hear it."

"Do you want a lift to the interview?"

He laughed bitterly. "And sit in that car next to you, thinking about how much I want you the entire way? No thanks." He spun on his heel and stalked away.

I watched him go. Then looked up at Harold Coker's office.

The man gazed down at me, making sure I knew he'd

seen everything. I stared right back, hating him with everything I had.

Like he fed on my emotions, Harold smiled, slow and calculating, before stepping back from the window and disappearing from view.

18

REBEL

I printed as many copies of my accusatory flyer on the home printer as I could before it ran out of ink. It wasn't enough. A burning need to find the woman Caleb had kidnapped or maybe even killed spurred me on, so I took the flyer down to the local Walmart and had them print hundreds more.

The woman behind the counter had glanced at the flyer and frowned. "You sure you want to do this, honey?"

I nodded fiercely.

She hummed her disapproval but printed the copies anyway, until I had a full stack of them bundled up in my arms.

The heavy weight of them was satisfying.

They represented a thousand women who would be warned to stay away from Caleb and his friends. Each one had the potential to save a life or help me find the one who was missing.

I wouldn't forget. She'd said nobody else was

searching for her, so that responsibility was one that now fell to me. I wouldn't take it lightly.

Vaughn's car was missing from the driveway when I got home, so I called him, but it went straight to his voicemail. "Hey. Where are you? I thought you were coming with me to hand out these flyers? I went a bit overboard and have about a thousand of them printed, so I'm going to plaster every car in the hospital lot, as well as any car or lamppost within a three-mile radius of Black Industries. I'm too hopped up on Starbucks and red food coloring to hang around waiting for you, but if you get this and want to come give me a hand, you know where to find me." I paused, then added, "PS, thanks again for the orgasm. We should do it again sometime."

I ended the call and smiled the whole way to Black Industries. But the minute I saw Caleb's building, the lightness left my body. I wanted to storm up the elevator and announce to every person there what Caleb and his right-hand man were into. That they raped women for fun. Held parties so other men could do it too.

But I knew if I did, I'd find myself sitting in the back of a cop car within minutes. If I could even get up the elevator at all without some sort of security card. I could have called Bliss and asked her if there was one, she should know, considering she'd been engaged to Caleb before she'd come to her senses and seen him for who he truly was.

But I didn't want her coming down here. I didn't know where Caleb was. War had pulled his guys from sitting around outside his house when he hadn't returned after a few days, and I doubted he was coming in to work when he had to know there were people after him. But I didn't want to take the risk either. Nash, Vincent, War, and Scythe weren't the only ones concerned with Bliss's safety. Especially since she was pregnant.

I walked the city streets around the building, handing out flyers to every woman I passed, imploring them to be careful if they hung out in bars or cafés Hugh and Caleb might frequent. When my feet got sore, I went into the café next door to Black Industries and ordered another coffee, handing over a ten-dollar bill along with a flyer to the young woman behind the counter.

She glanced down at it, then back up at me, her eyes wide. "I know them. Those two guys. They come in here regularly. Is this true?"

I nodded. "I wish it wasn't."

"They're assholes. They make comments about the women who work here. Which of us they'd fuck. Which of us they'd fuck but have to put a pillow over our heads. They think we can't hear them, I guess, or maybe they don't even care."

I pressed my lips into a line. She was so young. Probably not even eighteen. Caleb and Hugh were grown men in their thirties. They had no business even glancing in this girl's direction. It made my blood boil.

I grabbed her hand. "Don't ever be alone with them, okay? Have someone walk you to your car after your shifts if you finish late. Can I put a flyer up on your noticeboard?"

The young girl glanced over at an older man, working behind the counter. "I can't let you do that. He'd have a fit."

"I understand. But please at least let your co-workers know." On impulse, I grabbed a pen from my purse and scribbled my cell phone number across the top of the flyer. "If they ever make you feel unsafe, and your boss isn't doing anything about it, then you call me, okay?"

She took the flyer. "I'm Amanda."

"Rebel. It's nice to meet you, Amanda. But I hope you never have to call me."

She folded up the flyer with my number on it and tucked it into her apron pocket. "Me too."

With a renewed determination, I strode back through the café.

The bell above the door tinkled before I could get to it.

Hugh walked in, navy-blue suit pants encasing his legs. A pale-blue shirt buttoned over his chest, with a jacket slung over his shoulder. He had an earpiece in and chatted with the other person like he didn't have a care in the world.

His gaze met mine then kept on going. Like he didn't have a clue who I was.

But he would. Oh, he would.

He walked up to Amanda, and she shot me a nervous glance.

I stood there watching Hugh order coffee, silently waiting for him to say something to her so I could make a scene. But clearly, he was too preoccupied by his phone call to harass Amanda any today.

Which only made me more suspicious. Was it Caleb on the other end of that phone call?

"Rebel?"

I jumped at my name and spun around, not expecting to see my father standing there.

He beamed at me. "Hi!"

"What are you doing here?" I spluttered, completely taken by surprise at his sudden appearance.

He pointed at the register. "Same thing as you, I assume. Getting coffee."

Something about that didn't ring true. "There's coffee in Saint View too. Why come all the way into the city?"

The man bit his bottom lip then let it go slowly. "Okay, fine. You busted me. You drove past me when you were leaving Saint View. I couldn't help but follow. Don't be mad."

But I was mad. At least a little bit. "I said I'd call you if and when I was ready."

He dropped his gaze to the floor, his shoulders slumping. "I know you did. I'm so sorry. It's just hard for me to see you again. I know you're a woman now and you don't need me, but in my mind, you're still five years old."

"Could you two move? You're blocking the entire exit." Hugh pushed past me without even waiting for a reply, jostling me forward. My coffee sloshed around inside the cup.

"Hey," my dad complained, catching my arm to steady me before the coffee spilled everywhere. "You just knocked my daughter because you were too impatient to even ask politely. That was uncalled for."

Hugh just kept walking, leaving my dad staring after him with a scowl and muttering about needing to be raised with better manners.

Something in me softened at Torrence being protective.

He noticed me watching him and cringed. "I'm sorry. I know I'm not your dad in any way other than biologically. I shouldn't have said anything to him."

"No. It's nice, actually."

The guy looked so pleased by the tiny scrap of praise, I couldn't help but give him another. "Do you have time to drink one of these with me?"

His eyes went wide. "Now? Really?"

I gave a little laugh. He was sweet. "Sure. If you don't have anything else going on?"

He half bowed and gestured for me to go ahead. "What can I get you?"

I held up my coffee and a brown paper bag with the café's logo on the front. Inside was a rapidly cooling muffin Amanda had heated for me. "I'm good. But I would like to sit and talk. Maybe you could tell me about my..."

Torrence beamed. "You want to know about your family?"

It felt so weird to even think about. That there was more than just me and my mom. I'd never really thought of the two of us as a family. It was always just her and me. But I had siblings and a stepmom. Cousins, maybe. Aunts and uncles. That had a different ring to it.

Torrence led me to a table. "You have four sisters. Alice Elizabeth, Samantha Jane, Naomi Melissa, and Jacqueline Kay. They're all younger than you, obviously. I didn't meet their mother until about a year after I moved back to Texas."

"Is your wife nice?"

He nodded emphatically. "She's nothing like your mom. Not that your mom wasn't nice, of course. She could be. But we made each other miserable, I think. Brought out the worst in each other. The only good thing that came from us was you."

A warm feeling settled over me. "I wish you'd stayed," I admitted. "I feel bad for saying that because, clearly, you're happy in Texas, and you have a whole family and life there. But I was a kid…"

His face fell. "Me leaving was never about you. I had no money. Not a cent to my name, Bel. Nowhere to live. No job. When my brother said he had room for me at his place in Texas, I had to go."

He covered my hand with his. "I wanted to take you with me, but your mom flat out refused. I didn't have the money to fight her in court. I'd planned to just make enough money to come back and get you, but by the time I did…"

"You had a wife…"

"And a baby on the way. I couldn't leave her. By then, so much time had passed, I wasn't even sure you'd remember me. Was that the wrong decision?"

His face was so open. So vulnerable. I didn't have the heart to tell him I'd spent years hoping he'd come back. That someone, anyone would come and just help me deal with my mom. I didn't want to be the adult in my house. I wanted to be the six-year-old kid who had no responsibilities or worries.

I loved my mom. I wouldn't have swapped her, even if I could have. But I had never wanted to be her parent. She'd never given me the choice. She'd relied on me so heavily she'd crushed any chance of a childhood. She hadn't meant to. But she'd been inherently selfish and immature.

Too young to have a child because she was still a child herself. Her and my father both. He couldn't have been much older than she was. Even now, he could pass for late thirties, though he had to be at least forty-five.

"The two of you were babies raising a baby. That couldn't have been easy with no support."

He nodded. "It wasn't. But I shouldn't have left it all to your mom either, no matter how much she insisted. I should have fought harder to take you with me. If I'd known what was in my future, I would have. I swear it."

"I understand."

"I don't expect you to forgive me."

But I shook my head, running my finger along the edge of my coffee cup instead of looking at him. "Water under the bridge now."

But Torrence wasn't letting me brush it beneath the rug that easily. "What if it's not? I would like a relationship with you, Bel. Sally-Ann wants to meet you. The kids do too."

I raised my coffee to my lips and took a sip before I could respond. "They do?"

"Of course! They're so excited. They're in the middle of the school year though, and we place a lot of importance on their education. I know it's a lot to ask, but do you think you would consider coming to visit us at some point? I'd love to show you around and get to know you again. Maybe not as father and daughter. But as something else."

I swallowed down the emotion clogging my throat. His offer lit my inner child up. She came crawling out of the darkness inside me and smiled at him.

I couldn't deny her. "I'd love to come. Dad."

Tears glistened in Torrence's eyes, and he beamed at me with the pride I'd always dreamed of. "Okay, daughter. Okay."

19

VAUGHN

Rebel called not long after Kian stormed off and I did nothing to stop him. I let her call go to voicemail because I knew I had to have the same conversation with her. Harold's shadow standing in that window like some god, deciding my future, was still fresh in my mind.

I knew what had to be done. I just didn't want to do it. Not two times in one night.

I listened to her voicemail though, and with every word, I had to grip the wheel tighter to try to keep myself grounded. "Bloody hell, Roach. You kill me."

She was so freaking impatient. I'd told her I'd go with her to plaster her flyers everywhere. I didn't want her going anywhere near any of her attackers alone.

But there was nothing I could do about it. The woman was more headstrong than any person I'd ever met. It was like she overcompensated for how petite she was by being a dog with a bone in all other areas of her life.

It was admirable really. Except for when it increased the chance of her being killed.

I put my foot down harder. When the phone rang again, I answered it without looking at the caller display. "Roach."

There was a pause, then my mother's voice came down the line. "Vaughn? Is that any way to answer the phone?"

I sighed, my breath lifting the hair falling across my forehead. "Sorry, Mom. I thought you were someone else."

"Who on earth do you call Roach? That's a terrible nickname."

"I thought it was Rebel."

She paused. "Miranda's daughter Rebel?"

Was there another? "Yes."

"Oh. Why would she be calling you?"

I wasn't getting into the whole story with her. I couldn't explain the woman had gotten under my skin since the moment I'd spotted her in the bar. My mother certainly didn't need to know I'd spent weeks wanting to do unspeakable things with her. Or that she'd let me, right on the middle of my father's desk. "There's inheritance stuff to sort out."

"What does your inheritance have to do with her?"

I turned on a blinker, getting off the freeway at the Saint View exit. "You didn't read the will? Dad left her money."

Mom sniffed. "Your father was a good man. Of course he left her a little something."

"I wouldn't call half a little something."

"Half!"

"Yeah, but it's fine. I'm sorting it out. Dad wanted her taken care of, and I'll make sure I honor his wishes." I didn't know what that would mean for my wife, who was expecting me to financially bail her out. Again. I wasn't sure I cared, despite the unpleasant package of her hair I'd been trying to forget about.

For the tiniest of seconds, I considered I could just let the guys after Brooke have her. If they killed her, she wouldn't be my problem anymore. I could stay here, with Kian and Rebel.

I could be fucking happy for the first time since high school. Broke maybe. But happy.

But then Brooke's blood would be on my hands, even if I wasn't the one who killed her.

I couldn't live with that. "Sorry, Mom, but did you actually need something? I'm kind of busy."

"Right! I'm sorry. I was hoping you might come over for dinner over the weekend? I've barely seen you since you came home. You haven't even seen the renovations we did. I'd really like to help with the funeral arrangements too, if you'd like that?"

Relief filled me. The funeral planning had been hanging over my head for weeks. I didn't even know where to start. "I would. Very much. Thanks, Mom."

"Not a problem." She paused for a second then asked, "Would Rebel like to come for dinner as well? I can't call her Roach though. That name is dreadful. But it seems like the two of you have become friends..."

We were so much more than friends. Yet somehow less at the same time. I had no idea where I stood with her. But I couldn't imagine her wanting to have dinner with my parents, even if the idea sounded kinda nice. "I don't think so. It might be hard for her to be at a family event after she just lost her only living relative, you know?"

"Of course. Whatever you think. I just thought she might be lonely."

I instantly felt like a jackass, especially because my quick denial was mostly fueled by being scared of Rebel rejecting me. I wanted to sit at a table beside her, her leg warm against mine, my hand on her knee while we chatted with my parents about mundane things. I couldn't imagine her doing it, but I wanted it anyway. "I'll ask her."

I could practically hear my mother's smile. "Wonderful. I'll see you both on Sunday night then, okay? It'll be wonderful to get to know her. And to see you."

I hung up before she could get her hopes up any further. But mine were kind of up too.

I'd barely been off the phone a minute when my caller display lit up again. This time with Harold Coker's name. I cancelled the call immediately, but the damage had been done.

The dread wrapped around my heart had lifted while I'd been talking to my mom. For a minute, it had been nice to think about taking Rebel home to meet my parents properly. To what it might be like to have a real relationship with a woman, not one where I was just an accessory on her arm and a limitless credit card.

But one look at that caller display reminded me I wasn't free to offer Rebel anything. By the time I reached Saint View Hospital, asking Rebel to come to a family dinner with me felt like a very bad idea.

It would give me a taste of what a life with her could feel like.

Then Harold Coker would ruin the entire fucking thing, by faking evidence to throw at the two people I cared most about.

I pulled the car into the hospital lot with a jerky stop that had my seat belt straining across my chest. Floodlights lit up the cars parked in neat rows, spotlighting the woman skipping from car to car putting papers beneath the windshield wipers. She twirled every few steps, like she was a damn fairy, sprinkling moondust instead of rape accusation flyers.

I got out of the car and jogged over to her. "Rebel."

She flinched at the harsh way I said her name and spun around, her hand clutching her chest. "Jesus, Vaughn! You scared the hell out of me! What are you doing here, just sneaking up on a girl in the dark?"

I plucked a flyer from her hand. "You were supposed to wait for me to do this."

Her cute face scrunched up. "That's not how I remember the conversation going. I said I was doing it. You said you'd help. I never agreed to you standing there glaring at me like I'm doing something wrong."

"I think the cops might agree with me, don't you?" The words came out harsh, partially because I was frustrated over Harold, partially because what she was doing was dangerous.

She held a hand up in my face. "Nope. Not doing this with you tonight, Vaughn. Your grumpy ass can just go on home and quit raining on my parade."

She resumed her twirling, dancing to some beat in her head only she could hear.

"You drunk?"

"Not even a little bit," she called back gaily.

"High?"

"Only on revenge."

I squinted at her. We'd been slowly working on her revenge plan for weeks. It had never made her dance in the moonlight like she was now. "There's something else."

She stopped and shoved her hand on her hip. "Fine. If you must know, I had coffee with my dad today."

I stiffened. "Your dad? That guy you met at the movies?"

"Only one I got."

"You called him? You didn't tell me you decided to do that."

She shook her head in confusion. "Since when do I have to tell you everything I do? And for your information, Brother, since apparently that's what we've reverted back to, I didn't call him. I ran into him when I was out plastering cars with these around Black Industries."

I blinked at her, trying to digest all of that. "You went to Black Industries alone? Rebel! You could have run into Caleb or Hugh."

"I did actually. Hugh walked right past me and didn't even recognize me."

I breathed out a sigh of relief. "Good."

But that was apparently the wrong thing to say. "Good? No, Vaughn. Not good. I put all those beaten and bruised photos of me in his car, the same way I did to Leonn. Leonn nearly shit his pants. Hugh didn't even react. Now he doesn't even recognize me when I walk past him in the street? This revenge plan is pretty damn weak if he isn't scared!"

Jesus, she was impossible. I was all for revenge. I would support her in whatever damn thing she wanted to do to make these guys pay. But doing it impulsively like this? Putting herself in danger instead of just waiting a minute until Kian or Fang or I could go with her was reckless. She was going to end up dead in a ditch somewhere. I knew Caleb had it in him to do that. She was playing with fire, and we were all going to get burned. My frustration bubbled over, my voice raising. "What about me and Kian and Fang? Do you care how we are with you doing all this shit alone? Fuck, Rebel! You weren't the one who had to watch you drowning in the bottom of a pool."

Her eyes blazed. "No, sorry, I was just the one drowning in it!"

Fuck, she was infuriating. She was so reckless with her own life. She never stopped to consider the consequences of anything, even after what had happened with Caleb at the party. I understood she didn't want to admit she was afraid of him, but fucking hell. I was. She should have been. Now she was opening herself up to let another stranger take advantage of her.

"What did your dad want? Did he hit you up for money?"

She threw her hands up in the air. "Money? What, the seventy dollars I have left in the bank account from my last shift at Psychos?"

"You know you're worth a lot more than that."

"Am I? I haven't seen any of the money from Bart's business. Have you?"

She wasn't wrong. If Harold was to be believed, none

of us were worth anything. But I didn't trust the man as far as I could throw him. "I'm working on it. For both of us."

She nodded but I could tell we were back where we'd started, with her not believing I was looking out for her. In the beginning, she'd been right. I had wanted to push her out and keep it all for myself.

That wasn't the case anymore. I cringed at even the thought of her not having everything she needed. That house was hers, as long as she wanted it. I would get her the money from my father's business, even if it meant falling in line, doing as Harold Coker told me.

And staying with Brooke.

I still didn't trust Rebel's dad though. The fact he'd just popped out of the woodwork screamed of a scam. "Your dad has an ulterior motive, Roach. We both know it."

She slammed another flyer onto a windshield and dropped the wiper down to hold it in place. "We both know nothing about him. Especially you. You don't know he has a farm in Texas, do you? You don't know I have four sisters and a stepmom who all want to meet me."

I scoffed. "How surprising! They're country bumpkins whose long-lost sister suddenly came into millions. How funny they only now come looking for you. Where were they all this time? You're thirty, Roach. Did you even ask him why?"

"My mom kept him away."

"Convenient excuse. Blame the dead chick. Nice work, Torrence. You're a real class act."

She stormed across the parking lot and put both hands on my chest, shoving me backward. "What the hell is up your ass tonight? What happened between you going down on me in your father's study, where you couldn't get enough of me, to now, where you apparently hate my guts?"

I rolled my eyes. "I don't make a habit of licking the pussies of people I hate, Roach." But she was right. It wasn't all about her putting herself in danger. It was me fucking up with Kian. Again. It was Harold Coker. It was Brooke and the thought of having to go back to Cali, which had never felt like home and held nothing but bad memories. If I had it my way, I would never go back to that hellhole.

It was full of big, flashy houses and expensive cars.

Yet I'd rather live in Saint View.

"Sorry if I just don't want to see you hurt or taken advantage of," I muttered sullenly.

"Ugh! He's not taking advantage of me, Vaughn! He just wants the opportunity to get to know me. He invited me out to his farm to meet his wife and his kids—"

I widened my eyes at her. "You told him no, right?"

"I told him I'd come as soon as the funeral is done, actually. Or maybe even in the couple of days before it."

I gaped at her. "Are you insane? Do you want to end up on an episode of *My Daddy is a Murderer*?"

She cocked her head to one side. "Is that a real show? Sounds good."

I just stared at her.

She rolled her eyes. "He's not a murderer."

"You're so blinded by your need for family you're overlooking the danger signs. You are not going out there."

She was practically growling at me. "Actually, I am.

And I'm blinded by a need for family? Oh, I'm sorry, mister 'I grew up with two parents who adored me but took it all for granted to piss off to the other side of the country and never come back.'"

I snatched the flyers from her arms. "I'm coming with you to meet your family."

She snatched them back. "You weren't invited."

I glared at her, refusing to back down on this one. "Don't. Care."

She slammed her papers down on the trunk of a car so hard I was surprised the alarm didn't go off. Though this was Saint View. The car probably didn't have one. "I haven't met your family! Why do you get to meet mine?"

I wanted to close the gap between us and tell her I got to meet her damn family because she was mine. My girl. And if she was going to be a stubborn, pigheaded fool, then I was going to be the one standing behind her, backing her up, making sure she was safe and taken care of while she did it.

But we weren't there. Maybe we never could be. Not with Harold and Brooke in the picture, always holding shit over my head.

I would have to leave at some point. But she didn't have to. She didn't have to go running off to some middle-of-nowhere town to find the family she didn't have here.

"Come with me to dinner at my mom's house then. You want to meet my family? Fine. Meet them."

The more I thought about it, the more I realized it was a great idea, even if it would be torture for me. My mom was so warm and kind. I knew she'd wanted more kids than just me, but it hadn't been in the cards for her.

She poured all that extra love into her husband, her ex, me, and the causes she fought for.

It could extend to Rebel too. They were neighbors now, and I knew my mom's bleeding heart. She'd spend one evening getting to know Rebel, realize she was completely family-less, and take her in without another a thought.

That was the sort of person my mother was. Karmichael tolerated all her strays with love and compassion. They both loved Brooke, even though Brooke really wasn't very lovable, with her cold attitude and disinterest.

Rebel was the polar opposite.

She was easy to love.

I swallowed thickly, not wanting to analyze too deeply why that thought left me slightly breathless.

20

REBEL

I didn't know how, but I somehow found myself agreeing to go to dinner at Vaughn's mom's house. It had the desired effect of dousing the fiery argument with water, and Vaughn watched me walk around the parking lot, delivering the last of my flyers in silence.

I might have been quiet, but I wasn't happy with him. My conversation with my dad had been something nice to focus on. It had kept me from thinking about the fact Hugh hadn't even noticed me when I'd walked right past him in the café. It had kept that anger at bay.

Now that Vaughn had popped my bubble, that anger had room to move back in. It mixed with the healthy dose of annoyance I'd developed for Vaughn since he'd brought his bad mood back with him.

If I didn't want to jump the man's bones at all hours of the night and day, it would have made life a whole lot easier. Even now, with him leaning on his car, arms folded across his chest, his gaze following my every move.

It was hard not to be attracted to someone who

watched and watched out for you so intently. Especially when he looked that good doing it.

When my hands were empty, I held them up in the air. "All done. I'm going home."

Vaughn pushed off his car. "I'll drive you."

"And who's going to drive mine?"

He glanced over at my old brown junk bucket parked at the end of the lot. "Fine. I'll walk you to your car then."

"That's very gentlemanly of you, considering you're anything but." I knew I was giving him attitude, but I didn't care. He deserved it.

He kept walking, glancing all around us like the boogeyman was going to jump out of the bushes.

God, that was annoying. "You aren't in a James Bond movie, you know? You don't have to act like we're going to get ambushed at any minute."

A man stepped out of the shadows in front of us.

Vaughn glanced over at me. "Don't I? That's Leonn who just stepped out of the shadows next to your car."

I'd recognized the pudgy doctor as well. He was dressed in his green scrubs, a streetlamp farther down the line of cars casting a yellowish glow over him.

The last time I'd seen him here, I'd been completely frozen. Terrified.

This time was different. I'd seen how he'd reacted to those photos I'd put on his car. I saw the way he clutched one of my posters just now, his fingers crumpling the paper that trembled lightly in his grip.

He was no longer the terrifying figure from my nightmares.

He was a scared, middle-aged doctor who was in over his head.

I felt no remorse. "What do you want?" I called, stopping a few feet away.

Vaughn kept going, his gaze focused on the man who'd taunted me. Trapped me. Hurt me.

Even still, I grabbed Vaughn's arm and hauled him back to my side.

His biceps were stiff, tight with corded muscle, ready to be unleashed in the form of punches.

But he seemed to understand my silent plea for him to let me handle this.

Leonn held up the flyer I'd made with his photo and the accusation he was one of the men responsible for my attack. I waited for his anger. For the denials that would surely come. For the threats of suing or going to the cops.

I'd planned responses for all of them, knowing that this moment would arise eventually.

"I'm going to the cops," Leonn said quietly.

I nodded. "Good. I have the recordings from Caleb's house that night. I really think the cops will be interested to see those, don't you?" I was bluffing, but after Caleb's party, and being forced to sign a waiver that expressly said there were cameras recording everything, I was fairly sure there was a good chance I was right. Of course he was recording everything. He probably played those tapes over and over, getting off on forcing women.

Leonn shook his head.

The rage inside me swirled. "Try me."

"No, you don't understand. You don't need the tapes. Give them to the cops. Whatever. I don't think it matters anyway; they'll just conveniently lose the evidence. Caleb has made sure of that."

Maybe I was brave because I wasn't alone. Vaughn was right there at my side.

But maybe I was brave because I'd just had enough. "I've already sent copies to my lawyer. They can lose evidence all they want, but it'll still exist."

Leonn took a step closer.

Vaughn practically snarled at my side. I put a hand on his arm, but Leonn had his hands up, his expression weirdly sorrowful.

"You misunderstand me. I'm not reporting you to the cops. I'm turning myself in."

I blinked. "For what?"

He swallowed hard. "I'll tell them everything I did. To you. To the other women. I want you to know I'm sorry."

Oh, that made me freaking mad. "Excuse me if I don't accept your weak-ass apologies." I dug my fingers into Vaughn's arm. "I never wanted that. How do I even know you're going to go through with it? Talk is cheap."

Leonn nodded. "My wife found the photos you left in my car. I confessed everything."

"Good," I practically spat at him. "She should know what sort of scum she's sleeping next to every night."

"I'll tell the cops everything I did."

"And everything Caleb and Hugh did too."

Leonn paused. "Everything I did."

I narrowed my eyes at him. "So you won't tell them your scumbag friends are as bad as you are?"

He wrung his fingers and glanced over his shoulder at the brightly lit hospital behind him. "I can't. Please. Understand that I want to. I've wanted to for a long time. But I can't. The things Caleb would do to my family would be worse than anything you can dish out."

I was sure I was digging a hole in Vaughn's skin. "I could threaten your wife. Your kids."

Leonn nodded. "You could. But I don't think you will. I think you know they're innocent bystanders in all of this. They knew nothing about what I was doing. The sins I've committed are entirely mine. Please don't punish them."

I sighed. He was right. There was no way I would go after his wife and children. "You're right," I admitted. "I'm not a monster like you are."

He didn't look like much of a monster in that moment. He looked fucking pathetic. I couldn't even stand watching him anymore.

I turned around and got into my car.

But it did little to muffle Vaughn's voice, dark and deadly, when he said, "This doesn't absolve you of your sins, you piece of shit. I'm embarrassed to have ever called you a friend. Get the fuck out of my sight."

I smiled softly to myself.

Bad boy Vaughn was back, and he was really kinda sexy.

21

KIAN

The job interview had been a complete and utter bust. I was so preoccupied with what had gone down with Vaughn that I'd gotten completely tongue-tied and botched every answer I'd given. They'd thrown various worksite scenarios at me and asked how I'd respond, and even I'd known my answers were weak, if not completely laughable.

I was good with tools. Yet I'd acted like I didn't know one end of the hammer from the other.

Fucking Vaughn.

I caught the train back from the city, blaming Vaughn the entire way for the foul-smelling car that stopped at every goddamn station. I blamed him again when there was a group of teenagers talking on a phone using speakerphone, which was pretty much the most irritating thing I'd ever heard.

I could have been sitting in his dad's comfy ride if Vaughn hadn't been such a complete and utter jackass.

I wanted Rebel. I wanted to go home and find her

walking around the house in one of her oversized T-shirts, preferably the one with a rip in the hem because it showed off more of her legs. I wanted to lift her off her feet and just hug her, because I knew she'd hug me back.

But Vaughn was probably there, getting all her affection.

So I couldn't go home.

I could have gone to a bar. Found someone to leave with, but I was kidding myself thinking I could be with anyone else. If it wasn't Vaughn's two-day stubble scratching over my lips, or Rebel's soft sweet mouth on mine, I didn't want it.

I let the train bypass Providence and keep on going into Saint View. Thankfully, the boxing gym wasn't far from the station. I could walk the final few blocks. Because even if I'd had money for an Uber, they wouldn't come to this area for fear of getting jumped.

Darkness lingered here in so many ways, not only in the men smoking cigarettes at the end of the platform. The station was quiet. Dirty. Derelict. Razor wire topped fences around the tracks, designed to keep people from sneaking in without paying or loitering on the tracks. But they were so full of holes an entire army could have marched on through. Long shadows held secrets I didn't want to uncover. I stuck to the patches of light as much as possible, knowing even though I was a good fighter, I was still only one man.

I was also no match for a bullet or a knife.

I made it to the boxing gym without drawing any attention to myself and was grateful. It had been a long time since I'd lived in Saint View, but I hadn't forgotten the people I'd gone to high school with. There was so much anger. So much testosterone and aggression.

I'd been like that once too. Angry at the world for taking my mom. Angry because I had to live with the boy who I couldn't get out of my head, even though he had a girlfriend and was clearly not interested in me. As a teen, I'd never fit anywhere. I didn't fit with Vaughn's friends because I was just the son of the housekeeper. Too poor to be seen with. But I didn't fit at Saint View High either. As soon as they'd found I lived in a big-ass, proper house in Providence, I'd been on the outside. It didn't matter how much I explained it wasn't my house. All they saw was the fancy car that dropped me off at the gates each morning and the expensive cell phone Bart had bought me for my sixteenth birthday. They'd barely scratched the surface of who I was and judged me on it.

I'd been outgoing and had never had a problem making jokes at my own expense, so I'd had friends. A lot of them. But they weren't the true kind.

Vaughn was the only one who'd truly known me. He was the only one who saw my friends were as superficial as his were.

I'd been the one to call him on not really liking the girl he was with.

He'd denied it, of course.

But I'd known the truth.

I waved a hello to Gino, one of the owners at the gym, and went straight to my locker. I pulled out my gloves and a pair of shorts, quickly getting changed and strapped up.

Out in the gym, I strung up a boxing bag. There might have been no fights tonight, but it didn't stop my need to punch something. It was either that or self-combust.

Or cry.

Wouldn't that be the fucking cherry on top of the shit-day cake? Still broke with no job. Kissed a guy who then rejected me. Crushing on a woman who said she hadn't friend zoned me, but I didn't quite believe it.

I slammed a fist into a bag, sending it rocking back.

I followed up with a left hook.

A right.

Three kicks.

"Haven't seen you around much, Kian," Gino called from his spot behind his desk. "Where you been?"

I gave the bag another quick round of punches before I answered. "Around."

Gino sniggered. "Got anything to do with that short brunette you brought to the fights the other week?"

I couldn't help but smile at the mention of Rebel. "Yeah, maybe a little something."

"She's a hottie."

I glared at him, and he laughed.

"Damn, bro. It's like that, huh? Sorry, sorry. No more talking about your girl."

My girl. Vaughn's girl. Fang's girl.

Rebel wasn't anyone's girl but her own.

It was one of the things I liked best about her.

"You kicked that guy's ass the other night," Gino mused. "And you're pulverizing my punching bag right now."

I shook my hands out between rounds, breathing harder with each one. "That's what it's for, right?"

Gino nodded. "Everything else okay with you?"

I blew out a breath that lifted my hair from my sweaty forehead. I didn't want to tell him the truth about my complicated relationships. "Broke as fuck, but other than that, all good." I paused, watching him. "Hey, you got any work going here? I could teach? Boxing or fitness, whatever you prefer."

Gino screwed up his face. "Full up at the moment, bro."

"What about a women's self-defense class? You haven't got anything like that." I would make Rebel come.

Gino glanced over at the whiteboard that held the gym's already pretty packed schedule. "Maybe. But one class a week ain't gonna fix your money woes, Kian."

I leaned on the bag with one arm and gave it a vicious thump with the other. "Suppose not."

Gino gazed around at the rest of the gym. There wasn't much to see. Two guys on a couple of treadmills on the other side of the room. Another lifting free weights to our left. Still, Gino waved me in. "Come here. I need to talk to you about something."

Intrigued, I stepped in closer.

The shorter man grabbed my arm and dragged me a few steps farther away from the weights. "I might have a different sort of job for you... One that pays a fuck ton more than a self-defense class every now and then."

A fuck ton of money sounded good. "I'm interested."

Gino beamed and slapped me on the back. "Good. Good. I had a lot of interest in you after the last fight. It made you a favorite, you know? People keep asking when you're coming back, because no one has seen you lose yet this year."

I shrugged. "You have."

"Yeah, but I've known you since you were a runty kid.

The fights have been bringing in a new crowd lately. A lot of them have never seen you go down."

I unstrapped one of my gloves so I could run my fingers through my hair. "What are you getting at, Gino? Just get to the point."

"I need you to come in and win a couple matches."

"How is that a job?"

"Then throw one."

I paused. "Match fixing?"

Gino shrugged his slim shoulders. "You call it match fixing; I call it you had a bad day. It happens. No one can win forever, right? So maybe you just don't win on a night where we have a lot of bets for you as the favorite."

I shook my head. "That doesn't sit well with me."

"You'd get fifty percent of the profit. If we build you up enough over the first two matches, it should be a nice lump sum. I heard your truck is off the road."

"Yeah. It is."

"How you gonna get to your new job without a ride?"

"I'll fix it." Eventually. When I could afford the new parts the damn thing needed.

"Or you can throw one match and just buy a whole new truck. No one has to know. Stop being so straight."

I practically laughed in his face at that. I'd been kissing a guy in an elevator just hours earlier. Nothing very straight about that.

But Gino's face remained serious. "We have guys throw them all the time. Everyone does it."

I didn't doubt that. Saint View wasn't exactly known for its morals. "Doesn't make it right."

Gino sighed. "Fine. Think about it? At least come in

and fight the next two weekends, okay? You'll kick ass. We can discuss the third one after that."

I eyed him. "You paying an appearance fee?"

Gino snorted. "Nope."

I rolled my eyes. "Fine. I'll just come fight for fun. But it's a no on the match fixing. Okay?"

Gino backed off, his hands up. "Fine. Fine. You're a good boy. I got it."

I sighed, thinking about my damn truck in pieces on the driveway and having to ask Vaughn to be my taxi because I couldn't even afford one. Rebel had called me good too.

That was me. Always the good guy.

Being good sucked about as much as being broke.

22

FANG

The clubhouse buzzed with a nervous sort of anticipation. War, and Hawk, our VP, were locked away in church. Not the holy kind. The kind where my brothers and I gathered around a table to discuss club business. The rest of us hadn't been invited in, and I seemed to be the only one okay with that.

Aloha folded his arms across his broad chest and glared at the door that hadn't opened in hours. "What the hell do you think they're even talking about all this time? They've been in there forever."

Ratchet, one of our new prospects, sniggered around his beer. "Maybe they ain't talking. If you know what I mean."

Aloha raised an eyebrow at the cocky young shit who'd been hanging around for weeks. "I don't know what you mean at all. Why don't you tell us?"

Ratchet thrust his hips a couple of times. "You know. I heard Prez ain't fussy about who he takes into his bed. Women. Men. Whatever."

I was instantly defensive over War. Bliss too.

War once said it was his duty to look after Rebel because she was Bliss's best friend. That they were a package deal. If that were true, and Rebel was mine, I needed to watch out for her bestie too.

I glared at the new prospect. I didn't even need to say anything.

His smile faltered, then fell away completely.

"Who your prez takes to his bed is none of your fucking business. None of any of our business."

Aloha nodded in agreement, backing me up in putting the new kid in his place. "Prez loves his family, bro. Pull your fucking head in."

Ratchet dropped his gaze to his lap, suitably chastised.

Aloha nodded, satisfied, then leaned over and put his mouth to my ear. "You think they are though? You know? Making the boom-boom, bang-bang?"

I shoved him away, and he shifted back to his side of the couch with a chuckle.

War and Hawk had been best friends for as long as I'd been a part of this club. But there was nothing sexual between them. There was no spark. No chemistry. Nothing like the blazing connection War had with Scythe.

My phone buzzed, and it was a welcome distraction from staring at the door. We'd all been told not to leave. We were waiting on some sort of big announcement, and I had a feeling I knew what it was. But sitting around with nothing to do made me antsy.

If my brothers needed me, I'd be here. I owed them that after everything they'd done for me.

But there was a sexy little brunette waiting for me elsewhere, and she was a hell of a lot prettier than Ratchet and Aloha's ugly mugs.

Rebel: You coming home tonight?"

Fuck, I loved it when she said 'home' like that. Like it was mine too, even though I didn't officially live there. She was my home, and I think she was finally beginning to understand that.

Fang: Probably unlikely at this stage. Something is brewing.

Rebel: So you haven't seen Kian tonight then?"

I frowned at the screen.

Fang: No? Should I have?"

Rebel: He didn't come home either.

I glanced at the time on the top corner of my screen. It was after midnight. Though it wasn't unusual for me or Rebel to still be awake, Kian got up so early to work out that he normally disappeared into his room well before this time.

Fang: Maybe he's out partying?

Rebel: Or maybe he got laid.

A smile tugged at the corner of my mouth.

Fang: Doubtful. If he's not in your bed, Vaughn's is the only other one worth checking.

Rebel: I'm in Vaughn's room. Definitely no naked Kian in here unless he's hiding under the bed.

A tiny tinge of jealousy pulled at my emotions. Fucking hell. I wanted her well taken care of. I wanted her to have more than just me because I knew she needed it. I didn't want anyone clipping her wings. I'd watched my father do that to my mother, and fuck, if I was ever going to be like him. I wanted Rebel to have whatever she wanted, and if that meant she was naked in Vaughn's bed right now, that didn't matter.

A second later my phone buzzed, and an image of Rebel and Vaughn popped up. They were both fully clothed. Rebel beamed at the camera. Vaughn flipped it the bird with a scowl.

Rebel: We're funeral planning. Went to the graveyard and picked out plots earlier.

Fang: Grim.

Something had been playing on my mind ever since the day Vaughn had called me and told me to hightail it home to get Rebel off. I shifted slightly on the couch and willed my dick to keep itself under control at just the thought of the sex we'd had that night.

I had to take a couple of deep breaths before I could write my question.

Fang: Has Vaughn watched the tape?

Rebel: He said he started, but didn't get far. I don't know if he watched any more.

Fang: So ask him.

Rebel: Uh, no. Talk about awkward. I can't believe we did that.

Fang: Did you watch it?

Rebel: No!

Rebel: Wait. Did you?

Fang: Fuck, yes.

Rebel: OMG.

Rebel: Okay but...Was it hot or completely awful?

Fang: I've about worn the skin off my dick from jacking off over it. I get hard even thinking about it, Pix. Are you kidding me? Any tape of you, fully blissed out, is better than any other porn out there. Watch it. You'll see what I mean.

Rebel: I wish you were here. Thinking about you watching that and getting off... Now I'm the one who's horny.

Fang: Me too, Pix. Me fucking too.

The church door opened, and War stuck his head out, his face like a thundercloud.

"Shit," I mumbled. "That doesn't look good."

War glanced around the room at all my brothers sitting around, waiting on his command. "All of you in here. Now."

Queenie, Aloha's old lady, paused in making margaritas behind the bar. "Everything okay, sugar?" she asked War.

She and Aloha had been two of the originals when War's dad had started the Slayers MC Saint View chapter. Fancy, War's mom, might have been top dog amongst the women, but Queenie was the mother hen. Fancy was tough and rough around the edges. A tiny skinny woman with hard eyes that had seen too much. Queenie was the opposite. Sweet. Kind. Caring. She had the biggest heart, and though none of the younger girls would have dared to ask War a question like that, Queenie knew War was about as soft as a marshmallow for those he loved. Queenie was one of them.

War's jaw went tense. "Get all the girls here."

Queenie set down her margarita mix. "Amber's at her night course...you really need her here? She's been doing so well..."

War nodded curtly. "We're going into lockdown."

Kiki, one of the young girls sitting across the bar from

Queenie, cocked her head to the side. "What does that mean?"

Lockdowns weren't called often. Only when there was an extreme threat to the club members, and Kiki hadn't been here when the last one had gone down.

Queenie pushed a drink in her direction. "It means settle in, honey. Because shit is happening outside and we're club bound until the boys sort it out."

All the guys filed into church while the women watched on with worried eyes. I let all my brothers go ahead of me, so I could be the last one to enter.

"Lockdown?" I murmured to War. "Do I need to get Rebel in here? You know how much she'll fucking hate that."

War gave a slight shake of his head. "I'm leaving Bliss at home because Nash and Vincent are there. If Vaughn and Kian are with Rebel, let her be for now, just give the guys the heads-up. But, brother, prepare them. We might need to get them all in before this is over, no matter how much they might hate it."

Shit. I could only imagine how that conversation with Vaughn and Kian would go down. Like a ton of fucking bricks. "Can you give me a minute?"

War jerked his head. "You got one exactly. Then I'm starting this meeting, with or without you."

"I'll be there."

I stepped around the corner and tried to calm the shaking in my hand. Fuck. I'd been through lockdowns before and never thought twice about them.

Because I'd never had anyone I cared about.

Now the fear was overwhelming. I wanted to get

Rebel in here immediately, where I could watch her at all hours of the night and day.

Except I probably wouldn't even be here to do that. Whatever was happening, War would need me. I sure as fuck didn't trust some dumb prospect to stay here and protect my girl.

She was better off at home with Vaughn and Kian. At least until I knew exactly how bad the danger threat was. I trusted War's judgement.

If War changed his mind, I'd bring them in. All three of them. I wasn't risking anything else happening to someone Rebel cared about.

I called Vaughn's number. It rang out, and I swore beneath my breath before ringing him again.

The second time, he picked it up on the second ring. I didn't even let him get out a greeting. "Jesus fuck," I spat down the phone. "Answer the fucking phone next time."

"Hold on a minute, I just time-warped back to being fifteen when I broke curfew and my dad rang five hundred times until I answered the phone." Vaughn's sarcasm dripped down the line. "What the hell, man? Since when do you call me anyway?"

I didn't have time to argue with him. "Listen to me. Shit is going down with the club. I don't know what yet, so don't ask me, but it's got War spooked enough to call a low-level lockdown."

"Which means what? I don't speak biker."

"Which means I need you and Kian to watch out for her."

"Since when don't I do that?"

I shook my head, even though he couldn't see it. "More, Vaughn. I need you to have Kian's back too. And vice versa. I don't have time to call him, but promise me you have this handled."

"Kian hates my guts and is probably out somewhere getting laid just to spite me. I can't have his back if he's lying on it for some other guy..."

He wasn't getting it. "I don't care, Vaughn!" I yelled. "Get him back or I'm dragging you and Rebel here and locking you in this damn clubhouse myself."

He paused, and this time when he spoke he was quieter. "What's going on?"

I probably wouldn't be able to tell him even if I knew. I was out of time anyway. "Just do it. And next time, if I call, answer the fucking phone. I can't warn you of shit if you're letting my calls go to voicemail. Promise me."

"I promise."

A relief settled over me, and I strode through the church doors right before War closed them. "Oh, and Vaughn?"

"Yeah?"

I settled into my seat at War's left-hand side. "Watch the fucking tape. As you once told me, the girl has needs, you know."

23

REBEL

I lay across Vaughn's bed on my stomach, a laptop, a yellow legal pad, and a couple of pens scattered around me. While Vaughn talked on the phone, I scribbled down a list of potential songs to play at Mom and Bart's funeral. Vaughn had picked a bunch of traditional, depressing songs I thought would make everyone cry, even more than they already would be, so I was determined to find some Bart and Mom had loved.

I texted Kian again, asking where he was and telling him I needed his help in song selections before Vaughn had me sobbing and rocking in a corner.

Kian didn't answer.

I bit my lip, not sure whether to be annoyed with him for ignoring me or worried that he'd gone AWOL. Neither was like him.

Vaughn ended his call and tossed the phone onto his nightstand again. His expression was a whole lot more thoughtful than the smart aleck tone he'd started the conversation with.

I tapped the end of my pen against my list. "Who was that?"

"Fang."

I raised an eyebrow. "What did he want?"

Vaughn shook his head, his brow furrowed in confusion. "The club is in lockdown."

I gasped.

"That mean something to you?"

"Nothing good. They don't do that unless something bad is happening." I groaned, realization hitting me that this lockdown would affect me a whole lot more than any of their other ones. "Fuck. Was he demanding you take me in there?" I knew how lockdowns worked. Everyone the guys cared about was marched down to the clubhouse and had to stay there for as long as it took to eliminate the threat. Sometimes it was only a night. Sometimes they put their entire lives on hold for weeks.

But to my surprise, Vaughn shook his head. "He did threaten to drag us all down there. But looks like for now, Kian and I are enough to satisfy him."

I gaped at him. "Seriously?"

Vaughn shrugged. "That's what he said."

I let out a low wolf whistle. "Wow. Good for you. He respects you."

Vaughn seemed baffled. "How did you come to that conclusion? It definitely didn't feel very respectful when he was telling me to shut up and listen."

I rolled onto my side and propped my head up on my arm. "He kinda likes me, if you haven't noticed—"

"Blind men would have noticed, Roach."

I grinned at him. "And he respects you enough to take

care of me. That's a big thing for a guy like Fang, you know."

Vaughn sat on the edge of the mattress. He threw me a sidelong glance. "He also said I should watch the tape."

My mouth dropped open in outrage. "No! That little shit! He told me to watch it too."

Now it was Vaughn's turn to be surprised. "You sent me a sex tape that you hadn't even watched? Fuuuck. You're brave. What if it's horrific? What if it's like, close-ups of your butthole?"

I punched his arm as hard as I could. "You're the worst. For the record, close-ups of my butthole would still be a cinematic experience."

He chuckled, his gaze dropping to my booty.

I slapped him again. "You did not just check out my ass!"

He shrugged. "I did, and I'm not sorry. Your ass is sweet."

I didn't know whether to take it as a compliment or be offended. "Thanks? I think?"

Vaughn laid out on the bed beside me, mirroring my position with his hand propped up under his head. "So... want to watch it?"

I gaped at him. I'd thought about him watching it alone, in his room, in the dark. I'd been able to convince myself that was sexy rather than mortifying.

But watching it with him right next to me, where I could see his reaction was an entirely different situation.

Then why was I flushed with heat at the very thought of it?

Vaughn sat up so quickly it was like someone had

poked him with a branding iron. He pointed at me. "Fuck! You do want to watch it!"

I scuttled back on the bed, putting my back to the headboard and crossed my arms over my chest. "I never said that!"

"You never said no either!"

I was sure the heat in my face had turned my cheeks pink. "Well, you're the one who brought it up!"

"Because I want to watch it!"

My mouth fell open. "You do?"

He gave me a cocky half grin. "You sent me porn, Rebel. Starring you. Of course I fucking want to watch it."

I really hoped he didn't notice the full-body tremble that took over me. "Okay, so fine. We're watching it."

"Fine." He closed the laptop and put it to the side, along with the other bits of stationery.

We both stared at each other awkwardly.

"So," I mused. "How are we doing this? Like, do I make popcorn? Do I turn out the light?"

Do I get naked in the hopes that the video inspires other activities...

Vaughn palmed the back of his neck, and I wondered if he were having the same thoughts. "No light. No popcorn."

I nodded, scurrying over to switch the light off, while Vaughn flicked on a lamp on his bedside table. It cast a soft yellow glow around the room. "Okay?" he asked.

I had no idea how much lighting was right for watching homemade porn with your stepbrother.

I went and sat back next to Vaughn, both of us with our backs to the headboard, both of us very careful to keep to our own sides.

It wasn't like we'd never fooled around. But this...this was intimate in an entirely different way.

"Should I cast it to the TV, or we can watch it on my iPad?"

Despite assuring Vaughn my butthole would be a cinematic experience, I did not want to see it on the huge screen hanging opposite the bed. "iPad is good."

Vaughn took it out of a drawer, and I inched closer to him so our shoulders brushed. He put the iPad down, half on my thigh, half on his.

"You ready for your acting debut?"

I leaned across him and switched off the lamp, deciding darkness would be better at hiding my blush. "I'm ready. But just for the record, there's no acting when Fang makes me come."

Vaughn's chest made a grumbling sound. I wasn't sure if it was because he was jealous or turned on, but he hit play on the video before I could ask.

The little screen flickered to light in the dim room.

The video started with me sitting on my bed in a towel, and Fang walking back across the room to sit beside me. As soon as he sat, I reached over and undid his fly to free his cock.

Fang had situated the camera like a pro, even zooming it in a little so I was better framed on the screen.

Vaughn shifted on the bed next to me. We could see every inch of Fang's long, hard dick.

I nudged him. "That doing it for you?"

He snorted. "Only one dick that gets me going, Roach. It's not his."

I stifled a laugh. "I'm betting Fang won't be too upset by that—oh."

On the video, Fang had tugged at my towel and set it unraveling so I was completely bare to the camera.

Vaughn snuck a look my way. "Nice tits."

"You've seen them before."

"I know, but they deserve being complimented twice."

I was oddly pleased by that.

"Spread your legs for him, Pix. Let him see what he's missing."

Video me spread her legs like a good girl.

Beside me, Vaughn groaned and pulled a pillow over his lap.

I shoved the pillow off the bed so I could see the bulge growing in his pants. "Should I ask you again if that's doing it for you?"

He adjusted himself, clearly hard behind his gray sweats. "I think it's pretty obvious." He dragged his gaze away from the screen, where Fang was rubbing my clit. "You're so beautiful. You know that, right?"

I tried to laugh off the too-sincere compliment because I wasn't good at taking them. "I bet you say that to all the girls who make sex tapes for you."

He leaned over and kissed the side of my neck. "Only you."

I tilted my head to one side, giving him better access. "I'm still mad at you, for the record. You were a dick at the hospital."

He tucked his fingers in the hem of my hoodie. "Fine. But be mad naked."

I let him lift it over my head. I had a tank top beneath it. His fingers brushed my nipple through my shirt. "No bra. Hot."

"Comfortable," I corrected. "Bras hurt like hell. The

underwire stabs in places no woman wants to be stabbed."

Vaughn glanced over at the iPad still playing my sex tape, then dragged my tank top down to reveal one nipple. "Complains about bras digging in but does not mind having her nipples clamped. Make that make sense."

I shot a glance at the screen. Fang was adjusting clamps on my nipples while I had my head thrown back in pleasure.

"Tighter."

Vaughn clamped his fingers around my nipple, mimicking the clamps.

I moaned, much the same way I had in the video.

"I love how much you like this." Vaughn lowered his head to suck me into his mouth.

He was right. I did love it. It was something most guys in my past had overlooked. A half-assed boob grope was all I got before they were trying to shove their dicks in.

But not Fang. Not Vaughn either.

They'd taken the time to test my body. To work out what I liked.

I definitely liked having Vaughn's tongue on my skin.

He groaned with my nipple still in his mouth. "He clamped your clit?"

It gave a throb at the very pleasant memory. "He did."

Vaughn got up on his knees, and with one quick yank, pulled me down the bed so I was flat on my back. "Did it hurt? Want me to kiss it better?"

It hadn't hurt. I'd freaking loved the sensation.

But I absolutely wanted Vaughn to kiss it better.

"Yes."

Another sharp tug on my sweatpants, and they slid right down over my hips.

Vaughn pushed them off my legs while shaking his head. "No panties either? Did you come in here tonight, planning this?"

I watched him spread my legs and take up his position between them. "If I'd been planning it, I would have worn something sexier."

His gaze raked up and down my body, resting on the junction of my spread legs. "Nothing is sexier than you completely naked, Roach. Your pussy wet and glistening. Damn, I want to taste you."

Since there was nothing stopping him, he did.

Vaughn buried his face in my pussy, licking and sucking every inch of it. My lips, my clit, and my opening. He tongue-fucked me until I was squirming, begging to come.

On the video, Fang was doing the same thing.

"You're wet enough to take us both. We could both be in your sweet slit with how wet we have you. Or do you want one of us here? Fucking this sweet little ass until we fill it with cum?"

"Fuuuck me." Vaughn let out a heavy breath that blew over my wet, sensitive areas, making the whole thing tingle all the more. "If that's how Fang dirty talks, I change my earlier statement about only one man doing it for me."

"Don't tease me with the idea of something if you aren't going to follow through." I tugged at his shirt, needing him as naked as I was.

He lifted it over his head, and then tugged the cord on his sweatpants.

Eagerly, I drew them down his hips, laughing at the fact he had no underwear on either.

"Both. I want both."

I froze.

I'd completely forgotten I'd said that.

Vaughn notched his dick at my entrance and brought his mouth down on mine again. "Did you mean what you said in the video?"

I was sure I was blushing. My face was burning. It was freaking ridiculous to be embarrassed about what I'd said in the heat of the moment. Normally, I was super open about what I wanted.

But nobody had ever filmed me saying I wanted two men inside me at once.

Nobody else had ever made me want it like Vaughn and Fang did.

"I meant it," I whispered.

Vaughn dropped his head to the crook of my neck and shuddered. "If he were here right now, I'd give it to you. Do you have a vibrator?"

My heart hammered at what I thought he was maybe implying. A new flush of arousal coated the tip of him that was barely nudged inside my pussy. "Several. In my top drawer."

With more restraint than I thought possible, he pushed back and stood. "Give me two seconds."

Without even bothering to grab a robe or to check if Kian was home, Vaughn strode out down the hall, headed for my room, his thick erection leading the way.

I shivered in anticipation, putting my fingers to my clit and rubbing slowly to keep me on edge while I waited for him to return.

He was back in under thirty seconds, all three of my vibrators and a dildo clutched in his arms.

I raised an eyebrow at him. "Where exactly do you think you're going to put all of those?"

He tossed them onto the bed and climbed on top of me. "Wouldn't you like to know?"

"I very much would."

I was practically panting in anticipation of him using more than one toy on me. Vaughn ran the tip of one up and down my slit.

I whimpered, need rising within me, and he fulfilled that wish, pushing the toy inside me while it buzzed.

An orgasm built deep inside me, tingles building and rising in time with the way he played with my pussy. "I'm going to come."

His phone rang.

Vaughn paused, looking over at it.

I grabbed both sides of his face and yanked it so he was staring down at me. "If you even think about answering some business call when I am this close to orgasm..."

"It's Fang."

"As much as I love the man, I think he'll understand if we send it to voicemail, don't you?"

Vaughn groaned and kissed my mouth. "I'm so sorry, Roach. I promised him."

I watched in shock as he reached over and answered the video call. "This better be fucking good, Fang."

Fang's voice echoed around the room. "We're— What the hell are you doing?"

"Anyone else with you right now?" Vaughn had his arm outstretched, phone angled on his face.

"No, but—"

Vaughn, literally no shame, moved the phone so I could clearly be seen beneath him.

I squeaked and covered my bare breasts on instinct. "Vaughn!"

Fang swore low under his breath.

"What?" Vaughn laughed, clearly too delighted by the situation.

I could hardly blame him, after the stunt Fang and I had pulled with sending him the sex tape.

"You're the one who told us to watch the tape. You had to know it would end like this." He propped the phone up on the bedside table so we could both see.

Fang's low growl was so sexy it made me want to dive through the phone and right onto his cock. "You better be keeping my woman satisfied, Vaughn. If she hasn't come twice before you do, I'll rescind my invitation to share."

Vaughn held up my buzzy little friend. "Oh, don't worry. Even if my skills were subpar, which for the record, they are not, you aren't the only one with toys." He shot Fang an arrogant grin. "If this isn't some safety emergency, excuse me while I get back to it."

He leaned over to end the call, but Fang stopped him. "Wait."

Vaughn waited.

Fang adjusted the phone so it skimmed down his body. In the background, I recognized the pillow and quilt from his bed at the clubhouse. The camera rolled over Fang's tight white T-shirt that clung to his abs, then lower, to where he was one-handedly undoing his fly, a huge bulge behind it. "You watched me fuck her. Now it's my turn."

He took his cock out and stroked it slowly. The camera was fully focused on his glorious length, and for a moment, Vaughn and I both watched in fascination.

"Still only hard for one dick, Vaughn?" I breathed.

He rolled away from the camera to hover over me again, his weight rested on his forearms and knees. He licked his way up my neck. "You're the only dick I'm hard over right now, Roach." He pushed into me with one long thrust that had me gasping at his size and clutching my fingers in the sheets.

"Oh!"

Vaughn fucked slowly, dragging out of me so gradually it was torture, before leisurely pushing his way back inside. I grabbed his ass, toned and muscled, and tried to force him to go faster, but he refused, torturing me with a pace that drove me wild.

It was barely a minute before I was right back where I'd started, on the verge of an orgasm, pleasure spiraling within me, fueled by Vaughn's girth, his pubic bone grinding on my clit.

And by the occasional glance at Fang on the phone, sprawled out on his bed, getting off watching another man fuck me.

Oh my God.

I came with a mess of blinding light and Vaughn deep inside me. I clutched him, begging and pleading for him to give me more, my pussy fluttering and clamping down on his dick, but not for one moment did he falter.

He pulled out when my pants and cries dulled down to regular breaths, but he was still hard.

I was confused. "You didn't come."

His grin was nothing short of wicked. "Fang said you

had to come twice before I did. Seemed like good advice." He picked up a vibrator.

Oh, sweet Jesus.

It was one of my smaller ones, designed for anal, though I'd never used it as such. I liked it for clit and nipple stimulation while I masturbated with the bigger dildo.

But Vaughn had other plans.

He grabbed the tube of lube he'd brought from my bedroom drawer stash. When the vibrator was well covered, he ran it down through my slit, then lower to prod against my ass.

Fuck, it felt good. My nerve endings all came to life once more, pleasure coursing through my body and causing new pussy flutters that mimicked the orgasm I'd just had.

Fang groaned through the phone, and I looked over. Vaughn's phone was an expensive one, and I might as well have been watching Fang masturbate in full, high-definition. Precum beaded at his tip, and he swiped his thumb over it.

My clit throbbed. Every intimate area of me begged for more.

Vaughn leaned down to whisper in my ear, so only I could hear, "He's huge, Roach. If you're going to take us both, you need practice. Do you still want that?"

God, I did. I knew exactly how big he was, and Vaughn was no slouch in the dick department either. "I want it."

He groaned. "Good girl. Flip over and get on your knees."

I did.

He kneeled behind me and drew my hips back so my ass was in the air. Leaning over me with one hand, he rubbed my clit. The other stroked over my ass, cupping and massaging, his fingers edging closer and closer to the center.

He worked the tight hole until I was mewling for mercy and grinding back against his thumb, desperate for more. Every touch of him there had me trembling, my knees shaking, my muscles struggling to hold my weight, so I dropped down on my forearms.

Vaughn's hand ran down my spine and then trailed off, returning with the vibrator.

The tip nudged my ass, and I moaned at how thick it was in comparison to his finger. Nowhere near as big as his cock and not even close to Fang's, but it was exactly what I needed. He moved slowly, letting the vibrations work their way in while I shoved my face into the mattress, trying not to scream out at how much it heightened every bit of pleasure already floating around my body. I grasped one of my nipples and tweaked it as hard as I could, gasping at the sharp sting of pleasure that only encouraged the vibrator farther into my ass.

Vaughn was patient, never stopping on my clit, even when I begged and moaned.

"Let me get you there, Roach. You're already close."

I was. So fucking close I could practically taste the orgasm he teased me with.

He pushed his dick inside me, taking my pussy again.

The noises that left my mouth were indecent.

Vaughn's breaths were warm on my back. He gripped my hips, using them as leverage to go deeper, harder. The vibrator matched his tempo. Everything felt *more* than just having him in my pussy. The orgasm building was one on steroids.

I turned my head and watched Fang's face, twisted in something between intense pleasure and agony. My head hit the padded headboard over and over again as Vaughn's thrusts propelled me up the bed.

I was so close. So ready to go over the edge in free fall.

"Slap her ass," Fang instructed. "She needs more to get over the line."

Vaughn's palm across my ass cheek was exactly what I needed. I fell into a second orgasm, shouting his name into his mattress and pushing back against his every thrust so each one hit as deep as possible.

His moans mingled with mine. He spilled himself inside me while saying my name over and over again.

My real name.

Not Roach.

On the screen, Fang came with us, white jets of cum spreading across his lower belly. I watched through half-mast eyes, too full of desire to fully open. He didn't stop stroking himself until Vaughn and I collapsed on the bed in a tangle of arms and legs.

"Fuck," Vaughn groaned. "Just...fuck."

I couldn't have said it better myself.

He held me tight and gently removed the vibrator.

Vaughn placed a kiss to the side of my neck and tucked the blankets tight over me. "Gonna get something to take care of you." He stuck his head in front of the phone camera. "Sorry, big guy. You're on your own for clean-up."

Fang stuck his middle finger up. But then the camera

was back up at his face and he was studying me intently. "Are you okay?"

I nodded sleepily. "I'm great."

"He was gentle?"

"Where I needed him to be."

Fang made a gruff noise of satisfaction. "Good."

I grabbed the phone from the bedside table. "What's going on there?"

"We've got a lead on the Sinners. A house they're using to hole up."

I smiled at him. "That's great, baby."

Except Fang didn't smile. "They have women. Ones who aren't there by their own free will, we believe."

A sick feeling took over the lovely tingles of pleasure. I instantly wanted them back, but I couldn't grasp them. "You think they're being trafficked?"

He bit his lip. "I don't know. But, Pix? That's not all. They've seen Caleb there. He's using them for protection."

I gasped. "The girl? Is she there with him?"

He nodded. "At least we think so. We've been looking into it, and she arrived there the day after you nearly drowned."

I sat up. "Fang! You have to go in and get her! I promised!"

His teeth mashed together, but he nodded fiercely. "I'm on it, Pix. We'll get her. I promise."

24

KARA

She was the most perfect baby I'd ever seen. With tiny rosebud lips, the prettiest shade of pink, and a soft dusting of fuzzy blond hair. She was so sweet it was hard to believe she was even real, until she woke up and cried.

I wasn't sure the other girls felt quite as enthusiastic about the crying, but I loved it. When she was quiet, it was too easy for the dark thoughts to taunt me with the fact she might not actually just be asleep.

I watched her every minute of the night and day, barely sleeping, refusing the help the other girls kept trying to offer. I needed to soak up every moment with her. Commit it to memory, because at any moment, I knew Caleb would ruin it for me.

Georgia and Winnie watched me nurse my daughter from the corner of our room, the two of them deep in discussion about something.

"What is it?" I asked, a tremble in my voice. "What do you know? Did you hear something?" All the nightmares

I'd been trying to hold at bay came crashing down over me, threatening and dark. I clutched my daughter closer, as tight as I dared without hurting her.

Winnie rushed to my side and knelt in front of me to stroke the baby's downy head. "Oh no, nothing like that. We're just worried about you."

"No need for that," I assured them. "As long as I have her, there's nothing else I need."

I meant it with every beat of my heart. Having her in my arms was all that mattered. I just wish I'd known that before I'd stupidly turned up on Caleb's doorstep and demanded money from him. Mama was right. I was greedy and selfish and now I was being punished for those sins.

"I'm so sorry, baby girl," I whispered. "I wish I could take it back."

I would, in a heartbeat.

A knock at the door had us all freezing, but it was Hayden who opened it. His gaze flickered around the room but came to rest on me, and then my daughter. He smiled softly. "How's the little one?"

I couldn't help but smile at him. He was the only reason I'd survived her birth; I was sure of that. While Caleb had been ready to leave me for dead, Hayden had encouraged me right up until she'd been born, brushing my hair back off my face, breathing with me, reminding me I was strong and I could do this. When it was over, and Winnie had placed my daughter in my arms, Hayden had brought in a woman who hadn't looked happy but had stitched me up after he put a large wad of cash in her hand.

"She's great," I assured him.

Hayden nodded. "You pick a name for her yet?"

I shook my head. I didn't know why I was holding off. But the right name would come to me, I was sure. "Not yet."

He had a hoodie on today, paired with ripped jeans and loosely tied work boots. His blue eyes and cute smile did things to my insides I had no business feeling. I had to remind myself he was as much the enemy as Caleb was.

Hayden crossed to the corner of the room and checked the rickety secondhand changing table he'd brought in the day after I'd had her. He knelt and rifled through the array of diapers, baby wipes, and tiny clothes he'd filled it with. "I'll get more diapers today."

"You really don't need to," I said quickly. "There's plenty."

He acted like he hadn't even heard me. "What about blankets? Do you think she's getting cold at night? Are you sure you don't need that baby milk powder thing? Bottles?"

I shook my head. "We're fine."

We weren't. We were anything but fine, really, but in the scheme of things, we weren't in any immediate danger. Despite his support through my labor and delivery, I didn't want to feel like I owed this man anything.

Georgia beamed at him though, her smile bordering on flirtatious. "We're taking care of her. Don't you worry about that."

He nodded. "Good. I'm glad."

Georgia touched his arm. "Do you have kids, Hayden?"

"Me? No."

Georgia was practically a puddle at his feet. "Oh really? I thought you must have. You knew exactly what to get for this little one."

Hayden shrugged off her touch. "I called my brother, Liam. His partner, Mae, had a baby not long ago. He told me what to get."

Georgia acted like this was the most fascinating information she'd ever had shared with her. "Really? So you have a niece or nephew then? That's lovely. What about a wife? Girlfriend?"

Nova snorted softly. "Could you be any more blatant, Georgia? Jesus. Please take this painful attempt at flirting into another room where I don't have to listen to it."

I bit my lip to keep from laughing. I kind of felt the same way, I was just not as blunt as Nova.

I didn't quite understand why I was a bit disappointed Hayden didn't actually answer Georgia's question.

Of course the man had a girlfriend. Or a wife. Probably one who walked runways somewhere, because a guy like him would have a beautiful woman on his arm for sure. He screamed bad boy, plus he was tall and hot enough to model himself. I doubted his bed was ever empty for long.

A shout from somewhere within the house cut short any further discussion. All of us turned to the open doorway, and the sudden rush of big men thundering up and down it.

"Chaos! Get out here! We got ninety-nine problems, and every single one of them are the Slayers."

Hayden swore low under his breath and stormed to the doorway. But then he glanced back over his shoulder. "Stay here. Get away from the windows. Don't open the door unless it's me. Got it?" His words seemed to be for all of us...and yet he was only looking at me.

The other girls squeaked out scared yesses, but he didn't leave until I nodded.

The door locked behind him, an audible reminder that no matter how attractive he was, no matter how sweet he was in bringing me things for the baby, Hayden 'Chaos' Whitling was not a good guy.

All of us stared at the closed door, listening to the shouts and commands coming from beyond it.

Caleb's voice was one of them. Barking demands. Screaming at Hayden. I cowered away from the door, wishing there was a way of holding my daughter and covering my ears at the same time.

Nova shifted on the top bunk, peering out around the black curtain through the bar-covered windows. "Holy shit. There's a bunch of guys on bikes out there. More down the road, I think."

Georgia yanked the curtain from her grasp. "What are you doing? Hayden said to stay away from the window!"

Nova yanked it again. "Fuck that! I've been watching the road for days, and nobody ever comes down here. I'm hailing these mofos down and asking for a lift."

Winnie's eyes went wide. "Nova! You can't! We have no idea who they are!"

"They're a motorcycle club," Vivienne said quietly, staring out over Nova's shoulder. "Well known around here. They aren't the knights in shining armor you're hoping for. Trust me."

Nova glanced over at her. "Knights in cracked black leather then? Gotta be better than being kept prisoner in this fucking hellhole."

"What if it's not?" Winnie wrung her fingers. "Nothing bad has happened to us since we were brought here. We're fed. We have shelter."

Nova gaped at her. "Is that your standard for living the rest of your life? That you're fed and have a roof over your head?"

Winnie dropped her gaze to her lap, her voice suddenly hard. "It's more than I had before, Nova. So fuck off."

I blinked. Winnie had been nothing but soft and sweet and a mother hen since I'd arrived. I hadn't expected the F bomb. Or the sad admission about her life prior to coming here. My heart ached for her, that this was an improvement in her mind.

But similar worries plagued me. "What if they're worse than what we have? What if they split us up?"

Even Nova fell quiet at that.

Trauma bonded people.

I'd been trying to keep my distance, knowing this cozy arrangement wouldn't last forever. That eventually one of those men out there would come in and take whatever they wanted from us. Hurt us. Rape us. Sell us to other men who would do more of the same.

That inevitability seemed a little further away when Winnie was fussing over me and Nova was being a smart-ass.

"So what?" Nova eventually said. "We just sit here and do nothing?"

"Yes," Winnie said firmly. "Better the devil you know."

Nova threw up her hands. "Let's vote then. Whatever we do, it should be majority rules since the decision will affect all of us. Hands up if you're with me?"

Georgia raised her hand to join Nova's waving one.

She sighed when I didn't move. "Hands up if you're with Winnie?"

Vivienne raised hers.

I still did nothing.

"Kara!" Nova snapped. "You have to choose!"

I opened my mouth, but a round of shots exploded. All of us dove for the floor, the girls all burying me and the baby, now squawking in terror in my arms. Another round of shots came from somewhere, and Winnie's keening wail filled my ears.

"No, no, no. Don't let them take me." She repeated it over and over again, rocking in place, her arms wrapped around her legs.

It was a shock to see her like that. She'd been so calm and steady when I'd been having the baby.

But we all had our triggers. Our own deep-rooted fears that couldn't be pushed down. I moved the baby into one arm and put the other around Winnie's shoulders, drawing her tight to my side. "Shh, it's okay," I murmured, the reassurances for both my daughter and the woman next to me. "It's going to be fine."

The door swung open, and Hayden stormed in, eyes like fire, a gun shoved into the waistband of his jeans.

I cringed away at the sight of it, terrified he was going to put a bullet in each of our brains, just to save the guys outside from doing it.

But he went to the window and peeked around the curtain. "Fuck!"

Caleb appeared in the doorway, his eyes wide with panic. "What the hell are you doing, just standing in here? Do something!"

Hayden stood to his full height, spinning around and going chest to chest with the slightly shorter man. "What exactly do you want me to do?" he snarled. "Waltz out there and give myself up? They'll kill me before I even get a foot onto the porch."

"I paid you to protect me!"

"Are you dead? No. Then shut up and let me think."

"Think faster then, you idiot! Fuck me, this is what I get for hiring trailer trash from Saint View to do anything. You incompetent, useless waste of space."

Hayden drove his palms against Caleb's chest and slammed him up against the wall. "How about I throw you out there as a motherfucking sacrifice?"

I voted for that plan.

Caleb pulled Hayden's gun from the waistband of his pants and shoved it into his stomach. "You ungrateful shit. Get the fuck off me."

Hayden's jaw ground viciously, but his gaze slid to me.

I didn't know what expression I wore, but it was probably something close to pure terror.

Hayden stepped back and took a phone from his pocket instead, ignoring the gun trained on him.

Caleb shook himself and straightened his shoulders now that Hayden wasn't supporting his weight anymore. "That's more like it. I'll accept your apology later. Who the hell are you calling?"

Hayden stared at me, phone held to his ear. "Backup to come get them."

"What?" Caleb argued. "They're not going anywhere. The only reason this house isn't full of bullet holes is because of these stupid sluts and the Slayers' bleeding hearts."

Nova glanced silently at the rest of us. Her eyes quietly expressive.

Her message was clear. We should have made a run for it. Taken our chances on the MC with the bad reputation outside.

Maybe we still could.

In a panic, I shook my head no, but Nova turned away, pretending she didn't see.

Hayden spit out the address into the phone before Caleb snatched it from his grasp and threw it across the room. It hit the wall with a splintering crack and dropped uselessly onto the threadbare carpet. "You'd better hope they didn't catch that address. Those girls are worth more than your life, so watch me put a bullet in your brain before I give them up."

Another round of gunfire from the corner of the house lit up the night. Winnie screamed again; her trembling so intense it spread to the rest of us.

Nova pushed to her feet to shout in Caleb's face. "You can't keep us here!" She dove for the curtain, ripping it aside. "Help! Help!"

Caleb's smacked her across the face with the handle of the gun. "Shut up! Shut up! I can't think with you all screaming!"

Hayden caught her as she stumbled dizzily across the room, her eyes fluttering like she was fighting to stay conscious. He lowered her to the floor beside us.

"Keep her on her side for a minute."

Vivienne nodded, helping Hayden roll her over while smoothing Nova's pretty red hair back off her face.

A huge red-purple mark spread across her temple

and cheekbone. Her eyes rolled back, and her entire body shook viciously.

"She's having a seizure!" I hissed at Hayden. "Do something!"

"I already did," he whispered back. "There's an ambulance already on its way. When it gets here, you and the baby, and now her, will go with them."

I widened my eyes at him. "What do you mean? What about the others?"

Hayden glanced grimly at the other women huddled around me. "I'll do my best to make sure they're safe."

"Your best?" I spat out at him. "Your best is *trying* to make sure they're safe? That isn't good enough! You have a gun, Hayden! Get it! Use it. Shoot him in the head!"

For half a second, I thought he was going to do it too.

"Is that sirens?" Caleb screeched. He peeked out the window again, and red and blue lights lit up the room.

Hayden stood and shouted to the other men in the house. "None of you so much as touch those paramedics, you hear me? I don't care if all hell is raining down on you, you don't touch them. Get them down here now."

Hayden knelt again, checking on Nova who had stopped convulsing but hadn't regained consciousness.

"Where's the patient?" a man asked from somewhere down the hall.

Caleb waved the gun in our faces. "One word and you get a bullet. You hear me? You want to end up dead like your friend there? Don't try me."

Winnie wailed harder.

"She's not dead," I assured her. "She'll be okay."

I was reassuring myself as much as her. Nova didn't appear to be in good shape at all.

Hayden's gaze flickered to the baby and then to me. He smiled tightly. "When you get to the hospital, call someone to come pick you up. Then get the hell out of Saint View, Kara. Nothing good happens here. Take your daughter and don't look back." He stroked a finger over the baby's soft pink cheek. "Have a good life, little rosy-cheeked girl. I really fucking hope you don't remember any of this."

There was a click-clack of wheels along the hardwood floors, and two men came into the room. They did a double take at us all huddled on the floor, but I pointed at Nova.

"Please help her. I don't even know if she's breathing anymore."

The two paramedics knelt over Nova's lifeless body, poking and prodding and doing all sorts of things I'd never seen anyone do before.

"Let's get her loaded. Make way, please." He dragged the gurney closer and took a backboard from the top of it.

Caleb tore his gaze away from the window outside. "Not her. Take the one with the baby."

The paramedic glanced over at me and down at the tiny baby in my arms, who'd cried herself to sleep.

"How old is she?"

I shook my head. "A couple of days."

"You had her here?"

I nodded.

"She seen a doctor?"

I shook my head.

He peered over at my clearly healthy daughter and then back at Nova. "No. We only have one gurney. We'll call another ambulance, but this woman is the priority."

Caleb pulled out the gun again, pressing it hard into the back of the paramedic's head. "The priority is whoever I say it is."

The man flinched. "Sir. Please put the gun down."

"Then load the woman carrying my daughter."

Hayden looked at me sharply. "His daughter?"

I could feel the gazes of the other women too, each of them silently questioning me.

The paramedic let out a shaky breath, raising his hands when he turned to talk to Caleb. "This woman will die if we don't take her now. Her vitals are plummeting. Do you really want a dead body on your hands?"

The gunshot was so loud it left my ears ringing. The second was worse, the noise shattering through my skull until I was confused as to where I was.

But when it cleared, I wished for it to come back.

Both paramedics lay dead on the floor in front of us. A single bullet to both their skulls, their blood and bone and brains spattered across the women surrounding me.

Caleb was already tugging at their clothes, stripping them of their uniforms.

Men appeared in the doorway, but Caleb barked for them to piss off, and surprisingly, they listened. Hayden just stared down at the two dead men; his boots coated in their rapidly pooling blood.

"Get a uniform on," Caleb snapped.

Hayden blinked up at him. "What?"

"Get a uniform on. We're surrounded. You said it yourself. I just bought us a way out. You. Me. And the little slut carrying my child. Get the uniform on."

Hayden shook his head. "No." His arms went limp at

his side. "Fuck, Caleb. No. This isn't what I signed up for. None of it is. This isn't what you promised."

Caleb stopped and stared at him. "Liam Banks. Lawyer at Simonson Lawyers and Partners. Partner to Mae Donovan, Rowe Pritchard, and Heath Michaelson. Parents of a five-year-old named Ripley and a newborn baby named Jay. Your mother is Sarah, who drives a blue station wagon, license plate PPT-1680 and lives on Delilah Road in Saint View."

Hayden stared up at Caleb in horror. "How do you know my family? Liam and I don't even go by the same last name."

Caleb went back to tugging on a dead man's clothes. "Because I do my homework, Chaos. I know everyone's weak spots so when they turn into whiny, useless crybabies like you're being right now, I know how best to motivate them. So, you can either get on the uniform and protect me like I fucking paid you to, and your family gets to live on happily, or you can stay here and die in a mass shooting when the Slayers finally take this place and burn it to the ground. Your choice."

Hayden's eyes went hard. "You piece of fucking shi—"

Caleb waggled his finger in Hayden's face. "Now, now. Remember who's calling the shots here. Get your clothes on and let's go."

I grabbed Hayden's hand. "Don't let him take me," I begged. "He'll kill me. Or take my baby. Or sell us both. Please don't let him. I'll take my chances with the guys outside. They couldn't be worse than him."

Indecision flickered on Hayden's face. So long that Caleb grabbed the back of his head and pushed it down so Hayden was forced to stare at the dead bodies in front of him. "This is what your brother will look like. His woman. Your nephews. Maybe I'll let you explain to your mother how their deaths are all your fault before I kill her too," he sneered in Hayden's face, his eyes as black as the night outside. "Or would you prefer to watch me fuck her before I do that?"

Whatever light was left in Hayden's eyes shut down. He took my arm. "Get on the gurney."

I couldn't even blame him. I would have done the same.

The other girls wailed when I stood and waited for Caleb and Hayden to get dressed into the dead men's clothes and lift the gurney into position. Winnie clutched at my fingers while I got myself on and lay down with my daughter on my chest.

I couldn't bring myself to say goodbye to them as I was wheeled out of the room. All I could do was squeeze my eyes tight and hope the men outside were good to them. That they'd spare them. Maybe even set them free.

I didn't hold the same hopes for myself.

Caleb was never going to let me go.

25

VAUGHN

Rebel threw a pen across the room so hard it left a mark when it hit the wall and slid down to land on the floor. "I can't do this anymore, Vaughn! I'm losing my shit just sitting here."

I leaned backward on the kitchen chair, balancing it on two legs so I could retrieve the pen that had nearly taken my eye out. I placed it back on her side of the table gingerly. "If I give you this back, can you please promise not to use it as a javelin again?"

She blinked at me like she had no idea how her pen had even ended up where it had. She snatched it back and agitatedly scribbled on the mockup of the Order of Service we'd had designed for the funeral.

I winced and pulled the paper booklet out from underneath all the pen stabbing, replacing it with a notepad for her to destroy instead. "No news is good news, right? Fang will let us know as soon as there's anything to report."

She rolled her head from side to side, and her neck

cracked. It didn't seem to do anything to reduce her stress though. "What's taking them so long? Can't they just storm the place, guns blazing?"

"I'm guessing maybe they would have if the Sinners weren't hiding behind a group of innocent women."

Rebel sighed. "I can't even imagine what those poor women are going through. I can't stop thinking about them. Do they have families who are searching for them? Or did they target women who no one cared about enough to notice they were missing?"

"Probably the latter."

Rebel shook her head sadly. "That's somehow worse."

I wanted to put an arm around her and hug her close. I wanted to tell her it would be okay.

But I didn't know that it would.

I was pretty sure if I tried to hug her right now, I'd only be crowding her, making her anxiety worse.

She shoved her chair back abruptly and paced up and down the kitchen floor. "We need to do something."

I groaned. "Ah shit. Please don't say that. I promised Fang I'd keep you here, safe and sound while he took care of the problem. Please don't make a liar out of me."

She draped her arms around my neck and kissed my cheek. "Would I do such a thing?"

I rolled my eyes. "Fine. What are we doing? But it can't take too long. We've got that dinner at my mom's later."

"I know. But setting someone's house on fire doesn't take that long."

I laughed. "I thought I just heard you say you were setting someone's house on fire."

She was already moving around the kitchen, opening

drawers and cupboards, rifling through them for who knows what. "I did. Hugh's place to be exact. With him in it. Do you know where the matches are?"

I was sure my eyes were bugging out of my head.

But Rebel was a little tornado of action, collecting fire starters and anything that could have remotely passed as an accelerant.

I grabbed her arm. "Hey, pyro. Stop for a second."

She shook her head. "Can't. I have to do something."

"You don't. You have to stay here and be safe. With me." I swallowed thickly. "Fucking hell, Roach. Don't make me beg you."

She stopped and looked up at me, her eyes big and sparkling with unshed tears. "You don't understand."

"Then explain it so I do."

She took a shaky breath, breathing it out over a wobbly bottom lip. "It's my fault that woman is trapped with the Sinners. If I had just gone to the cops when Caleb had raped me..."

I cupped the side of my face. "That's not true."

"It is! If I'd just gone, maybe they would have arrested them. Caleb and his friends could be rotting in a prison somewhere. But I was selfish and said nothing. I didn't let Fang or War or Scythe go after him because I was so hell-bent on getting revenge myself. In the time I wasted, he took another woman." She kicked at the edge of a kitchen tile. "I might as well have abducted her myself."

She tried to pull away, but I grabbed the back of her neck, not letting her go. "Or you would have gone to the cops, and they would have blown you off, like they do to every other woman from Saint View who makes a claim of sexual assault against a powerful man. That's why you didn't go. You didn't go because you know the system. You've seen it too many other times to believe in it. It's failed your friends, your family, and it's failed you. Why would you keep trying when they don't lift a finger to help?"

She pressed her forehead into my chest. "You're right. I know. But it doesn't make it any easier to just sit here, knowing they're probably hurting her the way they hurt me. Leonn is turning himself in. Fang is dealing with Caleb. Someone needs to go after Hugh. I can't keep sitting on my hands. He didn't even recognize me when I was in that coffee shop, Vaughn. Did he even see my face when he pushed me to the ground? Didn't he see me cry when he ripped my clothes and scratched my skin? Didn't he hear me beg him to stop or my screams of pain?"

She hadn't meant to hurt me with her words. She'd just been venting, trying to get them off her chest. But every word she said was like shooting an arrow through my heart and twisting it, so the barbed edges did the maximum amount of damage.

She cared so much. She was tiny, but her heart was so damn huge. Who else would put themselves in danger for a woman she'd only spoken to via knocks through a bathroom wall? She didn't know anything about her, other than that she needed help.

Rebel hadn't deserved what they'd done to her. No woman did.

And Hugh was still out there, free as a fucking bird to do it all again.

While I was sitting here, in my mansion, scared to let

her leave. Scared to let her have her revenge. Scared she'd wind up as dead as my father.

She wasn't scared.

I didn't want to be the man who held her back.

"Fuck," I groaned, letting her go. "Jesus. Give me those and go upstairs and get something else on. Jeans. A sweatshirt. Got a couple of balaclavas?"

Her mouth dropped open. "You're coming with me?"

"Fang would probably run over my balls with his motorcycle if I didn't. Especially since Kian is slacking on the bodyguard duties."

She cocked her head. "That the only reason you're coming?"

No. I'm coming because you're beautiful. Because I can't think straight when you're not around. Because I have all these damn feelings and thoughts about protecting you, keeping you safe, and worse, making you mine. Because I tried to play them off as brotherly, or that I was fulfilling some vow to my father, but it's just because you're all I think about.

I couldn't get those words out, but they played on a loop over and over in my head, each one getting louder until I lamely said, "I like balls."

Rebel snorted.

"My balls. I meant I like my balls," I corrected quickly, but the damage had clearly been done.

"Cupping them or sucking them?"

I glared at her.

"Shaven or au naturel?"

"I really hate you."

She pulled on the string of my sweatpants and slipped her hand inside them, cupping me. "Just for the record, I like balls too."

She squeezed gently before moving her hand up to my cock, giving it a few slow strokes.

"You're a tease." I bent down so my lips were closer to hers.

She pressed up on her toes and pecked my lips. A second later, the elastic on my underwear snapped back into place and she guided me toward the stairs. "I know. But come on. I'll let you watch me get changed."

I trailed up the stairs after her. "Ooh. Fireproof clothes. So sexy. Can't wait."

She glanced back at me over her shoulder. "It would be so easy to push you down these stairs right now, Vaughn."

"So full of violence today," I mumbled. "I wish I didn't find that hot."

We split up, Rebel going into her bedroom to get changed, me going into mine. We met a few minutes later at the bottom of the stairs, Rebel's eyes bright.

My arms were full of all things required to make a fire. "We should cut through the woods behind the house and go the rest of the way on foot."

Rebel shook her head. "No. What if they use dogs to track us? We'll lead them straight back here."

Well, that was a point. "Okay, so we drive halfway, leave the car on a side street somewhere, and then walk the rest of the way in."

Rebel screwed up her nose. "I don't know. Maybe we should call Scythe?"

I stared at her. "And what? Ask for pointers on burning a man alive?"

"Unless you know someone more qualified? War and

Fang are already busy, so I don't think we should bother them."

"Not what I meant, Roach!" I shook my head. "How did I end up friends with you people?"

She patted my cheek. "Come on. If we're going to get to your mom's on time, we need to go now."

"Oh, yes," I grumbled, following her out of the house to my car because, apparently, she'd decided her plan was superior to mine. "Let's make haste so we can go kill a man and still get to dinner in time to set the freaking table."

Rebel tossed me the keys. "Even murderers gotta eat, you know."

I got behind the wheel of the car anyway and drove in the direction she pointed. We parked a few blocks from Hugh's house and got out, slipping into the darkness of the woods and using the tall trees for cover as much as possible until we rounded the back of his property.

"This is his." I pointed up at the million-dollar mansion.

Rebel panted beside me, completely out of breath. She leaned over, one hand on her leg, the other holding up one finger, indicating to give her a minute.

I shook my head. "Kian is right. You really do need to do more cardio."

She flipped her finger around.

Rude.

Between wheezing breaths, she jerked her head toward the house. "You sure this is it?"

"Worried you might set the wrong people alight?"

She glared up at me. "Actually, yes, Vaughn. That is

exactly what I'm worried about. Gimme the damn binoculars."

I muttered something about her lack of trust being insulting and passed her the binoculars that normally resided in my father's den. He'd used them for much more vanilla activities like bird-watching.

I stared up at the back of Hugh's mansion. Like many of the homes in Providence, most of the back wall was glass to take advantage of the view. He had lights on throughout, letting us see right into his bedroom, kitchen, living room, and what looked to be a gym.

Hugh himself was sprawled out on a couch on the second-floor living room, watching a big-screen TV.

"It's him," Rebel confirmed. "And there's no one else to be seen." She shook the box of matches at me. "You ready?"

"Just gonna say it one more time. This is insane."

At seeing Hugh, Rebel had lost the giddy laughter from her voice. Instead, her voice turned deep and cold. "This is revenge."

"This is murder."

She went quiet at that one. Until one little sentence came out as a whisper, "I don't care."

I did, until I let the memories of her bruises sink back in. They were quickly followed by Rebel sinking in the bottom of that pool, and the feeling I'd had ever since, the one I couldn't shake, that said if I lost her, nothing would ever be the same.

Hugh was a threat.

Not only to random strangers, but to the woman standing beside me. My heart hammered, but I held my hand out. "Give me the matches. I'll do it."

She was already making a run from the trees, leaving me behind.

"Oh, fucking hell, Roach!" But it was a whisper-shout, because the last thing I needed right now was Hugh hearing me cussing Rebel out because she was too stubborn and independent for her own good. I sprinted after her, reaching the edge of the house mere seconds after she did, because my legs were twice as long.

She tossed me a small can of gasoline. "Quick. Spread it around on anything that might be flammable."

She'd already made a start, squirting it around the door and window frames on the bottom level. Once she set those to light, they'd block the exits. "We need to get all the windows and doors."

Vicious.

"Give me a lighter." I held my hand out to her, as hopped up on adrenaline as she was. "I'm going to the front."

She passed me one from her pocket and grabbed my hand, not letting me go. Her eyes were wide, pupils dilated. "Don't get caught."

I leaned in and pressed my lips to her mouth. "You wait for me in the woods."

She nodded, kissing me back hard.

We split, and within seconds, I was at the front of the house, emptying out my can of gasoline on every surface I could find.

I didn't think about what I was doing.

About trapping a man inside his home and setting it alight.

I just concentrated on getting it done quick so I could get back to her.

I lit a rag from my pocket and dropped it into the puddles of deathly liquid.

It lit up the night in a tiny trail of flames, one that would have been pretty if it hadn't been so deadly.

I didn't stick around to watch. I put my head down and sprinted back to the woods. I didn't lift my head until I hit the safety of the trees, and by the time I did, the back of Hugh's house was illuminated with flames.

Shock punched me in the gut, and for a second, froze me to the spot. I was too stunned by what we'd done to move.

Only then I realized Rebel wasn't there.

I spun around frantically, looking side to side, trying to peer through the darkness. The only light permeating the trees this deep was that from the flames. "Rebel!"

No answer.

I didn't think my heart could beat any faster than it already was, but it somehow doubled its pace, panic setting in and clutching at my chest. "Rebel!"

A tap on the back of my shoulder had me spinning around.

My little roach grinned up at me. "Your sense of direction is awful. I was waiting about twenty feet down that way."

I didn't have time to feel relief. I found her hand and we ran, side by side, through the woods.

I couldn't get away from those flames fast enough. With every step I felt the heat of them at my heels, licking and curling their way up my skin, until I was sure I was burning too.

We burst out from the tree line, somehow right at the spot we'd left my car, despite Rebel's claims that my sense of direction was off. There was still nobody around. In the distance, sirens wailed, and the scent of smoke wafted in the air. We both stopped outside the car and stared back the way we'd come, not that we could see anything through the trees.

Rebel breathed hard again, but this time, my breaths matched hers. She stared up at me, her hands shaking violently. "What did we just do? Vaughn! Oh my God, we killed him, didn't we? We burned him alive in his own home! I'm a monster! As big a monster as he is! I—"

I grabbed her roughly and slammed my mouth down on hers.

Rebel froze, but then slowly her ice thawed. She kissed me back, her mouth hot from running, her tongue instantly seeking entrance to mine.

I needed her more. I pushed her back against the side of the car and kissed her fast, getting hard behind my dark jeans.

Adrenaline pumped through my veins, turning into a raging lust that couldn't be denied. If the way Rebel yanked at my pants was anything to go by, she felt it too.

She freed my cock, but we didn't have time for this.

Hanging around here any longer than necessary was suicide, and yet I found myself dragging her black jeans down her legs and hoisting her up onto the hood.

We were an awkward mess of arms and legs, Rebel's feet stuck in her jeans so she couldn't spread her ankles far, but she compensated with wide-open knees and propping her feet up on the bumper. She grasped at my shirt, yanking me closer, but I needed no encouragement, my dick spearing into her hard, bottoming right out on the first thrust.

"Oh!" she shouted.

I clapped a hand over her mouth and drew back, only to slam inside her again. My palm muffled her shouts as I fucked her hard and fast, using up the excess energy that was clouding my judgment.

The sirens grew louder, but I couldn't stop the need for her coursing through my body.

She reached between us for her clit, her moans still loud enough to draw attention, but there was no stopping either of us at this point.

She came around my cock, my name on her lips, and I replaced my hand with my mouth so I could kiss her.

"Hurry up," she moaned. "Come inside me."

I grabbed her sweet ass, hauling her in tighter and slamming myself inside her slick pussy. She clamped down on my length, my orgasm taking hold and milking every drop from my body.

An entire swarm of police cars could have circled us in that moment, sirens blaring, lights flashing, and I wouldn't have noticed.

Buried deep inside her, nothing else mattered.

I came hard, kissing her mouth, spilling inside her like she was mine.

Without withdrawing, I picked her up.

She wrapped her arms around me tight, burying her head in my neck, kissing the sensitive spot sweetly.

I didn't want to put her down, but I knew we couldn't stay here any longer. We had only wasted minutes, the sex a race to get off, but we couldn't just stay here kissing and hugging like we had all the time in the world. It wouldn't be long before news got out, and the two of us fucking like horny rabbits in balaclavas was kind of eye-drawing for anyone who might happen to drive by, even if it was dark.

The car's interior light turned on automatically when I opened the back door, and I bent down so I could lay her out on the back seat. I hovered over her for a second, her pussy still giving little flutters around me, then reluctantly withdrew.

Watching my dick slide out of her stretched pussy was the hottest thing.

Leaving my cum inside her, and watching it seep out of her cunt beat it.

I couldn't help myself. I scooped a little of it up and rubbed it on her clit.

Her moan had my dick threatening to get hard again.

Fuck. This woman. I'd never felt anything like the high I had going on right then. No drug I'd ever experimented with had come close to the feeling of wanting her.

It was dangerous. Reckless. Wild.

Everything my father's business partner had never let me be.

My brain shouted warnings, loud enough to force me to listen. But not before I grabbed her hand and put it to her cum-soaked pussy. "Make yourself come again before we get to my parents' house."

As I closed the door, I expected her to squeal and refuse, but by the time I got in behind the steering wheel, she had the balaclava discarded to the floor, her shirt lifted to expose her pert, round tits, and her free hand working furiously between her legs.

"Fuck," I groaned, my dick thickening again. I hadn't even had a chance to do up my fly, but I couldn't drag my gaze away from my woman on the back seat, pleasuring herself like arson got her going.

"Drive, Vaughn," she moaned.

I put the car in drive and hit the gas, taking the back way out, along the dirt roads I knew so well from growing up here. We came out on the far side of Providence, on the opposite side of town to where we needed to be.

We were late, the clock on the dash already reading quarter to eight, but I didn't care. The longer drive gave me more time to listen to Rebel's moans in the back seat, to inhale the scent of her arousal, and to sneak looks at her when she got herself over the line with a shout of release.

By the time I parked in my mother's driveway, just down the road from our own, Rebel had her pants done up and was trying to fix her hair, which looked like a flock of birds had nested in it. I got out and turned away from the house using the door as a shield. I tucked another erection into the low waistband of my pants and dragged my hoodie down over it. When I opened the back door to let Rebel out, she was sitting as demurely as she would have at Sunday school.

I took her hand and helped her out, straight into my arms. I didn't care if my mother was watching through the window. I kissed Rebel's mouth hungrily. "That was the hottest thing I've ever seen."

Her cheeks were flushed, her eyes bright. "That was reckless."

She was right, and we both knew it, but in that moment, if someone had asked me if I would change any of the last hour, I would have said no.

I would have done it all again in a heartbeat.

"I need a shower," she complained. "We should have gone home first. Your mom is going to know what we've been doing, I'm sure."

I drew her in tighter, some protective part of me needing to have her close. "No shower. I want to know your panties are soaked with my cum."

Her breath hitched as we walked to the door, but there was a relaxed happiness about her, despite the things we'd done that night. That fire had joined us. Bonded us in a way that we hadn't been before it.

I held her secrets now, and she held mine. That knowledge seeped its way into my chest and squeezed.

The feeling was foreign. I'd felt it only once before.

I was falling for her and I needed to tell her. The feeling was too big not to.

On my mother's porch, I pulled her to a standstill, the two of us bathed in a circle of yellow light from the bulb above our heads. She tugged at her clothes distractedly, nervously pulling at threads that weren't there.

I needed her eyes on me. Needed her full attention. I put my fingers beneath her chin and tilted it up, forcing her to watch me.

Her hands fell to her sides at the look in my eyes.

"Rebel. I think I—"

The door flew open.

"Vaughny!" My ex-wife stepped out onto the porch. "Hey, baby. I missed you."

26

REBEL

I stumbled back, shoved out of the way by Vaughn's long-legged wife, who towered over me like she'd been bred from giraffes. Nearly as tall as him, she threw her arms around his neck and rubbed her nose all over his.

Stiffly, he extracted himself from the prison of her arms, but if she was insulted by his lack of return of affection, she didn't show it. "Your mom and I have made our famous lasagna. We've been working on it all afternoon, and the house smells amazing. Come on."

She grabbed his arm, digging red fingernails into it and tugging him toward the door without so much as a peep in my direction.

He shook her off, his expression sharp with anger. "What the hell, Brooke? Get off me." He looked past her to me, his gaze searching me from head to toe. "Are you okay?"

My fingers brushed the back pocket of my jeans,

wishing my knuckle-dusters were in there. Though punching out Vaughn's wife might not be the best way to impress his mother. But what the fuck?

"Fine," I grumbled.

Brooke glanced over at me, staring at me blankly like she'd only just realized I was there. "Who are you?"

Vaughn answered before I could. "Rebel. This is Brooke."

"His wife," Brooke practically purred.

"Ex-wife," Vaughn spat out.

She shot me a smug look. "I don't remember signing any divorce papers."

Oh, fuck this shit. I didn't need to be here in the middle of one of their lovers' quarrels. "I'll go."

"See ya, Rachel," Brooke called gaily.

I shook my head at the name. It was clear she'd gotten it wrong on purpose.

Vaughn ground his teeth in her direction, but when he turned to me, his face was all puppy-dog eyes, and a little of my anger faded.

He picked up my hand, threading my fingers between his. "I'm so sorry. I had no idea she was going to be here. My mom didn't tell me. Let's go."

I blinked, shocked he was picking me over his mom and wife.

Clearly Brooke had similar feelings, if the flash of fury in her eyes was anything to go by.

But his mom stepped out onto the porch, wiping her flour-covered hands on a flowered apron. "What's going on?" Her gaze landed on me, and her arms automatically opened. "Rebel! Oh, sweetheart. It's really lovely to see you again. How are you?" She put a motherly arm around my shoulders and gave them a squeeze. "How are you holding up? It's been the worst couple of weeks, hasn't it? Please come inside. It's cold out here."

She'd already drawn me two feet over the threshold, so I didn't have much choice but to continue following into her home. I glanced over my shoulder at Vaughn, right as he flinched away from Brooke's touch again.

At least that was vaguely satisfying.

Riva steered me into a big open-plan living area, with a huge kitchen and an attached eating and living area. "Karmichael. Vaughn and Rebel are here."

Her husband dragged his gaze away from the TV and strode across the room to Vaughn. The two men shook hands, and then he turned to me, nodding coolly before going back to his game.

Riva tittered. "Excuse him. He's a man of few words. Come, sweetheart. Come sit while I cook. Vaughn and Brooke have a lot of catching up to do. They've been separated for so many weeks."

"Cali has been woeful without my sweetie there," Brooke said in the most annoying baby voice I'd ever heard.

I glanced at Vaughn and raised an eyebrow, as if to say, seriously? This is the woman you married?

Vaughn ignored me and scowled at his mother. "I don't know what you think you're doing here, but—"

Brooke put her hand on his arm. "I spoke to your father's business partner the other day. He said all is going well. That you're learning your place within his business."

Vaughn's laugh was bitter, but I seemed to be the only one who noticed.

Riva just nodded approvingly at her boy. "I always knew you were a good fit for that company. They need your young blood. Your father and Harold are...were...too set in their ways. You coming back here is probably the best thing that's happened to Harold in years."

Brooke gave him a pointed look. "He said he's working on getting you a salary and a sign-on bonus. A very substantial one, so I'm told."

Vaughn folded his arms over his chest. "Did he just?"

I had the feeling this was the first Vaughn had heard about any of it.

He stared Brooke right in the eye. "Is that why you're here? To make sure your grabby little fingers can snatch it up the moment it hits my bank account?"

Karmichael's head snapped around toward his stepson. "Vaughn! We did not raise you to speak to your wife like that. What's gotten into you?" His gaze darted to me, and for a second, I was sure I saw a flash of disgust.

I sighed. It was the same expression I'd seen my entire life once people realized I was the gutter trash from Saint View. It never mattered what I wore or who I was with. At the end of the day, to these people on the other side of the border, I was nothing but scum.

Riva seemed dismayed at the rapidly disintegrating dinner party, her gaze darting between her husband, son, and daughter-in-law.

I tried to smile at her. "Thank you very much for inviting me, Riva. Maybe another time?"

She nodded, a sad expression morphing on her aging

face. "You're welcome anytime, sweetheart. I'm very sorry."

I got up stiffly, but before I'd even gotten both feet down off the stool, Vaughn's fingers wrapped around mine. I tried to pull away from his touch, but he clamped down on my hand, refusing to let me go.

"It's called affection, Roach. Learn to like it."

A smile tugged at the corner of my mouth. It was the same thing I'd said to him when I'd hugged him for the first time.

When had we gotten close enough to have inside jokes?

I didn't know. Everything about Vaughn seemed to have crept up on me. Especially the way I felt about him.

At least when he wasn't being a douche canoe.

Brooke gave me a triumphant smirk as we passed, despite the fact her husband was holding my hand. Irritation prickled at the back of my neck, but her expression was mostly just baffling. I had no idea what she thought she'd won, until we got out on the porch again and I realized her expression was because Vaughn would be going back in. Back to her.

Which was probably where he belonged. Who the hell was I to get in the way of a marriage? "Thanks for seeing me out. I can walk the rest of the way home. I'll be fine."

But Vaughn led me over to the car and opened the passenger side door for me. "Get in. Did you forget Fang's orders? I can't let you out of my sight."

I didn't want or need a babysitter. "Last I checked, I wasn't a child, Fang isn't my dad, and he doesn't control you. I'll be fine." I gave him a little shove. "Go back inside."

But he caught my hands again and pulled them around his waist so they rested on the small of his back. He stared down at me, his brown-eyed gaze holding mine so tight I couldn't turn away. "What I meant to say is, I don't *want* to let you out of my sight. I don't *want* to go in that house without you. I don't want to be anywhere without you."

Some of the ice that had crusted around my heart melted. "You hate me though."

He chuckled. "I think we both know that's never been true." He brushed his lips over my forehead. "My wife in there, on the other hand, I kinda hate her right now. I'm so sorry about all of that. She was totally out of line. I would have never brought you if I'd known she was going to be here. I don't know what my mom was thinking, inviting her."

"Your mom doesn't know me. Brooke is her family."

"Only until the divorce is final."

"Brooke doesn't seem to agree with that."

He sighed heavily. "She's not the only one. My father's business partner is making all sorts of threats if I don't sort things out with her."

"What sorts of threats?"

Vaughn shook his head. "Nothing I want you worrying about. Let's go home."

I would have normally argued with him some more, but after the night we'd had, I just couldn't.

"Vaughn!" Brooked screeched, coming out onto the porch, and stomping across the grass to us. "If you're done saying goodbye to your whore mistress, your family is waiting for you."

"Excuse me?" I had been nice so far. More than nice. I'd put up with Karmichael's judgmental looks and Brooke's catty attitude. But fuck her calling me someone's mistress. Fuck her putting that shame on me when I'd done nothing to deserve it.

A low grumble of a growl started up in Vaughn's chest. "Turn around and walk inside, Brooke. I can't even look at you right now. I've told you before, and I'm telling you again. We're over. We were over the minute you lied and stole from me. You're a spoiled princess, and I fed into that for way too long. I can't do it anymore."

She stormed closer, grabbing at him, trying to get him to face her. When he wouldn't, she shoved her way between us. "So what? You're just going to let them kill me? Have you seen what they did to my hair!"

Brooke's hair was a short, stylish pixie cut that suited her high cheekbones and prominent jawline. I couldn't see anything wrong with it.

"They caught me walking alone at night—which I was only doing because you weren't there, might I add. Do you know how scary it is to have some strange man snatch you and shear your ponytail off with a knife the size of my arm?"

As much as I didn't like the woman, that sounded terrifying. A tiny amount of sympathy for her crept in.

Vaughn shook her off. "I can't keep doing this with you! You lie and cheat and steal. How am I even supposed to believe anything that comes out of your mouth?"

Her mouth dropped open in outrage. "You think I

would willingly choose a haircut like this? You think I want to look like your little slut friend there?"

Sympathy gone.

Not that Brooke noticed. "They're going to keep sending you threatening notes on white cards, and chopped up body parts, Vaughn. They told me they were going to, and they followed through, didn't they? You got the cards and the hair?"

Vaughn nodded tightly, grudgingly replying, "Yes."

"You see why I need the money! These aren't idle threats. They aren't messing around!"

"Then get it from your father."

"You know I can't go to him. He'd disown me if he knew."

Vaughn shook his head, his laugh dark. "Yeah, well, same."

Her hand cracked across his face, the slap so sharp it rang in my ears. "You asshole! You will do this, Vaughn. I know all your dirty little secrets. Does your whore know about all the dirty, disgusting things you've done in the past?"

He snorted. "Like what? That I was in love with a man? Yeah. She knows."

"She thinks it's pretty hot actually," I added in, not that anyone was paying me any attention.

They were too busy glaring at each other, eye to eye, the anger between them thick.

"You know what else she knows?" Vaughn threw back. "That I married someone I can't stand because I was too weak-willed to stand up to my father's business partner. Yeah, she knows that too."

"How dare you?" Brooke seethed. "How dare you

share intimate details of our marriage with some stranger. She doesn't know me! Or you! You've been together, what? Five minutes?"

He steeled her with a look that could have cut glass. "She's not a stranger. She knows more about me in a month than you've learned in ten years. And you know what? Maybe that's partially my fault, because I didn't love you enough to let you in and show you the real me. But don't ever fucking say she doesn't know me. She knows, because I actually fucking love her, Brooke. With every damn piece of my heart, I love her."

Brooke, finally giving up on getting anywhere with Vaughn, whirled and glared at me with blazing eyes.

I wasn't sure what my face was doing. I was a mess of confusion. Half shocked by Vaughn saying he loved me. A quarter confused and wondering if he actually meant it or if it was just to hurt his ex.

And a quarter smug.

Because I was petty like that.

She laughed bitterly. "You poor dumb bitch, in your cheap clothes, standing there thinking you won something because he claims to love you. He's *my* husband. It's me who lives in his house. Sleeps in his bed. Me who wears his ring. He'll never be yours."

Something inside me snapped. Any attempts at being civilized were thrown out the window. The Saint View underdog in me howled to be let free, and fuck if I was going to do anything to stop her. I stepped up, many inches shorter than the other woman, but I didn't care.

"That might be true but, bitch, my panties are still wet with his cum. Are yours?"

Brooke's mouth dropped open in outrage, but I was already sliding into the car and pulling the door closed.

It was a low blow. But sometimes a girl had to do what a girl had to do.

Vaughn got in on the driver's side and started the engine, revving it hard to drown out Brooke's shouts.

I leaned over and cranked up the volume on the stereo system, and in a roar of noise, we left Vaughn's old life behind.

27

REBEL

In Vaughn's bed, I slept until early rays of light streamed in, making sleep impossible.

For me at least. Vaughn seemed to have no such troubles, sprawled out on his stomach, back bare and warm to the touch, even though the morning was chilly.

I'd fallen asleep, emotionally and physically exhausted after running through the woods and the drama at Vaughn's parents' place. I'd barely even given a thought to the fact we'd set fire to a man's house with him inside.

Or maybe I'd fallen asleep so easily because I couldn't dredge up an ounce of regret for what we'd done. I'd had a moment of panic, but now, in hindsight, without adrenaline making me waver, I didn't feel regret.

Just power.

And a safety that came with knowing Hugh couldn't hurt anyone anymore.

I stuck my head into Kian's room, but he still wasn't home, his bed perfectly made. I ducked into our adjoining bathroom to pee and washed my hands with the fruity-smelling hand soap. My makeup bag sat on my side of the sink, my bright-red lipstick sticking out of it. I plucked it from among the mascara tubes and foundation sticks and uncapped it.

In big, blocky letters, I wrote on the mirror. *Where are you? I miss you.*

With a sigh, I tossed the now ruined tube of lipstick in the bin and wandered out into the house again. At the bottom of the stairs, in the entranceway, envelopes and junk mail had been shoved through the mail opening in the door. I scooped them up on my way to make coffee, sorting through each one and discarding them when they weren't of interest.

I switched on the machine and leaned a hip on the edge of the counter. "Bill. Bill. Junk. Bill." I tossed each offending item onto the countertop beside me. I had coffee steaming in my mug before I finally got to the bottom of the stack.

Beneath a flyer for a local plumber who claimed to have all my pipe needs covered, a white card had only one sentence typed on it in black ink.

You'd look pretty with your throat slit.

The card fluttered from my fingers, breath stalling in my lungs. I snatched it up again, flipping it over, but there was nothing else. No mention of who it was from. No postmark.

Whoever had sent this had been at my front door. While we slept inside.

The doorbell rang, and I screamed. Burning-hot coffee sloshed over the rim of the mug, cascading over my hand onto the floor tiles.

Vaughn came thundering down the stairs so quickly it was like he'd been shot out of a cannon. "Roach!" he shouted at the bottom, before spotting me in the kitchen. "Shit! Are you all right?"

He rushed into the room, took one look at my hand, and cringed. He gently led me over to the kitchen sink and turned the water on, so he could hold my hand underneath the cold stream. "What happened?

The doorbell rang again, and Vaughn glanced over his shoulder at it, then back at me. "Keep that hand there, okay? That burn doesn't look too bad but still worth keeping it under the water for a bit."

My skin was an angry red color.

I'd barely even noticed the sting. All I could do was stare at the card, sitting innocently on the countertop.

But before I could tell Vaughn about it, he had the door open, and there was a buzz of conversation from the entryway. When he didn't immediately let them in, I assumed it was a salesperson and went back to tending to my burn. It wasn't bad enough to need a dressing, but a bit of burn cream might take the pain out of it. I rifled through a couple of cupboards, wondering where Kian had stashed the first aid kit.

"Roach."

I pulled my head out of the cupboard. "Yeah?"

Vaughn's mom stood beside him; a clear glass baking tray filled with lasagna in her arms. She bit her lip worriedly, glancing up at the policeman standing next to her.

"Detective Richardson," I practically sang, voice full of fake sunshine. "Otherwise known as Detective Dickhead. I was thinking you'd forgotten all about me. But no, here you are, ready to ruin my day with your scowling presence. How lovely."

My nickname taunt didn't bother the cocky prick. "I'd like to have a word with you, Miss Kemp."

I didn't know where to look. At Vaughn, who had panic in his eyes. At Riva, who was probably wishing her son had never met me. Or at the detective, who was as smug as the cat who'd got the cream.

"I just wanted to drop off these leftovers..." Riva's sharp-eyed gazed moved from her son to me. "Should I call a lawyer? I have a good one."

I shook my head quickly, trying to downplay the entire situation, even though my gut knew this couldn't be good.

There were so many reasons a cop could be on my doorstep right now. I didn't even dare open my mouth for fear of admitting to something. "Call Liam," I said to Vaughn. "His number is in my phone."

But the detective shook his head. "No need for that. You don't have to say a word. I'll do all the talking."

I forced my face to remain neutral. "Very well then. Get on with it. We have things to do."

But on the inside, I was mentally running through the list of reasons why this detective would be standing at my door at eight in the morning.

He was here to arrest me for murdering Hugh.

Or he'd found a new way to pin my mother's murder on me.

Or he was going to tell me Kian's body had been found in a ditch somewhere.

I swallowed thickly, fighting to regain my composure.

Richardson rocked back on his heels. "A well-respected doctor and family man has turned himself into the police, claiming to have held you against your will and raped you."

I didn't react to the blunt way he'd announced it for everyone in the room to hear, zero compassion for what I might have gone through.

Riva gasped and put her hand on my arm, holding it tight. Her eyes watered. "Is that true?"

I lifted my chin. I wasn't the same woman I'd been when Detective Richardson and I had last gone head-to-head. I'd been barely a shell of my normal self back then, but day by day, I'd been learning how to come back from that place. How to rise from the darkness that had threatened to bury me. The one that had kept me small and vulnerable.

Fang and Vaughn and Kian had helped build me back into the woman I'd once been.

I was a fucking warrior.

I'd taken down two of my attackers, and I wouldn't stop until I found the third.

This detective wasn't getting in the way of that. If he thought coming here and reminding me of my attack was going to send me running for the hills, he had the wrong idea about me.

When I spoke, it was with complete surety and deadly calm. "He turned himself in because he's a piece-of-shit rapist who deserves to be in jail for the rest of his life."

Richardson narrowed his eyes at me. "He's one of the most valuable surgeons in his field."

"Does that somehow make him any less of a rapist?"

The detective folded his arms over his broad chest,

his thick biceps an attempted show of strength. "It makes him an easy target for women like you."

"A woman like me? What exactly does that mean?"

Riva vibrated with anger beside me. "How dare you?"

He ignored us both. "There's no proof Dr. Edrington did anything to you."

"Proof?" I squeaked. "What proof do you need? He admitted he did it. You can't just let him go."

Vaughn put a steadying hand on my shoulder. "Easy," he murmured.

Once upon a time, that might have sent me into a rage. But now I knew it came from a good place. This cop could arrest me if he wanted to. He'd already done it once.

The detective flipped open a little notepad and jotted something down on it. "Where were you last night?" he asked casually, abruptly changing the subject.

I froze. "Last night?"

He just raised an eyebrow and waited for me to answer.

My brain wouldn't come up with anything. I tried to force my tongue to move, to spit out an alibi. Shit, any damn alibi would do.

Riva answered for me. "She was at my place. She and Vaughn came for dinner."

Richardson raised an eyebrow at her. "Really? You know it's a crime to lie to a police officer."

Riva stared the bigger man down. She was fierce when she answered, "Yes, I most certainly do know that. My statement is still correct."

"Can anyone else corroborate your story?"

I cringed at the thought of Brooke having to be my alibi. She'd sooner throw me under a moving bus.

But Riva nodded firmly. "My husband."

He wasn't much better.

The detective smirked and closed his notepad. "I call bullshit."

Riva bristled, but he'd lost interest in her.

His gaze was firmly on me. "Did you hear there was a fire in Providence last night?"

I shook my head.

He chuckled. "Yeah, didn't think so. You know why?"

I opened my mouth to answer.

But he cut me off. "No, I'll tell you. More fun that way. You didn't hear about it because your pathetic attempt at arson was thwarted by the homeowner's automatic sprinkler system."

Shock punched me in the gut. The house had been alight when we'd left. I hadn't noticed any sprinklers.

Then again, I hadn't been looking for them either. It hadn't even crossed my mind when I'd been hopped up on adrenaline and revenge.

"The owner walked out a little on the soggy side, and with a few repairs for some minor damage, but otherwise I'm sure you'll be glad to know he was one-hundred-percent fine."

This disappointment that hit me like a truck was shocking. So much for taking my power back. I silently consoled myself with the fact it wasn't a completely wasted effort. Hugh knew now that I meant business. If I was willing to burn a man alive, I clearly wasn't playing.

There was at least some power in that knowledge.

I mirrored Richardson's posture, arms folded, head

held high. "Like Riva said, we were at their place. I'm glad to hear whoever's property caught fire was spared the heartache of losing someone. I know what it feels like to have someone you loved killed and the police be too useless to do anything about it. Wouldn't wish that on anyone."

Richardson leaned in, stiffening at my insults. "Troy Hugh called you out by name as a person who would want him dead, Rebel."

"Did you ask why?" I asked with so much fake sugar it could give the man a cavity.

"I did. He said you're obsessed with him. You've been stalking him, hanging around his place of work, leaving photos of yourself in his car."

I snorted at that. "Did he just?"

His fingers slid to the white card with the threatening note, picking it up.

I snatched it from his grasp, but it was too late.

His eyebrow raised. "Who are you writing such delightful messages to?"

"Actually, someone left that one in the mailbox for me. Maybe you should ask your friend, Hugh, about that?"

He tapped his short, blunt nails on the countertop before pushing off and moving toward the door. "Seems like you've made yourself some enemies, Miss. Kemp. Might want to think about coming into the station and confessing everything you know. We can't help you if we don't know what's going on."

Vaughn followed hot on his heels, clearly wanting the man out of our home.

Richardson saluted Vaughn, fake sincerity in his smirk, and Vaughn slammed the door closed behind him.

Riva had her hand over her heart. She slumped against the counter. "What on earth? That man was incredibly rude and completely out of line. I'll report him."

"Don't bother," I told her. "His superiors were the ones who trained him. They won't be any better."

Vaughn stormed back from the doorway and snatched the card out of my hand. He paled when he looked down at it. "What is this? Why didn't you tell me?"

"I literally saw it minutes before your mom and Detective Dickhead got here. I didn't have a chance."

The lines on his forehead were taut with anguish. "You think it was Hugh?"

I shrugged, knowing Riva was right there so I needed to be careful what I said. I didn't want to implicate her in any of this. Right now, she hadn't lied for me. We had gone to her place for dinner last night, even if we hadn't stayed long or eaten anything. I wanted to keep her out of it. It was bad enough I'd dragged her son into this mess; I didn't want to add any of his other family members. "Who else would it be? He clearly thinks I tried to kill him and he's trying to scare me."

Vaughn's expression morphed into concern. "Is it working?"

"No," I bluffed, with a fake laugh that was mostly for Riva's benefit because I knew Vaughn would see right through it.

I took the card from his fingers and crumpled it into a ball before tossing it in the bin. "I refuse to be scared, Vaughn. It's not who I am."

Except I was. Because Hugh had laid down the gauntlet again. I'd thought I'd had the upper hand, and now I was right back at the beginning.

I didn't think I had it in me to make a second attempt at cold-blooded murder.

28

KIAN

The stocky, dark-haired guy hit the dirt like a ton of bricks. The nose I'd just broken sent blood spraying in an arc across the people lined up in the front row, and they jumped back with a mixture of screams and shouts.

I cocked my head, waiting for him to bounce back up and send another punch my way, but the man didn't move.

Gino crouched and slapped his face a couple of times before he stood up straight and grabbed my arm, raising it into the air. "Ladies and gentlemen, we have a winner!"

The crowd went wild, but none of it sank in. Gino slapped me on the shoulder when I walked out of the makeshift fight ring and followed me as I pushed way through the throng of people who'd gathered to watch that night's fights.

As soon as we were out of sight, he handed me a thin wad of cash. "Good job tonight. Your cut."

It was barely enough to put gas in my truck. "Seriously? That's it?"

Gino shrugged. "Like I said, bro. You're the favorite right now. The payout is slim. You want a big payday? Win a couple more, then throw one. It'll be worth your while. You can see how many people are here tonight. Some of them have deep pockets. You see that guy over there in the suit? He bets big. If we can get him interested in you..."

I cast a glance in the direction Gino was indicating. "It's like he stepped out of a Mafia magazine."

Gino chuckled. "Would explain some things."

I didn't really think some Mafia head honcho would be hanging around the Saint View fights, but the guy's suit was really nice.

And I was really broke. "I'll think about it."

Gino beamed like I'd agreed to something and shoved me toward the gym doors. "Go inside and get a shower. You deserve it. You fought like a pro tonight."

Twenty minutes later, freshly showered, my hair slicked back with water, I headed out the doors once more. The fights were still going, the slaps of fists and feet hitting flesh echoed around the dark parking lot, but I wasn't interested in watching any more of it.

I pulled my phone out and checked it for anything I'd missed. But it was more of the same. Message after message from Rebel, asking where I was and if I was okay. The last one invited me to come hang out with her and Vaughn at a Psychos party that night.

"Yeah, because torture is my favorite," I muttered, clearing the message. "I really want to watch you and Vaughn slobber all over each other."

It wasn't a fair thought. She'd be working, so maybe that wouldn't happen. But then again, I didn't know what went on at these parties. Maybe on her break she'd be riding his dick in the middle of the room for any random person to jack off over.

"Fuck." What did I have to go and think about that for? The last thing I needed was getting hard over a woman who already had two men, and a guy who was so firmly in the closet I couldn't get him out, even with the key.

"Nice fight, Kian O'Malley."

I glanced up from my phone and did a double take.

The guy in the expensive suit. It was a deep blue, a crisp white business shirt poking out from beneath it.

He took a drag from a thin cigar, slowly blowing out the smoke while he studied me.

He was hot. Chiseled jaw. Tanned skin. Dark eyes.

A tattoo crept up the side of his neck, but it was too dark for me to make it out.

He was also no Vaughn.

Fuck, that annoyed me.

I nodded at the guy. "Thanks. Appreciate the support."

"Are you fighting again soon?"

I shrugged. "Not too sure. Maybe."

The man dropped his cigar, putting it out with the toe of his expensive leather shoe. "You've got talent. You could be great, with the right coach."

I jerked my head toward Gino in the middle of the ring. "Already got one of those."

The man shoved his hand in his pocket and produced

a business card. "I have better. If you're ever interested, give me a call."

I looked down at the card. It simply read Luca Guerra, with a number listed below it.

I tucked it in my pocket. "Thanks. Appreciate that."

His gaze rolled over me slowly before lifting to my eyes again. "I hope you call. Gino isn't bad, but he isn't great. He can't get you anything past this dirt lot."

I raised a skeptical eyebrow. "And you can?"

He gave a half-smile and pushed off the wall. "Call me and we'll talk."

He walked away, and for a second I stood there watching his broad shoulders that tapered down to a slim waist. His pants pulled snugly across his ass.

None of it did anything for me.

Because he wasn't Vaughn.

Was this what my life was now? Comparing every man I met to the one I'd never get to keep? I thought I'd been over this stupid infatuation. I thought when he'd up and left that I'd broken my own damn heart enough, and yet here I was, trying to kiss the man in an elevator, flirting with him, touching him, grinding on him, and getting off when he begged me to fuck him.

But when it came down to it, he was always just out of reach. No matter how many times he came back into my life, that was always what it narrowed down to.

Vaughn was a tease. A carrot dangled in front of me but one I was never actually allowed to eat.

I caught a bus home, not wanting to spend any of the lousy money I'd earned that night on an Uber. It all needed to go toward getting my truck back on the road so I could get to a worksite when I eventually found a job.

Vaughn texted again, repeating the info Rebel had already told me. They were at Psychos. That Fang wanted someone watching Rebel at all times. That I should go down there.

No thanks. Rebel was about as safe as she could be with Vaughn and an entire club full of people watching her every move.

Because she was that fucking beautiful, every man and woman there would turn their heads in her direction. She was fine. I didn't need to go down there and see the proof of it.

Rebel's car was in the drive, as was Vaughn's bike that he'd barely ridden since he'd arrived, preferring to take his old man's car instead. The lights were all off in the house, and it was late, so I assumed they'd driven to Psychos together.

I wondered what she was wearing. Lingerie? Topless? Completely freaking naked? I groaned. Fuck, I wanted to know.

The idea of grabbing Vaughn's keys from the hook by the door and jumping on his Harley was appealing. I could get back to Saint View in minutes.

But I'd only be torturing myself. If Rebel really was riding his dick in the middle of the room, I wasn't sure what I'd do.

I pushed open the door and blindly groped for the light switch on the entryway wall. When I found it, light flooded the open space, spilling over dark-gray tiles, as well as a blank white card that had been slipped through the mail slot.

"Freaking junk mail," I cursed, scooping to pick it up. I might not have been working at the house any longer, but it didn't mean I liked seeing a mess. I couldn't just walk over something on the floor and not pick it up and put it in its rightful place.

I flipped the card over, expecting to see an advertisement for a local electrician service or maybe a hairdresser.

Instead, I stared at the card, reading the neatly printed type multiple times before the words truly sank in.

You're next, bitch.

Below was a cut-out newspaper article, detailing Miranda's and Bart's murders.

I dropped my gym bag at my feet, my fingers digging into the white card stock. I spun around, like whoever had left the card might still be there, but saw nothing other than the dark night outside. When I paused to listen, the house was as silent as a tomb.

It did nothing to shake the uneasy feeling that swamped me.

I'd called Fang dramatic for wanting us with Rebel twenty-four seven.

Now I realized he probably hadn't been dramatic enough.

I grabbed my phone from my pocket and frantically called Rebel, but it went straight to her voicemail. Understandable, since she was working.

Without thinking about the fact we hadn't spoken since I'd fucked up everything with Vaughn and kissed him, I stabbed at my phone until it was dialing his. "Pick up, pick up, pick up, dickhead. You've been calling me nonstop for days and now you don't want to talk to me?"

The call rang out, and I swore at the top of my lungs.

I wasn't waiting around for him to call me back. I grabbed his keys from the hook and sprinted to his bike, throwing a leg over it. His helmet hung from the handlebars, and I shoved it on, snapping the chin clip together. I slammed my foot down on the kickstart, and the bike roared to life beneath me.

Any other day I would have admired the bike's power beneath me or the way it handled the corners I took too fast. But the Providence streets whizzed by, turning into Saint View streets, and I saw none of them. They were all a blur mixed with panic.

Whoever had left that note had been at our home. They knew where we lived. What if she'd been there alone? Would a note be all that we had left of her?

I fucking hated I hadn't taken Fang seriously when he'd told us there was a danger.

But was this even Caleb?

At this point, I wasn't sure who I suspected of murdering Miranda and Bart. Caleb hadn't even crossed my mind. They'd been killed just days after he'd attacked Rebel. She'd done nothing to retaliate at that point. She was just some woman he'd fucked over and forgotten about.

Until she'd sworn revenge on him.

He was capable of it, but it just didn't make sense.

I pulled up at Psychos and stormed across the parking lot, bypassing the line of people waiting to get in.

Scythe or Vincent, I had no idea which, stepped in front of me. "Join the line."

"I need to see Rebel."

He narrowed his eyebrows, his face stony. "Join the line."

I sighed in exasperation. Story of my life. I was easily forgettable in Vaughn's shadow. Not as smart. Not as attractive. I was taller, but that didn't seem to help much. "I'm Kian? We've met before, remember?"

A grin spread across the man's face so quickly it gave me whiplash. He reached out and shoved me in the shoulder. "Yeah, I know. I'm just messing with you. Go on. She'd twist my nuts if I left you out here in the cold." He grabbed my arm, his smile dropping into something deadly serious. "There'll be men in there looking at her. Touching her, even. While that's not on, unless she says it is, we don't do the jealous boyfriend thing here. Do you understand? Unless she tells you she needs your help, you sit and keep your hands to yourself... Can you do that?"

"I'm not her boyfriend."

I was already jealous though, thinking about the fact there might be men in that room looking at her or even touching her.

It was one thing for that to be Vaughn, or even Fang. But some random stranger?

Fuck no.

He sniggered, a wide grin spreading across his face again. "Oh, you're still in the denial phase, huh? Enjoy the blue balls. It's way more fun when you get over yourself. Trust me."

He opened the door for me and pointed to my left, where another doorway led to a very different side of Psychos.

Ceiling-high golden cages were spread around the room, a variety of performers inside. Each one was in various stages of undress, some still mostly clothed, and dancing provocatively for anyone who wanted to watch. Others going at it like rabbits, zero inhibitions, full-on sex without a care in the world who watched.

Or touched through the bars.

"We aren't in Kansas anymore, Toto," I muttered, dragging my gaze away to search the room for Rebel.

When they'd said Psychos was an underground sex club, I thought they'd meant it was some cheap, seedy place.

This was nothing like that. It was extravagant. Elegant. Sexy.

But none of it came close to Rebel sauntering through the crowd in a tiny bra and panty set that showed everything through the see-through material.

I stopped dead and groaned. "Fuck me."

Her gaze slid past me, then suddenly shot back. Her mouth fell open, and she dropped the empty tray she'd been carrying. "Kian!"

She sprinted the last few steps and threw herself at me. Like a koala, she wrapped her arms and legs around me, squeezing me tight.

On instinct, I caught her, hands against her lower back, her bare skin warm.

My blood ignited into fire. I was all too aware she was essentially naked.

So fucking perfect.

"Where have you been? Why haven't you been answering our calls?" She slid down my body to stand on her own two feet and glare at me. "I thought you were dead, you asshole!"

I shook my head. "Not dead, Little Demon. Just needed a time-out."

Her hurt was written all over her face. "From me?"

I felt like a fucking jackass. We'd kissed, and then I'd gone MIA. Of course she thought it was her fault.

I drew her into my arms again. "Never from you. I've just had a lot going on in my head. It hasn't been pretty."

She touched a finger to my split lip. "You've been fighting."

"A bit."

Vaughn appeared behind her, his face like a storm cloud. "Are you okay?"

I scowled at him. "Okay because I have a split lip? Or okay because I kissed you and you rejected me?"

He opened his mouth to answer.

I cut him off before he could. "Save it. I'm fine on both counts."

He clearly wanted to argue, and man, I would have loved that. Just seeing his stupid attractive face pissed me off.

He'd kissed me back.

He'd wanted it.

But it was just the same as it had been when we were teenagers. He was too fucking gutless to do anything about it.

I pulled Rebel a little closer though, and reluctantly gave her the card.

"What's this?" She stared down at it.

A second later, her gasp was audible, even over the sultry music pouring through the speakers and the groans and moans of people having sex around us.

Her fingers went limp, and the card teetered, threatening to fall from her grasp until Vaughn took it from her.

When he looked up at me, his expression was steel. "Where did you get this?"

"It was on the floor, put through the mail slot when I got home just now."

His fingers clenched into fists. "Fuck! You think they were watching the house? Waiting until we left?"

I shrugged. "I don't know."

Rebel dug her teeth into her bottom lip. "I need to tell you something. You aren't going to like it. So just remember that I give really good blow jobs and if you kill me, I'll never be able to do that again."

"I wouldn't know," I muttered.

"That would be a crime," Vaughn said at almost exactly the same time.

I glanced at him. "She blew you and you didn't tell me?"

He rolled his eyes. "Oh, now you want to be best friends who have sleepovers and braid each other's hair and share all our secrets?"

I glared at him.

Rebel patted me on the chest. "Just take my word for it. But this isn't the first threatening letter I've received. There was another one put through the door the other day."

I glared at Vaughn. "Seriously? I thought you were watching out for her?"

"That's rich coming from the man who hasn't been home in days and is spending all his time fighting and fucking."

"Fucking?" I choked out. "Who the hell have I been fucking?"

"Oh my God." Rebel rolled her eyes. "Would you two

go down to a private room and just screw each other? Your sexual tension is making me horny, and right now I don't have time for that. I have to come up with some sort of plan for oh, I don't know, staying alive when someone clearly wants me dead?"

Oh, yeah. That.

"This person is escalating. That's two notes in just about as many days. With that on top of the threat you could be used as a pawn in whatever is going on with Fang and the club, we need to get you out of here for a little while." Vaughn gritted his teeth. "I can't believe I'm going to suggest this, but now might be the time to take that trip to see your dad's family."

Rebel nodded slowly. "I liked the sound of that. He was pretty eager for me to meet the other side of my family." She sighed, the excitement in her eyes washing away. "It's not that simple though, is it? We aren't supposed to leave the state. And the funeral is at the end of next week."

Vaughn raised an eyebrow. "Since when do you care about breaking rules? We'll be back by then."

"My dad is still in Saint View. He's not even home," Rebel argued.

Vaughn was insistent. "If he wants you to meet his family enough, he'll make a quick trip back."

My head was a muddled mess with too many thoughts running through it in a constant loop. "I agree with Vaughn. Screw the cops and their 'suggestions.' Let's get the hell out of here for a little while."

She looked at me in surprise. "You agree with him?"

I thought it through slowly. Getting her out of Saint View and Providence for a few days seemed smart.

Whoever wanted her knew where we lived, and it was probably safe to assume they were aware of our cars and where she worked. If we stayed here, we were just sitting ducks. Some time on a farm in the middle of nowhere while we came up with a better plan seemed sensible. The fact it coincided with whatever was going on with Fang's club was just the icing on the top. "I'll take you. We'll leave as soon as you finish your shift. Drive through the night. I don't want you sleeping in that house tonight."

"I'm coming too." Vaughn stepped in, sandwiching Rebel between us, but his eyes were on me the entire time.

Fuck no. Not a chance. "I'm not sitting in a car with you for twelve hours, Vaughn."

Vaughn took a deep breath and held it for a second before he answered, "I'm the only one who has a car roadworthy enough to actually make it that far. So, I guess you are."

"Hey," Rebel complained. "As much as I'm enjoying being the meat between the bread here, don't insult my car."

"Your car is a piece of shit," Vaughn and I both said in unison.

Rebel's lips turned up in a half-smile. "At least you agree on something. You're also both rude."

I ignored her insults. "I'm driving."

Vaughn smirked at me. "Fine. I'll sit in the back with my girl and keep her happy the entire way there. We have a thing for the back seats of cars." He raised an eyebrow at me in challenge. "If you know what I mean."

Smug prick.

I leaned in, so only he would hear me, my lips barely brushing his ear. "Did you forget who taught you all about fucking around in cars? I know exactly what you mean."

Vaughn's cheeks when pink.

Rebel cringed. "The entire way? It's a long trip, Vaughn...that's a lot of orgasms."

He dragged his gaze away from me and looked at her. "What?"

She snorted. "Right. I see how it is. I'm the third wheel, huh?"

Fuck. She'd said it sarcastically, but there'd been a tiny hint of truth to the statement.

Vaughn had heard it too.

"Hey." He grabbed both sides of her face and tipped her head right back so he could gaze down at her, our argument clearly forgotten. "You are the first wheel, Roach. Always." He dropped an upside-down kiss on her mouth.

When he let her go and she straightened, her gaze landed on me. Before I could think about it too much, I traced the back of my hand over her collarbone, then danced featherlight fingertips over her skin.

She shivered when I trailed my fingers between her tits, and then lower to the barely-there scrap of see-through fabric that covered her pussy.

She gasped, and I played with the edges of the material, lowering it a little so my fingertips brushed her mound.

I leaned in and kissed her softly. "He's hot," I whispered over her lips. "And infuriating, and we have history.

But fuck, Little Demon. He's not you. You aren't ever second best to me. I want you both."

She glanced over her shoulder at Vaughn, but my words hadn't been loud enough for him to hear.

She grinned up at me. "This road trip is going to be fun then, isn't it?"

29

REBEL

Kian went home and packed bags for all of us, while Vaughn hung around the club as my own personal bodyguard. He'd been relaxed earlier, sitting on a couch near the bar with a glass of bourbon and Coke. His gaze had flicked around the room, taking in the scene, but it had continued to come back to me before wandering off again.

But after Kian's little bomb drop, Vaughn's gaze didn't leave me for a single second. He stopped drinking and followed me around the room, barely a few steps behind, like he was afraid at any moment, someone might pull a knife and run it across my throat.

I didn't even mind because after that second note, I was vaguely worried about that myself.

Bliss pulled me aside and cast an eye over my shoulder at Vaughn. "What's going on? He's stuck to you like glue all of a sudden."

"Much the same way Nash is following you around." I

waved to him hovering behind her. He was supposed to be serving drinks, but he was distracted as hell.

Bliss nibbled on her plump bottom lip. "The MC stuff has everyone on edge. War hasn't been home in days."

"Neither has Fang."

We both sighed.

I rubbed her baby bump gently. I didn't want to worry her any more than I had to, but she was my best friend. I didn't want to lie to her either. "I've had some threats come through my mailbox. Did you get anything like that?"

Her eyes went wide. "No. Nothing. What sort of threats? Do you think it was from the Sinners? Fang has made no secret of the fact you're his woman. They might come after you to get to him."

I shook my head. "I don't know what to think. But it's more likely they'd come for you, seeing as you're practically War's wife. He's a much higher-ranking member than Fang is. I think these threats are to do with my mom's murder."

Bliss's bottom lip trembled with worry for me. "Or Caleb and his friends trying to scare you..."

I laughed, but it had a hysterical tinge to it. "How did we get here? Where I have multiple suspects for the person stalking me?"

Bliss, being the best friend she was, who knew me better than anyone and had gone through many a wild ride herself, put her arms around me. "I don't know."

"I'm scared," I admitted, because she was one of the only people I could say that to. I tried so hard to be strong. I'd spent my entire life making sure nobody ever saw me as weak.

But this was getting to me. I'd only just built myself back up after the attack, and at every corner, there was something new, fighting to drag me down and drown me in fears and worries and disaster scenarios.

She pulled back to look me in the eye. "I'm scared too. But you know what? If I had a crystal ball that would have told me this was where I'd end up, I would still choose it, over and over again. I'd choose them." She jerked her head toward the door where Nash and Scythe were watching us. "I'd choose this baby. This life. I'd choose you."

Tears pricked the backs of my eyes. "I'd choose you too, Disney. Always and forever."

A tear spilled down her cheek, and I was pretty sure I had matching ones on mine. She grabbed me in a hug and held me tight.

I hugged her back, being careful not to squish her belly while sniffing and trying to smile all at once. "I love you. I don't know how I lived most of my life without you, but I'm damn glad I don't have to go another day like that. Even if all these lug heads we've accumulated fall off the edge of the earth, it's you and me, and mini Disney 'til the end, right?"

She laughed into my shoulder. "Always and forever."

I sobered. "I'm going away for a couple of days. To meet my dad's family." I screwed my face up. "That is if he'll meet us there. I need to text him. But either way, I need to get out of here. I feel like I jumped out of the frying pan and into a fire."

She nodded slowly. "You're coming back though, right?"

I was. "My whole life is here. You. Fang. My home.

Saint View is in my blood. But I need a minute to breathe. I'll be back for the funeral and to face whatever needs facing."

"I'll see you at the church then."

"Okay," I said as the house lights lit the room, signaling the club was closing.

Vaughn stopped behind me. "You ready to go? Kian is back. He's waiting outside in the car. I have your coat and purse."

Bliss squeezed my fingers one last time and disappeared into the crowd that was quickly emptying out. It was always a little confronting at the end of a sex party. When the lights came on and the illusion shattered, people left quickly.

Vaughn held my coat up for me, and I slipped into it. He put his arm around me and, like I was some sort of celebrity who needed shielding from the paparazzi, hustled me out of the club to his father's car, where Kian sat behind the wheel, engine already running. Vaughn put me into the back seat and went to follow me in, but I put a hand to his chest.

"Thanks, Kevin Costner, for giving me a Whitney moment, but I call dibs on the back seat. I've been working all night and I plan to make myself a cozy little nest back here. You're in the front."

He scowled at me, but I was already stretching out, ready to take a nice long nap. My feet were killing me, and my eyes were as gritty as sandpaper.

"Fine." Vaughn closed the door and tried to get in the front seat.

Kian jerked the car forward so Vaughn couldn't get a hand to the door.

Inside the car, Kian chuckled.

I shook my head. "You're an asshole."

He only laughed harder. "Oh, come on. He used to do this to me all the time when we were in high school. This is just payback." He zoomed the car forward again and stopped just as abruptly, forcing Vaughn to keep running alongside the car, trying to grab the handle.

"Kian!" Vaughn shouted.

"Run faster! You almost had it that time!" Kian waited until Vaughn caught up then jerked forward once more.

A howl of pain from outside had Kian slamming his foot on the brake so hard I nearly fell off the seat.

Vaughn thumped on the outside of the car. "You're on my foot!"

Kian peered back at him but laughed. "Yeah, sure I am, you faker. Come on, just get in. Let's go."

Vaughn glared at him through the back window. "I'd fucking love to. Do you know how to amputate the foot pinned beneath this tire so I can do that? Fuck, Kian!"

I widened my eyes at him. "I don't think he's joking!"

Kian jumped out and ran around to the other side, while I frantically slid across the back seat to lower the window.

Vaughn leaned heavily on the car, but when I looked down his body, sure enough, his foot was pinned beneath the tire.

I clapped a hand over my mouth and stared up at him in horror. "OMG. You aren't joking. Are you okay?"

"Been better."

Kian was already throwing himself back behind the wheel. "Fuck, fuck, fuck! I'll reverse!"

The car rolled back an inch, and Vaughn shouted again. "Forward, you idiot! You're making it worse!"

Kian slammed the car into drive and planted his foot on the accelerator. We lurched forward again, freeing Vaughn.

Kian and I just sat there, staring at each other in shock, while Vaughn limped to the passenger seat and jerked it open. He yanked his seat belt so hard it locked. He kept pulling it too fast, the seat belt protesting every time until he calmed down enough to pull it slowly.

I put my hand on Vaughn's shoulder gently. "Is it broken?"

He shook his head. "It's fine. Bruised for sure, but I don't think anything is broken. Let's just go."

Kian silently drove us out of Psychos' parking lot and onto the main roads of Saint View. You could have cut the tension in the car with a knife. We were almost at the freeway before he gave Vaughn a sheepish grin. "So...that never happened when we were in high school."

If looks could kill, Kian would have been dead on the spot.

30

VAUGHN

Fucking Kian. My foot throbbed from where the dumbass had squashed it. I was tired after being awake all night, but it ached like a mofo and made sleeping impossible.

Rebel, true to her word, had made herself a nest among my and Kian's jackets and gone right off to sleep.

Kian drove silently, eyes mostly on the road but occasionally glancing over at me awkwardly.

I wouldn't look at him. I was too pissed off to say a word. At least when I'd played that game with him in high school, I'd been a good enough driver to not run him the fuck over.

Uncomfortable, I stared out the window as night turned into day and the sun got higher and higher. Miles passed beneath our tires.

Eventually, Kian pulled into a gas station and got out to fill up the car.

I got out, too, favoring my good leg. "I'll drive for a while." My banged-up foot wasn't the one I needed for driving an automatic, and it would give me something to focus on. But pain shot through my foot when I put it down on the ground. Fuck. I hobbled around to the driver's side and quickly got back in. I was hungry and thirsty, but I didn't fancy putting weight on my foot again. Rebel was still asleep, and I wasn't about to ask Kian to get me anything. So, I stubbornly sat there, staring out the window while pretending I was anywhere but with him.

A few minutes later, he got back into the car, this time in the passenger seat, a rustle of packets in his arms. God, he really was a prick. Now I'd have to sit here and watch him eat while my stomach growled.

"Here." Kian threw something at me.

A little packet landed on my lap, and I turned it over so I could read the label. "What's this?"

"Painkillers for your foot." He passed me a bottle of water. "And a drink."

The stubborn part of me wanted to throw them back in his face. The injured part of me said stop being a jackass and swallow the damn pills.

So I did.

Kian sighed. "You know I didn't mean to run your foot over, right?"

I stared at him. "Yes, you did. You obviously wanted payback for what happened between us the other day..."

He shook his head, his jaw tight. "Fuck, you have your head up your own ass sometimes. I might have been pissed, but I would never deliberately hurt you."

I busied myself turning on the car and getting us back on the road.

Until a jumbo-sized Kit-Kat landed on my lap.

I didn't want to take it.

"Eat it," Kian demanded. "They're your favorites."

I hated he remembered that.

But I also kind of liked it.

He put a packet of salt and vinegar chips on the center console between us. "Also your favorite, if you're hungry."

Ugh. Damn him. A little of the ice I was feeling for him melted. I knew in my heart he hadn't meant to run me over. It had been an accident. I picked up the Kit-Kat and tore the wrapper off with my teeth. Then, stomach still protesting loudly, I took the biggest bite I could possibly fit in my mouth.

Kian groaned. "What are you doing?"

I chewed on my chocolate bar. "Eating? Driving?"

"You're doing it wrong!"

"Which one?"

He pointed at the Kit-Kat. "You can't just bite into it like that. What's wrong with you? You never used to eat them like that."

I looked over at him, baffled. "Please explain how I'm supposed to eat it then?" I took another huge bite.

Kian cringed then held up his own Kit-Kat. "Snap them into fingers, then bite into them. My OCD cannot with whatever you're doing over there."

I bit into it again. Wrongly, in his opinion, of course, just to piss him off.

He covered his eyes. "I can't even watch." He kicked at some rubbish on the floor of the passenger seat. "Also, what kind of slob have you turned into? Why are there so many wrappers and old drink bottles down here? There's no room for my feet."

I frowned. I'd been sitting on that side for hours, and there was maybe one empty Coke bottle and a burger wrapper. Both of which belonged to Rebel, who usually sat there, but I hadn't even really noticed.

Kian leaned over and plucked up the offending items and put them into the now-empty plastic bag he'd been given at the gas station. He shook it in my direction. "This is now the garbage bin. Rubbish goes in here. This car is a pigsty."

I glared at him. "Are you seriously insulting my car, after using it to run over and probably break my foot?"

His mouth dropped open. "You said it wasn't broken!"

"Well, it might be! Am I a doctor?"

We stared at each other for a long second, and I could have sworn I saw something more than anger and irritation flare in his eyes.

Or maybe it was just wishful thinking, because staring into his face did things to me I really wished it didn't.

He was the first to turn away. He put the bag of trash over the back into the floorboards Rebel wasn't using since she was sprawled out over the back seat, still dead to the world.

Then he reached over, covering my right hand on the steering wheel.

I batted him away. "What are you doing? Piss off, I'm trying to drive."

"Move your arm."

I glanced over. "What? Why?"

His face was insistent. "Move your arm so I can suck your cock."

I froze.

He was dead serious.

It took every ounce of effort to drag my gaze back to the road. "Stop messing with me."

But I let my hand fall off the steering wheel, navigating the car with only my left one.

Kian reached over and undid the button on my pants. A second later, he had my fly undone, and his fingers tucked into the elastic of my boxer briefs.

I grabbed his fingers. "Are you serious?"

He paused. "I tried saying sorry. That didn't work. I tried buying you your favorite snacks. That didn't work. I'm down to sexual favors. It's all I've got left to offer."

I shook my head. I didn't want a blow job because he felt guilty about a prank gone wrong. "It's fine, I forgive you. You don't have to do that."

Kian's fingers didn't move from my underwear. I glanced over at him.

There was no mistaking the heat in his eyes this time. It was there and it was blazing. "What if I just want to?"

I motioned back at Rebel. "What if she wakes up?"

A smile flickered across Kian's lightly freckled face. "I don't think she'd mind somehow."

He was right. Rebel had given so many hints about me and Kian screwing and how just the thought turned her on. I was tempted to wake her up just so she could watch.

Kian tugged on my underwear. "Lift your ass."

My brain hadn't even decided if we were actually doing this, and yet my body apparently had. My hips lifted, and my pants and underwear were around my knees in an instant.

Kian's fingers wrapped around my already half-hard cock, and it thickened beneath his touch.

God, it felt different. Not better than when it was Rebel's smaller hands around me, but different. His hands were bigger. Rougher. He jerked my shaft harder, more insistently than she did.

Fuck, it felt good.

My breathing picked up, and I fought to keep my eyes on the road. My gaze kept drawing down to my lap, getting off on the sight of him working my length.

"Keep your eyes on the road, Weston. I can't have you killing our girl back there."

Our girl.

Why did the thought of sharing her make me so freaking hot?

"I've missed your cock." Kian's voice was low. "Missed watching you get hard for me."

He'd been my first experience with dirty talk. My first experience with a lot of things, actually. The girlfriend I'd had in high school had taken a virginity pledge and couldn't even say the word dick, let alone touch mine.

Which worked out well for me because I'd never wanted her to. But at night, when Kian snuck into my room, I'd wanted his touch more than I'd wanted air.

Nothing had changed in ten years. I still wanted him as much as I always had. Only now, we weren't two dumb kids, fumbling around in the dark.

He leaned over and put his mouth on my cock.

I hissed at the warm wetness surrounding me and then groaned as he bobbed up and down, taking a little more of me each time.

I forced my eyes to stay on the road, but I was aware

of cars passing us. We were traveling at speed, but all it would take was one person to glance over and they'd see exactly what he was doing. The expression on my face was probably also a dead giveaway.

My hand dropped to the back of his head, and he grabbed his junk with his free hand, rubbing himself through his pants while he sucked me.

Heat sped through my blood, igniting every part of me. I was aware of my foot letting up on the accelerator and the car slowing down, but he was too good, and concentrating on anything else was a struggle.

He chuckled around my cock. "Drive, Vaughn."

Except it came out more like, "Dyge Gaughn," with his tongue wrapped around my cock and his voice sending vibrations down to my balls.

"Don't talk with your mouth full." I thrust my hips up.

He took my cock deeper, moaning his approval, encouraging me to keep thrusting up, pushing against the back of his throat.

He was so hard, the outline of his long, thick dick completely on display behind his pants. "Take it out."

If there had been any possible way I could have reached over and taken control for him, I would have. But he followed my instructions, hand moving into the elastic waist of his pants and getting his dick out enough that he could stroke it.

"Faster," I urged him, needing him to come with me, and needing it to be soon, because his mouth was more perfect than I remembered.

The last time he'd done this it had blown my teenage mind, but Kian at thirty was a different ball game altogether.

Fuck, I wanted to come in his mouth.

He worked his cock hard and fast, never stopping the rhythm he had on me. His free hand jerked my base at the same time, building us both higher and higher, while cars rushed around us.

The orgasm built deep inside me, a desperate need to be set free sparking to life. "Kian," I warned.

He kept going, just like I knew he would.

I came hard, spraying cum into the back of Kian's throat, which he swallowed down with a quiet moan. He came a second later, his dick spurting white onto his hand and lower stomach.

I pulled over onto the side of the road, the car barely rolling along, so I could watch him come with his mouth around my dick.

I wanted to kiss him. Wanted to drag him up from my lap and plant my mouth on his and claim him. His tongue, his lips, his cock, his heart. All of it.

Fuck Brooke and Harold Coker. Fuck anyone who said I couldn't have him.

He lifted his head as the car came to a complete stop and looked around, blinking in confusion. "We stopped driving?"

"Kinda hard to drive when your mouth is on my dick and I'm trying to watch you getting off."

Kian glanced down at the mess he'd made on himself. "Fucking hell. I shouldn't have done that. I've got nothing to clean up with and..." He gazed out the window. "Where the hell are we?"

I honestly had no idea. I wasn't even sure I'd been driving in the right direction for the past fifteen minutes or so. "I'll find somewhere to clean up."

A little packet of makeup remover wipes landed on the center console between us. We both glanced down at it, and then back at Rebel.

She grinned from the backseat. "You might need those, Kian. Nobody likes sticky hands."

Kian's cheeks actually went a bit pink. "How long have you been awake for?"

She stretched her arms over her head. "Oh my God. *So* long. Like, do you have any idea how hard it is to fake sleep as long as I did? I knew the two of you just needed to screw and get it out of your systems." She patted herself on the back. "Good job, me."

I cleared my throat. "So you saw the whole thing?"

"Saw. Heard. Got horny over it. All of the above."

I steered the car into the nearest exit. It was marked with a sign for food, gas, and accommodation in a town called Exetere. The car GPS system complained loudly. "Please return to the route."

I tapped a button to shut it up. "No can do." I glanced at Kian. "Our girl said she's horny."

He was in the middle of cleaning himself up but he glanced over at me. "That so?"

I put my foot down on the accelerator. "Time to find a motel."

31

KARA – 1 DAY EARLIER

Dressed in a paramedic's uniform, a beanie pulled down low over his brows, Caleb paused in the doorway. "Paramedics leaving the building," he shouted. "I have a woman and child. Don't shoot!"

I peered into the darkness beyond him, but there were no streetlights, and night had fully fallen. Those men were still out there. There was no doubt in my mind the moment we stepped out of the house, I could be killed instantly.

The baby in my arms let out a keening wail, and tears poured down my face. I didn't want her to die before she'd even had a chance to live. "Please!" I added my shouts to Caleb's. "Please let us pass. My daughter is only days old. Please let her live."

The baby only cried harder at the volume of my voice, but I held her to my chest while I sobbed. This was all my fault. If I hadn't been so greedy, I could have been sitting in my cheap apartment, broke as hell and probably contemplating going back to my parents, but at least she'd be safe. At least we wouldn't have guns trained on our heads.

"You're good. Go on. No one will hurt you." The voice from the darkness was deep and rumbly but sincere.

I believed him. "Thank you."

Caleb shoved the gurney forward, keeping his head down. Hayden took up the end closest to my head. I looked up at him, but he had his chin tucked into the collar of the thick jacket, and his eyes flicked left to right, assessing the situation. He didn't notice me watching him, focusing on him because I couldn't bear to think about getting into that ambulance with Caleb.

"Just keep walking," Caleb muttered. "Nobody make any sudden movements or try anything. You know what will happen if you do."

I held my breath while they wheeled me across the yard to the waiting ambulance. I waited for shots. For an ambush from the dark. For them to realize the paramedics weren't actually paramedics at all, but the two men the Slayers seemed to want most.

But it didn't come.

Caleb got the back doors open then went around to the front of the ambulance and got behind the wheel. He started the engine as Hayden loaded me and then followed inside, pulling the doors closed behind us. There were no windows back here. Both sides of the vehicle were lined with medical supplies and equipment, and Hayden slumped on a bench seat in the middle of it all, his gaze intent on me.

"Is she okay?"

I looked down at the little girl in my arms. "I think so. She's gone back to sleep anyway."

"Exhausted herself probably."

I hated she'd had to cry herself to sleep so many times since she'd been born. I'd read a lot of parenting books while I'd been pregnant, researching all the different parenting methods. I'd wanted to co-sleep and cuddle her when she cried. I wanted to try gentle parenting, so our days would be peaceful and calm.

I'd never wanted this. Her terrified and screaming because there were bullets exploding around us and strange men shouting. Her life constantly in danger.

Caleb drove the ambulance down the driveway, slowly and cautiously, and after a moment of flicking switches on the dash, he found the one for the siren.

"See ya around, you bunch of dumbass motherfuckers." Caleb laughed and stuck his middle finger up below the dashboard so no one watching from outside would see. "That's for you, War. You're even dumber than your old man. It was easy enough to have him killed when he didn't want to play nicely. You'll be next."

We turned out off the street.

Gunshots exploded into the night behind us, the Slayers and the Sinners opening fire on each other the moment we were out of the way.

I clapped a hand over my mouth, muffling the sobs I couldn't keep inside. The other women...they were all still inside. Sitting ducks.

Hayden stared at the wall opposite his seat, flinching with every gunshot. "This isn't right. I should be in there with them. I've known some of those guys since I was in high school and I just left them."

"You should be thanking me," Caleb called back. "The Slayers had you outnumbered. You'd just be another statistic of gang warfare if I'd left you back there. You'd be dead, and no one would even care."

Hayden's face was a picture of devastation.

On instinct, I reached out a hand to him. "Hey. Don't listen to that. People would care if you weren't here."

He dropped his gaze to mine. "They wouldn't. I'm a shitty son. A shitty brother. An even worse friend. Fuck!"

The expression on his face hurt my heart. It was the face of a man whose bad decisions had all caught up with him and potentially cost his friends their lives. I just wanted to take that look away. He didn't deserve it.

There was something good in Hayden Whitling. I saw it, even if no one else did.

"I'm a terrible parent," I blurted out, not even sure why. "If it makes you feel better."

Hayden squeezed my leg. "You're a great mom in a shitty circumstance. If anyone is a terrible parent, it's him." He jerked his head to the front seat.

Caleb sniggered. "Listen to you, all flirty with my sloppy seconds. You want to be the baby daddy, Chaos? Damn, slut. How good is your pussy that you have him so whipped in just a matter of days?"

Hayden's gaze lingered on me, then he took a gun out from beneath his jacket.

I opened my mouth to ask where he'd gotten it from, but he put a finger to my lips.

One tiny touch took my breath away so quickly the words died on my lips.

He climbed through to sit in the passenger seat and trained the gun on our driver. He didn't shoot, but Hayden's voice was deadly cold when he said, "You don't talk about her like that."

Caleb glanced over, then laughed. "Put your gun away, you idiot. You shoot me and the ambulance goes straight into a tree. Look around. You want me to drive us right off the road? We're surrounded by woods. What's going to happen to her then?"

Hayden didn't lower his revolver. "I'm done with this. With you. Any deals we had are over. I'm not doing your dirty work for you anymore. Pull the ambulance over and let us out."

I held my breath at the word 'us.' For half a second, I thought Caleb might actually do it. We'd be left in the middle of nowhere, but I didn't care. I'd walk all night to get back to town, if it meant getting away from him and keeping my daughter safe.

A roar of motorcycles behind us had Caleb and Hayden both checking their side mirrors.

"Fuck!" Caleb shouted, the debate with Hayden over letting us out instantly forgotten. "They must have realized you weren't in there."

"Me?" Hayden asked. "Why would they care about me?"

Caleb glanced over his shoulder. "Because they think you were the one who ordered the hit on their president."

Hayden stared at him. "That was you! I just gave you the contact."

Caleb waved his hand around. "Details, details. I might have paid one of your guys to drop the idea in their heads that it was you. Which was fun at the time, but not so much anymore, so now I'm gonna need you to get out."

"I'm not fucking getting out, Caleb. If they think I murdered their prez, they'll kill me on sight. You fucking bastard."

I didn't see Caleb draw the gun. Maybe he already had it firmly in his grasp and I just hadn't noticed.

But I noticed when he trained it on Hayden.

Without any of the hesitation Hayden had displayed over taking a life, Caleb pulled the trigger.

I didn't even have a chance to scream before a patch of crimson spread around the bullet hole in Hayden's chest. The impact pushed his body against the window, and he slumped, his eyes wide with shock and staring at the place he'd been shot.

"Hayden!" I scrambled to get the gurney straps off me with my one free hand, while clutching my daughter with the other. I got to my feet, unsteady in the moving vehicle but desperately spinning around for something to stop the bleeding. There were large, sterile packages of gauze in a drawer, and I ripped one open with my teeth, taking out the white fabric squares.

In the gap between the driver's and passenger seats, I crouched to push the gauze against the ragged hole in his skin.

It instantly filled with blood.

It was everywhere. Coating him. Me. The baby. I whirled on Caleb. "He needs a hospital!"

Caleb's attention alternated between the ambulance he was driving way too fast and the bikers following us. "Unfortunately, the hospital is not along our planned route of travel. So this is the end of the line for Mr. Whitling. If he'd like to get out here, I'm sure the Slayers back there will happily tend to his wounds." He shrugged. "Or let him bleed out for killing their prez. Could go either way."

"Caleb!"

I didn't even know why his callous words shocked me. They shouldn't have.

The man looked right past me, like I wasn't even there. "What's it going to be, lover boy? You getting out here and giving yourself up so those bastards leave me and your girl alone? Or you going to sit there and let her watch you die? Your call."

Hayden tried to say something, but blood dribbled from his mouth. He coughed and spluttered on it. His hand moved toward the handle.

I grabbed it, panic spearing through my heart. I wasn't going to watch him die. "No! You're not opening that door! At this speed, the fall alone will kill you. We're getting you to a hospital, and you're going to be just fine. They'll just stitch you right up and—shit! I need more gauze." I grabbed his hand and pressed it over the bloody patch that was completely soaked through. "Hold this, okay?"

He tried to talk again but couldn't get the words out. They were just moans of agony.

His expression ripped my heart in two. He was too young. Probably only a few years older than me.

All I could think about was the list of people Caleb had read out. Hayden's brother and his mom. They shouldn't have to lose him.

I didn't want to lose him.

I got up in his face, making sure his eyes locked with mine. "Hey. Don't you freaking die, Hayden. That's not happening, you hear me. Keep pressure on that wound, and I'll be right back."

I stepped away.

The instant I did, I knew I'd made a mistake.

The door handle clicked.

Cold night air rushed the cab of the ambulance.

And Hayden Whitling fell out into the night, hitting the asphalt with a bone-crunching thud I'd never be able to forget.

32

REBEL

"Soooo. Exetere is the legit actual middle of nowhere?" I got out of the car and twisted until something in my back cracked. As short as I was, sleeping awkwardly on the back seat of the car wasn't actually very comfortable.

Nor was it comfortable for watching your guys get each other off.

But I hadn't minded it so much then, once the touching and groaning and sucking had started.

So. Fucking. Hot.

Kian scooped me up and tossed me over his shoulder. "Not planning on seeing any of it other than the inside of this motel room. Vaughn, get the bags, will you?"

Kian strode toward the reception doors, with me dangling down his back, my bare legs kicking somewhere above his shoulders, his arm banded around the backs of my thighs tight to stop me from falling. If it had been anyone else, I probably would have fought them, but frankly, after the little show in the car, I was willing to be carried anywhere Kian wanted to take me.

Vaughn scowled after us.

I couldn't help but laugh as he opened the trunk and started pulling bags out.

Kian's palm crept up the back of my thigh, and he tapped my barely covered ass. "Do you know how hot it is that all you're wearing is underwear and that coat?"

I was finding it pretty hot too, especially with his hand resting there on my ass cheek, gently massaging it.

He pushed open the door to the motel, and a little bell chimed over our heads.

"Can I help...oh my."

Kian stopped. "Gonna need a room, please."

The woman paused, then said, "Did your friend agree to going to a room with you?"

Kian turned around so when I lifted my head, I was staring at the bewildered face of a young receptionist. I gave her a half wave. "Hi. Yep. I consent. I very much consent. But thank you so much for asking. It's really good of you to look out for me—"

Kian spun back around, cutting me off. "Really gonna need that room, please. Her talking about consent seriously gets me hot."

I covered my mouth, trying not to laugh.

Vaughn limped in, dropping all our bags at our feet with a huff.

Kian glanced back at him. "You need to go to the gym more if that tiny load of bags has you all hot and bothered."

Vaughn glared at Kian's back. "Seriously? All of that in the car and then you ruin it all thirty seconds later."

Kian glanced at the clock on the wall. "Was more like three minutes by my count. But please, the room, miss."

She tapped something on her computer. "Okay so, we do have three single rooms available—"

"One room," Kian announced. "Only gonna need one."

The woman looked up. "But there's only one bed in each room."

"That won't be a problem. We only need one for what I'm planning."

Vaughn shook his head. "Kian. You're embarrassing her."

I couldn't see whether the woman was embarrassed or not. I was sure we weren't the first ones to come in here, hoping for a bed to have sex in.

But maybe threesomes were less common. Even less common perhaps, was the two stupidly attractive men I was with.

There was a jingle of a key being handed over, and then the woman said, "Room seventeen. Go back out the door and along the path. You can't miss it."

Kian turned and strode across the room, back toward the door we'd come in.

Vaughn grumbled, picking up all the bags again.

"Thank you," I called to the receptionist.

She winked at me. "You're welcome... I get off at three, and I'm in the unmarked room next to yours if you need a fourth."

Oh my God.

"She's already got a fourth, actually." Kian held open the door so Vaughn could struggle through with the bags. "He's just not here tonight."

The woman shook her head. I was pretty sure I heard her mumble "Lucky bitch" below the tinkle of the bell as we filed out.

I slapped Kian on the behind. "Seriously? Do you have no shame?"

He slipped his fingers beneath my panties until his fingertips touched my pussy lips. "Pot calling the kettle black a bit there, aren't you? You're the one wearing lingerie beneath that coat and getting all wet and sticky watching me blow Vaughn."

His touch became a little more insistent, and he opened me up, slipping a finger inside me.

I gasped at him fingering me like this. Out in the parking lot where anyone could see if they happened to look out of their windows.

But I didn't want him to stop.

He paused at the door to our room and tossed Vaughn the key. "My hands are needed elsewhere."

His finger plunged back inside me, and I couldn't help but let out a moan.

Vaughn had the door open in seconds. He tossed the bags to one side, letting them land haphazardly, and slammed the door shut behind us when Kian strode in with me.

I almost didn't want him to put me down, though holding me in this position had to be uncomfortable. Hell, if he hadn't been slowly working me toward an orgasm, then I probably would have been uncomfortable too.

My pussy mourned the loss of his fingers, but my nipples got tight when he laid me down on my back and unzipped my jacket. His gaze roamed up and down my body, lingering over my tits encased in their see-through lace bra. He put his mouth to one and sucked me through it, his mouth warm and wet and perfect.

I speared my fingers into his hair, writhing beneath him when he tweaked my other nipple with his fingers. I slid my hands down to fist in the back of his long-sleeved shirt and pulled it over his head so I could see his bare chest.

He lifted his head long enough I got to take in the dusting of chest hair before he kissed me deeply, my head spinning at the intrusion of his tongue and the way I wanted more of it.

From the corner of my eye, I saw Vaughn take a seat in the single armchair. He twisted it slightly, so he faced the bed, but seemed content to let this be the Rebel and Kian show.

At least for now.

Everywhere tingled at the thought of what might come later.

"These see-through panties, Little Demon..." Kian kissed a trail down my belly until he got to my mound. He licked a hot path of lust along the waistband. "They do things to me."

"What sort of things?"

His eyes were fiery, burning into mine. "Like make me want to pull them aside and fuck you slow while you're still wearing them."

"Yes," I moaned.

I was already so wet. So turned on from watching them in the car. I could have taken him easily then, even knowing how big he was. But Kian had other plans.

He glanced over his shoulder at Vaughn. "All her toys and lube are in her bag. Can you get them?"

I raised an eyebrow. "I suppose it was too much to ask of you to just grab my underwear when the toys were all just sitting in the drawer too. But you seriously brought all of them?"

"Every last one, Little Demon. You have quite the collection."

I really did. Mostly courtesy of a toy party I'd thrown at Psychos a few months back. I'd gotten to keep the samples the sponsor of the event had sent.

Kian stood and undid his pants while Vaughn found the loot and tossed it onto the bed beside me. He pieced through it, while I lay there in anticipation. But then Kian was naked, and hard, and he was all I could see.

"You're so hot," I whispered shamelessly. "Like, really fucking hot, Kian. What are you doing in a seedy hotel room with me when you could have any woman...or man...you want?"

He knelt on the edge of the bed. "You're the only woman I want." He paused for a second then he looked at Vaughn, though his words were still for me. "And he's the only man I want. So I'm exactly where I'm supposed to be."

Vaughn seemed to be having trouble accepting the genuine moment Kian was trying to have. So I sat up and put my lips to Kian's, giving Vaughn a moment to get himself under control.

Kian's fingers sought entrance to my underwear again. He took up a spot on my clit, rubbing it before dipping lower to plunge inside me, then dragging my arousal back up and starting the process all over again. My breaths turned into pants of need as he worked me slowly and steadily, getting me hotter and hotter until I was sure something inside me would break.

But the minute I thought I was going to tumble over the edge, he backed off. "Not yet, Little Demon. Gotta get you ready for him."

I squeezed my legs together. He picked up the lube and a butt plug with a wide, diamond base. "You used this before?"

I nodded.

He swore softly. "Thank fuck. I can't wait to see you wear this. I want to come just thinking about it."

He squirted some lube onto it and shoved me up higher on the bed. With strong fingers, he pushed my thighs apart, baring my most intimate places to him again.

His mouth landed on my clit, and he sucked it hard.

I flinched at the cool lubricant on the plug, nudging my cheeks apart. But then he rubbed it up and down the crease, lubing me up, warming it with every swipe. My clit tingled with pleasure as he used the toy to play with my ass, gently nudging it.

I panted, trying hard not to come, because I knew it would be so much better if I could hold off until the plug...or Vaughn...was inside me.

Kian dragged his mouth away and watched the toy slide inside me.

He kissed the diamond base and then trailed his mouth back to my pussy, tonguing my entrance. "You have no idea how turned on I am, watching you take that like a good girl."

I moaned, thrusting my hips up to meet the plunges

of his tongue between words. I didn't have a praise kink, but who didn't like being told they looked good during sex? Kian calling me a good girl for taking a plug was never going to be a bad thing.

I was so ready for him. Ready for his cock. I needed more than just his fingers and his tongue.

The crack of the lubricant bottle opening again had us both glancing over. Vaughn trailed his fingers through the array of toys left on the bed.

Kian glanced over at him. "Vibrator on her nipples."

Vaughn picked one up and slathered it with lube. He touched it to my nipple, and I cried out at the sensation. He touched it to the other, and it was like being very pleasantly electrocuted, with the pulse of need and desire shooting from my nipples and landing right at my core.

He held the vibrator to my breasts, until Kian finally gave in and sank his cock inside me.

I shouted at the intense feeling of having him so deep with the plug as well. I pushed away the vibrator, the stimulation too much while Kian was slowly withdrawing and plunging inside me.

Kian's back muscles flexed and flowed, and I wrapped my arms around him, digging my nails into his flesh, scratching my way down his skin.

His mouth trailed off mine and down my neck, but he never stopped fucking me, each thrust perfect, his cock hitting my G-spot, his pubic bone grinding on my clit.

"Vaughn," he gritted out. "Gonna flip her over onto my cock so you can take her ass. You hard?"

Vaughn snorted. "No. I have magical superhuman powers and can stay soft watching the two of you like that. What do you think?"

"Then get naked. She's on the verge of coming."

We both turned our heads to watch Vaughn strip his clothes. He had a long, lean, swimmer's body I desperately wanted more of. I was so ready for him. Ready for both of them.

He leaned over and kissed me. "Not yet, Roach. I owe him."

Kian lifted his gaze to Vaughn.

With a wicked grin, Vaughn picked up the vibrator. "Keep fucking her. Don't come or I'll never do this to you again."

I peered over Kian's shoulder so I could watch.

Vaughn nudged the vibrator between Kian's cheeks, sliding the wand up and down, coating him with lubricant the same way Kian had done for me with the plug.

He shuddered and picked up the pace, jacking into me quicker, until I grabbed him, forcing him to slow down. "Eyes on me."

He stared down while Vaughn pushed the vibrator inside him.

He threw his head back with a roar. "Fuck! Don't stop."

I let him go.

Vaughn fucked his ass with the vibrator as Kian drove his cock inside me, over and over again. I stretched around the plug and his cock, taking everything he had to give. My orgasm bore down on me too hard and fast to stop.

I screamed his name when I came, the word hoarse and needy on my lips.

He kissed them, muffling my cries of ecstasy, and

continued pumping into me, while Vaughn matched his pace behind him.

"Need you, Little Demon. Need to come inside you."

I moaned my agreement, and he shuddered over the top of me, releasing his pent-up orgasm. He followed through with several more thrusts before he rolled us so I was on top of him. His cum seeped from the place we were joined, but neither of us cared. I leaned down and kissed him deeply, knowing Vaughn was getting a bird's-eye view of my decorated asshole.

He was behind me in a second, pulling out the plug and replacing it with his dick.

"Oh!" I shouted, taking the full length of him easily since I'd been well prepared by Kian. "Vaughn! Fuck!"

Kian rolled and tweaked my nipples. He was getting soft inside me but made no move to get me off him. I bounced on him, getting friction on my clit as Vaughn took my ass. He started slow but gradually built speed as we both found a rhythm.

"Arch your back," Kian demanded. "I want those tits in my mouth when he comes in your ass."

While his praises had done nothing in particular for me, his dirty talk was everything I could have ever wanted. "More," I whispered. "Harder."

He put his mouth over my nipple, nipping at the rosy bud and sending a jolt of energy through me.

I couldn't hold back any longer. I came for a second time, completely overstimulated and loving every second of it. My entire body sang, accompanied by Vaughn's moans of pleasure. He called my name and collapsed down on top of us, completely spent.

I was sandwiched between them. A hot, sticky, cum-coated mess but fully blissed out.

Kian rolled us to one side, all of us still connected, a tangle of arms and legs. He reached across me and stroked his fingers up Vaughn's arm, wiping away the sweat.

Vaughn looked at him. "Well?"

Kian chuckled. "Well, what? You want me to say you did a good job or something?"

Vaughn propped himself up on his elbow so he could glare at Kian over the top of me. "Maybe! You could at least tell me that was good enough to make us even."

I smiled softly into Kian's chest.

Kian's fingertips switched to trailing up and down my back. "Fine. We're even. Happy?"

But apparently Vaughn was not satisfied by that admission. "Say I've improved since high school."

Kian lifted his head. "You never fucked me with a vibrator when we were in high school."

"I know! So say I've improved."

"Jesus, Vaughn. Okay. You've improved. You're a sex god."

Vaughn settled back down on the pillow and nuzzled into the back of my neck. "Exactly. Thank you."

I sniggered, but I couldn't deny the praise was well deserved. "I second that. You were amazing."

Kian thrust his hips against mine, though he was too soft to do anything. "Settle down. You'll give him an ego and he'll stop trying."

I widened my eyes at him in pretend shock. "You're right." I twisted to toward Vaughn. "That was terrible. Try harder next time."

Vaughn pulled out and pushed me onto my back, covering me with his body and pinning me down on the bed so I couldn't move. "I hope you didn't plan on walking anywhere tomorrow, Roach. Because I've got all night to try harder with you."

33

REBEL

I called Torrence the next afternoon, after we'd all slept and showered and driven another four hours. The phone rang only once before he answered it eagerly. "Rebel. You called."

I drummed my fingers on the dashboard, suddenly a bit nervous. Meeting a bunch of people I was related to was kind of a big deal. "Of course. I said I would when we got here."

"So you're in Bedallen?"

"Just pulled into the main town. Are you here?"

"Got in last night. Caught the earliest flight after I got your message that you were on your way. I'm so glad you decided to come. Thank you. It means so much to me."

I didn't want him getting too excited. "I'm not here long, I have to get home for the funeral. I just wanted to meet my siblings."

"Absolutely. I understand," Torrence agreed quickly. "They can't wait to meet you either. If you're on the main road, take a left when you get to the gas station, then drive about five miles. Our property is called Ridgemont. There's a big white fence running right round it, a bunch of horses and sheep and cows in the pastures. You can't miss it."

I relayed the info to Vaughn in the driver's seat, and he made the turn. He didn't smile or comment. Kian was equally sullen.

I ignored them both. "We'll be there soon."

A silence fell over the car as soon as I ended the call. It grew thicker with every passing mile, until whatever the two of them weren't saying was very clearly the elephant in the room.

I sighed unhappily. "Okay. Just spit it out. Everything you're worried about. Lay it all out on the table."

"You don't know this guy from a bar of soap," Kian announced from the back seat.

"He's my dad."

Kian tapped his fingers on the center console distractedly. "Charles Manson was someone's dad too. Didn't make him a good guy."

"After what happened at Caleb's party, I'm scared of us getting separated," Vaughn said quietly.

That was a legitimate concern I could understand. I reached over from the passenger seat and squeezed his hand. "I kinda like when you're stuck to me like glue. Once we get there, we go everywhere together."

Kian let out a loud sigh, the leather seats creaking as he shifted around agitatedly. "Sorry, but I'm still stuck on 'this guy could have killed your mother.'"

I threw my hands up. "He didn't!"

"You don't know that," Kian argued. "Did you even ask him where he was in the weeks leading up to the murder? Was he here? Don't you think it's awfully convenient he just turns back up out of the blue now?"

Irritation prickled at me. They weren't even giving the guy a chance. He hadn't done anything other than try to be there for me. "He explained that, Kian. Jeez. Who knew you were so cynical? I thought you were all hippie love and everyone deserves a second chance?"

He frowned. "When did I ever say that?"

I huffed. "Fine. Maybe I just wanted you to."

Kian's mouth pulled into a line. "I don't trust this guy at all. I get why you want to meet his kids. I probably would too. But as an impartial outside witness, this all feels dodgy as fuck." He bit his lip, slowly letting it pop back out from beneath his teeth. "Which is why I did something you probably aren't going to like."

I twisted to narrow my eyes at him. "Talk more, Kian."

"I put your gun in your bag."

I leaned over and scooped up my purse from the floor and opened it. Sure enough, the little handgun I'd taken from my neighbor at the apartment house was nestled amongst my phone and wallet and a tiny mini vibrator.

I gaped at him. "Did you put the vibrator in there too?"

He grinned. "I thought you might need some stress relief on the drive home if this doesn't go well."

I shook my head at him in disbelief. "I'm not taking a loaded gun I don't even know how to use into a house full of children. That's dangerous."

"You know what's more dangerous? Going into a house unarmed when the owner is a suspect in a murder."

I glared at him. "You're a suspect in that same murder,

you know?"

He flashed me a grin. "But I licked your pussy so good last night that we all know you wouldn't shoot me."

Vaughn cleared his throat. "I wouldn't be so cocky. She has no shortage of men willing to go down on her, if you hadn't noticed."

I stifled a laugh, then pointed to the white fence that started up on a property line outside the window. I plastered myself to the glass, taking it all in. "There! That must be it. Wow. This place is so cute! I love it."

It was like a story book farm. Lots of wide-open space, with animals grazing among patchy grass and trees. A whitewashed fence ran the full length of the property, but about halfway along, we found a gate with a sign that read *Ridgemont Homestead. All welcome.*

Vaughn stopped the car, and Kian jumped out to unlatch the gate. He looked all around—down the road both ways, up into the clear blue sky, and thoroughly inspected the gate for I had no idea what, before he unlatched it.

"What is he searching for?" I asked Vaughn.

"No idea, but he looks like a try-hard spy kid."

I sniggered, but then Kian was pushing the gates open and we were driving through. Vaughn stopped again on the other side so Kian could get back in, and we trundled slowly down the driveway.

"There was a camera," Kian announced. "A small one, right in the middle of the gate. They know we're here."

I raised an eyebrow at him. "Why are you making out like that's some sort of big, ominous sign? Wouldn't you want to know if someone was entering your property? We could be cattle rustlers."

The look he gave me clearly said I was crazy. "Yeah, we're gonna steal a whole lot of cattle with Vaughn's dad's Mercedes. They're well known for having enough trunk space to rustle a cow."

He had a point.

Vaughn tapped the steering wheel, then pointed dead ahead. "House at twelve o'clock."

I just shook my head at their antics. "You two really gotta cut it out with the action movie wannabe shit. You're giving me secondhand embarrassment."

But I tucked the gun back into my purse anyway. It was ridiculous. But if it made the two of them feel better, then I would just make sure I had my purse on me at all times, so no small child could get a hold of it.

Vaughn parked the car just as the door to the house opened and Torrence walked out, a broad smile on his aging face, his hand in the air waving excitedly as he came to greet us. He stopped in front of me, beaming. "I'd really like to hug you, but I don't know if that's okay."

He seemed so hopeful I couldn't say no.

I nodded. "It's okay."

He acted as if I'd just handed him a winning lottery ticket, his grin wide. He wrapped his arms around me tightly and didn't let go.

Eventually, I hugged him back.

"Sorry," he said into my ear. "I know this is going on too long. It just reminds me of when you were a little girl."

Tears welled in the backs of my eyes. There was something familiar about it for me too. It prodded at memories pushed deep into the back of my mind. I found myself saying words I hadn't known I wanted to. "I wish you hadn't left. I wanted a dad so bad."

But what I meant was so much more. I wanted someone to be my parent. I wanted someone old enough and mature enough to tell me to be home by nine and to stay home and study because grades were actually important.

I wanted someone who gave a damn.

The realization hurt.

I loved my mother. But she'd been too young and immature and had no business raising a baby. She'd never been my parent. She'd never loved me more than she loved herself. She'd pushed away the only other person I might have ever had that from.

I didn't want to be mad at a dead woman.

And yet, I was.

He clutched me tighter. "I screwed up, Bel. I screwed up a lot. Please let me try again. I know you're too old to need a dad…"

Except I wasn't. I was so damn love starved that I was in some sort of weird four-way relationship that made absolutely no sense. I had daddy issues out the wazoo, clearly.

Healing some of them might be a good start to getting my head on straight.

Inside Torrence's farmhouse, the curtain slid aside, and three faces of varying heights peeped out through the second-story window. I waved my fingers at them, and they quickly dropped the curtain back into place.

Torrence hid a smile for his children. "I told them not to peep and to let you come inside in your own time, but they didn't listen, did they?"

I stepped away from him, happiness settling over me at just seeing their faces for a moment. "No. There was definitely some peeping, but I can't blame them for that. I'm curious about them too. Can we go inside?"

Torrence gestured toward the door. "Please. After you."

I slung my purse strap over my shoulder and double-checked it was zipped up tight. Then strode up the front steps. I didn't have to knock on the door. It opened before I could even raise my hand.

A woman who appeared to be in her fifties opened the door with a polite smile on her face. "Hello, Bel. I'm Sally-Ann. Your father's wife."

I stuck my hand out. "It's Rebel, actually. Not Bel." It was one thing for my father to call me that. He and my mother had given me that nickname. But I couldn't bear to hear another woman say it.

She frowned. "Rebel. Well, that is an unusual name, isn't it?"

Was it? I didn't really think so, but okay.

We stood there staring at each other for a moment, until Torrence cleared his throat from behind me.

"Are you going to let us in, Sally-Ann? Or are we going to stand out here on the porch all day?"

Sally-Ann bowed her head. "Of course. I'm so sorry. Forgive my lack of manners." She pushed open the screen door. "Come inside. We've made lunch..." She looked past me and Torrence. "Oh my. I didn't realize you were bringing company."

I realized I hadn't even made any introductions. I'd just rocked up with two stony-faced men who were ready take down anyone who breathed near me wrong. "Sorry.

Now I'm the one with no manners. This is Kian and Vaughn." I gave the two of them a 'smile please' sort of expression.

Neither of them smiled.

I fought the urge to roll my eyes and turned back to Sally-Ann. "I'm sorry. They appear to have swallowed something sour. Please ignore them."

She nodded and moved deeper into the house. "Kids! Please come down here and meet our guests."

It wasn't lost on me she didn't call me their sister. I tried not to let the hurt from that show.

The stomping of feet thundering down the stairs left no time for bruised feelings. A little girl who was maybe eight landed at my feet, and a moment later, three older kids joined her. Two appeared to be in their late teens, the other maybe slightly older. They were all neatly dressed, in clean, if not particularly stylish clothes. They looked like they'd come straight from church, with freshly scrubbed faces, hair neatly combed and tied back with ribbons.

They all had dark hair like I did, and brown eyes. All the older girls were an inch or two taller than me. The younger one super cute and mischievous-looking.

I gave them a wave. "I'm Rebel," I announced since no one else was introducing themselves. I wanted to call myself their big sister, but I wasn't sure what Torrence and Sally-Ann had told them about me, so I kept my mouth shut, not wanting to create an uncomfortable situation. I really wanted this to go perfectly.

Torrence cleared his throat. "Go on then. Introduce yourselves to your sister."

My heart squeezed. I'd never been called that in my

life, and it felt really damn good. There were some little similarities between me and the girls. Their noses turned up at the end, the same way mine did. Their bottom lips were full and pouty, same as mine. They were petite like I was too.

The eldest of the four stepped forward. "Hello. I'm Alice Elizabeth. This is Samantha Jane, Naomi Melissa, and Jacqueline Kay. We all go by our first names, except for Jacqueline. She's always Kay. Only our parents full name us."

I smiled at her. "It's really lovely to meet you. Thank you for coming down to greet me. I'm sure you'd all rather be chatting with your friends or watching YouTube, right?"

Torrence shook his head. "Oh no. We don't have Wi-Fi out here."

I blinked at him. "What do you mean? How do you order Uber Eats at three in the morning?"

He chuckled, leading me into a living room where a tray was laden down with a pot of tea, mugs, and some finger food. "Even if we did have Wi-Fi out here, there's no one around to deliver anything at that time of the morning. We only get deliveries of supplies once a week."

I gawked at him. "There's no shopping mall? We didn't see one in town, but I just figured there was one somewhere else nearby."

"Nope. Not unless you drive over an hour. Not much out here other than the freeway and farms."

I stared at the kids, baffled. "Where you do you all go to school?"

The younger kids all turned to Alice as their spokesperson.

"We're homeschooled," Alice explained. "We do a few hours every day. But we learn a lot being out here on the farm."

"Indeed," Sally-Ann replied. "They learn how vegetables grow and animal life cycles and all sorts of wonderful things. There really is a lot to be learned without ever stepping foot off the property."

A weird feeling settled over me. There was nothing wrong exactly. Of course, people homeschooled their kids, especially when they were super rural, like this family was. But something felt off about Sally-Ann. I glanced at Vaughn and then Kian, but their faces gave nothing away. I didn't want them thinking they were right about my dad or his family. I was being ridiculous.

The woman had strangers in her home. She didn't have to fall all over me with open arms, just because I shared DNA with her husband. She didn't know me, nor did she owe me anything.

I sat on the couch, and Torrence sat next to me, proudly listing off each of his children's achievements. The older girls were both gifted artists, and Torrence pointed out each of their artworks, framed on the walls. I gawked at how good they were while sipping on the tea that was shared around.

"You did this?" I asked Samantha. She couldn't have been any older than seventeen.

"Yes, ma'am."

I blanched at the term. "You don't need to call me that. We're sisters."

The girl looked at her mom, who nodded.

Samantha gave a small smile. "Yes, Rebel."

I smiled at her and then went back to admiring the

intricate brushstrokes on her artwork. "Damn. The only thing I was doing when I was seventeen was getting high and trying not to get pregnant."

I turned around to find everyone staring at me. Sally-Ann seemed especially horrified.

Embarrassment crept up my neck. I hadn't even thought before I'd opened my mouth. These people might have been my family, but it was clear we were not from the same world.

I ducked my eyes to avoid Sally-Ann's shock. How different my life would have been if my dad had taken me with him. Would I have found out I had some sort of hidden artistic or musical talent? Would I have ended up in a career that didn't involve pouring cheap beer or walking around a sex club mostly naked? I loved my job, but these kids weren't going to turn out like me. They were destined to be artists or doctors or lawyers.

I was only destined to close Psychos at two in the morning with a random guy vomiting in the gutter beside me.

Kay stared at me with big eyes. "Do you want to hear me play the violin?"

She was all of maybe eight years old and cute as hell. I'd never felt motherly toward any child. It wasn't that I didn't like them, it was just they were really boring, so I paid no attention.

But I could see me in Kay's big eyes. I'd been her age, or maybe even younger when my mom had kicked my dad out. I wanted to pull her onto my lap and hug her and tell her she was going to be okay. I wanted it so bad my fingers shook, and I had to dig them into the fabric of my purse to stop them shaking.

Kay didn't need that hug. She was perfectly safe and healthy and taken care of.

I swallowed thickly. "I'd love that. But could I use the restroom first, please?"

I needed a minute to get myself under control. To remind myself I was just fine the way I was, and growing up any other way wouldn't have changed anything. There was nothing wrong with me. I wasn't less than because I didn't have an education or a family or money.

Except deep in my heart, I knew I didn't believe that.

"I'll show her where it is," Alice announced.

"I'll get us some more tea while you're gone." Sally-Ann stood and motioned to her husband. "Come give me a hand, please."

It was said in a no-nonsense tone where you just knew she wasn't really asking for his help. She just wanted a chance to get him into another room alone. Most likely so she could ask him why he'd brought Saint View trailer trash into her pristine home.

"Thank you," I murmured. "More tea would be lovely." Though I'd barely sipped from mine.

I followed Alice up the stairs and down a hallway with many doors along both sides. The walls were lined with family photos, but I slowed down as we passed each one, noticing the little thin Post-it notes stuck on most of them. I paused at the third one. "What's with the Post-it notes?"

I peeled one off, but in the next second it was ripped from my hand.

Alice quickly stuck it back in place. "Don't touch that."

I dropped my hand to my side. "I'm sorry. I didn't

mean to intrude."

Alice continued down the hallway, her gaze firmly on the floor, the back of her neck flushed.

I didn't exactly know what I'd done, but I did know I didn't want to have upset her.

I pointed at the doors we were passing. "Are these all bedrooms?"

Alice nodded. "And bathrooms. That one there is mine."

"Can I see?"

She hesitated for a second and then opened the door. "Sure. I'm sorry it's a little messy."

The room was neat as a pin. Even Kian would have been impressed. The walls were painted a sunny yellow with white trim. There was a single bed with a flowered quilt and a white desk with a neat stack of textbooks on the shelf. It was nothing like the rooms I'd had at her age. Mine had been messy, every surface littered with makeup and clothes and the walls plastered with punk rock band posters.

"This is adorable," I told her.

She huffed out a sigh. "It's lame. You can just say it. It's a baby's room."

I didn't want to blow smoke up her ass, so I didn't deny it. "At least it's your own, though, right? Better than sharing."

To my surprise, her face fell. Water welled in her eyes so quick a tear dripped down her cheek before she could wipe it away.

I widened my eyes, guilt rushing in at making her feel bad. "Oh, shit! I'm so sorry. Don't cry. It's really not that bad at all!"

She shook her head. "No, it's not that. I just...I used to share this room."

I bit my lip. That made more sense. "With the girl who's covered up in those photos?"

Her eyes filled again, and she sniffed hard. "Her bed used to be over there, by the window."

I fought back fears of rejection and dared to pick up the younger woman's hand. Her palms and fingertips were calloused and scratched over mine, but I concentrated on her face. "What happened to her?"

She lifted her tearstained face to meet mine. "She died. I didn't even get to say goodbye. None of us did. It was too quick."

"Shit," I swore softly under my breath. "That's terrible." It explained a few things, though. Like maybe why Torrence had come searching for me after all these years. Was it really because he wanted to reconnect with me, or had he been hoping to fill a gap his other daughter had left? It would explain why Sally-Ann was so standoffish with me. I knew nothing about being a mother, but I was sure if I'd lost a child, I wouldn't want my husband bringing home someone to replace her.

"What was her name?" I asked quietly.

"Louisa."

Alice went to her desk and opened the top drawer. She took out a framed photograph and passed it to me. "Mom and Dad can't stand seeing any reminders of her. They took away all her things and covered up all her photos. I stole this one and hid it so I would at least have something to remember her by. We aren't even allowed to say her name. It makes my mom cry too much."

In the photo, Alice and Samantha beamed at the

camera. An older girl smiled with them. She had to be the eldest of the sisters, maybe four or five years older than Alice. Which probably made her only five or six years younger than me.

My heart broke for the older woman downstairs who was clearly mourning a very heavy loss. I knew how that felt. "I lost someone recently too. My mom."

Alice clapped a hand over her mouth. "I'm so sorry. I didn't know."

"It's okay. I just wanted you to understand I know how it feels to miss someone."

Alice ran her fingers over her sister's image. "I just want to talk to her. To tell her I love her one more time. I don't know if I told her enough. What if she died wondering if I was still mad because she used the last of my perfume?"

I put my arm around her and squeezed her tight. "She knew. I promise, she knew how you really felt."

I had to believe that for my own sanity. I had to believe my mom knew how much I loved her, despite all her faults. That hadn't changed, even knowing what I knew now. Nothing would ever change that sort of love. It ran too deep.

I wanted Alice to know something though. "I'm not here to try to replace Louisa. I just want you to know that."

Alice took the photo back. "I'm sure you're very nice..."

I laughed. "Nice is not generally a word people use to describe me."

She cocked her head. "It's not? Sometimes I wish I didn't always have to be nice."

"You don't."

Her shoulders slumped. "I do. It's expected."

I didn't know much about parental expectations since my mom had never had any for me, so I couldn't relate. But I could give her a safe space. "You don't ever have to be nice with me, okay? I'll give you my phone number before I leave, and any time you just want to do or say something bad or wrong you can call me."

Her mouth dropped open in horror. "Oh, I couldn't do that."

I laughed. "Honey, I promise you, whatever you're thinking or feeling, I've done worse. Stick with me, kid. I can teach you all the best ways to be corrupted."

I didn't really mean it. This kid was too sweet and innocent for her own good, and clearly still grieving too. But it made her smile, and that was all that mattered.

She leaned in, her voice lowering conspiratorially. "Can you teach me how to find two sexy men like you have downstairs?"

I widened my eyes at her in mock disbelief. "Did you just say sexy, Alice? My, my, not as sweet and innocent as I thought, huh?"

She stifled a laugh. "There's a boy next door. I think he's kind of sexy."

I could relate. "Those men down there are my boys next door too. Looks like we have something in common."

That was all it took for me to feel bonded to this family. An admission of loss, a cute eight-year-old, and girl talk about boys.

34

REBEL

I didn't want to leave my father's house, not after I'd realized what they'd been through. We drank the tea they offered, and though Kian and Vaughn were giving me evil side-eyes, I accepted when my father offered for us to stay for dinner.

"We'd love to." I smiled at him happily.

Vaughn cleared his throat pointedly. "We'll be pushing it to get back in time for the funeral if we don't get back on the road..."

I waved my hand at him. "Plenty of time. We have enough clothes to last a week, thanks to Kian's over-packing."

He grumbled something about clean underwear not being the problem. It wasn't like him to be so grouchy.

But I really wanted to stay. I'd barely scratched the surface with these people, and I desperately wanted to know everything about them. "Come on, please, Vaughn. Just a couple more hours and then I'll drive through the night if I have to."

Vaughn rolled his eyes. "Or you'll pass out on the back seat again while we drive, but if you really want to, we can stay a bit longer."

I put my arms around his neck and kissed his cheek. "That's why you're my favorite."

"I heard that," Kian mumbled.

So I kissed his cheek too.

Over his shoulder, I caught Torrence and Sally-Ann exchanging displeased looks.

I quickly dropped my arms. Sally-Ann probably didn't want to have to answer her children's questions about why I was all over not just one but two different men. I could wait until we left to do that.

I clapped my hands together now that it was decided we were staying a few more hours. "So! Maybe we could get a tour of the farm before dinner?"

My father stood eagerly, motioning for us all to follow. "It's a little muddy right now, so I hope you wore old shoes."

Vaughn's shoes had probably cost more than a month of rent on my old apartment, but he didn't complain. The three of us followed the rest of my family outside into the cool winter afternoon.

Alice fitted herself to my side and slid her hand into mine. "Come on. I'll introduce you to my horse."

We took a path that led away from the house and through a couple of other buildings that housed tractors and various other farm machines. "This is so weird for me," I admitted to her. "I've never been on a farm."

"Never? Not even on a field trip or something?"

"Nope. I haven't gone much of anywhere, really. I stick pretty close to Saint View."

"That's your hometown?"

I smiled over at her. "Yep."

"What's it like?"

I lifted a shoulder and spread my arms out, indicating the open sky and green pastures surrounding us. "It's not as nice as this."

"Saint View is a slum," Torrence announced bluntly. "It's full of prostitutes and crime and drugs and no-hopers." At the last minute, he glanced over at me. "Present company excused, of course."

Alice's eyes were huge when she looked over at me. "Is that true? You live in a place like that?"

I couldn't deny Saint View wasn't exactly glamorous. My father had lived there for years, and nothing had changed in the time he'd been away. But his viewpoint wasn't the whole story either.

"It's true," I admitted to my sister. "But there's also some great things about it. My job. My friends are all there. They're good people. The best people, actually. I just recently moved one town over, into a nicer house, but Saint View will always be my home."

Torrence asked Kian to help him with an oversized bag of feed that needed to be spread out among the horses, and Kian quickly rolled up his sleeves and got to work.

Vaughn stuck close to me though, taking the whole "not getting separated" thing extra seriously.

"I'd like to meet your friends one day." Alice tugged me toward a large black horse, its head hanging over a stall to stare at us curiously. "I don't have many here on the commune. Only Samantha really. None of the other girls are my age."

Vaughn shot a look at me.

Commune, he mouthed.

I'd heard it too.

Alice caught us and laughed. "You think we're weird hippies now or something, right? It's not like that. Ridgemont is just a community of people who like to be as self-sufficient as possible."

I patted the horse's silky nose. "That doesn't sound so bad, I guess. Growing your own food. Not paying a fortune in taxes to the city."

She nodded. "We used to have TV but not anymore. Not since Uncle Josiah deemed it ruined our brains. I missed it at first, but not so much anymore. Come on, I'll show you the chickens."

I went to follow her, interested in seeing anything she wanted to show me.

Vaughn pulled me back. "No TV? What's the bet there's no smartphones allowed either? This is weird, Roach. I've got bad vibes."

I pulled my arm away, laughing him off. "Not everyone has to be a slave to technology. I think it's kind of nice. Do you have any idea of the trouble I was getting myself into at her age? It would have been a lot less if I were out here with no phone or TV."

He scoffed. "You can't seriously be telling me you'd rather have grown up out here, completely sheltered and oblivious to the real world?"

His accusations cut. I didn't like that he was calling my sister sheltered. She was just a kid. Not even old enough to vote, probably. She didn't need to be worldly at that age. I'd learned young the world was cold and hard and would chew you up and spit you out. I'd got tough because of it. Alice was still sweet and kind. She reminded me of Bliss.

The world needed more people like them.

Vaughn was just being an ass because that was his usual state of being.

Alice waved me over to the chicken coop. "Rebel! Come on!"

Just beyond it sat an array of raised garden beds. A man straightened at Alice's shout and put a hand to his eyes to shield them from the slowly sinking sun. "What do you have here, Alice?"

She dragged me over to the man. "Uncle Josiah, this is my big sister, Rebel."

The man did a double take. "Big sister...wow. I had no idea you had another sister." He held a hand out to me. "Rebel, was it? Nice to meet you."

I shook the man's hand. He was maybe the same age as my dad. Somewhere in his mid-forties. "This is Vaughn."

Josiah offered Vaughn his hand, but Vaughn was very slow to take it.

He eyed the man warily. "Uncle, huh? So are you Torrence or Sally-Ann's sibling? Or married in?"

He gave a small shake of his head. "Neither, actually. But all the kids in the commune call the adults aunt or uncle as a sign of respect."

Vaughn nodded. "I see."

I nudged him with my elbow. The words he'd said were fine, it was more the way he'd said them. Like he was completely suspicious of the entire thing. He was being rude and judgmental and he knew it.

"Are there many other families here?" I asked. "I didn't see any other houses on the way in."

Josiah nodded. "We have a lot of land here. There are more houses over that ridge. Some others beyond that stretch of trees. There are a few different entrances too. My place has a driveway onto the street back there, instead of the one you would have come in to get to Alice's place."

"But you all share the land?" I asked.

Torrence and Kian caught up with us, the last of our conversation drifting back to them.

"Did Josiah show you the vegetables?" Torrence asked proudly. "Well, the gardens, really. We built these ones over the summer so it wouldn't be so hard on the backs of our older members."

I eyed the waist-high raised garden beds that looked to have been made from pallets. "They're great. Good idea. Nobody needs a bad back before their time."

Josiah nodded. "Indeed." His gaze wandered back to me. "Will you be staying long? We could have a big community meal tomorrow if you'd like to meet everyone and learn more about the place."

Alice grabbed my arm. "Can you stay? That would be so fun. I could introduce you to..." Her cheeks went pink, and she shot a glance at Josiah and then at her father. "Um...all the animals."

She clearly meant the boy next door she had the hots for, but I wasn't going to give her away. As much as I wanted to say yes, I shook my head. "I wish we could, but we really do need to get back on the road after dinner. We have a funeral back home we need to be at."

Alice looked so crestfallen it made my heart ache.

"I'd rather stay here with you," I told her, meaning it. I didn't want to go back. A big community meal sounded nice, and I would have loved to have met the boy she was crushing on. "I'll come back soon, okay?"

"Or maybe I could come visit you?" she asked hopefully.

"You're always welcome," I assured her. "You have my number now, so anytime you want to come to Saint View, just let me know and I'll make up the guest bedroom."

She whirled around to her father. "Can I, Daddy?"

"I think dinner might be ready by now." Torrence clapped Josiah on the back. "You're welcome to join us, brother."

Josiah wiped dirt off his hands onto the back of his jeans. "Seems like you already have quite the full house tonight."

"There's always room at our table for you."

"Come, Uncle Josiah," Alice chirped. "Rebel's going to tell us all about the gangs and drugs and prostitutes in Saint View."

Josiah looked at the younger girl sharply and then at me. "Excuse me?"

I laughed awkwardly. "That's not exactly dinner conversation."

Josiah was distinctly uncomfortable. "I should think not. A young lady like Alice doesn't need to hear of things like that. Brother Torrence, thank you for the invitation, but I'm required at home tonight."

My father's face fell, but he wiped the expression away quickly. "Of course. Another time, then."

"That would be nice." Josiah turned to me, and his mouth pressed into a line. "I hope you'll spend more time with us out here, Rebel. It sounds like your hometown is not exactly...desirable."

I didn't say anything. Just watched him walk away.

Kian cleared his throat, his gaze on Josiah too. "Well, that was awkward."

I shot him a look, but Torrence was already storming away, his younger daughter's arm gripped tight beneath his fingers. He spoke to her in low tones, but it was clear from his expression he was unhappy with her for what she'd said.

Guilt seeped in. I'd embarrassed him.

I'd spent half my life wondering why he'd left. My mom had said it was him. He'd said it was my mom.

But with that one conversation, it suddenly felt like maybe he'd never brought me here because he was embarrassed by me.

35

CALEB

The crying was incessant.

The high-pitched squealing of the baby. The lower sobs of the woman.

I couldn't stand either of them. "Shut the fuck up." I ground my teeth. "Seriously. Shut. The fuck. Up."

The woman, Kara, glared at me through watery eyes. "You want me to be quiet? Just let us go. What good are we to you? My family has no money if you were hoping for a ransom. I'm not going to tell anyone about what you've done. No one would believe me anyway. You're a respected member of society, and I'm a nobody. Just let me go and you'll never see either of us again."

I pressed my hands into the sides of my head, trying to think through the racket the baby made. It was a trick. A trap. A game the woman was playing, trying to one-up me. I didn't know what her endgame was, not yet. But something inside me wouldn't let her go. Some deeper instinct said I needed to hold on to this one until I knew more about her.

But fuck, she was trying my patience. "You're not going anywhere. You came to me, begging for money." I cast an arm around the room. "Look at this place. Thick carpet. Expensive furniture. This is what you wanted, isn't it? A fancy home? You greedy bitch. I give you what you want, and you still aren't grateful."

Hugh shifted on the couch, crossing his legs, his gaze bouncing between the two of us with interest. "She ain't staying here, Caleb. No fucking way."

I glared at him. "I bought you this house. What makes you think you get a say in who lives here?"

I'd ditched the ambulance after my little Chaos sacrifice to the Slayers. That had kept them happy enough to quit chasing me and pounce on him instead. But I couldn't go back to my place. Coming here probably wasn't even the best idea, but I was quickly running out of places to go. I hadn't been to my office in ages, and this hiding away thing was getting old fast. I had to come up with a better solution. I wasn't giving up everything I'd worked for just to abandon it.

Kara put her baby to her tit, and I looked away in disgust. But at least the feral thing was quiet.

"This place reeks," I complained to Hugh. "You need to get a cleaner in here."

He tossed a piece of popcorn into his mouth. "I did. Even they can't get out the smoke stench. Nothing to be done about that apparently, but they did say it would subside in time."

"What kind of shit cleaner can't get out the smell of smoke? Spray it with some fucking Febreze or some shit."

Hugh ground his teeth into his popcorn. "She was a specialist. A pricey one too. Gonna send that Rebel bitch the bill. I know it was her who set that fire. Her and Vaughn Weston."

I ran my tongue along my teeth. "Should have killed her when I had the chance."

"We didn't know she was going to turn into such a pain in the ass. Or that she was in with the MC."

Which just pissed me off all the more. I hadn't been thinking. I was too busy trying to get back at my bitch of an ex that I hadn't done my research. It was lazy.

I should have learned from the little slut sitting across the room with a baby she claimed to be mine. Not doing your research had consequences.

Fuck my life.

My phone rang, and I pulled it out of my pocket.

"Who's that?" Hugh asked, only barely interested. He was mostly ogling Kara's half-naked breast.

I groaned, "Harold fucking Coker."

"Who?"

"Vaughn's dad's business partner? Self-appointed manager of the old boys' club. What the hell does he want?"

Hugh went to reply, but I held one finger up, silencing him, and answered the phone. "Harold! So good to hear from you. How's that golf swing coming along?"

I wanted to roll my eyes at how fake I sounded, but Harold ate it up.

"Excellent, my boy. Excellent. The Bahamas was amazing. We played a lot of golf. Did a lot of business talk. Really do wish you could have made it."

I dug my fingers into the phone case so hard I was surprised it didn't crack. I would have happily played golf in the Bahamas if the old man hadn't rescinded his invitation. And all because I didn't have a wife to play happy family with like him and his friends? It was fucking bullshit. Now I'd missed out on all the business details I desperately wanted to grow my own company. Getting into the old boys' business club was proving harder than getting into Kara's tight little cunt.

And she'd fought me like a pro.

I smiled at the memory, though now wasn't the time to get hard over past sexual exploits. "Next time for sure," I assured the old asshole.

"That's actually why I'm calling. As you know, it's Bart's funeral tomorrow."

I didn't know that. But I wasn't going to admit it. "Of course."

"I'll be hosting a luncheon afterward, at the club. Just us boys. A gentleman's memorial to pay our respects."

My ears pricked up at the opening. "I'd love to attend."

"Good. Good. We've much to discuss and fill you in on. I'll see you at the ceremony then. I believe you and Bart's son went to school together? I'm sure he'll appreciate your presence."

"Yes, we were friends. I wouldn't miss it. I look forward to the luncheon afterward. Thank you for thinking of me, Harold."

"You're an up-and-coming star in this industry, Black. I only want to work with the best."

A slow smile spread across my face at his praise. "Thank you, sir. I'll see you tomorrow." I ended the call, grinning like a maniac.

Hugh raised an eyebrow. "What was that about?"

"We're going to Bart Weston's funeral tomorrow."

He stopped tossing popcorn into his mouth. "Are you insane? We can't go there."

I glared at him. "Why not?"

He started listing reasons out on his fingers. "Oh, you know, just that Vaughn and all the guys from the MC will be there. Pretty much everyone who is out for your blood and obviously mine too, since they tried to set my house on fire. That woman who died with Vaughn's dad was Rebel's mom. No fucking way, Caleb. We aren't going anywhere near that place. That's a death wish."

He had a point. The Slayers had only given up on me because I'd delivered Hayden to them on a platter. But that wouldn't tide them over for long. Plus, Vaughn and his friends were hell-bent on defending their bitch.

"Fuck," I mumbled. "Fucking, fuck, fuck!"

I wasn't missing out on another business opportunity. Getting an in with Harold Coker was exactly what I'd been working for ever since I'd first started Black Industries. I needed him and his friends on my side if I was going to take this business to the next level. There was no way around it. It was all about who you knew.

They were the gatekeepers, and I wanted in.

My gaze fell onto Kara.

The Slayers had bleeding hearts. I knew for a fact they wouldn't touch a woman. Their Achilles' heel was their females. Which made taking one with me a smart idea. What the hell could they do in the middle of a funeral anyway? Especially if I had a woman right there by my side. Especially one their girl cared about after their little basement encounter that night at my Halloween party.

Even if they wanted to kill me on sight, she wouldn't let them if I had Kara with me.

I motioned for the woman to get up. "Let's get you a party dress, slut. You're going to a funeral."

She raised her head from gazing at the baby. "I'm not going anywhere with you, Caleb." Her voice was a wobble and full of exhaustion.

Like I gave a shit.

I glared at her. "I don't know why you think I was asking."

She mustered up strength from somewhere. "If you force me to go to that funeral, I will scream to anyone who'll listen that I'm your hostage and you're keeping me against my will." She pushed to her feet, clutching the kid close to her chest. "This is over. I'm done. I'm leaving."

She strode toward the door.

Stupid bitch.

Like that was going to work.

I stepped in front of her. "You forget your place," I growled at her.

She refused to look me in the eye. Refused to back down. She tried to move around me, but I blocked her again.

"Sit your ass on the chair."

She raised her eyes to mine.

And spat in my face.

I recoiled at the vile act. Anger exploded through me, hot and fast, mixed with a healthy dose of pure embarrassment Hugh had seen it.

I backhanded her, cracking the backs of my knuckles across her cheekbones.

She spun around with the impact, a cry falling from her mouth, one hand clutching her face.

That just made it all the easier to snatch the baby from her arms.

"No!"

Her bloodcurdling scream rang in my ears, but I twisted, holding the baby out of her grasp.

She fought. She slapped and punched and kicked and scratched at me. "Give her back to me! Give her back! I'll do whatever you want! Just give her back to me."

She kept going and going until Hugh banded his arms around her from behind, hauling her away from me.

Tears streamed down her face, her posture defeated, her expression bereft.

It wasn't enough. I had to break her wholly and completely.

I wiped her spit from my skin. "You need to be taught a lesson, clearly. You'll come with me to this event. You'll dress pretty. You'll smile at my friends, compliment their wives, and you'll hang off my every fucking word like I'm your damn God. Do you understand me? You'll make me look good, Kara. I'll hold on to this in the meantime until you prove your worth to me. Got it?"

"No! Please! I'll do anything! Just don't take her from me."

But it was too late for that. She'd brought this on herself. I didn't trust her as far as I could throw her. I strode for the door and let myself out, the sniveling baby in my arms, her mother still screaming as I drove the baby away.

36

REBEL

We were barely on the road that led back to town when Vaughn twisted to stare at me. "What the fuck was all that?"

Kian, in the back seat, leaned forward in between us to stare at me too. "Seriously. Your dad is in a cult."

I laughed him off, though it was weak at best. "He's not in a cult. It's a farming community. It's not that weird."

Vaughn's gaze wouldn't let up. "That Josiah guy is a creep. Did you see the way he stared at Alice?"

I frowned. "He looked at her the way any aunt or uncle would."

"Only the pervert kind who jerk off to images they found on the dark web," Kian said quietly.

I glanced back at him. "You too? You agree with him?"

Kian was dead serious. "The way he looked at you wasn't much better."

I rolled my eyes. "You two need to curb your jealousy. Just because an attractive guy takes a peek my way, doesn't mean anything. Remind me not to invite the two of you next time."

Kian gaped at me, his eyes wide. "You aren't going back there!"

"Of course I am. They're my sisters. He's my dad. They're literally the only family I have, and I want to get to know them. Is that honestly so crazy?"

"Over my dead body." Vaughn glared at me, daring me to argue.

He should have known better. I'd never been the sort of person to back off just because someone else was getting uncomfortable. "Fuck off, Vaughn. Did you forget you aren't actually my brother? Or my mother for that matter, because you're starting to seem a lot like her. She wouldn't let me see him either. I didn't get a say in the matter with her. I do now. So, I am going back there to see my family. If that's over your dead body, then that can be arranged."

Vaughn shook his head. "You're blinded by your daddy issues you can't see your mom keeping him away from you was the best thing she ever could have done for you. That could be you on that farm, you know? You'd probably be one of old Josiah's five wives by now."

I rolled my eyes. "You've been watching too much reality TV."

"I'm with Vaughn. Sorry, Little Demon. That's a cult if ever I saw one."

I jerked the car to the side of the road and put it in park.

"What are you doing?" Vaughn asked.

I yanked off my seat belt and opened the car door,

stepping out to stand on the side of the road. "I'm done talking about this. One of you drive. I'm going to sleep."

Vaughn glared at me. "Get back in. I don't care if you don't want to hear it. It needs to be said until you quit being stubborn and see it for what it is."

I stormed to the back, jerking open the door. "Out."

Kian blinked.

"Get out, Kian! I'm not driving! If you don't give up the back seat, I'm walking."

Kian scuttled out, and I gave him a clear berth, which he clearly noticed.

He reached for me, his voice a lot softer than it had been a minute ago. "Hey, come on. Come here."

I danced around his outstretched fingers so he couldn't make contact with me. I didn't want his touch. I knew how easy it was to fall into it. They were being assholes, and I was mad. I wanted to stay like that. I dove into the back seat and pulled my hood up.

I so desperately wanted them to be wrong. I'd only just warmed up to the idea of having a dad and sisters and a proper family.

I didn't want that bubble to burst. It felt too good to be true, but I wasn't ready to let it go.

Kian sighed and got behind the wheel. He started driving again without a word.

That's how pretty much the rest of the drive home went. Me ignoring the two of them. Kian eventually giving up on trying to make conversation and putting on his 'Women of the 90s' playlist so he could sing along, while Vaughn cringed at every wobbly high note.

Eventually, I fell asleep to Kian's out-of-tune warbling.

I didn't wake up until Vaughn shook me.

"We're home. You've got about fifteen minutes to get dressed before we need to be at the church."

I blinked sleepily at him. "How long was I out for?"

"Hours. I'm serious. Go. I'll dump your stuff in your room while you're in the shower."

I glanced at the clock on the dashboard and then at the bright morning sun outside. Apparently, I'd somehow slept right through the night. "Shit!" I lifted one arm. "Do I really need a shower?"

He raised one eyebrow in the direction of my armpit. "Considering I have to sit next to you all day, yes."

Rude. "I thought you liked how I smelled?"

He leaned in close. "I like how you smell when you're turned on from me sucking your pussy. Not exactly the same as 'scent of road trip.'"

That was more like it. In the fresh morning light, after hours of sleep, and on the day of our parents' funeral, I didn't want to be mad. Today was already going to suck enough without him and me bickering. I could put that on hold until tomorrow.

I pushed past Vaughn but paused at the front door. "Fang's not here?"

Kian was piling bags into his arms. "His bike isn't here. You haven't heard from him?"

I bit my bottom lip. "Not for two days. Shit. I'll call him."

"Call him after you've had a shower!" Vaughn shouted after me, bossy as usual.

I ignored him, taking out my phone to call Fang's number. He didn't answer, but it did go straight to his voicemail. Disappointment hit me. I really wanted to hear his voice. I knew he was busy with his club stuff, but

I missed him. "Hey, handsome. It's just me. I know you have a lot going on right now, but I was kinda hoping you would be here today. It's my mom's funeral, in case you forgot. At the church in Providence. Anyway... I hope you can come. I love you."

Vaughn glared at me from the doorway.

I glared back. "Is that look of anger because I just told another man I love him or because I'm not in the shower?"

He sighed, dropping my things. He crossed the room and pulled me into his arms. "I love you, okay? Let's just go get this over and done with. We can make up later."

I raised an eyebrow. "Are you cruising for make-up sex?"

He chuckled. "Or maybe a make-up threesome. Kian is probably mad too, you know."

I kissed his lips. "Mmm-hmm. Nice try. See you downstairs in ten."

"Five, Roach."

I shoved him toward the door. "They aren't going to start without us. Get out of here."

I was vaguely worried they would though. I threw myself into the shower, rubbed my underarms with some soap, and jumped straight back out. I had zero time for hair or makeup, however, it fell would have to do. In my closet, I threw on a short black skirt, a black Guns N' Roses T-shirt, and classed it up with a cropped black blazer. My black Doc Martens completed the look.

Kian banged on the door. "Move it! Gotta go!"

I stepped out of the closet, and his eyes went wide. "You are so fuckable in that skirt. Please tell me you aren't wearing panties."

I raised an eyebrow. "It's a funeral, Kian. Of course, I am." Then I grinned at him. "Black ones, to match the theme of the day."

His eyes twinkled with mischief. "I don't care. Take them off."

My core gave a happy throb, and damn if I didn't find myself reaching below my skirt and hooking my fingers in my panties to pull them down my legs.

He grinned at me. "Better. Now let's go."

I followed him downstairs, where Vaughn was already waiting for us in the car.

"Rebel isn't wearing panties," Kian announced as we both piled into Bart's Mercedes.

Vaughn whipped his head around so fast he probably gave himself whiplash. "Are you serious?"

I lifted my skirt and flashed him.

They both groaned.

I laughed. "This is so inappropriate. My mom would have loved it."

She'd always been up for fun and mischief. That was what I wanted to focus on today. Celebrating her life, the way she would have wanted it.

It wasn't far to the church at Providence, and there were people already milling around in the parking lot, waiting for the service to begin. Most were men in business suits with smartly dressed wives on their arms. Acquaintances of Vaughn's dad, I assumed, because I was pretty sure they didn't run in the same circles as Miranda. Vaughn's mom waved from where she stood talking to her husband and another man I didn't recognize, but whoever it was noticed Vaughn and raised an eyebrow at him.

"Who's that?" I asked him.

"Harold Coker. My father's business partner. The one who told me I needed to stay married to Brooke and put on a show like he and his friends do with their trophy wives. Fuck that old bastard," he muttered. "I'm not playing his games. Not today." He glanced over at Kian and picked up his hand, threading his fingers in between.

I smiled at the little frown on Harold's face when he noticed. So satisfying.

Vaughn caught me next and dragged me in close. "Where are you going?"

"Putting on a show, are we?" I asked.

His lips were practically on top of mine.

He shook his head. "I just want to kiss my girl wherever I want to."

His lips dropped onto mine, and I smiled into his mouth, knowing Harold Coker was probably having a heart attack right now, what with all his business associates watching. He might have shoved Vaughn into the closet as a kid, but he couldn't hold it closed any longer.

"Mind if I kiss my girl too?"

I spun around to stare up into Fang's ice-blue eyes. "You came!" I spluttered.

Vaughn let me go, and I flung myself at Fang, holding him tight, accepting the kiss I'd waited way too long for. I don't think I'd even really noticed until that moment how much I'd missed him. But now my heart beat triple time to have him next to me again. I wanted to wrap myself around his body. Reassure myself he was here and safe and not dead in a gutter somewhere.

"I love you," I said between kisses, not caring I'd

totally outed this little foursome I'd found myself in the middle of. Fuck anyone who didn't like it.

When I pulled away from Fang, I definitely saw some disapproving looks sent my way. A few heads went together, no doubt gossiping about Bart's son and Miranda's daughter holding hands while she kissed another man.

Might as well pour fuel on the fire. I pressed up on my toes and brushed my lips over Kian's too.

Let them talk. I didn't give a shit what a bunch of gossipy old businessmen thought. Clearly, at least for today, neither did Vaughn.

He squeezed my fingers. "Let's go do this. I need it to be done and finished and put behind us."

I did too.

I spotted Bliss, War, Nash, and Vincent near the doors, and made a beeline for them. They all hugged me and exchanged greetings with the guys, and then we all went inside the church. Vaughn and I sat in the front row, Kian on his other side, Fang on mine.

Two coffins sat side by side in front of the altar. I swallowed hard, staring at the white one I knew held my mother's body. The priest came over and quietly spoke to Vaughn and me, but I wasn't really listening. All I could see was that white box.

Suddenly, I was right back on those courtroom steps, holding my mother while she died.

The grief hit me like a tornado, ripping me apart, ravishing me until I felt like I couldn't breathe.

Other people filed in, taking seats behind us, but I didn't dare turn around. If I did, I might run for the door.

I didn't want to break down here in front of everyone.

I didn't want their pity or their judgment. But I didn't want to say goodbye to my mom either.

For all her faults, she was the only one I had.

Fang picked up my hand and stroked his thumb over the back of it. I stared over at him miserably, wishing I didn't have to do this. Wishing she was still here so she could see these men sitting around me.

Damn, she would have loved it. Loved them.

Fang's hair was messed up from his helmet. His club jacket sat on his broad shoulders, his familiar scent of leather and smoke calming. I laid my head on his shoulder and looked down at our joined hands.

I froze. "Is that blood beneath your fingernails?" I whispered.

He swore softly, tucking his fingers into a fist. "Sorry. I thought I got all that off."

I widened my eyes at him. "Whose blood is it? What happened? Is Caleb...?"

Fang shook his head. "No, unfortunately. He's still very much alive. And he has the girl."

"The one from the basement?" I already knew what he was going to say.

He nodded. "Her name is Kara. There's a lot more I need to tell you."

"Tell me now!" I hissed.

"Can't." He nodded toward the priest. "They're starting."

I bit down on my lip, fighting the urge to drag him outside and demand he tell me everything right then and there.

But my mom deserved more than that. She deserved my attention, and Vaughn might need me too. His mom sat right behind us, on the same pew as Bliss and her guys. Now wasn't the time or place to start peppering Fang and War with questions about where they'd been and who they'd killed.

I'd never really thought of Fang as a killer before. Or if I had, it had been some far-off idea. Like he did that in another dimension. One I wasn't a part of.

Instead of thinking about that, I focused on the priest.

The service went on. Vaughn's mom got up and said a eulogy for Bart. It was lovely, and well worded, and she spoke so eloquently.

The priest asked if there was anyone who would like to say some words about Miranda, but nobody came forward.

I swallowed thickly, looking around, hoping my dad might say something, but I couldn't even see him in the crowd. The priest turned to me.

"You don't have to say anything if you don't want to, Pix. Nobody is making you." Fang squeezed my fingers.

But that really wasn't good enough. My mom might not have been wealthy or influential, but she was still a person. She deserved to have people say nice things at her funeral. I pushed to my feet. "It's okay. I'll say something."

I walked stiffly to the podium, and the priest leaned over and adjusted the mic to be closer to my mouth.

I couldn't look out at the crowd. I clutched the edge of the podium so tight my fingers went white, but I forced myself to clear my throat. Then finally, to speak. "My mother wasn't the most responsible of adults. Nor was she the best mom. She had me too young, she'd be the first to admit that. But that meant we grew up together.

We taught each other. We didn't have much, but that made us close. It was always me and her against the world."

I sniffed, fighting back the tears welling in my eyes. I battled to keep my emotions under control. I just needed to hold it together for a few more minutes, then I could fall apart.

I couldn't do it. One dripped down my face and onto the back of my hand.

My mother's voice echoed in my head. *You're Rebel freaking Kemp, and Kemp women are strong. You got this, baby. I love you.*

I raised my head, gazing out at the sea of faces, wishing I could hear her say those words one more time. But I couldn't. All I had was the memories.

Her memory deserved more than me staring down at my hands, sniffling like some timid little mouse.

I suddenly wanted everyone to know about how she'd been obsessed with hockey and that Jacob Rhodes from the Colorado Titans was her favorite player. Or how she loved Oreos, but only the double-stuffed ones because the original didn't have the right ratio of cream to cookie. I wanted them all to know that even though I hadn't gone to a fancy school, and I couldn't speak as eloquently as Vaughn's mom, I cared enough to try to do her justice.

My gaze came to rest on the back row.

I froze.

Hugh and Caleb sat side by side, identical smirks on their faces.

The edge of the podium snapped beneath my grip.

"Pix?" I spun and found Fang standing behind me. "Are you okay?"

I shook my head. They couldn't be here. They wouldn't dare. I looked back at where I thought they'd been, but the pew was completely empty.

I stared at it. Had they left?

Or had they never actually been there at all?

My head hurt from trying to make sense of what I'd seen. I stumbled, grasping at the podium so I didn't fall down the altar steps.

"Come on. You don't need to do this." Fang put his hand to my lower back.

My entire body trembled. I couldn't remove the image of Caleb and Hugh, sitting in that back row, like some sort of demons, risen from their grave to taunt and torment again.

I'd tried to kill Hugh in cold blood. I'd gone to his house and set it alight with him inside.

Who did that?

What the hell was wrong with me?

Too shocked to argue, I let Fang lead me away from the microphone. I sat heavily in my seat but couldn't stop glancing back over my shoulder at the empty spaces.

My chest tightened with every second that passed. I clutched my purse to my stomach, silently begging the feeling to go away. The walls of the church closed in on me until my lungs screamed for air.

Until I couldn't just sit there a moment longer.

I ran for the exit.

I burst into the midmorning sun, but it did nothing to stop the out-of-control feeling. So I kept going, weaving my way through the church graveyard, where that afternoon, my mother's coffin would be put into a hole and covered with dirt. I dodged around tombstones and mausoleums and remembrance monuments. There was no one around. Not a soul in sight. I powered up a hill, pushing my body harder and harder in the hopes my lungs would right themselves and I'd be able to breathe again.

But I heard them behind me. My guys calling my name. Bliss and her guys following too. Their shouts mixed amongst the organ music that floated from the church as my mother's funeral dragged on without us.

I crested the hill and headed down the other side. This was familiar. Vaughn and I had come here with the funeral director and picked out side-by-side plots for our parents. We'd parked our car at this end of the cemetery and walked through, inspecting the various available plots before picking two beneath a weeping willow with branches so long they almost touched the ground, making the spot quiet, shaded, and private.

Bart and my mom would never get to spend their lives together, but they'd be here beneath a willow tree for all of eternity. That was the least we could do for them.

Sobbing, I swept the branches aside and found the two holes, already dug and waiting for their coffins.

On the other side of the empty graves, two men and a woman cut through, making their way to the parking lot.

I gasped. "It *was* you!"

Caleb, Hugh, and the woman turned around.

If they were surprised to see me there, they didn't show it.

The two men were as arrogant as ever, in expensive suits and sunglasses.

I couldn't take my eyes off them. Not even when my guys surrounded me, and behind them, Bliss and hers.

"Caleb?" Bliss gasped.

"Can I kill him now?" Scythe growled from the back of my group. "Please fucking let me kill him."

His knuckles cracked. Or maybe it was his neck. I didn't even know.

"Only after I do," Fang spat out, his voice deep and feral, like he barely had a hold on himself.

In unison, Hugh and Caleb both drew guns.

Scythe didn't move. Neither did Fang. Bliss didn't say a word. A deathly silence fell over us all.

They were waiting for me to give the okay. Out of all of us, it was me he'd hurt the most. Me who needed revenge. Me who needed to give them permission.

None of them were armed, though. None of them were a match for a bullet.

The woman standing behind Caleb, let out a tiny sob, drawing my gaze to her.

I did a double take, recognizing her instantly.

The woman from Alice's photo. I was as sure of it as I was sure of my own name. The sister she'd told me was dead.

I clutched my purse tighter. "Louisa?"

The woman's gaze snapped to mine. Confusion flickered all over her face. But she gave a tiny nod. "Louisa Kara. But I just go by Kara now. How do you know my name?"

My head spun. Alice's sister was the woman I'd spoken to in the basement?

I couldn't put it all together quick enough.

But Caleb did. His laughter echoed in my ears. He slowly walked backward to his car, holding the gun on me the entire time. "This is so great. You two are only now working out you're sisters? I have to admit, I didn't know either, until yesterday when I finally took the time to do my research on both of you. What a coincidence, huh? I guess I have a type." He looked me up and down, taking in my slight frame. "I think I liked fucking you better though, Rebel. Your sister is a fat bitch, just like my ex over there, hiding behind you."

My sister.

She'd been there all along, and I hadn't even known.

Caleb grabbed her arm, twisting it roughly. "If you'll excuse me, we have a business meeting to attend. Was nice seeing you two again."

Anger rolled through me. Hot and fast, adrenaline spiking in my blood until it rushed in my ears, trying to drown everything else out.

"Let the girl go," Fang growled at Caleb. "So help me fucking God, you piece of shit, I will kill you where you stand. Let her go."

Hugh turned the gun on Fang.

I didn't hesitate. It was one thing for them to aim guns at me.

I wasn't losing any more of my people. I grabbed the gun from my purse, lifted it, and fired.

The crack was thunder, the gun recoiling so hard my arms jerked with the force.

The single bullet struck Hugh in the chest.

His eyes went wide with surprise, and he stared down at the ripped hole in his shirt, a large circle of blood spreading around it. He dropped to his knees, face-planting in the loose soil around the edge of the grave.

A hush fell, all of us staring at the man dying on the

ground, gurgling, and making pitiful noises as he drowned in his own blood.

My fingers trembled so bad I could barely hold the gun, but I took aim again, this time at Caleb.

He had my sister by the arm, dragging her backward toward the car.

But I wasn't letting him go. Not again.

I didn't care if he shot back at me. As long as it wasn't at someone I loved.

I strode forward, arms out, steadying the gun with every step I took. Each one filled me with power. He could shoot me if he wanted, but that would be where it ended. If he shot me, he'd have six guys on him in an instant. He couldn't shoot them all.

There was no escape for him now. I drove him backward, striding forward like I was seven feet tall instead of five. It didn't matter.

This was the revenge I'd wanted all along.

The one I'd obsessed over.

It was mine for the taking, and we all knew it.

Caleb's back hit the side of his car. He let go of my sister long enough to fumble for his keys.

"Run!" I screamed at her, finger hovering over the trigger. I didn't trust my aim to shoot with her so close to him. She just needed to take two steps to her left. Two tiny feet, and this could all be over.

Instead, she stepped in front of him.

Her arms spread wide, shielding him, and putting herself right in the path of the bullet I was so close to firing. "Don't shoot! Oh God, please! Don't shoot!"

"Move, Kara!" I screamed again. "This needs to end. He needs to die!"

Caleb's laughter echoed back from behind his human bodyguard. "She's not going to do that. I've got your niece and I'm the only one who knows where she is." His eyes glinted with the evil that came straight from his soul. "You kill me, her baby is dead too."

The end...for now.

Rebel's story concludes in Rebel Heart, Saint View Rebels #3
Get it here: https://mybook.to/SaintViewRebels3

Want a bonus Rebel and Fang scene from before this series started? It's got a public spanking...
https://www.ellethorpe.com/fangrebelbonus

SAINT VIEW READING ORDER
EACH TRILOGY CAN STAND ALONE, BUT IF YOU WANT TO BINGE...

SAINT VIEW HIGH
REVERSE HAREM

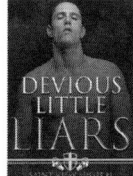

- Devious Little Liars
- Dangerous Little Secrets
- Twisted Little Truths

SAINT VIEW PRISON
REVERSE HAREM

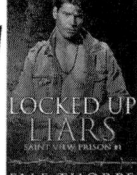

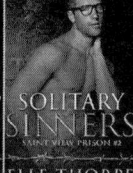

- Locked Up Liars
- Solitary Sinners
- Fatal Felons

SAINT VIEW PSYCHOS
REVERSE HAREM

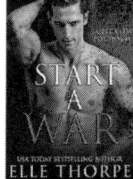

- Start A War
- Half The Battle
- It Ends With Violence

SAINT VIEW REBELS
REVERSE HAREM

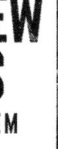

- Rebel Revenge
- Rebel Obsession
- Rebel Heart

SAINT VIEW STRIP
MALE/FEMALE
(BEST READ ANY TIME AFTER PSYCHOS)

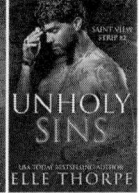

- Evil Enemy
- Unholy Sins

PLUS SHORT STORIES AND BONUS SCENES AT
WWW.ELLETHORPE.COM

WANT SIGNED PAPERBACKS, SPECIAL EDITION COVERS, OR SAINT VIEW MERCH?

Check out Elle's new website store at
https://www.ellethorpe.com/store

ALSO BY ELLE THORPE

Saint View High series (Reverse Harem, Bully Romance. Complete)

*Devious Little Liars (Saint View High, #1)

*Dangerous Little Secrets (Saint View High, #2)

*Twisted Little Truths (Saint View High, #3)

Saint View Prison series (Reverse harem, romantic suspense. Complete.)

*Locked Up Liars (Saint View Prison, #1)

*Solitary Sinners (Saint View Prison, #2)

*Fatal Felons (Saint View Prison, #3)

Saint View Psychos series (Reverse harem, romantic suspense. Complete.)

*Start a War (Saint View Psychos, #1)

*Half the Battle (Saint View Psychos, #2)

*It Ends With Violence (Saint View Psychos, #3)

Saint View Rebels (Reverse harem, romantic suspense)

*Rebel Revenge (Saint View Rebels, #1)

*Rebel Obsession (Saint View Rebels, #2)

*Rebel Heart (Saint View Rebels, #3)

Saint View Strip (Male/Female, romantic suspense standalones. Ongoing.)

*Evil Enemy (Saint View Strip, #1)

*Unholy Sins (Saint View Strip, #2)

*Book 3 (Saint View Strip, #3)

Dirty Cowboy series (complete)

*Talk Dirty, Cowboy (Dirty Cowboy, #1)

*Ride Dirty, Cowboy (Dirty Cowboy, #2)

*Sexy Dirty Cowboy (Dirty Cowboy, #3)

*Dirty Cowboy boxset (books 1-3)

*25 Reasons to Hate Christmas and Cowboys (a Dirty Cowboy bonus novella, set before Talk Dirty, Cowboy but can be read as a standalone, holiday romance)

Buck Cowboys series (Spin off from the Dirty Cowboy series. Ongoing.)

*Buck Cowboys (Buck Cowboys, #1)

*Buck You! (Buck Cowboys, #2)

*Can't Bucking Wait (Buck Cowboys, #3)

*Mother Bucker (Buck Cowboys, $#4)

The Only You series (Contemporary romance. Complete)

*Only the Positive (Only You, #1) - Reese and Low.

*Only the Perfect (Only You, #2) - Jamison.

*Only the Truth - (Only You, bonus novella) - Bree.

*Only the Negatives (Only You, #3) - Gemma.

*Only the Beginning (Only You, #4) - Bianca and Riley.

*Only You boxset

Add your email address here to be the first to know when new books are available!

www.ellethorpe.com/newsletter

Join Elle Thorpe's readers group on Facebook!

www.facebook.com/groups/ellethorpesdramallamas

ACKNOWLEDGMENTS

First of all, a big thank you to my readers. I really hope you're enjoying Rebel's series. Scale of 1-10, how annoyed are you that Caleb is still alive? Hahaha.

Extra big shout out to the Drama Llamas. You guys make my days fun. If you aren't already a member, it's a free reader group on Facebook where I share all sorts of stuff. Come join us, everyone is welcome. www.facebook.com/groups/ellethorpesdramallamas

Thank you to Montana Ash/Darcy Halifax for writing with me every day.

Thank you to Sara Massery, Jolie Vines, and Zoe Ashwood for the constant support, friendship, and book advice.

Thank you to my editing team:

Emmy at Studio ENP and Karen and Barren Acres Editing.

Dana, Louise, Sam, and Shellie for beta reading. Plus my ARC team for the early reviews.

Thank you to the audio team:

Denise and Troy at Dark Star Romance for producing this series in multicast audio! Thank you to Troy (again), Michelle, Michael, and Gregory for voicing Kian, Rebel, Vaughn, and Fang.

And of course, thank you to the team who organize me and the home front:

To Donna and Ari, for taking on all the jobs I don't have time for. Best PA's ever.

To my mum, for working for us one day a week, and always being willing to have our kids when we go to signings.

To Jira, for running the online store, doing all the accounting, and dealing with all the 'people-ing.' Not to mention, being the best stay at home dad ever.

To Flick and Heidi, for helping pack swag, and to Thomas, who refuses to work for us, but will proudly tell everyone he knows that his mum is an author.

From the bottom of my heart, thank you.

Elle x

ABOUT THE AUTHOR

Elle Thorpe lives in a small regional town of NSW, Australia. When she's not writing stories full of kissing, she's wife to Mr Thorpe who unexpectedly turned out to be a great plotting partner, and mummy to three tiny humans. She's also official ball thrower to one slobbery dog named Rollo. Yes, she named a female dog after a dirty hot character on Vikings. Don't judge her. Elle is a complete and utter fangirl at heart, obsessing over The Walking Dead and Outlander to an unhealthy degree. But she wouldn't change a thing.

You can find her on Facebook or Instagram(@ellethorpebooks or hit the links below!) or at her website www.ellethorpe.com. If you love Elle's work, please consider joining her Facebook fan group, Elle Thorpe's Drama Llamas or joining her newsletter here. www.ellethorpe.com/newsletter

- facebook.com/ellethorpebooks
- instagram.com/ellethorpebooks
- goodreads.com/ellethorpe
- pinterest.com/ellethorpebooks

Printed in Great Britain
by Amazon